S0-AKZ-754

"MOVE, DUMBO!"

Benton pushed the big dog away from Eleanor. "If there's any kissing to be done, I'll do it, okay?" The dog plopped down beside them on the floor, where he'd knocked Eleanor in his overly enthusiastic display of affection. "In fact," Benton added suddenly, "I think I will."

She felt his big hand on her hair, turning her head. She had a quick glimpse of his mouth only inches from hers before he claimed her lips.

At first the kiss was casual—warm—pleasant. She wasn't sure when it changed. But it did change, and she found herself cradled in his arms, heard him murmur against her mouth. She clung like a mindless idiot as he struggled to his feet and drew her to him, so she could feel the whole length of his body against hers.

She also felt him—suddenly—freeze. Then, in her ear, he said, "Whoa!"

But he didn't let her go; he still held her tight. His mouth moved against her cheek. "Cease and desist," he whispered. "I don't know what's going to become of this, but if something does happen between us, Eleanor Wright, it's going to happen with class—not in the middle of the kitchen floor with a dog on top of us. But meanwhile," he went on whispering, "I may just—kiss you again. One more time . . ."

And he did.

IT'S NEVER TOO LATE
TO FALL IN LOVE!

MAYBE LATER, LOVE   (3903, $4.50/$5.50)
by Claire Bocardo
Dorrie Greene was astonished! After thirty-five years of being
"George Greene's lovely wife" she was now a whole new person. She
could take things at her own pace, and she could choose the man she
wanted. Life and love were better than ever!

MRS. PERFECT   (3789, $4.50/$5.50)
by Peggy Roberts
Devastated by the loss of her husband and son, Ginny Logan worked
longer and longer hours at her job in an ad agency. Just when she had
decided she could live without love, a warm, wonderful man noticed
her and brought love back into her life.

OUT OF THE BLUE   (3798, $4.50/$5.50)
by Garda Parker
Recently widowed, besieged by debt, and stuck in a dead-end job,
Majesty Wilde was taking life one day at a time. Then fate stepped in,
and the opportunity to restore a small hotel seemed like a dream come
true . . . especially when a rugged pilot offered to help!

THE TIME OF HER LIFE   (3739, $4.50/$5.50)
by Marjorie Eatock
Evelyn Cass's old friends whispered about her behind her back. They
felt sorry for poor Evelyn—alone at fifty-five, having to sell her
house, and go to work! Funny how she was looking ten years younger
and for the first time in years, Evelyn was having the time of her life!

TOMORROW'S PROMISE   (3894, $4.50/$5.50)
by Clara Wimberly
It takes a lot of courage for a woman to leave a thirty-three year marriage. But when Margaret Avery's aged father died and left her a
small house in Florida, she knew that the moment had come. The
change was far more difficult than she had anticipated. Then things
started looking up. Happiness had been there all the time, just waiting for her.

*Available wherever paperbacks are sold, or order direct from the
Publisher. Send cover price plus 50¢ per copy for mailing and
handling to Penguin USA, P.O. Box 999, c/o Dept. 17109,
Bergenfield, NJ 07621.Residents of New York and Tennessee
must include sales tax. DO NOT SEND CASH.*

PROMISES TO KEEP

MARJORIE EATOCK

ZEBRA BOOKS
KENSINGTON PUBLISHING CORP.

ZEBRA BOOKS are published by

Kensington Publishing Corp.
475 Park Avenue South
New York, NY 10016

Copyright © 1994 by Marjorie Eatock

All rights reserved. No part of this book may be repro-
duced in any form or by any means without the prior
written consent of the Publisher, excepting brief quotes
used in reviews.

If you purchased this book without a cover you should be
aware that this book is stolen property. It was reported as
"unsold and destroyed" to the Publisher and neither the
Author nor the Publisher has received any payment for
this "stripped book."

Zebra and the Z logo Reg. U.S. Pat & TM off.

First printing: April, 1994

Printed in the United States of America

To Alta Claus
And the memory
of Betty Ionson
Both of whom have always been cordial,
willing, and unfailingly helpful
to an amateur "antiquer"

One

Eleanor Wright awoke with a start, jerked upright, glanced at the clock, and scrabbled bare feet from the warm covers to the cold floor before reality hit.

Whoa.

It didn't matter that it was past seven!

Her son no longer had to have his medication on the dot, or suffer awful consequences. Bobby was dead—gone a year. And for six beautiful, peaceful months she'd been here, in this lovely, serene, old Victorian house of Julia Bonford's—her partner, her friend, her surrogate mother.

She sank back against the pillows with a deep sigh, sticking her legs far under the rumpled blanket for warmth against the autumn chill, and trying to still her thumping heart.

How long was it going to take, O Lord? Even now those abrupt, nerve-shattering awakenings came at least once a week. During the days she had come to terms with Bobby's death, was even glad that the struggles of a brilliant young man with multiple sclerosis had finally ended. But the night terrors persisted. And the heart-rending awakenings . . .

Taking a deep breath, pushing the brief swing of silver-ash hair from over sleep-sticky eyes, she made herself listen to the sounds around her. Outside her window in the yellowing leaves of the big old syca-more, starlings were quarreling with cheeky little sparrows over the choicer seeds in the bird feeder. Other than that, quiet reigned. Absolute quiet. No distant radio giving the weather, nor bathroom sounds down the hall.

Could Julia have gone to the shop al-ready?

Eleanor knew the answer even as her mind asked it: yes. Julia was spending every available hour refurbishing the beautiful old John Belter living room suite, glorying in each renewed shine of mellow wood, ignoring the fact—Eleanor thought with a loving smile—that no Belter piece of furniture made had ever recognized the normal bends of the human frame.

Finding it complete in the elderly lady's attic had been akin to finding buried treasure. But that wasn't what spurred Julia Bonford on. Unlike that ratlike Marvin Coles in his pseudo-antique shop on the opposite side of the town square, Julia simply loved old, classic furnishings. And she delighted in giving them renewed life.

As she has given me renewed life, Eleanor thought. A reason for going on.

Widowed early, with Bobby struck down by MS, out of money, out of hope—until Julia hired her at Bonford Antiques, gave her a chance.

And then, when Bobby's astronomical medical bills and funeral expenses finally lost Eleanor the house, Julia insisted she move in with *her.*

Let Marvin Coles and some other townspeople laugh, call Julia a funny old maid—and a few other things not so nice. What Julia has done, Eleanor would never be able to repay.

The sound of the big old clock in the hall bonging a mellow seven-thirty brought Eleanor upright again, but more calmly.

She'd better get going, too. Julia wanted her to run out to that farm where an auction was scheduled next week. It was rumored the lady had some nice old pieces. And she had said Bonford Antiques could have a look before the scavengers descended.

Besides, Eleanor was hungry.

And that was a change. For how many years had she just grabbed a cup of coffee and a chocolate cookie—if she remembered even to do that.

On the other hand, Eleanor thought wryly, shucking off the old cotton nightshirt and eying herself in the mirror, there is a downside.

She had added a few pounds—on the butt, especially.

She sucked in, didn't notice any appreciable difference, and thought, Who cares?

Her eyes no longer looked like two burned holes in a napkin. Her silvered hair was getting some shine and some life back. She was fifty-something years old, for cryin' out loud. A little late for beauty contests.

When her clothes got tight, she'd knock off on the cheesecake.

With that firm resolution, she took some clean underwear from the old Empire chest of drawers and padded along the dim, quiet hall to the bathroom.

Later, slacks on, with a bulky blue pullover sweater against the fall chill, she trotted down the long stairs, reminding herself—at the bottom—that neither she *nor* Julia should descend quite so carelessly. A fall would screw up the routine for either of them pretty seriously, with autumn sales coming on. She went into the cheerful, sunny kitchen, found it empty but the coffee pot full.

Julia had left a note. It said, "Eat the last bagel. And stop by the shop before you go to Crane's farm."

Eleanor disdained the cream cheese, and sat down comfortably on the old bentwood chair at the table by the sunny window. She sipped her coffee, realized the bagel needed something, and leaned backward to fish the orange marmalade from the fridge. This dislodged a calling card stuck on the door with a magnet, sending it fluttering to the floor.

First Eleanor spread marmalade on the

bagel. Then, munching, she retrieved the card.

Wow! Anthony Mondaine was really going first class. The square of cardboard was gold rimmed, beautifully embossed, and said only MONDAINE'S. No telephone number, no address, as if anyone in the antique business who mattered already knew.

Which, she acknowledged, they probably did. She added more marmalade—the bagel was dry—no wonder Julia wanted it eaten. Anthony Mondaine was the foremost dealer in antiques in St. Louis, and possible in the entire Midwest.

Julia had visited his shop a few days ago; she must have picked up the card then.

Eleanor had a mental picture of Anthony—tall, distinguished, suave. Yes. Very suave. Sometimes one could almost spread it with a knife. But one also learned to watch those black Sicilian eyes—and when they flashed fire, look out!

Rumor had it that his interests were not purely antique—that he'd bed anything with boobs if the opportunity offered.

Julia had laughed at that. "Of course he would," she'd said. "But honey, I'm seventy-six years old. Coming on to me would have no advantage to Tony Mondaine. I've got his number and he knows it. So we just get on with business."

She put the card back on the refrigerator door, poured a second cup of coffee—she'd inhaled the first—and checked out the window to see if the van was there.

It was. Julia had walked to work.

But she hadn't taken her pills.

"Drat!" said Eleanor aloud, and put the dosage in her shoulder bag along with her own. Both she and Julia had terrible blood pressure; also Julia owned a tricky heart, yet felt she'd live forever. What was she to do with the woman. She wanted her to live forever. She couldn't imagine life without Julia.

As a matter of fact, she had no life without Julia.

It was a sobering thought, and not one Eleanor particularly cared for.

She put the coffee in an insulated mug, snapped the cap, unplugged the pot and went out the door.

The van keys were, of course, already in the ignition. She climbed inside, shoved the large bag of cat food onto the passenger seat and moved her own seat forward six inches. She did not have Julia's long legs. She did, however, have more expertise in backing the van, as was testified by not scraping further bark from the sycamore tree as she maneuvered out into the street and headed south. Julia had also done a pretty good number on the light pole at the curb. It had a definite northerly lean.

Bonford Antiques bisected the south side of the small town square, as did Marvin Coles's junk shop on the north, Porter DeKalb's car agency on the east, and Mountain Insurance on the west. They all faced towards the soaring turrets and crenellations of the fairy-tale castle called the county courthouse. Turning into the narrow, dingy alley between their shop and the hardware store, Eleanor parked the van next to her own elderly Chevrolet. Leaning against the weathered loading dock was an ancient bicycle which meant that old Ben Fulmer was early also; he was as hot on doing the Welsh dresser as Julia was on the Belter set.

Smiling to herself at the disparate things that constituted people's personal pleasures, Eleanor climbed out of the van. As she reached for the bag of cat food she heard a very impatient and complaining meow at her feet.

A tiger-striped tomcat was looking upward indignantly, his tattered tail in an accusing spike, his yellow eyes saying quite obviously, It's about time.

Eleanor said, "Oh, cool it, Thomaseen; you've never starved yet." She hoisted the bag out and carried it up the creaking wooden steps to the dock. The cat followed; as the door opened with a complaining rasp at the push of her shoulder, he shot inside and sat down pointedly by an empty bowl.

"Spoiled, spoiled, spoiled!" Eleanor said. "That's what you are, cat."

A denim-clad arm waved from behind the half-polished Welsh dresser. Ben's voice announced, "Mornin'—I tried him on m' dog's crunchies, but he didn't care for 'em. Picky is what he is. If you're lookin' for the ma'am, she's up front. Someone was bangin' on t' door."

Eleanor said, "Good lord, it's only eight-thirty!"

The denim arm echoed the motion of a shoulder shrug and disappeared.

Now she could hear Julia's calm voice beyond the door to the showroom. Perfectly in control as usual, she was saying, "How nice to hear of your interest. Do come back later, when we're open, and we'll have one or two other pieces to show you, too. Good-bye."

Eleanor thought ruefully, I would either have ignored the door, or become a wet noodle and let them in.

Standing up, she could see her employer wending her way through the shuttered dimness of the closed shop. Even wearing paint-smeared, baggy coveralls, Julia Bonford was regal—in the grace of her thin hands as they readjusted the lotus shade of a Tiffany lamp—in the set of a well-shaped white-crowned head on erect shoulders. But her smile as she saw Eleanor was warm, and her voice cheerful.

"Good news," she said. "We may finally unload that awful Victorian stuff we had to take to get the Regency chest. Ben, bring a piece or two in from the storeroom, will you? Good morning, Ellie dear. Did you eat the bagel?"

"Yes," said Eleanor. "But you didn't take your pills."

She held them out.

Julia grimaced. "Bother!" she answered, and took the pills in her own hand.

"I probably forgot them yesterday, too. Pour me some coffee, dear, then come look at the settee."

As Eleanor turned, she dropped the medication into a desk drawer and ignored Ben's frown. Shaking his balding head, the old man disappeared into the further room, snapping on a light as he went. Eleanor turned back with a steaming pottery cup in her hand, stepped over a contentedly munching cat and followed Julia through the organized pandemonium of loose-spindled chairs and shaky-legged tables. The Belter settee stood, in all its curving glory, beneath the glare of a work light.

"Done," said Julia. She unbuttoned the coveralls, shrugged them to a heap about her feet, stepped out and accepted the coffee cup. "I think we'll move that suite of Federal furniture to the far wall and put the Belters on the Aubusson carpet."

Eleanor was smiling, but it was really more of a grin. "You mean you'll put them out in full view for someone to buy?"

"Don't get smart!" said Julia, acknowledging her own propensity of only selling to people she liked. "There's a lot of work hours tied up here. I'm certainly not going to sell the set to some klutz to use in a bar."

Eleanor was looking through the open door into the showroom. She frowned. "That Federal stuff is heavy. You will let the boys help move it?"

Julia shrugged. "I suppose." She sipped coffee, shoving a long hand through the white hair slipping over one eye. "Why don't you open up? It's almost nine. I'll go tidy myself a bit, then you can run out to the farm. There's a checklist on my desk. Ben says they used to have some nice old primitives."

Eleanor nodded and obeyed, refilling the conspicuously empty cat dish, a plastic margarine container. Thomaseen had hopped up on a shelf over Julia's desk where he now reposed languorously, licking one paw.

"Spoiled!" said Eleanor again. She raised the roller blind on the window and waved at the two guys next door loading a hot-water heater into the back of a pickup truck. Then she snapped on the showroom lights, punched up the computer, and opened the ancient roll top on her desk. Its measured rattle suddenly brought her up short.

Routine. She was doing the same thing, every morning.

18

So what was wrong with that? It was safe, it was sane, it was useful. It was stress-free.

When in her entire life has she ever had it so good?

Get real, you idiot, she said to herself sternly. For being almost sixty you're in good health, Julia's made you a partner in a business you enjoy, you're almost on top of your financial problems—this month will do it—and you work with people you like.

What the hell else is there?

Ignoring the answer to the rude question that there just might be something else, she slipped the rubber band off the morning paper. Skipping the headlines, she went directly to the back pages where the ads were sandwiched in between the local items and obituaries. One caught her eye. John Cass had died. At one time John had owned the hardware store next door. Recognizing nobody else, she scanned the ads. There was the Crane farm auction bill, and it gave directions. Around the bluff road, then left at the junction. Now she knew where she was going this morning.

The sound of a shuffle and the smell of stale tobacco told her Ben was peering over her shoulder.

"Well, well, Johnny Cass," he said, dusting an overly ornate claw-footed chair with a red, crumpled bandanna. "Poor man—brain-dead as a turnip, he was. Knowin' nothin'. Maybe his wife and that military feller will get married, now. Hope so; they're sure nice folks. Help me rearrange that table and sideboard, Ellie, so's I can put these out."

Eleanor followed him to the front of the shop and obediently tugged and hefted until the furniture was set to the old man's satisfaction. She didn't quibble. Ben had a good eye.

She did, however, feel a warning twinge in her back, and rubbed it carefully as she returned to her desk.

Julia was standing there, now impeccably groomed from dark blue slacks to snowy head, running one finger down a typewritten list.

"Forget the washstand," she said, as Eleanor approached. "We have three good ones and they're a dime a dozen around here anyway. But look at the buffet. Anthony Mondaine's wanting a nice one for some project of his. And," she added, smiling, "I owe him a favor. He just doesn't know it, yet."

Eleanor wasn't going to touch that. She said, "Okay," and picked up her shoulder bag. "The van or my car?"

"Your car. Since this is Saturday, after we close at noon I may need it to get some firewood. It's supposed to turn colder over the weekend. Pork chops tonight?"

"Sounds fine. I'll mash some potatoes."

"Good. I thought I'd ask Mary Ann and Leonard."

Eleanor grinned. "Then perhaps Mary Ann will bring her German chocolate cake."

"I didn't say that."

"No. But we were both thinking it. Okay—I'm on my way."

If Eleanor had glanced back, she would have seen Julie sit down suddenly, rubbing both sides of her neck. But she didn't. She retrieved her insulated coffee cup from the van, got in her car, and drove out into the street heading east.

Insulated or not, the coffee was cold. She went through the Bunny Burger drive-up, got a hot refill, and readjusted her car seat before going out into traffic again. Her back still hurt a bit.

Age, she thought. Or stupidity. You know you can't lift a lot of stuff, idiot!

For long, long years she'd lifted Bobby daily, and it had taken its toll on her muscles. But she didn't regret a thing.

She had passed the long line of stately old houses marking the city limits, and was into the country now, driving between level fields of golden grain. Ahead, the river bluffs loomed, their rocky crags covered with blue-green firs and blazing, crimson sumac. As she turned south off the highway, a huge combine chuffed its way towards her in the dry, brown rows of a bean field; the driver waved a long arm, and she waved back.

A creek ran clear and sparkling over limestone. When she crossed its bridge, she glimpsed a deer contentedly lapping water. The shadow of her car brought his head erect with a snap. She automatically braked, but he merely looked at her serenely with calm eyes. Driving on, she saw in her rear-view mirror that he'd resumed drinking again, and that three others were sauntering out of the tree line with the same possible intent.

But the road ahead was clear, and she resumed her speed. Hitting a deer with a car improved neither the deer nor the car.

Nor the attitude of the insurance company, she added, turning sharply left at a leaning mailbox and driving carefully up a rutted country lane. She was boxed in by thick chokecherry trees and tangled wild grapevines along each side of the road; she turned into the clear space before the fenced-in yard before she saw it was already occupied. By a shabby van, lettered, Coles Collectibles.

Eleanor said a short word not generally attributed to ladies. It was too late to back off. A stooped little old woman in a bib apron was standing on the sagging house porch next to the well-known ratty figure of Marvin Coles, and they'd both seen her.

Mrs. Crane waved, and the relief on her face was as obvious as whiskers on a cat. The look on Marvin Coles's thin visage was a mixture of satisfaction and curiosity; satisfaction, because he'd got there first; and curiosity, because he wanted to know specifically why she was here.

Mrs. Crane was chirping, "Ellie, how nice to see you! Let me go put on some coffee."

Marvin Coles said, "Whoa! You never offered me none, May."

"Didn't think you drank anything but 'shine," the lady rejoined crisply and disappeared inside the house. Her last visible movement was a head jerk at Eleanor indicating acidly, "Get rid of him."

"Ain't it hell to be popular?" Marvin grinned, and leaned against the paint-blistered porch railing. He shook a cigarette from a generic pack and offered it to Eleanor.

She shook her head. He shrugged, lit up, and tossed the burnt match over into the grass where it sent a thin trail of smoke into the morning sunshine. "Been meanin' to talk to you, Ellie."

"Be still, my heart."

"No foolin'. Take me serious."

"All right, Marv. What is it?"

"You know I do a right good business."

"Yes." She had to concede this was true. People would always buy collectibles—and junk. To each his own.

"But I need to spread out. Add some class."

Sweeping up his shop would help. But she didn't say that, only, "Okay."

"I want you to come to work for me."

Her jaw must have clicked. But she was too stunned to notice. He went on hurriedly, "Don't say no. Don't say anything—not just now. Think on it."

24

"Marvin, I—"

He cut right across her, glancing back to be sure Mrs. Crane wasn't listening, "Now hear me out. Since you moved in with that—that queer, Ellie, people are startin' to talk. And you don't need that. Not a nice lady like you—and I can stop it. In a flash. Yes, I can. Jus' come over to work for me, and there won't be no problem—"

The problem was that if the porch railing beneath her clutching hands had been loose she would have brained him with it and set herself up for a charge of manslaughter—or justifiable homicide.

But it wasn't loose.

And he was already sidling off the porch, ignoring her stunned face, saying, "Jus' think on it, Ellie. 'S all I ask."

Through her set teeth, restraining herself as best she could, detesting the skinny, ferrety little man before her, Eleanor said, "Julia and I are partners."

"You're partners?"

"Yes."

He shrugged, clapping a shabby ballcap on his head. "Hope you got that in writin'," he said. "Anyway—like I said: think on it. I'll talk to y' later."

Like when hell ices over.

But Eleanor didn't say it aloud. She could hear May Crane's footsteps inside, and she turned, putting a smile on her face, hoping the Coles-induced freeze wouldn't crack her cheekbones.

Perhaps she did need a change from routine—or something—but Marvin Coles certainly wasn't it.

May Crane asked from the dim living room, "He's gone?"

"Going."

"Thank goodness. Can't stand the man."

The elderly lady emerged with a tray bearing two coffee cups and a saucer of obviously sinful cookies. She put the tray on the small metal porch table, and gestured Eleanor to one of the chairs. Eleanor sat.

"That was fast."

"I had it made. I just didn't want him getting any."

Mrs. Crane took the opposite chair, smoothing her apron over her knees. "My husband couldn't stand him, either. Like the underside of a log, Clyde used to say. Anyway—I heard what he said about Julia."

Eleanor winced. "Oh, dear."

"I know. But I don't believe it, hon. Most of us folks don't. The world had just turned plain vicious. Great day! I suppose next year my grandson can't take an apartment off campus with another guy 'thout folks talkin'." She passed the saucer. "Try one. Out of a tube from the grocery store, but I never made better, myself. Listen— while we're still chattin' on it—that gossip about Julia—jealousy. Pure and simple. Jealousy because she took a store from nothing and made money. By herself. No menfolks helpin'. That's the worst crime."

Eleanor munched chocolate chip, and nodded.

Mrs. Crane went on, shooing off flies with a corner of her apron, "Besides, I knew the fellow she had a hankering for— he got killed on Omaha Beach. And I don't think Julia ever looked at another guy. People forget things like that. Mostly because it suits 'em. And that Marvin Coles—he should talk. Dodged the draft because of his poor, helpless old mother on the farm alone. Pish-tosh. Soon as he could, he sold the farm, chucked mama in a home and married Gracie-Bell Manton because her daddy had money. Which he

27

did," she added, picking loose chocolate chips from the saucer and eating them with relish, "until he lost it all gamblin', and Marvin was stuck."

"He's divorced."

"That's why. Honey, I didn't ask—sugar or cream in your coffee?"

"Black. Thank you. And thank you about Julia. She's been so kind to me."

"You're a good gal. Everyone who watched you with that poor boy of yours knows that. No other family, I guess?"

"A few cousins. Back in Ohio."

"Figured. Since nobody ever showed up to take an interest. I'm so lucky. Got my son and a nice daughter-in-law and three swell grandkids."

"Is that where you're moving?"

"Sort of. A little house next door. With them, but not with them, if you get my meaning. My boy will keep on farming the place, but I'd like him to sell it. He isn't getting any younger, either. Have another cookie."

"I've had three."

"Have another, and I will, then the plate'll be empty."

That was immutable logic in Eleanor's

book. Glossing over her morning memory of her butt in the mirror, she cooperated.

Mrs. Crane munched hers. "Julia's alone, too. Her only brother's been dead for years. Of course they didn't speak when he was alive, and folks said that was Julia's fault, too—but it wasn't. He totally screwed her out of their pa's estate, and she never forgave him. I wouldn't have, either. Spoiled rotten, he was. Had a nice wife, though. And a cute little boy—good gracious, he'd be in his fifties, now. How time does go. Of course, when they were both killed in that car accident, maybe he was, too. I disremember."

She shooed vigorously at another fly. Eleanor finished her coffee, thinking in amazement, I have learned more about Julia in five minutes than in all the years I've worked for her.

"Done? Let's go look at my stuff."

Mrs. Crane stood up, downing her own coffee as she did so. Eleanor rose, too, wincing at the twinge in her silly back. She asked, "Did Marvin find anything he liked?"

"Shoot, girl, I didn't even let him in the door. He can come to the auction like everyone else. We'll do the front room first.

I seem to remember Julia liked my grand-dad's rocker, but that's going with me."

"Do I hear the telephone?"

They both listened. It definitely rang again. Mrs. Crane waved Eleanor into her sunny parlor and went to answer.

Alone, Eleanor stood and looked. Tall, narrow, draped windows, with a caged canary in one, busily throwing seeds onto a worn nondescript carpet. Comfortable, upholstered and use-misshapen sofa and chairs. Blond 1950 end tables, crowned with department-store lamps and burgeoning with flourishing green vines—plastic. Huge TV. Scarred coffee table with one wiggly leg, and a knitting bag open on it. And—between the kitchen and bedroom doors—a really lovely Chesterfield sideboard, cringing under layers of darkened varnish. Bingo.

Eleanor got out Julia's list, and looked. There it was.

Mrs. Crane was still on the phone. Eleanor bent, peered underneath at the dovetails and the bracing. Perfect. Straightening up again, for the first time, her eyes came in contact with the large, framed picture on the wall. It was Mrs. Crane, her husband, her son, his wife, and the "three swell grandkids." Looking straight at the camera. Relaxed. Happy. Smiling.

Tears came to her eyes, brimming on her lashes, and she turned away, suddenly, inexplicably unable to bear the sight. A family. Together.

Why? What had she done wrong, that she couldn't have had that?

"M' neighbor," Mrs. Crane said, bustling in.

Eleanor had hurriedly bent, turning her traitorous face away, fingering the nice brass pulls on the drawers. "This is lovely," she said, hoping her voice wasn't as strange to May Crane as it was to her.

"It is, isn't it? I had to fight m' mom to keep her from junking it, though. Said she was tired of seeing it around; wanted one of those new open bookcases from Sears put there. Try the bedroom, hon. Ain't much, but there is a nice old dresser. Daddy bought it in about 1937 secondhand from an old German fellow."

Daddy should have saved his money. But Eleanor didn't point out the failing veneer, nor the house-nail repair job on the back. She smiled, made herself nod, and they went on.

Twenty minutes did the survey job.

Back on the porch, Eleanor returned her list to her bag and thanked her hostess. "We'll call you Monday," she said. "You really have some lovely things. I know Julia will want them."

She was accompanied to her car by a friendly lanky-legged coon hound, and was watched by three amused Jersey milk cows as she tried to back around in a very confined space without crunching the old wooden fencing. At last, waving at May Crane still standing on the porch, she finally got the Chevy straightened out, and headed down the lane.

It had been a useful hour or so. Julia would be pleased.

And certainly it had also been one in the eye for that disgusting Marvin Coles.

The nerve of the man, thinking she might leave Julia to go to work for him. She'd rather be employed by a packrat.

The coffee in her cup was cold again, but even an insulated one could hold heat only so long. It didn't matter, though; she'd already had enough to float a rowboat.

No cars were in sight. She slowed, looked speculatively at the jungle of trees and bushes along the roadside, saw poison ivy turning red in the sun, and decided she could make it to the shop.

The bicycle was gone, but the van was still parked. Strange. It was well past twelve-thirty.

But her first priority was, of necessity, the bathroom.

Calling out cheerfully, "It's only me!" she turned into the small cubbyhole, left of the door.

Her next priority was fishing Julia's list out of the shoulder bag she'd left in haste in the Chevy.

Thomaseen, basking in the sun on the dock, indicated it would be acceptable to have his fluffy ginger tummy smoothed. She acceded to this briefly, then went back into the shop.

The lights were on. But it was quiet.

Very quiet.

She called, "Julia!"

No answer.

"Julia, it's me!"

Still no answer.

Oh well. Perhaps she's run over to Bunny Burger for a quick lunch. Julia was always casual about locking doors.

But she wasn't casual about her purse.

And there it was, lying on the desk.

Then Eleanor knew something was wrong.

Her heart pumping in her chest, she ran to the showroom door. "Julia, answer me! Julia!"

First she saw the huge old Federal chest-on-chest askew from the wall as if someone had started to move it. With intense relief she also saw Julia, sitting in a chair, her white head bent. She started, "Hi—there you are! Wake up, sleepy, I saw the buffet and you don't want it, but there is a Chesterfield that will simply knock your eye out—"

Then she stopped. Frozen. Knowing the truth: Julia Bonford would no longer care about Chesterfields.

Julia Bonford was dead.

Two

In civilized countries there is often a fortunate if temporary side effect to the social rituals of death and burial. It is a self-induced numbness that holds the pain and uncertainty in check until the proper ceremonies are over. One smiles, although sadly, makes the prescribed responses to well-meaning people, moves automatically through the ceremonial pavane. The hurt, scared little creature inside is caged. Concealed. But it waits its times.

In the ensuing three days, Eleanor Wright made the proper arrangements, said the proper things, endured the proper procedure. She'd done it with Bobby; she could do it again. That her insides were churning was not obvious to either the truly concerned or to those social buzzards of death who feed on signs of grief. There were dark rings beneath her eyes. Her hands were frequently closed, one in the other. But her voice stayed calm. Her mouth smiled.

She remained in Julia's house. It was her home, also. Against the well-intentioned pleas of Mary Ann and Leonard from the shop, and Matt Logan, Julia's longtime friend and attorney, she went back there each night, smiled, said, "Thanks for everything. I'll see you all tomorrow."

Those friends needn't know of the night terrors, the clammy awakenings, the desperate pacing of bare feet down a cold, silent hallway, the frantic beating of fists on Julia's vacant bed—nor the final gulping of sedatives left over from Bobby's death as she steeled herself for the dread of the forthcoming day.

She was, in fact, so tightly buttoned into her own necessity for hanging on that she failed to see the increasing tension in Matt Logan's distinguished old face, the pressure on his arm from his wife as he opened his mouth, then closed it again.

Only one thing penetrated: the nephew of whom May Crane had spoken had survived his parents' car crash. He was a farmer upstate, but commitments of some sort prevented his attending the services.

Big hairy deal. If Julia hadn't needed him before, she certainly didn't need him now.

The surprise that did affect Eleanor's protective fog was the appearance of Anthony Mondaine.

Julia's funeral-home visitation was on Tuesday night, and very well attended. For four hours people streamed into the hushed atmosphere of the mortuary, smiled and waved at friends, shuffled past the open casket, and patted Eleanor's tight shoulder as she stood six feet away, her back to the softly lighted view of Julia's serene profile. She found herself once wondering why she hadn't thought to print a large poster saying, "Yes, it was a heart attack. Yes, she does look lovely. Yes, we'll miss her, too. No, we are *not* closing the shop."

Why, why had she acceded to Matt's advice and allowed an open casket? Local customs go hang—it was barbaric. What the whole thing really constituted was a social event. Look at those people from Donald Antiques in Jacksonville—they're not talking about Julia; they're closing some sort of deal with the folks from Ancient Treasures in Monmouth.

Feeling the anger surge, Eleanor took a deep breath, made herself smile at the little old lady from Art's Crafts, forced herself to nod, got her moved on, then half turned, right into the expertly tied knot of an exquisite silk paisley necktie.

Anthony Mondaine. All six Sicilian feet of him, smiling down at her gently, putting one arm about her shoulders, feeling the tension, saying in her ear, "When can I get you out of here before you scream?"

She shook her head, smiling. "Is it that obvious?"

"To me. Sorry I'm late. I just heard. I was out of town." No value in telling this uptight woman he'd had a disaster of his own—a potential calamity that would have brought him here whether Julia Bonford had died or not.

He'd felt enormous respect for Julia. They'd sparred for years; when she won, she laughed, and when she lost, she shrugged and smiled and said, "Next time, Tony." This time she'd almost won—at least he hoped fervently it was "almost."

As for the graying but attractive widow at his elbow—she was still an unknown quantity and had kept herself so. To him. He was not accustomed to have women, particularly in small towns, distance themselves from Anthony Mondaine unless, as some gossips avowed, she had been Julia's partner in more ways than one. And somehow he just didn't buy that premise. He'd developed a good sense for those off-key things, and this example didn't play.

One thing for damned sure, though: he'd better find out.

And fast.

Eleanor had turned, was patiently countenancing shoulder-patting from an elderly gentleman with a Van Dyke beard.

"Doc McCreary," the gentleman said, thrusting out his free hand. "Up-county vet. Specializin' in hogs. Don't reckon you got any."

Anthony, whose experience with the porcine variety was limited to an occasional bacon and tomato sandwich, agreed that this was so, and with a deft, gentle tug of his hand managed to move the veterinarian by. Then as a reward he found himself faced by a ratty, squint-eyed character in a rumpled suit.

"Mondaine, ain't it?" the man asked. "Marvin Coles. Got the place across the square. Interested in a real nice Federal corner chair?"

"Not today," Anthony answered pointedly, having caught a glimpse of the intense dislike on Eleanor's face. "Get in touch with my people."

"Got an eight-hundred number?"

To get rid of him, Anthony gave him a card.

"Wow," Coles said, "These things ain't cheap. Makes my scribblin' my phone on the back of a charge slip look pretty tacky, don't it? Look honey—" and this was to Eleanor, who—consciously or unconsciously—had moved closer to Anthony, "keep in mind what I said tother day. Okay? The offer's still good."

Tightly, Eleanor answered, "Thank you."

Marvin Coles moved on. Eleanor said to Anthony with a laugh that shook, "Julia used to say about Marvin that she never knew whether to stomp him or spray him. Oh, Mrs. Williamson—thank you for the soup. I did appreciate it last night—and Don's bringing it over."

"We can't do much," the little elderly lady said. "Everyone will miss her. Don sends his apologies. He had to go to St.

Louis to pick up his wife—but they'll both be at the church tomorrow. Why don't you go on home, hon? You look pooped. People will understand."

"Splendid idea," said Anthony, and his brilliant smile made the little lady almost blink.

Then suddenly she said something swift in Italian that made *him* blink.

He replied, laughing, and while Eleanor listened in uncomprehending amazement they rattled back and forth for fully a minute and a half before Mrs. Williamson said in English, "All right. Enough. Ellie's head's whirling. Thank you, sir—that was good exercise for me. I don't get to do it very often. There's my ride. Okay, Erma, hold your horses—I'm coming!"

As she bustled away out the door, Eleanor asked, "What was that all about?"

Anthony turned his attention back to her with an amused smile. "She asked if my parents came from Italy. I said yes. She asked if it was Catania. I said yes, also. And then she said so did hers."

"Wilma?"

"If that's her name. Her mother insisted she learn the language. But she says there's not much use for it in Pike County."

"I guess there isn't," Eleanor murmured, too tired to be further amazed at how little one sometimes knew about people seen every day. There was probably a moral in that, but she was beyond caring at the moment.

The mortician was locking the doors and dimming the lights, looking pointedly at the last few lingerers. He said, "There's coffee in the sitting room, folks. Ellie, why don't you run along home?"

Eleanor sighed, realizing how tired she was. At least tomorrow this ordeal would be over.

Or was it only starting?

"I think I shall," she said. "Thanks Mike. I know Julia would be pleased. And she'd appreciate your coming, too, Tony."

Anthony Mondaine did not intend to be dismissed. His hand on her arm was almost possessive. "Have you eaten today?"

"I—I don't remember."

"That figures. Your car here?"

"Y-yes."

"Leave it. We'll get it later after we dine."

"Tony, that's kind, but I don't want—"

"I didn't ask. I said. Come along, like a good child."

He retrieved her coat from the hall rack, draped it about her shoulders. Matt Logan, the attorney, thrust his white head around the corner and asked, "Are you okay, Ellie? Shall we pick you up tomorrow? We'd be glad to do it."

"I shall," the tall Italian interposed swiftly while Eleanor was still forming words with a tired mouth. "Thank you, sir. Watch the step, my dear—it looks as though it's been raining."

He'd opened the tall door, letting in a damp wind, and deftly guided Eleanor through it. He hadn't seen the dismayed and apprehensive look in Matthew Logan's eyes that had his wife asking, "What is it, Matt?"

"That bastard wants something," he answered softly. "Or knows something. He's never paid attention to Eleanor before. God damn, hon. I wish tomorrow was over."

Eleanor, being guided down the wet and shining steps, was silently wishing the same thing. She was too numb to give much cogent thought to Anthony Mondaine's sudden attentions. Frankly, she didn't care one way or the other. All she wanted to do was get through the next twenty-four hours.

One step at a time. That's all she could manage right now.

Anthony Mondaine's low-slung red Porsche was gleaming wetly beneath the streetlight, very hard to miss in the parked row of Chevys, Buicks and pickup trucks. A light wind skittered dry leaves across the sidewalk before them. A tabby tomcat, intent on something in the barberry bushes, merely twitched its tail as they walked by. Eleanor had the momentary thought that she hoped Ben had been feeding Thomaseen.

But of course he had. Ben was as reliable as sunrise. Thank God she had Ben to help her with the shop.

Opening the door, Anthony tucked her expertly inside, admiring the glimpse of very acceptable legs beneath the soft silk flow of dark blue skirt. Of course, with the complications in his life just now, he'd have to come on to her if she ran on rollers—but it was reassuring to know she didn't. Life had to have some niceties.

The Porsche purred to life. He drove it up the narrow street where flanking porch lights shone orange through the fine mist, onto the small city square, and around the side of the brilliantly lighted courthouse. There, more parked cars, and hanging lamps shining through the grace of green ferns marked the only restaurant uptown.

Eleanor came out of her self-absorbed funk, looked, and demurred. "Oh, Tony, this is nice of you—but perhaps I shouldn't—"

"Would Julia expect you to starve?"

"No, of course not. But—"

"Then be a sensible child."

He was out, around the elegant hood, and opening her door, a compelling silhouette against the opalescent mist.

She shrugged and obeyed. There was certainly no one waiting on her in that silent old house three blocks away.

Never again.

Sensing her desolation, and not totally self-serving, Anthony guided her up the two cement steps by his warm hand on hers, and opened the door to the sound of voices, the warmth, the light and the smell of conviviality.

The real world, Eleanor thought dimly. Where no one has died yet.

But that made no sense. Oh well . . .

Marvin Coles was sitting on a tall stool

at the bar. He waved his beer glass at them as they passed. Neither noticed—or cared—that he suddenly did not look too pleased.

They sat down at a small table behind the ferns. Anthony ordered two *aperitifs,* sighed at the waitress's blank look, changed his order to vodka tonics, then sat back, stretching out long legs in immaculately creased trousers.

"Now," he said. "I command you. No moans and groans. Relax."

"It's not that easy."

"Of course not. I'm not a totally unfeeling fellow. But try. What's the status on the Belter set? Julia was telling me about it a few days ago when she was in St. Louis."

"It's—it's done. She finished it."

"And now?"

"We'll move the Federal pieces over and put it on the Aubusson. It's what she wanted us to do."

"Julia had a good eye." He sipped his vodka tonic. "But will you sell it?"

"I—I don't know." She almost added, "What does it matter?" but realized he was probably just making conversation.

Casually he went on, "My brother said she was looking for some paintings last week. Did she find them?"

"I don't know that, either. If so, I didn't see any." Caught by his words, she was searching her mind as she idly turned her glass in cold fingers. She totally missed the intense point of fire in those dark eyes. "Of course she was always looking for Guy Wiggins or someone in that school. I'll ask Ben."

"No problem. Just idle curiosity." About as idle as a cobra behind a log. Damn the wench! Didn't she pay any attention to what went on in that shop?

"I'm a Wyeth man myself," he went on easily, and led the conversation into that area. She liked Andrew Wyeth also, and he was gratified to see a little color come into the rather nice curve of cheek, and some sparkle in the smoky eyes.

All in all, she wasn't too bad for fifty-some, he conceded, ignoring the fact that he'd never see that number again himself. Men were different. They could be randy at a hundred—but a hundred-year-old broad on the make was a patently ridiculous picture in Anthony Mondaine's mind. He preferred his women lissome and fortyish.

He gave the chubby waitress his generic Mondaine smile as she put plates of steaming chicken teriyaki before them and he encouraged his weary-faced companion, "Chow! Isn't that what they say here in the boonies?"

She smiled but picked up her fork. "What do they say in the streets of St. Louis?"

"You don't want to know. Damn. Not too bad."

"You were expecting alfalfa in it?" Eleanor's tone was a little sharp. As far as she was concerned, he could get off the ultra-sophisticated kick. His background had hardly been on a par with that of Julius Caesar. Julia had told her so.

But he only grinned—a surprisingly disarming look. He said, "Listen, lady. I only discovered good food that didn't have garlic nor oregano in it a couple of years ago—and my stomach has been saying, Thank you, thank you, ever since. Now, I don't mean to pry; I want to help. What's after tomorrow?"

Eleanor looked at the soy sauce container as though she'd never seen one before. To it, she answered slowly, "Life goes on. Isn't that the right cliché? We open the shop, we go to auctions, we deal with customers, we get on with it."

"No plans for change?" Had she noticed, his voice was very, very bland.

"Why? Julia had a good formula. Why screw with it?"

"No heirs?"

"To the business? Just me."

"You're an heir?"

"I'm a partner."

Vistas opened up to Anthony Mondaine. The initial problem with Julia that had brought him to this small burg suddenly began to solve itself. Eleanor was a partner—ergo, now she owned the whole business. And the whole business was an antique shop with a potential for making big bucks unparalleled in the Midwest—when, of course, it was under the aegis of Anthony Mondaine.

The adamant, laughing negative that was Julia Bonford existed no more.

All he had to do was secure the allegiance of Eleanor Wright. And that should be no problem. Not to him. Good God, he'd even marry the woman if he had to. Bonford Antiques his—his brother's idiotic screw-up swept quietly beneath that Aubusson carpet.

With an effort so enormous he thought his heart would jump out of his black-curled and lean chest, he made himself say quietly, "Congratulations. I didn't know that."

"Oh, Really? We went on a partnership basis more than a year ago. Except—the house. I really don't know about the house." She made herself smile, although it was an effort. "I may be out of a home. Matt Logan will have to tell me that, after the services tomorrow. He said he would. But—that's no problem. There's temporary room in the back of the shop and a lot of places for rent. I just—hope I can manage as well as Julia did. She taught me so much—and I'll try. I'll try hard."

"Will you need to hire? I can recommend—"

But she shut him off there, shaking her head, making the silky silver bang slide across arched brows. "Oh, no. At least not at first. I have Ben—and Mary Ann. That's enough. For now."

He shrugged broad shoulders, and accepted her words. For now, he thought, echoing her. But don't underestimate me, lady, when I want something . . .

Instead, he asked, "Dessert? I seem to remember they do a fantastic apple pie."

She shook her head again, and glanced

at her watch. "No, thank you. But I guess I did need to eat. I feel better. And I'll not keep you any longer; take me back to my car."

"You're not keeping me, my dear. I have a motel room for two nights, and more if I need it. And that very good, circa 1900s regulator clock ticking away on the wall behind you says barely nine. Come along. We both need to relax. I've had a hard week, too."

Acknowledging to herself that she was chicken, that she didn't want to go back to that silent, empty house, Eleanor went to the rest room instead while Anthony paid the tab.

Glancing at herself in the mirror, she forebore replacing her lipstick. Why should she? If he wanted a glamour girl, let him drop her off and go out to the local bar.

The chubby waitress came in, folding her ruffled apron, and leaned toward the mirror with a lipstick of her own.

"Hi," she said. "Who's the Romeo, El-lie? He looks like something from an old Cesar Romero movie. Wow."

"Antique dealer," Eleanor answered, pushing the buzzy hand-dryer.

"For an old gent, he's not too bad!"

"I'll tell him," Eleanor lied, but had her first real laugh in days as she went back out the door.

Anthony was waiting by the door, both coats over his arm, not totally oblivious of the admiring glances of the six older-vintage ladies eating pie at a corner table. Their eyebrows went up and they leaned towards each other communally as he took Eleanor's arm and escorted her out the door.

Eleanor said softly, "The widows' club."

"What?"

"The widows' club. Those girls at the table. They'll all be on my case tomorrow."

"Envy, no doubt."

"Maybe. Mostly information."

"Information?"

"If you're not mine, then you're fair game."

"The buzzard brigade."

"They won't poach. They're ethical. Nice girls, really. Just lonesome."

"It is not," Anthony said, opening the Porsche door for her, "an exclusive emotion."

Long strides took him around to his own side. He tossed the coats in the back, and started the motor purring. His handsome profile appeared etched against the restaurant lights. Beyond them she could see the widows peering around the ferns. Yes, indeed. There would be inquiries.

And they probably wouldn't believe she didn't give a damn.

"It's stopped raining," he said, backing out into the shining street. "I'm driving you out to the lake. It's not closed yet, is it? And perhaps we can learn something from the high-school kids."

He was laughing. She said in reply, "Not likely on a Tuesday night," but didn't demur further. That empty house haunted her. At the moment Anthony Mondaine seemed merely a handy port in the storm.

On the way they talked quietly of Chippendale and Oriental rugs and the sudden, incredible surge of interest in depression glass. She told him of the local elderly lady who, when asked by a twittering guest what she *did* with six genuine Hepplewhite chairs, replied dryly, "Mostly, I sit on them." He laughed, pulled with a soft spray of gravel over to the marge of the quiet lake, and turned off the engine.

They were both silent for a moment.

Eleanor was leaning her tired head on one hand, looking at the serene, shimmering water, shining silver as part of the moon peeked coyly through scudding clouds.

Anthony Mondaine was looking at her, wondering when he should make his move, and discovering it wasn't going to be too unpleasant. Eleanor was really quite an attractive lady. She obviously had all the components; the line of soft breasts was very acceptable as she leaned her chin on her hand. And a back-buttoned dress never presented a problem.

And face it: she'd been married, had a kid. Perhaps in sex she could go both ways. He didn't really care—as long as she went his . . .

Across the narrow inlet, four deer stepped from the trees and made their way gracefully to the water's edge. The three does drank, making slurping noises and sending silver ripples outward. The stag, his proud head erect, watched carefully. Then they melted back into the dark of the timberline.

Eleanor sighed, a soft sound in the silence. Then she noticed that Anthony's long arm had gone around her shoulders. When had that happened?

But—it was very comfortable. He was warm. And quiet. And *there*—not lying in a dark box like Julia. And Bobby.

"Perhaps," he was saying with a deep chuckle, "we don't need the high-school kids. For examples."

His long fingers stroked her throat. Gently. Softly.

My God, she thought, it's been years—years since a man did that to me. Since a man even got close—or wanted to get close.

I'm in a box, too. A box of my own making.

Do I want out? Is this step one?

She didn't answer herself. Not then. The same long, gentle fingers tilted her chin upward. He put his mouth on hers also gently—at first, then with a searching force. And the hand slid down, pushing her amazingly unbuttoned gown off bare shoulders, cupping around warm, soft breasts, teasing their rosebud tips, stroking them.

"Where have you been?" he was murmuring in her ear, "Why have I only seen Julia? My God, Eleanor Wright, you're like a Botticelli."

Her body was responding, her breasts swelling, her heart beginning a dizzy thud.

And she couldn't believe it. This couldn't be true. Not now.

He perceived withdrawal; first cursed it—or his rampant body cursed it—then accepted the situation gracefully, although not without a certain concealed smugness. He had got a reaction. It was there. The woman wasn't dead. So, okay. Back off. There'd be a next time.

"Sorry," he said gently into her ear, sliding his hand from those temptingly velvet breasts, restoring the gown to her shoulders. "Poor timing. I apologize. But not for finding you so lovely."

He was pushing her forward, buttoning her dress, giving her shoulder a little squeeze. His voice came to her wryly: "I think I'd better take you home, Circe. We'll continue this at a later, more conventional date. All right?"

And he was starting the car, backing around, heading for the lake road exit.

All right? Was it? She didn't know. She didn't know—anything.

In a barely audible voice, she said, "I—I—"

Then, taking a deep breath, she did manage coherency. "Yes. All right. Other than that, I—I don't now what to say."

"Nothing." His lean hand came over, patted hers. "Absolutely nothing. It was old Mother Nature's timing that was poor. But—keep this in mind, lady—it will happen again. More appropriately. I guarantee that."

And he put the hand back on the wheel.

It was only a ten-minute trip, but for Eleanor it went on forever. He knew. As he pulled the Porsche into the shadows cast by tall Victorian turrets beneath an October moon, he laughed.

"Don't run," he said. "You needn't. Try to sleep, Circe. Shall I follow you home?"

"No, thank you. I'll be fine."

"What time tomorrow?"

"The funeral? Ten o'clock."

"Right. I'll be there at the house about nine-thirty. Okay?"

Kanawha Public Library
Post Office Box 148
Kanawha, Iowa 50447

"Yes."

He was letting her get out by herself, merely leaning over to pat the cold hand unlatching the door. Then he said, "Good night. Remember—try to sleep."

And with a parting wave, he drove away.

Grateful for his careful detachment, not knowing who might be watching from curtained windows, she went stiffly to her own shabby car, slid onto damp seats, started it, drove home.

But *was* it home now? Was this tall, dignified old house of Julia's really her home?

Did she want it to be?

Well. Matt would tell her. Tomorrow. After the services.

Right now, Anthony Mondaine was right. She'd better try to sleep.

She went up on the small kitchen porch and through the kitchen itself, disdaining lights. She knew the way. The vagrant moon was sending hesitant shafts of silver through tall windows into the hallway. Her shoe heels clicked, echoing behind her, out of sync with the ticking clock. Suddenly and painfully not able to bear the dissonance, she bent, took them off, and mounted the half-dark staircase, coat, bag, and shoes in one hand.

Her room was the first on the right. She turned into it, leaving the door open. Who cared? The big bed was unmade, from last night. Or the night before. She didn't remember.

Blindly she stripped, dropping clothing where it fell, shrugged into the crumpled mass of a flannel nightgown, and crawled

inside the sheets, pressing her fr...
against a cold pillow.

Her whole body was rigid enough...
splinter. She tried to relax it. She failed.
She got up, padded down the hall, took
the last of the sedatives, went back, made
herself shut her eyes.

After forty-five minutes of self-recrimi-
nating hell, the drugs worked. She slept,
with only soft anguished sighs which no
one heard but the busy mice in the blanket
closet, until six the next morning. The day
of the funeral.

The end? The beginning? She didn't
know.

She did know one thing: she was scared.

Three

There is a level of numbness after which the human body refuses to accept any more disasters.

I, thought Eleanor wearily, am at that level.

I thought I'd reached it yesterday. I hadn't.

This is it.

Matt Logan is looking at me.

Tony Mondaine is looking at me.

Both, in their own way, are as shocked as I: Matt, because he'd had no idea Julia had been so careless with her business affairs; and Tony, because last night when he almost seduced me, he probably thought he was making love to the new and sole owner of Bonford Antiques.

Well. I'm not.

The midday sun is shining through Matt's office window. Outside, the maple trees are rustling their last rags of red and gold. There's a crisp tang and a smell of burning leaves in the air. By now, Julia's grave in that small cemetery is heaped with floral wreaths, petals fluttering in the wind. And on Bobby's, the urns need to be emptied of dying geraniums, replanted to evergreens.

But those are details. They help preserve sanity, but do not affect reality.

Reality is here. In this law office. Where I am suddenly and unexpectedly back to square one.

"Eleanor—"

One of them was saying her name. It was something she did still recognize in a reeling world. Anthony's lean hand came out, covered hers. But it had been Matt who'd spoken.

He said, "I'm sorry. I'm so damned sorry. I had no idea until I got out her file. Damn Julia! Damn her for being like that—high-handed, assuming that wanting something automatically preempted all previous decisions and made it so. Julia never intended this to happen. She meant you to own the shop. But there's not a damned thing any of us can do until the nephew comes."

The nephew. Someone Eleanor had never even heard about until a casual conversation three days ago. But nonetheless—under the terms of a will made fully twenty years ago and never changed, he owned the shop. Lock, stock and barrel.

An enigma, an unknown quantity, a man who had made some trumped-up excuse for not even coming to his only aunt's funeral.

Well, he was coming, now.

Anthony, darkly tanned and impeccably clad in the gray suit that had heads turning even at Julia's funeral, tightened his fingers on hers. He said,

"Hang in there. We'll work something out. The nephew may be a perfectly reasonable guy. I mean—what does a hog farmer know about antiques?"

His resonant voice showed his easy contempt for the picture in his own cosmopolitan mind: a hulking peasant type with muck on his boots.

Eleanor had a little clearer picture of the twentieth-century farmer than that. But nonetheless, he had a point. Julia's shop might not be a pleasure to someone who lived upstate. It could be an unexpected burden.

Or a windfall.

Oh God, please—not that! Not just quick money from a buyer like—like Marvin Coles, while she, herself, could only stand by helplessly with no finances, no means of counter-offering.

Misery caused her fingers to tighten convulsively on Anthony's.

Matthew Logan noticed, misinterpreted, and frowned. He disliked Anthony Mondaine. This absolutely sudden attention to Eleanor on Mondaine's part had his antenna up and beeping.

He cleared his throat—a courtroom sound.

They both looked at him: Eleanor, with affection; Tony Mondaine with a shuttered appraisal—the old man was smart, and he mustn't forget it.

Matt said, "I was able to talk to him on the phone. Just an hour ago. The nephew."

"And?"

The question came from Anthony. Matt pointedly addressed his reply to Eleanor.

"He'll be here today. Sometime. When he can."

Tony laughed—a dark laugh. He said derisively, "Sure. He couldn't make the trip for his aunt's funeral—but he damned well can come for the loot."

Matt frowned. "No, no. Not at all. We misunderstood. The woman I got on the phone originally—his wife, I assume—didn't make herself clear. He's been out of the country. He just heard about Julia. And he said he'd get here as soon as he could."

Anthony made a wry face at Eleanor. "He probably won a manure-pitching contest, and the Handy Dandy shovel people gave him four glorious days in the Bermuda Triangle. Lighten up, baby. We'll deal with the guy."

Easy to say. But Eleanor supposed Tony was trying to cheer her so she gave both him and Matt a watery smile. However, a fact was a fact: She was out; Benton Bonford was in. So on with the dance, Eleanor. Four days ago she'd thought she needed change. Well. She was certainly going to get it.

She asked, "Where is he coming? The shop?"

"Julia's house," Matt answered ruefully. "He was in it once, when he was ten. He says he hates motels."

"Marvelous," said Eleanor. "Since I live

64

there. Or did. I wonder what I should do first: lay on the fatted calf or start packing?"

Matt said, Ellie, dear, you know Martha and I would love to have you any time—"

"You and Martha may get me," Eleanor interrupted. She blew a small, expressive jet of air. "Oh, well. In the meantime, as they say in the soap operas, life goes on—even while we wait for the axe to fall. I'd better go and see if Ben has opened the shop. We still have the people coming for that seminar on depression glass this evening."

"You didn't cancel?"

"I couldn't. I just couldn't, Matt. Julia had worked for weeks getting it organized. Besides, the visiting expert is booked up clear into the next year. If we didn't have her tonight it would be months before she could come again. I—I guess I thought Julia would want us to go on as usual."

"You're probably right."

Eleanor knew she was. Work had always been Julia's panacea for problems. Now she suspected she also knew why Julia had spent such late, long hours on the Belter set. She'd been in pain. She'd known the reason.

But retrospect was useless, as well as the pain of Julia's not confiding in her, and the guilt of sensing somehow *she* should have noticed.

But she hadn't. Since Bobby's death, and the comfort of living in Julia's house, she'd simply been floating, avoiding all personal stress. Well, the free ride was over. She'd pay for it, now.

She took a second deep breath. "How about the bills, Matt?"

"For her funeral services? Prepaid. She did some things right."

"Then I guess we just wait until this— this—Benton Bonford—is that the name?" At his nod, she went on, "Until he arrives— and we go from there. Matt, did you get any idea on the phone about what he might do?"

Matt shook his white head, taking off his glasses and rubbing tired eyes. Fine print bothered him these days. "None. He didn't seem to be much of a conversationalist."

Eleanor was getting up. So was Mondaine. Damn the man. He seemed to be suddenly sticking to Eleanor like glue. What was his game?

Eleanor smoothed the gray skirt down over thighs, a little rounder than they used to be, and going to Matt behind his desk, she bent and kissed the thin cheek.

"Thank you," she said, "for everything. If you think of anything useful, call me. I'll be at the shop. Other than that, I guess I just play it by ear."

He walked them to the door, shook hands perfunctorily with Mondaine, feeling a petty grudge that the man was a full head taller than he.

He was frankly worried to death. Julia had had a streak of toughness in her. He wasn't certain Eleanor did. That look she had given him at the news of the nephew was like that of a homeless kitten. And even though Mondaine had a St. Louis shop as elegant as Sotheby's the reputation preceding him said he ate small-town women as canapés. His gentle, Sydney Carton-ish sniffing around Eleanor was scaring Matt Logan spitless!

Sighing, he gave them a last wave, closed the door, went to call Martha—then stopped. Damn. He'd forgotten to take his heart pills. And he certainly didn't intend to do a Julia Bonford.

While Matt Logan dug in his pocket for his capsules, Eleanor was allowing herself to be stowed away in Anthony's Porsche.

He fitted himself into his own seat, put his long legs into the proper slots, leaned to give her a quick and unexpected kiss, then started the engine with its particular sound of growling superiority. The motor was not unlike the man, Eleanor thought wearily. They were both the best, and there was hence no need for further discussion.

Ordinarily she could handle it. But in the cold light of today, last night was beginning to loom a little large. He hadn't pressed her—she gave him enormous credit for that—and a good thing it had been, too. She was shocked at how grief had stripped her social defenses without her knowing, and left a vulnerable, primitive woman. She remembered too well how the touch of his mouth and the caress of his lean hands on her breasts had sent them swelling, desiring, heedlessly available. Now, this afternoon, she recognized it as one of nature's dirty tricks on females, probably designed to assure perpetuation of the species. Well. The species could damned well perpetuate further without her help.

She had never been one for the classic quick roll in the hay. Some things made no sense. Last night was one of them.

In that light, she did appreciate his drawing off, not pushing an obvious advantage—and thinking so, she gave him a smile a bit warmer than its actual intent. Misinterpreting this smugly, he reached, took her hand, kissed it, laid it against his lean cheek, and gave it back. Then he sent the Porsche purring down the small-town street, as out of place as an orchid in a petunia bed.

The nephew, he admitted to himself, was a bit of a clinker. Last night things had looked so clear. Gain possession of this broad—marry her if he had to do so; she had enough innate class—with his coaching, of course—to make a good impression on his various international associates, a few of whom for some archaic reason still valued the married state. Add Bonford Antiques with its money-making potential to his string of achievements. Let her run the place, if she desired to do so. And—*numero uno*—quietly reclaim that fake Picasso painting his incredibly stupid brother had sold to Julia last week *before* the discovery of its fakery damaged their reputation to an extent that boggled his mind.

What in living hell had Julia done with the thing?

Dom said she'd packed it in her van and driven away with it.

To where, for God's sake?

Well. No matter. Not now. He'd find it. No one was looking but him.

And Eleanor knew nothing about it. He'd swear to that. So time was on his side.

He wheeled his car into the dingy, ratty alley behind the antique shop, parked next to Eleanor's elderly Chevrolet, but didn't turn off the engine. He said, cheerfully, "I'm dumping you."

Eleanor answered, "Oh, my wounded heart."

"Only until later. I'd better get back to the motel and make a few calls so I can be free this evening."

"You mean you're coming to the depression glass seminar? That's like Mr. Fostoria drinking from a Dixie cup."

She was opening the car door, thrusting out feet in high-heeled pumps, knowing that if she didn't get into something more comfortable shortly, the backs of her legs would cramp painfully. "The ladies," she added over her shoulder, "will be so agog.

Anthony Mondaine among the pink glass sugar bowls."

"My sweet Eleanor," he said soberly, "I am not interested in agogging ladies. I am interested in Mr. Benton Bonford."

Eleanor gathered up her bag and her own copy of Julia's disastrous will. "So," she said wearily, "am I. If you're staying to offer support, Tony, thank you. I'll probably need all the support I can get."

"You have mine," he said, "totally." He put out that lean, brown hand again, cupped her chin. His brows were black bars, silver frosted and his eyes were liquid ebony. His fingers softly caressed the line of her face. "But you know that," he added, "of course."

He leaned, kissed her.

It was a very warm, very loving, but gentle kiss, full of promise. Unfortunately, in the bright thin light of this particular autumn day, no bells rang, no birds sang. He didn't know that, of course, so it didn't bother him. But Eleanor knew.

It bothered her. Twenty years of comparative chastity had not dried up her interest in the opposite sex, and Tony Mondaine was about as opposite as a man could get. She strongly suspected that

Tony's propensities, when truly unleashed, could make Rudolph Valentino look like Mr. Magoo. Last night he'd had her vibrating like a wild Irish harp. Why not now?

Some of her stark uncertainty must have reached him. He raised his head. His face was very close. Beneath the dark moustache, the wide-lipped mouth was smiling. Swiftly it touched each of her eyes in butterfly kisses. Then he let her go. Reluctantly.

Soft in her ear, he said, "Flee, madam, lest I be indiscreet."

She opened the door, stood up. Some sudden, primitive reluctance to be alone made her say, "I make a remarkable cup of instant coffee."

"Preserve it in amber; I shall return."

He put his car in gear, backed away.

She waved, then with a cold feeling, turned slowly around to face the old, splintered beams, the cement loading dock and the faded sign that still read in Gothic letters, Bonford Antiques.

But Julia Bonford was gone.

How could she be?

She was, though. She was. Eleanor had still refused to accept Julia's death this morning, through the flowers and the choir singing and the pressure of people's hands. Even the sighing hemlocks in the cemetery had had no relevance, nor the larks wheeling overhead in the vivid Picasso blue that Julia had loved so much.

She accepted it now—here, on this bare old dock. A cold truth. Julia was dead. Gone. Forever.

"Meow!"

It was an angry voice, a demanding voice.

Through blinking tears, Eleanor looked down at her feet. She saw the ragged, tiger-striped tom, one eye swollen shut, tattered tail in an accusing spike, whiskers bristling.

"Meow!"

It was a peevish accusation from a deprived cat, an abused cat, one separated from home comforts by a cruel world.

Eleanor said, "Oh, for heaven's sake, look at you!"

She shifted her bag, and scooped up the shabby, sulking feline. "When are you going to learn? That marmalade tabby isn't worth it, Thomaseen; she fluffs her fur for a shag rug. Wait until I get unlocked, and we'll take care of your eye."

As she pushed awkwardly at the heavy door the smell of ammonia hit her nose. Old Ben Fulmer rose from beside the Welsh dresser and waved his stripping brush. "G' afternoon."

"Ben! Bless you, but you needn't have come in today."

"You're here, aren't you?"

"Yes, but—"

He shrugged bent shoulders in faded blue overalls and sent a sour look towards the battered tomcat. "Wondered where he'd got. Hadn't seen 'm since yesterday. Took a lickin', didn't you, buster?"

He climbed out, took a scoop of cat food from the bag, bent over and poured it into the empty margarine container. Thomaseen wriggled from Eleanor's arm and crouched over his ration, mingling crunching with sinuous hisses, his ragged tail lashing.

"Dab at his eye when you get a minute. The ointment's on the shelf."

He nodded. She put away her purse in the rolltop desk, and avoided looking over at Julia's where the cascade of receipts, orders, notes, and the leaning row of shabby, much-thumbed reference books all annotated in a firm, upright hand, spoke of nothing but yesterday.

Blinking wet eyes, running one heedless hand through her hair, Eleanor said in a tight voice, "I'd better open up. They'll start coming soon."

"Been a carload at the door already. I told 'em to come back. No loss, probably. Grazers."

"Grazer" was Ben's term for the aimless browser.

Eleanor added her own term: vultures. At least, today. Julia's death had made all the local papers. But if anyone thought her dying had put the merchandise up for grabs, they had better think again.

Unless—oh God—the nephew!

What would he do? Would he value the deep shine on a Chippendale corner chair? Or would he plaster garish FOR SALE signs all over everything, and let his aunt's entire life go down the tube for a quick buck?

Gritting her teeth at the idea, forcing it back behind the more immediate necessities of the day, Eleanor pushed open the second door and went on into the shop. She felt very old and very alone and not just a little cheated.

She threaded her way down the central shaft, a dim tunnel behind drawn drapes. Her feet made no sound on the faded rose carpet strips, but each lamp clicked as she turned it on, sending warm rays from beneath the Tiffany lily and wisteria shades and making the hand-rubbed patina of old cabriole legs and gracefully carved slats shine like lustrous dark honey.

The front of the shop opened to the town square with a door centered between two modest windows. She swished the drapes on the right. The noonday sun poured in. It caught the crystal sparkle of round goblets and transformed itself into slender rainbows spraying across the artful toss of violet velvet to highlight the jewel-like tips of the green fronds of hanging plants.

Eleanor loosed the night chains on the beveled door and moved to open the second window curtain. Here, the sun glanced from the brilliant cobalt blue of fiesta ware filling an old Dutch kas, and lovingly traced the petit point peacocks on the seat of a fine Queen Anne sidechair.

Then she turned, and looked back towards the rear. Her lip trembled, and she swallowed, closing her eyes.

Ben and Leonard had moved the Federal furniture to the far wall and arranged the Belter set on the Aubusson as Julia had wanted. It looked beautiful in all its graceful curves, as Julia had known it would.

And—from the Gustav Stickley rocker to the immense oil painting of snow in New York City with the magic signature of Guy Wiggins in one corner—this was her shop, damn it!

What right did some horny-handed cow jockey have to walk in and take it all away?

Every right in the world that the law allowed.

Eleanor took a deep breath. She said aloud a very succinct but dirty word that the horny-handed cow jockey would have recognized immediately and she went to unlock the side doors.

One led to a graveyard of unrestored and shabby furniture. She left it shut, going instead across the slippery old carpet to unlock the other—then the tears did come, silently, painfully.

Setting up for the seminar was one of the last things Julia had done. There were two long, laden tables. In the brightness of overhead chandeliers the amber and blue and rose and amethyst pieces of glassware sparkled like translucent bouquets of flowers. Eleanor, who had no great love for depression glass, could never have achieved that look of singing violet, of crystal green. Only Julia, with her patrician fingers and her eye for the effect of slender stems and frozen, delicate lace.

But of course Julia had had genius. And Julia was gone.

Whatever came after tonight was up to the dipstick nephew.

Would he sell it? And to whom? Oh, God, please—not Marvin Coles! Herself? Ben? Ben was eighty, on a slim pension. And the only way she'd stayed off public aid had been through Julia's generosity. Would a bank even look at her or Ben without laughing?

Anthony Mondaine. Anthony would probably back her. But did she want to be obligated to Anthony? That much of an obligation?

Turning the pink glass of an Adams compote in her hands, Eleanor thought, Better Anthony than Marvin Coles.

Or would it be? Particularly in the light of last night. Playing games with Tony was all right, something she could handle. But being owned by him was something else—something scary.

Eleanor gave a small, wounded gasp of anguish and put down the compote, thinking desperately that Anthony Mondaine would be a last resort. She wasn't sure why. She didn't even want to think about it right now. But please, God—make the nephew a nice, reasonable, easygoing male, willing to forget that his father and Julia hadn't spoken for years. Make him a pleasant man—one with human sympathy for her dilemma. Was that too much to ask?

Gently she pulled the plastic sheets off the display tables and folded the cover of the refreshment bar. Everything was ready for the caterers except fresh flowers. Also, perhaps she'd best add a few more chairs. Julia's death might bring in some ghouls and she may as well be prepared. There were scavengers in every trade.

But she could deal with scavengers—without a tear, without compunction. They were known quantities. It was the unknown that scared her—like an upstate farmer. She was assuming he wouldn't know a John Belter chair from a Grand Rapids. But—what if he did? Would that be better? Or worse?

Suddenly she realized: Ben probably hadn't heard about the nephew. Ben was as entitled to bad news as she. She'd better tell him now.

"Sit a bit," he said after she'd delivered her bulletin, and she had to admit she needed to obey. His shocked face had melted her matter-of-fact tone and his old hand patting her shoulder had turned her back almost thirty years to the frightened young widow who hadn't known a Shaker chair from a slat back, but who had desperately needed a job. Any job. Ben had been gentle with her, then; he was gentle now.

His old denim jacket lay on the worn cushion of a rattan rocker waiting to have its spindles reglued. Thomaseen was curled on the jacket, purring and kneading his paws. Ben lifted both cat and coat, pushed the rocker forward, saw her into it, tossed the coat into a corner and the cat into her lap. Wearied into amiability by his night's carousing, Thomaseen resumed his purr and Eleanor had her unhappy face in his striped fur.

Ben extracted a tatty bag of tobacco, rolled a skinny cigarette, licked it shut, opened the alley door.

"A nephew," he said. "Yeah."

He struck a match along his shoe sole and lit the cigarette. "Happen I do remember him. A wispy kid, all jaw and carrot hair. His folks got killed about 1940—Julia's only brother, that'd be. He was being sent upstate to live with his grandpa on the farm. He stayed here overnight. Ain't seen 'im since."

He blew a jet of smoke out into the alley and met Eleanor's startled eyes. "But that was him. Has to be. She only had one brother. God Almighty. That little boy. Orneriest kid I ever met. Carved up the dowels from a Windsor chair for Indian arrows. And the gutsiest. When I found him in a heap crying for his folks he said he'd stuck his finger in his eye—and stuck a finger in his eye to prove it. Poor scared, lonely little shaver. I often wondered what happened to him. Julia never said."

Eleanor puffed her cheeks in a sigh. "He survived to own this shop."

Ben shrugged.

"Reckon so. It has to be the same young'un. And he's a farmer upstate you say? Son of a gun. That's why he made the arrows. The kid was a New Yorker, scared spitless about the country. Thought he'd

81

be scalped by Indians. Guess he found out differently. Since it appears he stayed."

"I guess. But why hadn't we heard of him? Julia never said a word—not in all these years!"

"She probably never thought of him again. Bein' on the outs with her brother and all."

"But her will—"

"When was it made? Before you came along, I bet."

"Yes. A year or so."

"That tallies. Julia got sick about then, thought she was going to die. Old Mr. Lawson—that would be Matt's daddy-in-law before Matt married and went into the firm—he probably advised her to settle her affairs. She had no other kin. Bonfords aren't a hardy lot. Then—" Ben took the cigarette from his mouth, looked at its soggy end, made a wry face and threw it into the alley. "Then she got well—or seemed to—and thought no more about it. She wouldn't. Ellie, I'm sorry. I figured you and me could run this place pretty good."

"I thought so, too, Ben."

He patted her shoulder again. "There, now. Let's not borrow trouble. See the bright side. Maybe he'll not change anything at all. Maybe he'll just go away again and let you run the place for him."

But somehow Eleanor could not shake the awful feeling that it simply wasn't going to be like that.

Thomaseen rolled to his back, all four paws waving, and requested that she fluff his pale ginger tummy. She fluffed, but her mind wasn't on it.

It was on the nephew. A "skinny kid with carrot hair." An "ornery kid."

But all grown up now. Late fifties, early sixties. Probably a wife, and ornery carrot-headed kids of his own. Or grandkids. She would never have any.

And coming today.

All right. She'd be "nice." From their first how-do-you-dos. Be pleasant. Capable. Make a good impression. Maybe wear plain skirts and tailored blouses and put her hair in a bun. Put on her glasses, too—if she could find them; she was always leaving them on a table somewhere.

Anyway, show him she was sensible. Astute. Discuss the books, project expenses, estimate profits . . .

The old man, watching affectionately, thought, Poor little Muffin. To him

Eleanor was still the grieving young widow of thirty years ago, vulnerable and naive. All our lives are upset, he went on, but especially hers—and she's the one Julia loved the most.

He thought of the delicate Picasso painting put away for Eleanor's birthday next month, but bought two weeks ago, from Mondaine's shop in St. Louis.

"It's the blue of her eyes," Julia had said. "I had to buy it for her. Tony doesn't know—his brother sold it to me. I may even have whipped it out from under Tony's nose; it was a real steal. But that's all right. Tony's done me a few times, I'm sure. We'll keep it a secret until the party."

The painting had arrived with a shipment from Mondaine's place; they'd whisked it out of sight before Eleanor had caught so much as a glimpse.

It was hidden, now, but Ben knew where. On the proper day he'd give it to Eleanor— then he reckoned they'd both cry. Julia Bonford had been a first-class human being.

As for Anthony Mondaine—he could do without Anthony. He devoutly hoped Eleanor could do without him, too. She'd turned into a prime-looking woman. She had class. If Benton Bonford would leave them alone, they'd make out in this shop just fine.

But somehow, from what he remembered, Ben doubted that would happen.

Strangely, at that moment, on the telephone in the mundane privacy of his motel room, Anthony Mondaine was saying almost the same thing.

Wrapped in a heavy silk, full-length robe, his wet, silvering hair curling darkly around his ears, and red wine in a stemmed Venetian goblet held between two brown fingers, he was saying impatiently, "Of course it's serious, you idiot! This guy is an absolute ringer—God only knows what he'll do. The worst is that he'll decide to sell, lock stock and barrel. . . . Of course, I'll offer to buy it. But what if he insists on calling in some appraisers I can't influence and they find that garbage Picasso before I do? Then we are really screwed up. A fake painting with a fake provenance and my name signed attesting to its authenticity. God! It makes me sick to think about it. Twenty years of credibility down the drain, the Mondaine reputation gone to hell. Why did I ever let you talk me into this racket?"

Far away, in the clutter of his small workshop, Anthony's brother Dominic said quietly, "I think it's called 'greed.' "

Anthony's hand tightened on the glass. Then he slammed it down, trickling ruby drops on the table top.

"All right. All right. But fat businessmen gloating in private over fakes they think were stolen from the Louvre is one thing. Julia Bonford was another!"

"I told you. It was a mistake. I didn't know who she was."

"Well, you know now."

"So find it."

"My God—you think I haven't tried? Eleanor doesn't know anything about it—I'll swear to that—nor the old man. So Julia fiddled it out of that shipment, herself, and I don't know why except she really didn't like me much; maybe to play some game of her own. But Julia is dead, and that fake hangs over me like a knife blade. I don't know when I'll get back to town. I'll be in touch."

He slammed down the receiver, picked up the wine, downed it, wheeled and looked at himself in the long mirror.

His mother's Sicilian eyes in his father's Palermo face looked back. All the polish, all the carefully cultivated veneer dropped away; he was once again fifteen years old, ragged, tough, boiling with anger at his trashy neighborhood, the drunks in the gutters bombed out on cheap red wine, the stinking stairway to his own place, the car that never ran, no matter how many parts you stole, the clean, pretty girls in the parish school, looking down their damned Anglican noses at a guy who didn't even own a belt and underwear.

Well. All that had changed. He'd found St. Louis, he'd found Italian Hill, he'd made the right connections and he'd made the bucks—and he wasn't going back.

Four

Eleanor found herself that afternoon not arranging asters in the old stone jar by the door so much as poking them so they looked like angry question marks.

At four the nephew still had not yet arrived.

Each time the brass bells on the main door jangled, her heart dropped into her shoes. Had he come?

But he hadn't.

So she made herself sit at her desk, methodically check a long list, and write thank-you notes. So many people had been thoughtful. Kind. Mike and his wife at the funeral home. The merchants around the square—those who were left after the mall had appeared on the highway. The ladies who catered the noontime meal at the

Episcopal church. All the fellow antiquarians who'd driven miles to express their sympathy. There were still some nice people in the world.

Anthony had not yet reappeared, and she was grateful, although she did appreciate his staying around. If nothing else, it certainly enhanced the reputation of the shop in the eyes of peers. But neither did she really need the complications to her own life he seemed suddenly determined to pursue.

She'd known him casually for years. He'd never seemed to give her a second glance, before. Why the hell was he doing it now—especially since he knew that the shop was not hers? It was the nephew's. And where was *he*?

She dashed home for a moment in the middle of the afternoon, suddenly seized with the idea that he might have gone there to just sit, waiting.

But he hadn't. Nothing was changed but the half gallon of milk she'd forgotten to put back in the fridge the night before—and the handful of mail on the hall floor beneath the brass door slot—which meant more notes to write.

And the house was too silent for her to

linger if she didn't have to stay. She went back to the shop, wrote the notes, suddenly realized she could have left one taped to the door of the house directing the nephew to Bonford Antiques. She wrote one, sent Leonard back with it. Worried. Looked at her watch. Fused with the centerpieces on the evening buffet table. Told a thin lady with an acid face that a pressed glass pitcher was Philadelphia when it was really feathers and fans, lost a sale. Didn't care.

Suddenly she found Mary Ann and Ben each taking one of her arms, sitting her down, putting a cup of tea in her hand.

"Don't move," said Ben, "lest y' break something. You're a damn hazard. Mary Ann'll mind the store."

Mary Ann, a chunky lady in elastic-topped slacks with a pleasant smile, blatantly black-dyed hair, and efficiency unparalleled, both with cleaning mop and customer, said indeed she would. Thomaseen indicated that if she'd just sit still she could have the privilege of smoothing his back.

She sat. And smoothed.

And thought.

That was the down side to sitting.

One month would have put her out of her financial difficulties and in the black. Julia had been going to take her to St. Louis to dine, for a celebration.

Now she'd lost Julia—and very probably the rest of it, too.

Bobby, whose high-school passion for baseball had been cut short by his illness, used to laugh at his mother's smaller perplexities. He'd say in that careful, slurry voice, "Remember, Mom—when you don't know what to do—take two balls and hit to right field."

Well—this was hardly a small perplexity—and where the hell was right field today?

The caterers for the seminar came in, bearing ice chests of food and immediately attracting Thomaseen's interest. He hopped down, stretched languorously, and trundled after them.

Admonishing him to mind his manners, she glanced at her watch. Four-thirty. Okay. Time to run back to the house, and find something to change into for the evening. Perhaps poke in some laundry—now a necessity. She'd been avoiding it before, knowing painfully that some of the clothes were Julia's.

She called out to Ben, "I'll see you in about an hour. If the nephew arrives, keep him."

Ben nodded, wiping varnish off old hands with a smelly rag. "I brought m' change of clothes. I'll be here."

Leaves flew from her Chevy as she nosed it out of the alley, and all up and down the streets she saw people raking stolidly, making amber piles of leaves. A cluster of small kids were laughing and thrashing about in a pile of their own, leaves stuck to their jackets and bright stocking caps.

Next Saturday, she thought, I'll get to ours—then she acknowledged the painful truth that by Saturday "ours" might be even less a truth.

As she neared the graceful peaks of the old Victorian house set deep among towering sycamores, her heart began to thud.

Would he be there already—the nephew?

In possession, as it were?

But no cars sat on the graveled drive by the weather-beaten garage. The note appeared to be gone, too. Yet it could have blown away. A searching jet of autumn breeze was sending a chill crosscurrent over the high veranda.

She stopped beneath the wooden-lace canopy of the porte-cochère, hurried up the steps and entered the small side entry. Poking her head into the narrow-windowed, gray and green drawing room, she called cautiously, "Hello?"

The Belgian lace underdrapes had stirred in the errant breeze as she'd opened the door. That was it.

The TV was silent. There was no luggage tumbled in the hall, no coat tossed over the back of the tall, damask porter chair. The rest of the mail lay on the table where she'd left it.

Guiltily relieved at not having to face such an unknown quantity alone, she picked up the mail and went upstairs, sorting as she climbed. Bills, of course. A notice of an estate auction. Two notes from other dealers about farm sales. One inquiring about a Belter catalogue, offering five thousand dollars for an original. Wow. Undoubtedly in some old attic at this moment five thousand dollars was gathering dust.

Wishing she knew the whereabouts of such an attic, Eleanor laid the handful on her bedroom desk, stripped, wrapped herself in a thick, terry robe, and dumped the laundry down the shaft that had once held a dumbwaiter but was now a laundry chute. She shut her eyes momentarily, envisioning the heap below on the basement floor and promised to deal with it tomorrow.

In most houses of this vintage the bathroom was merely the hall end with a door added and plumbing installed when such niceties became available. Julia's house was no different. Even though she could use the shower over the tub, the floor space was necessarily cramped. But Eleanor was used to it. Sidling between the sink and the toilet, she wrapped her wet head in a towel, redonned the robe against the chill, and padded back to her room again. Blow-dryer in hand, she faced the fact she needed a haircut, shrugged, and got on with it, trying to remember to remind herself about checking the thermostat. The house seemed unusually cold.

But when she glanced out the window, she understood. The world above the tree-tops was rosy purple with an angry sunset, and a few vagrant raindrops were already splatting against the ancient pane. Great. Just what the seminar needed. Trying to close her mind against the picture of that lonely, flower-heaped mound in the cemetery going sodden and crushed with wet, she told herself to hurry. People would probably be arriving now. Antiquarians always came ahead of time; it must be their acquisitive instincts. The early-bird syndrome.

Eleanor put her feet back into the same dark pumps and eased on the blue silk dress. The one she'd worn for the visitation would have been more appropriate, probably, but she didn't even want to look at where it lay in a careless swag over a chair back. The blue one was now silently telling her bustline that a little less butter on the morning bagel might be a good idea. There were no buttons. Just a side zipper.

She'd used a cover-up on the violet beneath her eyes, but the dark still showed. So what? She was worn. She had been through trauma. No one expected her to look like Shirley Temple.

Put on the pearls. They were her one good claim to quality jewelry, and the people this evening knew quality when they saw it. Handbag. Shop keys. Raincoat.

Down the stairs again—halfway, before she froze.

The doorbell was chiming.

Damn, she said between her teeth, it's him.

And I have to answer. My car is right outside.

Her heels clicked on the bare floor of the hall. She put a stiff smile on her face, her hand on the brass latch, pulled—and received Anthony Mondaine's pointed forefinger full in her middle as he reached to ring again.

She stepped back, gasped, said, "Oh! Thank goodness it's just you."

One black brow dipped. "The word 'just' blunts your enthusiasm somewhat," he said, "and from the look in your eyes, dear love, I rather sense that it's more relief than passion anyway. Whom else did you expect?"

Then his dark face changed swiftly. Answering himself, he went on, "Oh, him. The nephew. Poor baby—if you could have seen your expression—as if you were set for the guillotine. Is the man's coming bugging you that much?"

He stepped inside, closing the heavy door with his foot, and put his arms around her before she could move away. His rich voice against her soft, clean hair, murmured, "Don't, Ellie. He's not going to eat you alive—I won't let him!"

It was momentary temptation to stay there, warm in his arms, held against his custom-tailored suit, let herself be cherished and petted and made all better, as she vaguely remembered a shadowy mother saying. But Anthony's arms were scarcely maternal, and the absolute silence of the empty house behind her was a reminder that things could get out of hand very easily if she allowed them that leeway.

She released herself, moved away, laughed, but also put up a definite wall between herself and the masculine, lean, muscled warmth that had awakened such sensuous response yesterday.

"Yes, he's bugging me," she answered. "He'd bug you, too, if you were in my place."

She had a clear sense that Tony had not liked being stopped. There was that quick, star-bright flash of red in his eyes she'd seen before. When he was angry. More pertinently, when he was controlling his anger.

But if it had been there, it was gone immediately. His own answer was in an easy tone: "But I wouldn't let him get to me—

and don't let him get to you. Let him cut up rough. We're all behind you."

"I know." She said it gratefully. "And I do appreciate knowing. I suppose it's because he's such an unknown quantity—and Tony, my life is in that shop. I can't help being scared. Oh, well. I'd better run."

"I know. That's why I came to fetch you. Ben is holding the caterers at bay; he seems to think they'll put clam dip in the finger-bowls if Eleanor isn't there to supervise. Don't you lock this place?"

In the act of closing the door behind her, Eleanor stopped and looked up at him, startled. "Why—no. We never have. Not here. Not in this small town. I don't even know where there's a key."

"Good God. The Lord does indeed look after babies, idiots and small-town people. If this were St. Louis, my child, you'd not get around the corner before the chop boys would have everything portable in a moving van, including the Eastman Johnson over the mantelpiece. Unless it's a reproduction. They don't take reproductions."

He followed her down the sagging wooden steps, opened his car door, and admired the glimpse of nylon-stockinged calves as she got in.

Folding her coat on her lap, she answered lightly, "Julia never had reproductions. She used to say the only repros in the shop were Ben's teeth."

Oh, thanks a lot, he said to himself, but not out loud. He got the car into the street before he even pursued the subject: "You mean Julia had no funny Fabergé nor pseudo-Picasso?"

"She didn't particularly like Fabergé's knickknacks. And although she loved Picasso—as do I—neither of us could afford him."

Maybe you couldn't. But she could. Or did.

Another dead end?

He had to pursue it further: "You don't have any?"

Why had his voice lowered half a tone? Wasn't the idiot listening to her? A little patently patient, she answered, "No. But perhaps someday—if I ever get a bit of money ahead."

"Shall I look for something—affordable?"

Her yellow caution lights went up. In exchange for what?

99

And at the moment she didn't care for what. She was not in any mood to play games, amatory or financial, if that was his intent. Games were for people whose lives did not lie shattered on the ground.

She answered the cold, non-maneuverable truth: "It depends on the definition of affordable. At this point I could hardly spend five cents even if I could focus my mind on the subject—which I can't."

"The nephew?"

"The nephew."

"I told you not to worry—we'll work things out."

The temptation to inform him that it was really none of his damned affair was almost too hard to overcome. But she might need this man on her side. She made herself smile and answer, "Yes, I know. It's good of you, Tony. We'll just have to see. Turn into the alley again. There's more room to park, and I'd hate to have one of your lovely fenders bumped by someone who only knows a Miss America pattern from a sunflower. And are you really sure you want to stay for this thing? You are going to be bored to the eyeballs."

A sudden idea had struck him. She saw it almost as tangibly as if she'd seen the blow. But she had no inkling what the idea was. She did know, though, that she was correct when he answered, "You could be right. I'm really only here to meet the nephew. Why don't I just wander in and out?"

"Fine. Do that."

Personally, she couldn't care less. And she did realize there would be fewer distractions for the speaker to deal with if he was not there. Deliberately or inadvertently, Anthony Mondaine didn't share limelight well at all.

She climbed out, said, "But do come back for the clam dip," found that the repugnance on his dark face made her feel better somehow, and she hurried up the wooden steps.

If she'd glanced back long enough, she would have seen the Porsche turn right at the street—towards Julia's unlocked house, and a fervent search for a bogus Picasso.

But Eleanor had other matters on her mind.

Feeling well rid of the Mondaine distraction, she went into the workroom and dropped her coat on her desk chair. Ben appeared in the doorway, clad in one of the world's few remaining "leisure suits."

"He hasn't come yet?" she asked.

"Who? Oh—the nephew."

Ben shook his head, loosing a potent draft of Christmas aftershave. "Nope. I haven't seen anybody but the food folks. Look out—" this, as a streak of ginger stripes suddenly shot towards them from the shop, followed by a highly irate flow of invective.

Thomaseen, it appeared, had walked across two trays of anchovy canapés to reach the liver pâté. He hated anchovies, and was partial to liver.

Making the safety of the alley in two leaps, he now sat atop the shop van, calmly licking his whiskers.

Recommending to the battered tom that he stay there, Eleanor closed the door on further forays and went to soothe the caterer's feathers—an effort necessarily brief, since guests were already entering from the front.

For her, it was a difficult evening from the very beginning. Everyone felt they must make their condolences, and after an hour of them Eleanor knew that the expression on her face could be peeled off and put on a shelf.

But people did mean well. And some of

the older acquaintances had lovely things to say about Julia. Eleanor hoped that in some celestial corner Julia was able to listen. She also hoped that she, herself, could gain the same respect someday. If she didn't find herself next week making egg sandwiches at Bunny Burger.

And still no nephew.

How long did it take to drive down from upstate? And what was he driving—Clydesdales?

She did hope he wasn't simply back at the house, just waiting. She'd left another note on the hall table—a polite, civilized note, merely asking him to join them at the shop.

Had that been such a good idea?

Perhaps it would be better just to leave him there. Cooling his heels, as it were. On the other hand, she didn't want him to feel unwelcome.

Fortunately, at that point, the depression-glass expert arrived, and things began to proceed per plan. Eleanor seated herself in a quiet corner. Terms like "Adam" and "American sweetheart" and "Doric with pansy" floated by her chair with the gossamer touch of light fingers. Suddenly she realized to her surprise that she was imminently in danger of going to sleep.

She couldn't do that.

She moved in her Stickley rocker, recrossed her legs, breathed deeply. But old Gustav Stickley had known too much about the contours of the human frame, and the drowsiness of comfort remained. Quietly, she moved to a deeply carved Gothic side chair whose golf-ball sized knobs would keep the dead miserable, and began to count noses, skipping the empty place left for the Country Cupboard representative who had yet to appear. After she'd counted the two from Quincy twice she had to give that up. Perhaps food would chase the drowsiness.

She arose quietly, sidled around to the refreshment table by the door, picked up a canapé, discovered a definite pawprint on it, discarded that one hastily for a crustless ham sandwich, turned, and found herself eyeing the fourth button on the shirt of a barrel-chested, surly looking, white-haired gentleman in an Irish squash hat. This, she thought wearily, has to be my week for regarding men's middles.

The gentleman was looking down at her with no particular pleasure. He must be the one from Country Cupboard, she thought.

He muttered grimly, " 'So the funeral baked meats do furnish forth the marriage table.' "

Eleanor had never been strong on Shakespeare. She stared, not comprehending the allusion to *Hamlet*, and decided to ignore whatever it was he'd said. Whispering, she said, "They saved a chair for you. If you'll just follow me—"

"Damned nice of them." He did not sound, however, as though he really thought it was damned nice. "Which one is Eleanor Wright? I suppose it's the frowsy broad in the Mother Hubbard?"

His voice was not noticeably restrained. A small ripple went down the conference table as heads turned, the lecturer paused uncertainly in her verbal blow, and the "frowsy broad" in the Mother Hubbard glared.

Eleanor's soft mouth went into an ominous line. It wasn't poor manners enough to be late; now he had to be rude as well.

Through her set teeth she answered tensely, "I said they'd saved you a chair." Which was more than she'd have done. "If you'll just sit down—"

"Sit down, hell! My aunt's dead and everyone is having a party. From where I come from, we find that just a little inappropriate. Once more with feeling, tootsie—which broad is Eleanor Wright?"

Oh God, thought Eleanor Wright.

In a cold fury, she shoved him out the door, successful in this maneuver only because she caught him off balance. Otherwise, he'd be as easy to move as a cemetery monument.

"Hey!" he said, catching at the corner of an oak settle, "What the hell's going on around here?"

First she made sure the door to the seminar was closed behind them. Then she wheeled on him. Her nostrils were pinched white. Her blue eyes shot sparks.

"I'm Eleanor Wright," she said with acid crispness, "and you're an uncouth, ill-mannered, loud-mouthed bonehead! Get on over to Julia's house where you belong, and later this evening—*maybe*—if I calm down enough—we can talk this over like two civilized human beings. But don't count on it."

She threw out one arm, a pointing finger at the end. "Now get going!"

His eyes narrowed. He sucked in his

breath and for one long moment she really thought he was going to scoop her up and break her into three neatly stacked pieces.

Then he shrugged, turned, and walked away.

In amazement she watched him, threading his path through the golden glow of Tiffany on beeswax polish like the classic china-shop bull. Dishes rattled and chairs moved. Once he paused. Her breath caught in her throat. But he only picked up a delicate Venetian cruet—looked at the price on the bottom, said audibly, "Holy horses!"—put it gently down and walked on.

When the back door went shut behind him she sat down. Fortunately, a Georgian armchair was beneath her as she had no choice; her knees were suddenly composed of inferior gelatin.

That had been the nephew.

And what had she just done?

Five

Torn it good! That's what she'd done. Bad-mouthed her bread and butter. Told Julia's nephew to get out of his own shop.

Well—rudeness was rudeness, whatever the reason. He'd no right to jump in feet first as he had, make false assumptions and boorish allegations.

And tootsie—he'd called her tootsie!

What a tootsie was—especially in his head—she damned well was not.

At least, she thought angrily, he woke me up. I am certainly not sleepy any more.

She leaned back against the thin stuffing of the chair, closing her eyes. She found she was shaking. That wouldn't do. She had to get herself under control.

But there were already hot tears beneath her lids and they slid out, rolled down her cheeks. How she needed, how she wanted Julia—her warm presence, her voice with its hint of laughter saying, "Never mind, Ellie—we'll find a way."

Eleanor's grief was, for the first time, a physical ache, and—for the first time—she was genuinely close to giving way.

But she couldn't. She had guests and responsibilities.

Thomaseen strolled in, weaving his sinuous way through the forest of table and chair legs. He hopped up on Eleanor's lap, put two furry paws, claws neatly tucked inside, on her shoulders, kissed her ear. He smelt of pâté, and the rolling rumble inside his fluffy chest was a song of repletion.

She hugged him a moment, stroking his silky striped coat, then with a sigh put him down and stood up, smoothing the blue silk of her dress.

Priorities, Julia used to say in times of stress. Place your priorities. Do one thing at a time.

She mopped her cheeks, flipped the last wet drops from her lashes with a shaky finger—blessing waterproof mascara—and was glad she'd been quick. The door from the storage room opened and both Ben and Anthony appeared. They brought with them a definite smell of smoke and cognac.

Anthony asked, "How's it going in there?"

"Fine," she said. She was reluctant to tell them that Benton Bonford had arrived—particularly, she was reluctant to tell Anthony, although she hadn't the faintest idea why this was so. Of course, no one likes to admit to making a royal ass of oneself—and she had certainly done that.

Ben asked, "Think I could go home?"

Eleanor nodded. "Of course. You've put in a long day."

Ben nodded back, peeling the outmoded jacket to reveal an outrageous Hawaiian shirt. The day wasn't over yet, but Ellie didn't know that. He did. He was going to go by his favorite beer joint, wash down the taste of that French stuff with an honest brew, and mull over his conversation with Mondaine while it was still bright in his mind.

Mondaine had kept leading the talk around to paintings, and particularly to Picassos; Ben had stubbornly refused to bite. Julia had wanted Ellie's birthday Picasso to be a secret, and a secret it was going to be. Even with Julia dead, there was no reason not to respect her wishes.

But it was damned curious because Mondaine's forte had never really been art objects. Furniture had been his game. Up to now.

Eleanor was saying, "Good night, Ben. I'll see you tomorrow."

"I'll be in early. That Sheraton sideboard is ready for another rub."

Anthony waited until the far door had closed behind Ben's thin figure, then cupped Eleanor's face in one hand, lifting it. "Tears, love?"

Eleanor spoke the truth—or part of it: "Julia. Tony, I do miss her."

"Of course." He kissed her lightly, moved the hand from face to elbow. "Of course you do. Come along. Let's join the herd. Have they fed yet? Good. I'll ask some fascinating questions to show how amateur I am on the glassery, then reward my humbleness with a cracker or so of the green gunk, and perhaps a sandwich. I do intend to take you out to eat later, so make up your mind to it."

Eleanor's silent reaction to this was dismissive. But she said nothing. Number one, the decision as to what she did or

111

didn't was still hers to make, although after last night he might not think so—and truthfully, she wasn't certain she wanted to eat, anyway. In fact, perhaps never again. Unless it was crow.

She'd been right about Anthony's impact on the seminar. On his entry the ladies unconsciously patted their hair, the men's profiles remained forward, but their eyes slid sideways, and the speaker's vowels got broader, her treatise on the advisability of putting depression pieces in the dishwasher became a bit more portentous.

Of course Anthony recognized all this—and probably, Eleanor thought, took it as his due. He was the first to reach the speaker at her conclusion, modestly introducing himself, and congratulating her on her expertise—underplaying, of course, his own knowledge of the subject.

Eleanor thought to herself, He ought to run for governor. Then she acknowledged that possibly he already had that idea shelved for future pursuit. Anthony obviously recognized no limitations in his own personal goals.

The buffet proved popular, and the guests tended to linger, chatting idly over

Julia's thin Chinese export porcelain cups. Eleanor wished they would go. But she smiled, and nodded, spoke endless inanities and tried hard to be patient.

Her stomach was tied in knots, the primary one being in the shape of an Irish squash hat. She did wish that Tony wouldn't be so patently the supportive swain. Of course, fortunately no one else knew just yet about the nephew; everyone present was assuming the shop was hers. The truth would come out soon enough and she'd have to cope with it. In the meantime the people present might not know about Benton Bonford but they did know Anthony Mondaine—and his attentions to her were causing quite a few nudges and smiles.

Also, private speculations. Lots of private speculations.

It really would be amusing to hear the discussions in darkened cars speeding homeward about whether or not Ellie Wright was going to let herself be suckered by the suave and urbane Anthony—and what advantages there might be to either of them.

Ellie Wright, however, was not amused. When the last person was finally eased out the door, she locked it with almost a spiteful snap. Then she proceeded to the rear, turning off lamps as she went, at least remembering to call to the caterers, "Nice job, guys!"

"God, those folks could eat!" said one of them cheerfully, dumping empty containers into a garbage bag. "I thought old ladies were dainty."

Since the remark was directed to her, Eleanor assumed she should take the tacit exclusion of herself as a compliment. And apparently he hadn't noticed three of them quietly scooping leftover canapés into little plastic bags which then went into their purses.

She replied only, "But they're nice people," and picked up her raincoat. "Is it still misting outside?"

"Nope. Not for the moment. And the weather channel on TV says colder by morning, so maybe it won't. Run on if you want. We'll lock up."

"Fine. Got the bill?"

"On your desk."

"I'll take care of it tomorrow."

"First of the month will be okay. You've had plenty on your plate already this week. 'Night."

" 'Night."

Shrugging into her coat, she went out the door he held open, realizing suddenly and poignantly that she didn't know whether she could write payroll checks or not. And they did need to be done. Ben, Mary Ann and Leonard were on pretty slim incomes. Not to mention herself.

Moonlight shone with cold clarity on the cement of the dock area. It cast a staggered shadow of corner posts down to the alleyway, and blackly fringed the weeds turning brown in the cracked concrete. There was a glint of wet on the trashbin, and more than a hint of chill fall weather in the night air.

Eleanor shivered inside her coat. Anthony was holding open his car door, the engine already purring. She slid inside, appreciating the surge of warmth.

Now the next hurdle—the one in the custom-tailored suit.

He was sliding in on his side, closing the door with its genteel "thunk," and reaching to turn the fan up a notch.

His voice came calmly: "No sign of the nephew?"

"Oh, yes. He's here."

"What? When?"

She told him, her anger still barely disguised.

He said, "Shit! That must have been the big oaf I saw stomping down the steps and roaring off in a dirty red pickup. Where'd he go?"

"I don't know. I was too mad to ask. The nerve of the man, crashing in like that, saying those things!"

"Well, I'll tell you right now, dear girl, that if he's camped at Julia's house, you aren't."

Was that what she wanted? Was that how she took charge of her own life—crying on Tony's shoulder?

Good grief, Eleanor thought ruefully, I'm showing the diplomatic skill of a baby chicken.

She made her voice calmer: "I have to deal with him sometime."

"Right. Tomorrow morning. When you've had a good night's sleep. Good God, girl, you haven't stopped in four days. It's time."

There was validity in that. She compromised . . .

"First, let's see if he's there."

But, to all appearances, he wasn't.

No pickup sat in the drive. There was a

light gleaming through the lace curtains of the sitting room, but it was an automatic switch, coming on at eight.

Eleanor's watch said ten-thirty.

Conscious of enormous relief, she said, "Good. He's gone to a motel."

"Or a bar."

"Whatever. Tony, I'm too tired to eat. Pull in and drop me off."

"Only if I stay, too. I'm not leaving you in an unlocked barn for that moose to come on to."

Oh, for heaven's sake! What did he think she was—a vestal virgin with spaghetti for brains? Clinging to her fast diminishing patience, she said, "I can lock, Tony—from the inside. And I will. I promise. I am so tired . . ."

She let the words trail off—convincingly, she hoped. She was very aware of a more elegant "moose" with perhaps the same intent he envisioned in Benton Bonford. Her idiocy last night had certainly given Anthony no reason to think otherwise.

He slid the Porsche in beside her dented old Chevrolet. The golden light through lace dappled his smiling face.

"It's not precisely what I had in mind."

"This entire week was not precisely what

I had in mind," she answered, and thinking gratefully she'd won, she reached for her purse. Not yet.

One dark arm with the dazzling white of a shirt cuff and the flash of antique diamond cuff links came around her, scooping her cold body next to his.

He murmured in her ear, "Come on—just a little reward for being a good boy," and put his searching mouth on hers. His other warm hand was already on her throat and sliding down she well knew where.

Against his lips her own said, "No. No, Tony."

His hard cheek caressed hers. "Not tonight? No reruns? I was so looking forward to it."

"Not tonight." She made it firm, but did not say aloud, Nor ever. Hard facts might dictate that she need this man.

He sighed, an exaggerated sound, kissed both cheeks and released her. "Think of me, then, in my lonely and indifferent motel room. Crushed. Deprived."

"That will be the day."

"Cruel hussy."

He was leaning across her, opening the

car door. "Go, then, fickle maiden. I'll call you in the morning."

She got out. He gave her a friendly pat and drove away. It would not have improved her mental image of herself to know she was already out of his mind before he made the corner. He was thinking about the damned nephew.

If he *was* in a bar, he'd find him. Make the encounter casual. But they needed to have a chat. . . .

Eleanor stood for a moment in the chill, damp shade of the kitchen porch, trying to get herself together. That Anthony Mondaine had been put off far too easily never entered her mind. Perhaps she'd been out of the dating game too long—at least the *whoopee, into bed we go* phase of it. She'd had a few casual engagements after Bobby died—antique dealers, mostly, trading dinner for picking her professional brains. After she'd moved in with Julia they'd dropped off almost completely—although until now she'd never wondered why. And if now she knew, she certainly and angrily didn't want to think about it.

Besides, she was conscious that her heart was thumping anxiously, and not because of Anthony Mondaine.

Was she right? Was the nephew not there?

The scudding clouds obscured a wan moon as she crunched across the gravel drive and checked the old garage. Two garbage cans, a lawn mower, and stacks of unwanted magazines. No pickup truck.

Okay.

And nothing in the alley beyond except puddles with leaves drowning in them from the sycamore trees.

So. He wasn't anywhere.

Good. Perhaps she didn't need to face up to anything else until tomorrow. All she really wanted to do was to go to bed, close her gritty eyes, and forget everything.

She'd emptied the sedative bottle last night, but there was one more in her bag.

Thinking this, holding it out as a reward, she went up the sagging kitchen steps, her heels clicking hollowly. She grasped the doorknob.

It didn't turn. It didn't even budge.

An awful suspicion knitted her brows and she said softly, "Oh, my!"—innocuous words, but portending a major problem.

Retreating from the kitchen porch, she hurried along the wet gravel to the porte-cochère, mounted those steps, tried that door.

Locked.

Now very concerned, and a little angry, she came down again, went along the weedy walk around the side of the big old house. Her skirts brushed the tall curling stems of the dying hosta plants. Her heels made staccato clopping noises that were a little faster than before.

The front door was also locked.

She was tempted to kick the thing and say, "Open up, damn you!" She thought better of it, both for the benefit of sleeping neighbors and the useless expenditure of energy.

Back to the kitchen, again.

This time she put coat and bag on the small wooden bench and tried the door with both hands.

No way.

So—at last she had to accept the truth: she was locked out.

Ergo: the nephew had locked her out. Innocently, or in revenge. Whichever. It didn't matter at the moment. What did matter was that she was outside. He was, presumably, inside. Even if there wasn't a car.

She sat down on the damp bench next to her bag, pulled the coat back around cold shoulders, and took a deep breath.

Well. What were her options now?

Her watch, squinted at in the dim moonlight, said past eleven. Not a good time to wake up Matt Logan or his wife. Nor get a motel. She'd already given townspeople enough to speculate upon. Sleeping in her car would be murder on her shoulder as well as cold.

She could go back to the shop.

The hell with it!

This expression came into her mind with unexpected venom.

He was not going to run her off like a whipped puppy. If that was his game, forget it, buster!

And she remembered: the pantry window had no lock.

It was just beyond her to the left of the porch. She leaned over and eyed it speculatively. If she lugged this bench there and put it beneath the pane . . .

The hosta plants weren't improved, although she tried to be careful. The high-heeled pumps were a handicap, as well as the raincoat. She removed them both, put them on the bench with her bag, then stood up stretching, trying to get her fingers beneath the sill. This cost two fingernails—one of them broken far enough down to hurt.

She said the same word that once more would have been recognized by the cow-jockey nephew, muffled by the finger in her mouth.

She needed something to pry with.

There was a screwdriver in the Chevy glove compartment.

She got it, paddled back over the sharp gravel in stockinged feet and climbed up on the bench again.

That did it.

The window rose with an almost undetectable groan, about a foot—as high as she could reach.

Now what?

The sill was just beneath her chin.

If she got her elbows on it and quietly wriggled and pushed with her feet—

This was not easy. The knees of the pantyhose went quickly, followed by the toes, and her hair blew across her face tickling her nose.

Compelled by the need to be quiet, she hastily dropped down and muffled the sneeze.

Then she tried again.

Almost.

One more time.

Grimly she scrabbled her knees up the side of the house, trying not to huff and puff. Something inside the pantry fell and rolled to the floor. Her dress caught on a sliver of the sill and ripped. She banged the top of her head on the window sash.

One more good, thrashing pull with everything behind it—

"Do let me help," said a grim, deep voice.

Hands grasped her shoulders and pulled roughly. Her knees scraped. Her dress tore in another place with a loud, ripping noise. Once clear of the window ledge, the hands dropped her, and she fell in a tangled, ungainly heap on the floor. Simultaneously, the pantry light came on and she found herself looking up into the round, mean hole of a gun barrel and the angry eyes of Benton Bonford.

Without the squash hat, his tousled hair was a thick cap of white. The bathrobe inadequately wrapping his middle exposed a great deal of chest matted also with white—the legacy of red-haired parents—

and considerable length of hairy legs, the size and girth of large trees.

The threatening look on his square face faded, however, to one of pure disgust, and he lowered the gun.

"Damn!" he said. "The Wright broad! What the hell are you doing here?"

Being disheveled and on the floor was a tremendous psychological disadvantage. Mustering what shreds of dignity she could summon, she got to her feet unassisted and said very coldly, "I live here."

"You what?"

"I live here! You locked me out."

"How the hell was I to know? Nobody told me."

"You didn't ask."

"I didn't have a chance to ask. As I recall, I was told in no uncertain terms to get out and go home, so by God, I got out and came home."

She said, "Oh!" which was a general indictment of all the obtuse men in the world, white-haired or not. She gritted her teeth and climbed painfully erect. He leaned against the pantry counter with enormous Popeye arms folded across his chest, that scary gun still dangling. He also made no effort to help.

It was hard to be dignified when one's dress was ripped, one's hosiery shredded, and one's feet unshod. But she tried. She pulled her torn dress together—over an unnecessarily lacy display of decollétage—with one hand and pushed back at untidy hair with the other. Almost bitterly she said, "You didn't have to be rude."

"Rude!" And he looked even more disgusted. "Listen, lady. I just spent three weeks of valuable harvest time in whatever they're calling Russia these days trying to work a grain deal that will benefit everyone else but me. I come home and find my wife—the lovely, two-faced Jill—has taken the opportunity of my absence to go to Las Vegas or some damn place where they start divorce proceedings thus ending my second shot at marital bliss. My aunt has died—the only relative except Grandpa who ever gave me a decent shake, whatever her personal proclivities. She's left me, the guy says on the phone, an antique store which of all things I need like another hole in my head. When I come to investigate, I then discover a large group of citizens apparently celebrating her demise with cakes and ale. Surely you understand that I am not too thrilled. When a tootsie in a blue dress tells me to get the hell out, I get. Then—upon hearing funny noises in the dark—I find the same tootsie breaking into my aunt's house. So you must admit, Mrs. Wright—if that is who you are—that the logic of the situation, in the heat of the moment, does tend to become obscure."

It had been a long speech.

Eleanor shut her eyes briefly, waiting for it to be over. Her head ached abominably. Her knees and elbows were oozing blood. Her body felt as if the rude trip over the window ledge had almost dragged it in two.

When he finally shut up, she answered between her teeth, "I am tired. I am beyond arguing logic. Or anything. Welcome to our town, Mr. Bonford. If you want something to eat, there's ham and milk in the fridge—"

"I found the ham, the milk smells funny, and I don't drink light beer—"

"—and bread in the bread box," she went on, ignoring the interruption. "We can continue this exhilarating discussion in the morning. At the moment I am going to bed."

"Yours or mine?"

Her eyes snapped open. He smiled, but there was little humor in it.

He said, "Just wanted to get the lines straight. That's one thing Jill did teach me—don't take anything for granted. Get it in writing."

He looked as unlike Marvin Coles—who had said the same thing—as a pot roast and a wiener. But they had the same mentality.

It popped out before she thought. "You must have had an interesting marriage."

"Like yours," he answered. "If what I picked up at the town bistro tonight has any validity."

It totally missed her. Get it in writing. Get it in writing. Would people ever let her forget that she hadn't? That because she hadn't, she was in this awful position today?

Damn him! Damn Marvin! Damn everybody!

Through her teeth again, she said, "Good night, Mr. Bonford."

"Good night, Mrs. Wright."

As she went slowly up the shadowy staircase she had a sense that he was either watching her or following her. She wouldn't give him the satisfaction of looking around to see, but she did wish desperately to make a less ridiculous appearance. For all of her efforts, her dress tail still flapped, and her toes were sticking out of her pantyhose. She must look like an aging Weary Willie.

But it was his fault.

At the top of the steps she permitted herself a swift glance downward.

He was still in the lower hall, looking up, backlighted by the diffused glow of the night lamp. His expression could only be described as "bemused." Not that he cut such an elegant figure himself. With those enormous legs under the inadequate robe and those enormous arms still folded across his wide chest he looked for all the world like an elderly Bluto from the Popeye cartoons.

Then he caught her look. And he smiled. A raffish, toothy smile.

It so disconcerted her she caught her toe on the loose edge of the hallway carpet and almost broke her neck as she bounced off the old acorn balustrade ornament.

He called up, then, "Hey—okay?"

"Yes!" she snapped. "Thank you!"

On top of all her problems she was showing herself to be about as graceful as a fat lizard.

Well—the hell with it, she muttered silently in her head, and plodded onward, waiting until she was out of sight to rub at her newly wrenched shoulder—the one that gave her fits, anyway.

Maybe it served her right. Maybe she *wasn't* fit to be loose without a keeper.

And it was only then that she remembered: her shoes, her coat and her purse with everything important she owned in it were still on the bench beneath the pantry window.

Six

Setting her jaw, she plodded on. She would not go back down there again. At least, not now. Perhaps after he went to sleep.

Which bedroom had he chosen?

The light streaming out of an open door told her that it was the one with the Chippendale highboy. Besides, she could see clothes scattered helter-skelter over the foot of the low, rumpled bed and the place reeked of smoke. Julia would have had an absolute cow. No one had been permitted cigarettes in her house for years.

The fact that her own room was directly across the hall annoyed Eleanor momentarily. Then she decided she had more important things to pursue than worrying about that. There was a lock on her door.

She assumed it worked. And her arm was not broken.

She went inside, closed her door, switched on a lamp and began to strip off her tattered apparel hurriedly. Sharing a bathroom with Julia had been comfortable, but running down the hall in her flimsies with this clod in the house did not strike Eleanor as too cool.

No luxurious soaking of tired bones tonight.

Damn the man!

A quick survey showed her the dress was irretrievable. Fifty bucks down the drain, even if it had been on sale three years ago. She stuffed it in the waste can with the pantyhose. Then, grabbing her longest, thickest, most sexless old brown robe, she wound it about her, took a quick glance, found the hall still mercifully empty, heard the sounds of water running in the kitchen, and pattered down the hall to the bathroom.

Her dentist would not have approved of the quick tooth brushing, but what did he know? He'd never had to dodge the roving eye of an aging macho bear in a shorty bathrobe.

Her hand on her own bedroom door,

she paused, puzzled by her own thoughts. Why in the world had her mind chosen those particular words—macho, roving?

Tony Mondaine. Yes, indeed.

But the cow jockey?

He looked like a retired Green Bay Packer—macho.

But—roving?

Well—he'd had two marriages already. He'd said so. That indicated some sort of marital distemper. And also, sometimes, she decided cogently, the subconscious knows what the thinking mind misses—and no matter their age, wise women alone in large houses with king-sized men do well to heed their subconscious.

As she reached out from her bed to turn off the light it suddenly dimmed briefly, accompanied by a sudden roll of distant thunder. Great. Another one of those quick, cold fall thunderstorms coming up.

The electricity returning to its full brilliance didn't deceive her. The local power substation routinely developed some sort of technical glitch during rainfall. The power would probably go off again. It wouldn't stay off, but it would go.

Should she tell the nephew?

Why, goody two-shoes? Let him find out for himself.

Another thought struck—should she lock her bedroom door?

Under the heading of "Better safe than sorry," she hoisted herself out of bed, flinching as her shoulder twinged, padded over and pushed the button.

She had to push twice before it clicked. Lord. She hadn't locked her door since Julia had entertained both the lady auctioneer and her pet boa constrictor, and that had been three months ago.

In the dark she almost tripped over the long legs of Bobby's old flannel pajamas. They were a little large, but a safety pin held the pants up pretty well. Besides, if on some awful chance, she had to encounter the nephew again that night she certainly wasn't going to be wearing any skimpy pullover job, which was all she had left until she did laundry.

Laundry.

She'd forgotten.

Tomorrow. Before she went to work.

Hopping back into her high tester bed, she started to pull up the covers, stopped, and sniffed.

The room smelled odd—almost doggy.

Strange.

Oh. No, it wasn't strange. It was the new finish on her small taboret. Ben had warned her the lacquer needed a week to dry, but she'd lugged it home anyway—mostly to keep the thing safely out of Marvin Cole's sight. He'd tried to buy it ever since they'd outbid him at a household auction.

Perhaps if she opened a window. Just a crack. To let in some fresh air.

Out of bed again, she padded over and raised the old sash a few inches. Beyond the pane was only blackness, and the sound of wind soughing through that tall elderly pine by the garage. One of its tattered branches was rubbing the garage roof. Julia had meant to have it sawed off.

Now Eleanor would have to see to it—or someone, she amended grimly.

And it was going to rain again for certain. If it would only hold up until Bluto got to sleep and she could sneak down for her poor coat, shoes and bag. The coat would probably fare all right, but those were the best pumps she had, even if they did hurt her feet—and a good wetting would undoubtedly reduce everything im-

135

portant in that canvas purse to an unlovely pulp.

Damn the man. Again. For whatever time. She'd lost track.

Once more she slid between the light covers, stared up at the black ceiling and told herself the shoulder really didn't ache too badly and she'd best save the last sedative for a real emergency.

She breathed deeply, counting slowly to ten.

Wind swept through the window crack, blowing the sheer curtains and chilling her cheeks even through the layer of night cream.

Again. One—two—three—

Even with the breeze the room smelt doggy. She'd have to tell Ben about that.

Seven—eight—nine—ten. Forget it. Forget the deep breathing also. It wasn't helping.

She sighed, reached out and snapped the lamp back on. Twisting enabled her to see the tiny French clock whose wheels and springs had been lovingly assembled long before anyone ever heard of radium dials.

A quarter of one. This was ridiculous. She had to get up at six; Ben had reminded her of people coming to the shop at seven-thirty to look at that rosewood divan. Selling it would mean many bucks.

For someone.

She made a small, but totally exasperated sound.

Perhaps if she sneaked down and got her shoes and bag. Perhaps it was that piece of idiocy that was bugging her most.

Surely by now the nephew was asleep. He'd driven a long way. He must be tired.

She sat up again and put one toe on the little prayer rug by her bedside. Then she noticed—because of the squeak.

Her doorknob was turning.

Grimly she called out, "Good night, Mr. Bonford!"

"Mrs. Wright—"

"I said, good night!"

"I think you ought to—"

Really angered at the sheer persistency of the man, she cut him off in as chilled a voice as she could muster: "Sleep well!"

There was no further answer, but it didn't matter. The knob had stopped turning.

She lay back down—again—and flopped over, closing her eyes, vowing silently that tomorrow someone had to go. Either him—or her. But this was nonsense.

In the silence of the old house she thought she heard his heavy body creak the springs of his chosen bed across the hall. Then thrash over. And thrash again.

Tough pickles if he couldn't get to sleep either. She really bled for him.

The storm was coming. The lightning was flickering in her window and the thunder rolls were no longer muted.

How long was it one counted between lightning and thunder to find out how far away it was?

She made herself try to remember, and in counting she managed to at last drift off in a listless, gentle fashion just as rain started to patter against the old, whorled glass panes.

Then the horrible thing happened. There was a vicious rip of lightning that shook the entire house, a Wagnerian roll of celestial kettledrums, the lamplight died, Eleanor tried to sit up—and was helplessly flattened by something huge, something enormous, something making obscene noises and trying to get between the covers with her.

Totally berserk, she screamed, tried to reach out but found her arms trapped, felt hair and a wet tongue against her bare throat.

A frantic twist took her from beneath the burrowing heap above her, sent her body with a teeth-rattling bump under the trailing covers to the cold floor. She rolled, got to her feet running, with sheer luck punched the door-lock button the right way, threw open the door and collided thumpingly with the very substantial frame just dashing across the hall.

Large arms caught her smack against a bare, silk-matted chest. They both reeled, doing a sort of strange pavane in the pitch dark of the hallway while she gibbered and hiccoughed and he finally steadied them both with his back against the clammy wall.

Then the lights came on again.

She looked, screamed once more, tore away, shrank against the opposite side of the hall, grabbing the bronze Remington statue from the console table and waving it threateningly over her disheveled head as if she were an untidy Valkyrie wielding a spear.

She said through clenched teeth, "You disgusting, degenerate plow jockey!"

At the same time he said, "Dammit, put

139

that thing down! Maybe the next time you'll listen to me."

"You listen to me! One more step and I'll shell that thick skull of yours like a pod of peas!"

"Oh, for God's sake!"

He stepped back against his own side of the hall wall and put his huge arms in their favorite position, locked across his chest. He looked at her with a scowl as thunderous as the weather, and she looked back with blue eyes darkened by fury and fright to the black of the night outdoors.

In a titanically calm voice he continued, "I said—put it down before someone gets hurt—and you may be damned sure it won't be me. I'm sorry Charlie scared you. If you'd listened—"

"Who's Charlie?" she asked, gasping in horror at the idea there might be two of them. Her grasp on the statue tightened.

"My dog."

That monstrous behemoth that had climbed into bed with her? She grated angrily, "Oh, come off it!"

He shrugged, looked beyond her into the lamplit bedroom and whistled between his teeth.

On huge, furry feet, with dejected head

and tucked-under tail, a large brown and white Saint Bernard padded from her room and sank into an abject heap on Benton Bonford's feet.

Eleanor gasped. She swallowed. She also lowered the bronze statue.

With obnoxious patience the man with the fur footwarmer said, "You can't say I didn't try to tell you."

With no patience Eleanor cried, "Tell me what?"

"That he was probably under your bed."

"Under my—"

"Right. I missed him from my room when I came back upstairs—with, by the way, your shoes, coat and purse, which are there behind you on the hall chair—and which I found when I went to close the pantry window—which you forgot. Anyway. Remember that first bolt of lightning? While we were still downstairs? It spooked him. I knew it would. He's scared pea green of storms. My bed was too low to get under, so he found yours. You must realize that Charlie is a devout and practicing coward—aren't you, old boy? Look at him shiver. You dumb broad, you've got him scared to death!"

"I've got—" Then she stopped. She

opened her mouth like a gaping fish, and to her horror she found her entire defensive system short-circuiting at last—failing utterly, making up for the last horrible four days of being brave. Large tears spilled crookedly down her pale cheeks and trickled a taste of salt into the corners of her unhappy mouth.

Benton Bonford made a noise, too—of teeth grinding. He said hoarsely, "Stop that!"

She put her hands to her wet, woebegone face, shook her mussy head, mumbled, "I'm sorry—I can't. Don't look. Just go away."

Her answer was a resounding smack as Bonford turned and drove his doubled fist into the wall. It left a shallow dent in the old paper and a startled look on Charlie Saint Bernard's upturned muzzle. Benton Bonford, himself, leaned on the fist, undoubled and braced against the dent. He breathed deeply. Rhythmically. Consciously. Over his broad shoulder, not looking at her, he said with careful articulation, "*You* go away. You lock your door. You put a chair against it. I'm telling you."

Then, when—startled—she didn't move, only stared with the glisten of wet on her face, he swung around and his deep voice was taut as a wire: "God damn it, woman, I haven't slept with my wife nor any other wench for eight weeks. And I may be sixty years old but I'm sure as hell not dead yet. Don't you realize how sexy you look?"

Then—only then—did she see that in her frantic wrestling off her bed, the overlarge pajama top had unbuttoned, the safety pin had been lost, the large bottoms had been shed on her dash to imaginary sanctuary and lay puddled beyond her on the floor, and worse, far worse, her deep, incredulous gasp had just increased the soft, round tilt of breasts to be nearly bare.

She also knew something else—she knew with a blinding, dizzying flash that she had never seen a man so beautiful—that from his broad, deep barrel of a chest with its fine silver mat to the brief white, molding jockey shorts and those huge, muscled thighs beneath, he was a Herculean god and his wife must be out of her mind—

There was a different danger here, different from anything she'd ever encountered—either in her short, married span, or in her conservative widowed years—perhaps in her entire lifetime.

The lightning flashed again, dimming

143

the light to a fuzzy glow, but something entirely different was crackling between the tired man and the exhausted woman in the hall, locking their eyes, stopping their breath.

If he had held out his arms—or if she had—either of them, either way—it would have happened, as irrevocably as the tides. Perhaps one of them did—or both. But they'd never know, for at that moment the light went out entirely and through the harsh, painful sound of two breaths came the abject whine of a terrified dog—and it broke the spell.

The man said in a mutter, "Oh, Christ," and stooped through the dark to comfort the huddled mass squirming between his massive legs and the wall. The woman said nothing.

But there was the added sound of a door. Closing. Locking.

Unlocking.

Seven

The storm was passing. The whip and thrash of the pine trees had lessened again to gentle soughing. The crisp, drying sycamore leaves still skittered across the old wooden veranda, but the moon occasionally shone for a brief moment through their patchy parent branches. The air was chill, wet-washed. It swept in through the window crack with the peculiar brown smell of sodden bark and dampened earth.

Eleanor lay flat in bed, staring up at the dim plaster rosette in her bedroom ceiling. The thought of sleep was now laughable. If someone plucked her, she'd twang.

Back to square one. Damn the man!

And double damn the unexpected frailties in her. Reacting like a schoolgirl ingenue. Good God!

But why suddenly feel this way?

Grimly, she suspected Mother Nature, up to her tricks again. Tony had turned her on; she'd resisted, but she had been weakened. Enter, of all people, the nephew—and almost finishes the job.

It's not fair, she railed silently, to an unequal Providence, firmly entrenched in centuries of adamant procedure. And it's not going to happen to me. Unless I choose. And I don't choose. I'm too old for that nonsense.

She thrashed over and saw the lamplight glinting on the Remington statue where she'd put it on her night table. The superb bronze mustang reared, silently pawing the air. She could almost hear the breath snorting from distended nostrils.

The stallion. Always the stallion. No matter how old.

She did her own snorting and felt better—until through the sound of the breeze and the dry leaves and the fluttering curtains came that of authoritative knocking on her unlocked door.

Then she froze.

From the other side a deep voice said, "I'm sure you're not asleep. God knows, I'm not. Get up and put on a lot of clothes.

146

We have to talk. I'll be down in the kitchen."

"I don't think there's anything to say at two o'clock in the morning."

"Don't be an ass. There's everything to say. Don't worry. I've got a lot of clothes on, too, and Charlie will chaperone. Get up. I'm making the coffee."

Incredulous, she heard his feet, shod, going down the stairs, accompanied by a furry schlumping sound that was probably the Saint Bernard.

Had he tried the door? What a frustrating man to not let her know. And what an egoist, to think she'd obey. Be sensible, Eleanor. Stay in bed. Wait until tomorrow, talk to this exasperating man through Matt Logan who knows the proper words to say.

Yet—perhaps that was the point. Tomorrow *would* be Matt Logan, and probably Tony Mondaine, and God only knew who else—and this was, after all, Julia's nephew. This might be the only chance she'd ever have to talk privately, eye to eye. To present her own case, without legal pressure.

Knowing she might be walking a fine line right into another disaster, Eleanor slid out of bed.

A lot of clothes. That's what he'd said.

Grimly she fished in her closet, pulled on a shapeless flannel jogging suit in battleship gray and enormous fluffy house slippers. That should do it.

She shuffled towards the door in the big shoes, then suddenly—on an inexplicable impulse—turned back, picked up two pink hair rollers, stuck them in her top hair with bobbypins. There. "Come back, little Sheba," she said to herself, grimaced at the pale face in the mirror and went down the stairs.

The bright lights were on in the kitchen, and the fine rich smell of fresh coffee caught her nose even as she shuffled across the parquet floor.

The back door was open. Beyond it she glimpsed Charlie, feathered tail a waving banner, trotting about, adding his portion of precipitation to each pine-tree trunk. Benton Bonford leaned against the jamb, cup in hand. Over faded jeans he wore a huge sweatshirt, the back of which was ornamented with the fat south end of a pig going north. With the cup he waved at the coffee maker. "Help yourself. All I could find was decaf, but tonight I figured any port in a storm. Okay, Charlie, come on in."

She ignored the remarks about decaffeinated coffee, chalking them up to another one of his male stupidities. Rinsing her own cup, she poured and tasted cautiously. It was coffee, all right. Yes, indeed. What had he measured with—a fruit jar?

He was grinning. "My kind of coffee," he said. "Too thick to stir, too thin to plow. Sit down. Please."

The last word was probably an afterthought, but she accepted it. However, the ball was in his court as to further action. She pulled out one of the bentwood chairs and sat at the table with that premise in mind.

Benton Bonford closed the door, told his mountain of a dog to lie down. The dog obeyed with a reproachful roll-up of eloquent brown eyes and a *thunk* that rattled dishes in the cupboard. Then he sat down, also. The old bentwood stayed the course; it was sturdy.

If only he doesn't try to lean back on the rear legs, Eleanor thought. That glue won't hold in the joints. It might be gratifying to have *him* embarrassed for a change, but not at the expense of splintering a bentwood chair.

However, he was being merely silent,

clasping both hands about his own cup. She observed that the front side of the enormous sweatshirt showed the same pig, smiling, with a daisy dangling from its snout. Then she looked at the hands. They were not only huge enough to encompass a sizeable coffee mug, but they were red-brown, faintly freckled, and definitely callused. Capable hands. Work-hardened hands.

Inevitably she thought of Tony Mondaine's. They were capable hands, also—hard, lean, brown. And deft. Knowing.

Out of the blue she felt heat surge to her cheeks, and thought in dismay, Oh please—don't let me blush.

But Benton Bonford wasn't looking at her. Not at all. His eyes seemed almost glued to the circles he was idly making as he swished the coffee in his cup.

Out in the hall the old clock melodiously bonged two—or was it three? Eleanor never knew, because the man was suddenly grimacing, white brows drawn down. And he said, very carefully,

"I was thinking. Up there." His head indicated the stairs. "Thinking that—that I might have been a—a bit of an ass."

A bit! echoed Eleanor silently. Try, a lot!

But she said nothing aloud, psyching herself up for another sip of the liquid loam he called coffee and letting him trap himself.

"Logan—that's the lawyer, right?—gave me your name as being in charge of the business. You say you live here—in this house—which obviously puts you in my Aunt Julia's top drawer. What—arrangements you may have had are not—not relevant at the moment."

Was he ignoring her sudden, sharp gasp of surging anger because she'd had about enough of that crap or was he just genuinely trying to sort things out?

He went on, "My Aunt Julia did not 'suffer fools lightly.' Did she?"

Tight-lipped, Eleanor answered, "No."

"So you've had a—relationship of long standing?"

"Yes."

"You were partners?"

"I thought so."

"Why?"

Trying desperately to be calm, Eleanor made herself answer: "Because she told me we were. Because we shared all sides of the business."

"And this house."

She had had about enough. She answered coldly, "Only since my son died. I was losing my own home and everything else I owned to his medical bills. Julia took me in. She was—she was one of the most generous women in the world."

"That's what I remember, too."

"You should."

"I hadn't seen her since I was ten."

"She hadn't changed." Suddenly, despite herself, it was all welling up. Turning her face to the window, drinking from the cup that would shake no matter how desperately she clutched it, she said in a voice thick with tears, "Damn this town! Damn those people in it with minds like sewers! What are they trying to do? Can't they see it's hard enough to have her gone, without having to listen to their lies?"

His answer was to heave his mass erect, get the pot, and top off her cup as well as his. Very quietly, almost compassionately, he said to her, "Don't worry about them. Just help me get my lines straight—then we can go from there. Okay?"

She gulped, swallowed, took the swatch of paper towel from a large hand to mop her traitorous eyes. "Okay."

He sat again, and the chair creaked. "So.

She *meant* to make you a partner. She treated you as a partner."

"Yes."

"But you weren't."

"No. Matt says—says she just—never got around to it."

Had she looked, she'd have seen a gentle smile tug the corners of his mouth, crinkle his eyes at the corners. "That follows. I never got my Christmas presents until July. Anyway. So now I turn up. Legal heir. And you appear to be down the tube."

"Yes." What else was there to say? What did he want her to say? Oh, please, kind sir—or throw herself on the floor, clasping his knees?

She didn't have to do either. One big hand unclasped from his cup, fisted, and suddenly thumped the tabletop so hard both coffees slopped.

"God damn it all to hell!" Benton Bonford roared angrily. "Couldn't someone have told me?"

"You never asked."

"What was to ask? The turkey on the phone merely said my aunt was dead, I'd inherited her antique business so kindly get my tail down here. Now I admit that I am already not too cool, what with Jill splitting to Las Vegas, eighty acres of prime seed corn up to its kazoo in river water, hog futures out of sight, and just off the plane from Russia. None the less, I came. Not even unpacking. Just loading up Charlie and hitting the road. So—I was not, as noted, too thrilled to find at the shop what appeared to be a party. Was it?"

Eleanor shook her head, glaring at him through tear-streaked eyes. "No. And once again, you didn't ask."

"True. And for that, I apologize. I do not apologize for locking the house, although I didn't mean to shut you out. I don't approve of leaving house doors open."

"Doors open. But I didn't—"

"Someone did. The front one was ajar."

There didn't seem to be too much point in telling her at this moment that someone had definitely made an exit out the back as he'd entered the front. She looked genuinely upset as it was. "Anyway. I am here in good faith, although already guilty of at least two bloopers. And, Eleanor Wright, I have not come—" and this he was saying gently, "—to deprive the orphan nor rob the widow. Surely we can work something out."

Eleanor took a deep breath. There it was—what she'd hoped to hear. And the big guy was sitting there looking at her, waiting for an answer.

She took a deep breath. Cautiously she said, "I think we can. I—I hope we can."

Benton Bonford echoed her breath, puffing out his cheeks. The overhead light caught the faint rough beginnings of tomorrow's beard. At his feet Charlie stirred, turning over with his ermine white tummy up and all four, platter-sized paws in the air. Bonford stroked the ermine with a scuffed, booted foot the size of the box Eleanor's shoes came in. Through the half-open window came the rattling sound of dry leaves across the porch. She shivered. He reached out a long arm and closed the window.

"There. The rain's made it chillier."

"Yes. And—there's the sound of—of winter coming."

"Change. I'll bet you don't like change, do you? Even in the seasons."

She started to deny it, then ended by answering honestly, "No. I guess I don't. I've had to deal with enormous change all my life. After a while, you get tired of—of dealing."

He nodded. Stretching one long leg, he fished in his pants pocket, pulled out a battered pack of gum. "Want one?"

"No. Thank you."

"It's supposed to keep me from smoking."

"Does it work?"

"When I'm out of cigarettes. Like now. You have any?"

"No. Julia never smoked. I've quit."

"And survived?" He was giving her a wry smile, shrugging massive shoulders.

"So far."

He peeled the gum stick, poked it in his mouth. "I didn't think I saw any ashtrays. Anyway. What changes?"

"Pardon me?"

"You said you'd dealt with enormous changes. In your life."

Confession time, was it? Oh, well, no harm in telling him a little. After all, he had said the magic words about "working things out." Perhaps if he understood a bit more about her, things would be patently clearer for everyone. She certainly wasn't going to bring in the violins, but there was no point in being obstinate.

She sipped her coffee, finding it cold but she was not willing to ask for more. "I

156

suppose there's not so much. My parents divorced and no one wanted me. So I sort of—just grew," she said. "I married at sixteen. My husband was killed on a motorcycle. My son developed multiple sclerosis. He—died a year ago. What little income I had I managed to screw up. That's when I went to work for Julia. She—she felt sorry for me."

"But not enough to make you a partner. *Per se*. I think I knew that much about her. You must have earned the partnership."

"We worked well together. And I learned to love the business. It is, in fact, the only thing I know."

She smiled, but felt it was a valid point. She had to play the percentages, if only for sheer survival. If the man before her would allow her to run the place. Would that be too much to ask?

But his mind seemed to be elsewhere. Slowly he said, "A drunk driver killed my wife and boy."

Startled into unguardedness, she said, "Oh—but I thought—" then stopped, embarrassed.

He answered her stuttering with a wry smile of his own.

"Years ago. Jill is my second wife. A mistake in judgment on both our parts. I thought she would like the farm, and she thought because I farmed I was rich."

"Oh."

It had been a very small sound. He grinned at her discomfiture, wiping back white hair with one hand. "You obviously don't know much about me, either."

I never heard of you until a week ago, she thought.

But that was hardly the thing to say. She shook her head.

"No. I don't."

"Grandpa Bonford left me his farm. A good one. I haven't hurt it. I raise hogs, a few cattle, and a lot of grain on the bottom land. Right now I'm between a rock and a hard spot because the state wants to put in a recreational lake that will flood a good part of it."

"Oh my. Do you have to sell?"

"No. Not at the moment. But I am trying to look at the big picture—one item of which is that I'm sixty years old with no one to leave it to when I'm through farming."

He took a deep swig of his own coffee, and Eleanor knew by his face that it was cold, too. He muttered, "Damn," and reached back for the pot. "Want some more?"

She shook her head.

He poured, replaced the pot, then smiled at her wearily.

"Want the rest of the story?"

"Why not? You heard mine."

"I get sent with a bunch of other pork producers to Russia—on what they called consultation. They're a mess over there. It just makes you sick at your stomach. Then when I come back, my wife has split and my only aunt is dead. Now I am, admittedly, one of the lucky farmers just now—which is to say the bank doesn't totally own me. However, I must also admit that when I heard about Aunt Julia's antique shop what it did mean to me was a little margin for error. I didn't," he finished quietly, looking directly at her, "know about Eleanor Wright. The one time I saw my aunt, she was in the shop alone. That seems a hundred years ago."

He was trying to be honest. Eleanor tried it, too.

"The shop has potential," she said soberly. "Or it could have. It could make a lot of money. Or sell for a lot of money. There will be buyers—and Julia was very

159

well known." She swallowed, with Marvin Coles's greasy face and Anthony Mondaine's handsome one before her eyes.

"You?"

"No. I couldn't afford it. At least, not by myself."

"Would you want to? Could we work a deal?"

She hesitated, her past financial agonies foremost, and forced to acknowledge silently that with the banks her credit was probably nil.

"I—I don't know."

He was considering her from beneath half-lowered lids.

"How long have you worked with my aunt?"

"Almost thirty years." And she was almost like my mother. But should she say that? Would he believe it? And with the terrible things going around, why should he?

He sensed her hesitation. He leaned forward suddenly, Bluto arms on the table. "Damn it, lady, I'm not going to eat you! I'm just trying to get the picture—and I have only about a week before I have to get my tail home to start my combine on the beans. Which, incidentally, is the one thing

I do owe the bank a bunch for, as my old one died last year?"

"Beans?"

"Combine. Almost a hundred thousand dollars worth of machinery—most of which I have already paid off. The bean crop should pay the rest."

"Or the money from an antique shop." She may as well say it—he'd obviously thought it.

He shrugged massive shoulders. "You said it—I didn't. What I said was that we'd work something out."

She nodded, but she didn't believe. How could the shining treasures of an antique shop possibly equate in importance to a—a *combine* to the man before her. How could he even understand? Why should he understand?

Her head was aching again, and she pressed her fingertips to it.

He looked across at her—the swing of silver ash hair with the two ridiculous pink rollers secured by bobby pins—and beneath it the pale curve of a very tired face. He said suddenly—and gently, "You poor gal. You've really been through it, haven't you?"

She knew a stark truth. She could handle anger—but not sympathy.

Go away, Benton Bonford—upstairs, out, anywhere. Just please go away.

He was stretching out a massive leg, digging in a jeans pocket. She found an enormous white linen handkerchief tucked into one of the hands holding her head. In the same gentle voice he went on, "Go ahead. Cry. You probably need that more than anything. And I don't mind."

In painful, desperate truth she answered, "That's all I've done today."

"But only in dribs and drabs. No good, loud, high-water bawl. Have at it. I'll tell the neighbors I beat you."

He had reached over, was sympathetically stroking her shoulder.

They both felt something else—a chill draft as the kitchen door behind them opened.

Anthony Mondaine's voice, as cool as the wind, said, "I do hope I'm not interrupting something."

Eight

He meant to sound as though he was joking. But anyone who knew Anthony Mondaine would realize immediately that he was not. Eleanor was one of those, and the instant depth of her resentment alarmed her.

She did not belong to Anthony Mondaine—not now, and not ever. She hated the subtle implication to Benton Bonford that she did—and Benton was no dummy; he was getting the message. He had glanced in surprise at Tony, then—as swiftly—back to her. His green-hazel eyes had gone blank. He waited.

All day, Eleanor's emotions had swung wildly from right to left, and now was no different. From grief was but a short step to anger again, and it surged up inside

163

her. Yet, she was no fool; she knew it mustn't show. She needed Tony Mondaine and she needed Benton Bonford—she had to have on her side both of them.

Yet, if two men were ordained to be in opposite camps, they were the urbane Tony and the jeans-clad Benton Bonford who stood facing each other right now.

Mentally she swallowed, forcing back the dismay she felt at having Benton think men were free to appear on her doorstep at any hour of the day or night, and at her indignation at Tony's obvious suspicions, both so rampantly male and—and Sicilian.

Damn each of them. She didn't need complications of this sort.

What she replied to Tony's question was quite different from the knot of exasperation in her stomach. She said calmly, "Of course you are interrupting. Mr. Bonford and I were just planning to fly to Rio for a mad weekend of utter debauchery. Benton, this is Anthony Mondaine. He owns a terribly elegant shop in St. Louis, and has been an invaluable friend to both Julia and me."

They shook hands, saying each other's names, and the handclasp could well have been a physical contest—was, in fact, nearly that—but both men had second thoughts and refrained, for their own, individual purposes.

Eleanor went on, "Sit down, Tony, although I warn you about the coffee. What in the world are you doing out and about at three in the morning?"

Tony sat, next to her, crossing his long legs in their impeccably creased slacks, and declined the coffee. He said in his calm, resonant, faintly amused voice, "I couldn't sleep and was just—driving about. I saw your light and thought perhaps you had the same problem."

He was implying, of course, that he felt free to drop in on her at any hour of the day or night. Eleanor tried hard not to react but in truth she could have kicked him. The Saint Bernard, however, created his own diversion by rising from his position as a throw rug and curiously sniffing Tony's pants.

"Good God, what an enormous beast you are," Tony said.

He was patently displaying no particular affection for enormous beasts. Benton said chattily, "His name's Charlie."

"Charlie?"

"From Prince Charles, of yore—the one

they found up a tree after the battle was over. He is not a noticeable hero type."

Benton was leaning against the kitchen counter, long legs crossed at the ankles, big arms folded, as usual across his chest. He was, also, a bit amused and not at all unhappy at the long, loose hairs that were transferring from Charlie's coat to Mondaine's elegant pants. He went on casually, "I must confess that Eleanor's being up and around is my fault. We felt that there were a number of things we needed to discuss."

"I'm sure," Tony answered, and gave Eleanor an openly questioning look.

She refused to reply with any sort of signal. She said, forthrightly, "We think we can work something out." Let him put that in his pipe and smoke it.

Tony answered, "Excellent." He was averting his eyes from his furred pants.

Reluctantly deciding this dude had suffered enough, Benton said quietly, "Charlie, go lie down."

Charlie padded into the hall, and flopped with a sigh on the cool marble floor.

Benton went on, "And I think I'll take

my own advice. Good night, Eleanor. Good night, Mondaine."

He nodded pleasantly to both of them, went out. They heard him say, "Come on, boy." Charlie rose again with an audible sigh, and both large specimens ascended the stairs. Eleanor was abruptly—and curiously—aware of how suddenly big the kitchen had become.

She knew she was supposed to say something to Tony. Perversely, she didn't.

She watched Tony swallow his irritation. He leaned over, plucked out the two pink hair rollers and asked with obvious amusement, "Did you really need these?"

"What?"

"For protective coloration. These, and the jogging suit: did you really need them? Poor darling, isn't he too ancient to be *that* much of a jock?"

She gave a long, honestly tired sigh. "I don't know. Tony, I really don't. Go home. Please go home. I have to get some sleep. In my own bed. Alone."

He said. "Of course," although to which of her pronouncements she wasn't certain. But he did stand, grimacing at his pants, and muttering, "Damned mutt." Then he bent and kissed her—not swiftly, but lingeringly, lovingly.

Both of them wondered if Benton Bonford was secretly watching.

He went on, "Good night, baby. Are you sure you're all right?"

"I'm fine—just dead on my feet. Tony—"

He stopped, halfway out the door, and—framed against the vagrant moon he had to be the most handsome, sensuous man she'd ever seen—almost. She went on, "He says there may have been someone else in the house."

His mouth tightened. "I told you," he answered patiently, "that not to lock this place up is almost criminal. Now do you believe me?"

"I guess."

"Perhaps you need a dog. Not *that* animated bathmat, God knows, but something. I'll get you one."

"I'm not sure I want a dog."

"What do you want, Eleanor?"

The question was, suddenly, very serious.

She answered painfully, "I don't know!"

He was turning back, holding out his arms, and she was too tired, too hurt, needing human comfort too much. She couldn't resist, she went into them. They closed around her and he said softly into the top of her silvered ash head, "I know. And I'll show you. Sometime."

The smug look on his face vanished as he released her.

"Right now, go to bed. As you said—your own bed. Alone. I'll see you in the morning."

She waited until she heard his Porsche purr off into the night before she switched off the kitchen light. Then she stood for a moment in the dappled, leaf-ragged moon rays, eyes squeezed shut, angry at herself, at Tony, at the world.

Damn! What was happening to her? She'd never been one of those limp-spirited women who absolutely couldn't make it without something male to lean on. Never. Not even in her worst times. In fact she'd intimidated the various men she'd gone out with over the years. Midwestern, small-town girls were supposed to be in need of support—at least those of her generation. She'd been told that.

And laughed to herself.

So what in the world ailed her now? Whatever it was—forget it!

Filled with holy resolution to stand on

her own feet, she put them in motion, one shaggy foot after the other, crossed the hall where moonlight through the high, leaded transom cast ruby and sapphire jewels on the parquet floor, mounted the stairs, clinging with one weary hand, gained the quiet upper hall.

It was quiet, but hardly empty.

Benton Bonford was leaning against the door frame of his room, arms crossed, of course, and face obscured by the hallway gloom.

He said in a deep voice of grim calm, "When you told me about yourself, you failed to mention him."

She had simply had it—with both of them. She snapped, "Why should I have mentioned him?"

"Because, damn it, I want to know all the rules, not just part of them."

Anger surged inside her. "Then, damn it, here's Rule One: I sleep in my bed, Tony sleeps in his, and you sleep in yours! Got that? Good night!"

Slam went her door.

Then she stopped, and listened, the blood pulsing in her ears. She'd not chicken out! She wouldn't lock herself up like a virgin in a convent. She had to cope, and, by God coping started now.

Slam went his door.

More than that—quite audibly, *click* went his lock.

Her jaw dropped. The blood surged, but not in her ears. Not this time. She said, "Why you—" and added a very dirty word not generally used by nice women.

Then, at last, she went to bed, jogging suit and all.

It was not a success.

For one thing, she'd been there before.

For another, it still smelled doggy.

She sighed, got up, reopened the window and leaned into the clean, refreshingly cool air for a moment, hoping it would clear her head. Then she realized that what it probably *would* do in her lightly clad condition was give her a head cold of major proportions. And when she got a cold it was with sniffles, drips, red eyes and wheezes—which would really be great while trying to settle the rest of her life.

One silly hair roller had fallen out. She removed the other and tossed it on the dressing table along with the two bobby pins. Bobby pins. Ye gods! Who else had bobby pins these days? Perhaps she'd better mat them for wall decorations, or bronze them, or something.

Silly—that's what she was getting—and at almost four in the morning.

She could go down and start the laundry.

No, she couldn't.

Her ears had just picked up the click of a door, padding feet, and a muttered male voice saying, "Awright, Charlie, awright, come on, damn it."

They came out on the lawn beneath her window. She watched them guiltily, feeling almost that she was spying—but this man held her future in his big hand. Surely any little nuance she could see was fair game for her side.

Of course what she did see was a large dog happily trotting about, lifting his furry leg on every tree in sight, and a tired man wearing an unbuttoned shirt over faded jeans and staring into space.

Once he looked up, and she ducked back so fast she almost broke her neck over the dressing-table bench. After that she crawled into her messy bed and listened again to the six heavy feet, this time ascending.

The bedroom door didn't lock.

Perhaps he forgot.

Who cared?

But one thing was certain. Somebody had to go. This old house might have fourteen rooms, but it was not big enough for both of them.

Realizing the probable truth—that the departure would undoubtedly be hers—she finally went to sleep.

Nine

Eleanor awoke to the sweet, silver chime of her French clock and opened gritty eyes reluctantly on a pearly morning. She felt, not too inaccurately, that she'd just got to sleep.

Inanimate for just a few brief moments, she stared at the plaster ceiling rosette, trying hard to get herself organized. Her mind also felt as if someone had filled it with marbles, rolling in all directions—but, at least, it was different from yesterday, when she woke to a silent house, with painful memories, each empty corner echoing with a beloved voice that would never be heard again.

Today the house was not by any means silent.

A dog—a large dog—was somewhere at

a window, barking a large bark. As she lay there, listening, another voice—also large—bellowed, "Charlie, damn it, shut up, or I'll open the window and let that squirrel inside!"

It was obviously a potent threat, for the bark ceased. Then the door across the hall opened, bare feet thudded bathroomward, that door slammed, the water went on and there came the buzz of an electric razor.

It was all rather—nice, Eleanor thought, then scowled, not happy with her sap-filled streak of latent Susy Homemaker or with the insidious way the owner of those feet had dominated her dreaming.

The sound of water streaming turned to that of water spraying. The buzz of the razor stopped, a deep voice dum-dee-dummed tentatively, then broke into something vaguely resembling "The Volga Boatman," interspersed with a few Russian words that were patently ribald in intent if not in articulation.

Obviously he hadn't spent all his time in Russia soberly consulting with grain farmers.

He was turning out to be a man of many parts, this Benton Bonford. Refusing to fit the mold of the upstate hog farmer was only one of them. And the idea of his standing in the shower soaping bothered her. She could envision the water flattening the thick white hair to the back of his sturdy neck, pushing lacy suds in wet scallops down, down, cleansing the broad chest with its curly mat, the huge muscled flanks—

She was out of her everloving mind.

Eleanor hit her pillow one resounding thump with a doubled fist, swung bare feet to the cold floor, stuffed them into the fluffy shoes. The oval mirror above the Regency dressing table stood in full morning light. She shuffled to it, made herself stand, take a long, hard look at the faithful image thus displayed.

You idiot, she told herself bitterly. What are you trying to have—a second childhood? Who the hell do you think you are?

I'll tell you. Not a dewy rose, kiddo. You're going to have a birthday in six weeks and it's not going to be twenty-one. Furthermore, right now you are in a scrap for sheer survival—and don't try to gloss it into being anything else.

If you have to *pretend* you're just a lil' ol' helpless sweetiepie, that's one thing, because the name of the game right now is getting what you want. But going all squashy because a white-haired cow jockey has been deprived of his regular roll in the hay so long that even you looked good—that's different. *That,* you cannot afford.

When Benton Bonford came out of the bathroom, he found her swathed to the eyes in the heavy robe and leaning against the wall. Waiting. Obviously. This was called "trying to establish a pecking order in the facilities."

It failed. He only breezed by, wafting a smell of soap and aftershave, and saying, "Hi. Hurry up. I went down and made the coffee."

He'd also used up all the hot water.

When at last she descended the stairs it was grumpily, with the use of the curling iron not a success on hair that needed cutting, and the blue, heavy sweater hopefully distracting attention from the mud stains on the bottom of gray slacks. She *had* to do laundry.

Benton was at the table, tucking away a stack of toaster waffles. "Hi. Want some?"

"I don't eat much breakfast."

"City girl. If you were on the farm you would."

Ignoring that, she poured a cup of coffee, took a tentative sip and waited for the initial jolt to her taste buds. It came. After that, they were so numb it didn't matter, and she drank hastily, her mind on the laundry.

In a polite voice he said, "I hope Charlie didn't wake you."

Charlie, if he put his canine mind to it, could probably wake the dead. "Oh, no. I had to get up. I've a seven-thirty appointment."

"At the shop?"

"Yes."

"May I come?"

Dandy. She needed this man breathing down her neck while she tried to make a sale about as badly as she needed measles.

But he owned the place.

"Of course. First, I have to put in some laundry."

"That stuff on the basement floor? I already did. I hope you don't mind—but I came off in a hell of a hurry and kind of shortchanged my wardrobe."

Sudden, horrible visions of good sweaters shrunk to the size to fit Barbie dolls must have frozen her face, for he laughed and went on gently, "I set the water on cool—and sorted stuff. No pink T-shirts, nor pantyhose stuck on zippers. Promise. The first load is in the dryer."

What time had he gotten up?

That must have shown on her face also, because he dropped his eyes to his coffee cup and said to it, "I—I didn't sleep well. I was—wandering around, and thought I might as well be useful."

She nodded, a movement that must have looked both affirmative and sympathetic because the tension between them suddenly left. "I appreciate it. I really do. I guess I'm just not back on track, yet."

"And some of those things were—are—Aunt Julia's."

"Yes."

"That's hard. I know it is. Shall I fold them for you?"

"No, no. I'm a big girl. And I know where they go." At least for now. But she didn't say that. One thing at a time.

Still, he met her at the top of the basement steps, and took the sweet-smelling armload from her. "I have to get my gear. Where shall I put these?"

"On—on the chest in the hallway."

"Right. Then are you ready to go?"

"Yes. That last load will be fine until this evening."

"Okay. Be right back down."

The stairs creaked as he ascended them. She didn't look but she heard. They'd never creaked for Julia.

Last night's cups were already in the dishwasher, but on the opposite side from where she and Julia put them. Absently, she moved them over—then stopped stock still. What was she doing? Who in the world cared where they were, as long as they were washed properly? Had her world become so set in stone as to be endangered by misplaced cups?

When he returned, he was shrugging a denim jacket on over his shirt and jeans. He went to the door, whistled Charlie in from the yard, gave him a bowl of dry food and a bowl of water, and told him he'd be back. Charlie hunkered down quite happily into the shape, if not the size, of a muff and almost instantly went off to sleep.

"His middle name," Benton said, grinning, "is Insouciance. Ready? Let's go. Hey—what about the doors?"

"Oh." And she grimaced, a little sheepishly. "I forgot. And I have no idea where there are keys."

He shrugged. "Okay. No sweat. Charlie!"

Furry ears raised.

"Guard, Charlie. Guard."

Eleanor said, "Surely you jest."

"No. Not at all. It's the unknown that spooks Charlie. He understands about people. He won't let anyone in this house now except you and me—and that guy, last night—what's his name?"

"Tony. Tony Mondaine."

"Yeah. Him." He was opening the door and pale, golden sunlight spilled across his broad shoulders, making his eyes almost green. A little sheepishly he said, "I hope I can ride with you. My pickup's down the street a block—out of gas."

Well. That answered that question.

She laughed. "I guess neither of us had a particularly good day yesterday."

"May the rest be better—since the only way to go is up."

"I hope so," she replied fervently, and preceded him out the door.

His truck was where he'd left it—at the curb, drifted with yellow cottonwood leaves. It was bright red, with Bonford Farms painted on the door and some baling wire for a tailgate latch.

As they drove by, Eleanor said, "Ben can bring you back over with some gas."

"Ben? Who's Ben? Good lord. Not the same cranky cuss who worked for Aunt Julia when I was a kid."

"That's him."

She parked the van in the shop shed because there was another one backed up to the loading dock with its doors open and a stack of old, tattered quilts already laid out. It would appear that her customer was intending to deal.

He was. He came to the back entrance with a broad smile, a stocky man whose hairpiece hadn't quite kept pace with the aging fringe beneath it—but nevertheless a nice man, and a shrewd one. He knew a good thing, and the rosewood set was that. He said cheerfully, "Mornin', Ellie. Fine day."

Climbing from the tall van, she answered, "Good morning, John. Sorry I'm late."

"Hell, girl, you ain't late. My damn gallbladder wouldn't let me sleep last night, so I just got in the rig and came on."

"When are you going to tend to that

thing? John Moss, this is Benton Bonford."

"How j' do. Sorry about your aunt. She was one of the best."

Benton said, "I agree."

But once the handshake was over, John Moss was through with amenities. Looking beneath his salt and pepper brows at Eleanor, he asked, "You still saying fifteen hundred?"

"Absolutely. With what we've got in it, that's not much margin."

"Couldn't talk you down to twelve?"

She laughed but shook her head.

"Damn. You're a hard lady."

"I learned from the best."

He laughed. "That you did. Sold. Let's load 'er up, Ben."

They disappeared into the shop. Eleanor and Benton stood on one side, out of the way, as they reappeared carrying a curve-backed, velvet covered divan. Benton said to Eleanor quietly, "I presume that wasn't as easy as it sounded."

Eleanor shook her head. The cool morning breeze sprayed silver hair across one cheek and she pushed it back absently. She was remembering the auction where she'd first seen that divan. It had been in a back yard beneath an ancient lilac bush, weathered completely gray and smelling of cat. The matching chairs had finally been found on the rafters in a tool shed, seatless, with the stringers wired together.

"No," she said. "It wasn't that easy."

How could she explain to this towering farmer the hours spent—the loving hours—bringing rosewood back to the glowing beauty it showed this morning in the pale sun. He probably wouldn't even be interested. And why should he?

She merely added, "He's been dickering for it since July. And the price is fair. John knows that. Besides, he'll take it into that place of his in Springfield, sell it to some dimwit with more cash than brains and double his money."

"Is that what Mondaine does?"

She hesitated. "I guess. In effect."

He let that pass—for later. He went on, "Don't the—the dimwits ever come here?"

"Oh Lord, do they ever! But you see—" She drew her brows down, kicked with her toe, tried to find the right words. "You have to understand Julia. How she was. Julia rarely sold anything she valued to someone she—she didn't like. She put too much of herself into a piece to tolerate its going to some bonehead who'd reupholster it with Ninja Turtles and leave it on an open patio."

She didn't notice how careful his voice was: "That doesn't sound like good business."

Her voice short, she answered, "We didn't starve. Look out, Ben, you'll catch a corner."

Ben mumbled, "Got it." He was concentrating on hefting his end without barking the varnish. At times like these he had to realize he wasn't getting any younger.

Carefully he put his part of the love seat on the carpeted floor of the van and turned away, mopping his face and leaving the positioning to the purchaser. He found himself looking at the middle button of a blue shirt, let his eyes travel upward, stared, and said, "Good gravy! It ain't!"

Benton grinned, thrusting out a big hand.

"It is," he said. "I grew. How are you, Ben? Good to see you again."

They shook hands heartily, no contest. Ben chortled, "Did you scalp any Indians?"

"What?" Benton looked startled, then

laughed. "No. No Indians. But I did get two chickens and the ear on a yearling before Grandpa broke my arrows over his knee and didn't do too badly with my backside. Can I help?"

Ben stepped up inside the van. "Hand in those quilts. Hey, John, this here is Julia's nephew."

"We met." The dealer stuck his mismatched head out and took an armload of quilts. As he carefully wrapped his purchases, he asked casually, "You in the business?"

"No. I farm."

" 'Round here?"

"Up north."

"Any good stuff like this up there?"

Eleanor saw a strange look of almost pain go across Benton's face. He answered quickly,

"Not any more. My wife's not—into this sort of thing."

"Modern type, I suppose."

"You could say that."

John jumped down, slammed his doors, dropped the bar and locked it. "Okay. Now the hurty part. My check's all right?"

"Of course."

He wrote it briskly, bending over Julia's

186

old desktop, and waved the results in the air to dry. "There you are. Now—just don't get to the bank before I do."

Everyone laughed politely. Eleanor said, "Come again, John."

"You better believe. Call me when that Welsh dresser's done."

"Got a hankerin' for it, have you?" grinned Ben.

"Not me. And my wife's on a Shaker kick—says anything hung on t' wall is easier to dust under. But there is a guy, just got promoted to something real important, and now he's wantin' to furnish his house like the big boys do. We might deal. As I said, give me a call."

He got in and started his motor with a series of backfires that shot indignant starlings from beneath the shed roof.

Benton grinned. "Sounds like my Farm-all," he said, which meant nothing to Eleanor. "Sure hope he makes it home."

Ben said casually. "He will. If he has to push. John just don't particularly like to spend money on frills—like fixin' cars. My God, boy, you sure growed!"

He was looking up at Benton. Benton was grinning down.

"Well, I've stopped now," he said, "except maybe for here." He slapped his stomach.

Ben replied, "Oh, pshaw. That ain't nothin'," and slapped the protuberance the size of a muskmelon above his own belt.

Not a part of this love feast, Eleanor looked at her wristwatch. "Eight o'clock. I'm here. I may as well open."

"You are open," Ben said shortly. "A couple came in when John did. I told 'em to go graze. The man's not bad, but the woman's a real dinger. Money, though. *Wall Street Journal* type."

Eleanor shrugged. "Onward and upward," she said, and turned towards the shop door. It was already opening. A tall, thin, elderly man stood there, flanked by a short fat woman with too many necklaces and a painted, petulant face.

Eleanor said politely, "May I help you? I'm Eleanor Wright."

The man answered, "How j' do." The woman said crossly, "We were here yesterday, but the place was locked."

Eleanor made no effort to explain. She only said pleasantly. "Is there something you're interested in, Mrs.—uh—"

"Smith. J. Calder. This is my husband, Calder. And yes, there is something I am interested in—those Queen Anne things in the window—that is, if they are not reproductions. We don't care for reproductions, do we, Calder?"

Calder replied something like, "Mmmf."

His wife was already leading the way, waddling back across the Aubusson carpet towards the front window, beads jingling and ample fanny bouncing in the fairly lenient confines of a stretch-denim sports skirt. She wore pink yarn-balled golf socks which also bobbled as she walked—a fact that Eleanor failed to notice, but Thomaseen, lazing off the night's excesses beneath a wicker basket chair, took great interest in watching. Perhaps they looked, to the cat's eyes, like small baby mice.

"These," said Mrs. Smith, indicated with one pudgy hand the lovely round, small table and the two side chairs with their petit point peacock seats. "How much?"

Eleanor said, "There are three more side chairs, and an arm chair." She was wondering what Mrs. Smith meant by reproductions—or if she *knew*. Grand Rapids repros, perhaps. Grand Rapids repros, to a lot of people, were synonymous with junk.

The lady's plucked eyebrows had risen at the news of four more chairs. She said, "Oh." She hesitated. "They're a set?"

"Yes."

"You have the provenance?"

Eleanor smothered a smile. Mrs. Smith had been reading too many antique magazines. "I'll have to check. I believe we only have them dated back to 1858."

"Are they—I mean—did they—"

Her husband interrupted in a faintly weary voice, "Emily wants to know if they were owned by anyone famous."

"A governor and two senators." And a bankrupt cat house, which was where Ben found them. Somehow, Eleanor sensed that Emily wouldn't care for that.

"Oh. Indeed." The arched eyebrow bit again. "May we inspect them?"

"Of course. Shall I get the others?"

"If it's no trouble."

"Not at all. Excuse me a moment."

From the corner of her eye as Eleanor went to the back, she saw Mrs. Smith open her bag, take out some small objects.

Ben and Benton Bonford were swinging their legs off the tall dock and apparently having a cozy chat, the subject matter of which she wasn't sure she'd care about from their self-conscious faces as she approached.

It annoyed her a little, although she knew Ben was on her side. She said, "Another mail-order expert. She was getting out her tape measure when I left, and I'll bet Calder already has lint on his knees trying to see the screws and the dovetails."

Benton frowned. "What's the tape measure for?"

"The table. Wood only shrinks in one direction. If the top is perfectly round it's new. Old ones are oblong. Ben, I need those other chairs."

"Think she's serious?"

"It's worth a shot. Anyone who wears designer sports shirts in size 44 can't be too poor."

Ben hauled himself erect. "Okay. Come give me a hand, boy."

Thomaseen was gathered lightly into a plush crouch, his tail tip just flicking. He was interested in those pink mice. What he had to do was worm his way through the forest of furniture legs and get just a little closer.

"Only two dovetails," Mr. Smith was reporting as Eleanor returned to them. His wife had put away her tape and was holding a small magnet to the table drawer pull. It was responding exactly as a solid brass pull should respond—by doing absolutely nothing. Mrs. Smith looked, if anything, a little disappointed. She probably preferred to pick. She asked rather sharply, "What about the seat covers?"

"We have a craftsman who does them for us from the original design," Eleanor answered smoothly. The Jasper twins had put themselves through three years of college so far with their needlepoint, even though they were full time footballers. "If you'll just step to the back again, the men are bringing down the other chairs."

She turned to lead the way, and found Anthony Mondaine coming down the aisle. The Tiffany lamps turned his hair to frost and made his teeth almost blue-white beneath the heavy moustache. The dark blue golf sweater completed the picture, making him so handsome it fairly hurt to look. Eleanor heard Mrs. Smith suck in her breath—and her stomach. She was probably patting her hair. Tony had that effect on women.

"Good morning," he said.

Mrs. Smith cried, "Do you own this shop?"

Tony grinned. "No, madam. He does."

He pointed with blank-faced relish to a dusty giant in blue shirtsleeves, stripping brown paper paper from a sidechair.

Mrs. Smith said, "Oh." Then she said, "But I know you. You—You're that Mondaine man. In St. Louis. The one my daddy bought the painting from."

Ten

No one even noticed the slight freeze to Tony Mondaine's smile—not even Eleanor, who was trying to decide whether or not she was glad to see him.

Fortunately, for this small hiatus in Anthony's charm, the plump Mrs. Smith gushed on, "Daddy buys those things then simply squirrels them away. Mummy and I find it so annoying. What's the use of having something if one can't show it to one's friends, we always say."

"He shows them to no one?"

"Well—his men friends, occasionally." She made a small moue.

Tony looked—just fractionally—relieved. "Ah. Well—to each his own."

"But a Van Gogh!"

"I'll tell you what," Tony went on and

his white teeth flashed. "Come into my shop and I'll sell you one for yourself. Good morning, Eleanor darling. You're looking fetching."

Such lavish praise for the gray slacks and pullover was laying it on a bit thick, Eleanor thought, and knew the well-larded Mrs. Smith was thinking so, too. The lady half turned and gave her a somewhat more respectful look.

Eleanor only smiled. "Mr. and Mrs. Smith are looking at the peacock chairs."

"Indeed. Are they meeting my price?"

Well. Sly Tony; he knew all the angles. He needed those chairs in his place like she needed bubonic plague but that was a piece of information the Smiths were lacking. She turned, smiling, to them, "I don't know."

Mr. Smith said hastily, "We're thinking. Come, Emily, they've got the others ready for us."

Tony stood aside and let them go by. He grinned down at Eleanor. "That'll cost you, darling," he murmured.

"Do you remember them?"

"I remember 'Daddy.' Many bucks." He was still speaking quietly. "How are you doing with the tractor jockey?"

"I don't know." That was God's truth. "As soon as I get a chance, I have to call Matt and set up a meeting."

"Scared?"

More—or yet? She compromised. "A little."

"Shall I take care of it?"

"By doing what? Dropping him off the nearest cliff?"

"That's a possibility. But, no. Let me buy the place and you run it. If he'll sell."

There it was: a solution, right smack in her lap. Why did the adrenaline start to pour?

Eleanor knew why. It was the look in his liquid ebony eyes, the sensuous feel of his hand quietly stroking her back. What an easy out. Let Tony take over.

Take over everything. The shop. Her.

Because that's how it would be. What did she have going for her, besides a ten-year-old car? Nothing. The expertise she'd learned from Julia meant nothing to Tony either—he could hire a dozen people with expertise. Basically, she was an Indian, not a chief. And if he got the shop, what guarantee would she have of staying on when he tired of their deal—or tired of her? She could still go down the tube—

Unless she played it right. Got something legally binding.

That was the solution. That's what she'd have to have.

If what Tony Mondaine offered was better than what Benton Bonford said he could "work out." If "working out" did not include Marvin Coles.

Abruptly she caught Benton Bonford's eye. Clear down the length of the shop she caught it as he towered over the Smiths and looked her way. It was a quizzical eye, a curious eye, and the heavy brows were peaked.

Then she realized the tableau she and the elegant Sicilian must present—the close stance, the tilted faces, the possessive arm about her shoulders. And the arm tightened. From the corner of his own eye Tony had also caught the gaze.

Hating herself, she deliberately played both sides of the fence. Standing on tiptoe, she kissed Tony's cheek lightly, removed herself from the half embrace and started down the aisle. Over her shoulder she said, "It might be worth a try."

Tony was no fool. Even without seeing, she knew the red star had flashed. He didn't follow. And he said, "The offer is limited."

Of course it was. Men like Tony Mondaine did not wait forever.

They didn't have to stand still. They were men.

Damn them all, Eleanor said silently, and gave Benton Bonford an innocent, brilliant smile.

He had stepped back, was leaning against the tall Welsh dresser, arms folded, while the Smiths went through their little examining routine again.

Unnoticed, Thomaseen skulked between his legs and the wall like a striped shadow. The target kept moving, those enticing pink morsels just beyond his paw. If they'd only stay still a moment.

They did.

Unfortunately, due, perhaps, to the previous night's excesses, Thomaseen's aim was a bit off. He got, not only a pink yarn ball, but a nick of Mrs. Smith. She screamed. She grabbed her foot. He fled, a striped wraith. She turned around, hopping, and saw the John Belter suite.

So it was really Thomaseen's fault.

She stopped hopping. She put the foot down and said, "Calder—it's that man—

what's his name—four pieces. I want it. I must have it. No, no, I'm all right; I must have backed into something. That doesn't matter." She swung on Eleanor. "How much?"

Eleanor's heart had pulled itself into a small cold ball. Not the Belter suite—not to this pursy, ridiculous woman with the gimlet eyes. She thought desperately, Julia, Julia, what are the words you would have said?

No words came. She blurted, "It's not for sale!"

"Nonsense. It's on display. This is a shop, isn't it? You—you in the blue shirt—how much for this?"

Benton replied calmly, "Whatever Mrs. Wright says."

She wheeled on Tony. "Mr. Mondaine, help me!"

Tony shrugged. "The lady says it's not for sale."

"Ridiculous. This is ridiculous. Calder, be quiet. You know I have Daddy's birthday money. If you think I will haggle, Mrs. Wright, you're quite wrong. I do not haggle."

Eleanor took a deep breath, made her voice quiet. "No, Mrs. Smith." She may as well tell the truth—not that this woman would believe it. "You've found the only thing in the shop for which we have a sentimental attachment. It is—simply not for sale. If we decide to sell, you may have first chance."

"But—"

Calder Smith's hand went quite firmly over his wife's, and his voice said above hers, "Fair enough. Fair enough, Emily. Are you taking these chairs?"

"I don't know. I don't know." Her eyes were still on the Belter suite. Then suddenly she snapped, "No. I think I want Mummy to see them."

Her husband's eyes apologized but his voice did not relent. "Very good. Thank you for all your trouble. We'll go on, now. Come along, Emily."

"But I'll be back!" Emily called as they went towards the front entrance.

The brass bells rang out their peculiar heavy chime as they left. Eleanor, staring after them, was too upset to notice the short strand of yarn trailing from one heel in lieu of a ball. She was miserably aware of having handled the situation badly. But the reaction had been instinctive. The Belter set was still too imbued with Julia's essence, her loving craftsmanship. She couldn't see it in the hands of Emily Smith.

Nonetheless, it had not been a particularly practical attitude for a merchant. She was conscious of Benton Bonford standing there, seeing a large amount of money flounce out the door—his door. And Tony—Tony was probably laughing to himself.

Ben was calmly restoring the sidechairs to their wrapping.

"There went a nasty female," he said, to no one in particular. "And she's right. She'll be back. Hell-bent for the Belter set. You'll see."

Benton Bonford asked of Eleanor Wright, "Was that simply psychological warfare to jack up the price?"

An out—a genuine out—and he was handing it to her.

But Eleanor was too honest to accept. "No," she said. "But it can work that way. If you like. Ben's right; she'll be back."

Benton tore off a long strip of brown tape and handed it to the old man on his knees wrapping cabriole legs. His voice was quiet. "Then will you sell it to her?"

Eleanor's voice was equally quiet. She

had herself in hand again. "It will be up to you. It should have been up to you, this time."

"No it won't," he answered, making her heart quicken. Then he straightened, and turned to Anthony who was leaning indolently against a cherry highboy. "Would you have sold it?"

Anthony shrugged. "As myself," he said, "probably. I'm a middleman. I have no involvement with the things in my shop. As your aunt—no. Julia was involved with her things, and she frankly didn't give a caramel damn about getting rich. In her terms," he added, and smiled at Eleanor, "she was rich already."

It was true. It was also a bit thick, Eleanor thought, and wished he'd get off the privileged-old-friend kick because he really hadn't been that at all. A privileged business associate, indeed, but not beyond—at least, not to Julia.

It was the not-to-Julia part that brought her up short, reminded her honestly about her own dependence on Tony these last few days. She had to be fair. Whatever he was thinking now, she'd probably started it. By being weepy. A clinging vine. Bite the bullet, Eleanor, she concluded, and smiled back.

Satisfied, he glanced at his wristwatch, saying, "Anyway, I came to take you all to breakfast, and it's still not too late."

Without thinking, Eleanor replied, "We ate at home."

Tony looked startled. "Good God. Darling, you mean you cooked?"

Benton Bonford answered smoothly, "No. I did."

Now he was grinning at her, managing to convey a spurious sort of—of intimacy. Damn both of them! They deserved each other—and she'd see they got each other!

"I have things to do," she said. "Clear out—the both of you. Eat again. Come back in an hour and we'll go see Matt Logan."

To her amazement they went—and she found that, even more disquieting.

She was right. She wouldn't have liked what was being said.

Holding a cup of hot coffee with both, long-fingered brown hands, Anthony Mondaine took a cautious sip, and looked directly across the booth table at Benton Bonford.

"Sell me the place, Bonford. I'll make you a good price. Cash."

Benton who had nothing against eating twice, took a forkful of restaurant hash-browns, found them, as usual, wet, shredded cardboard on the inside—and tackled his egg instead. He hardly seemed to glance up.

"Why you? Why not someone else?"

"Because I'll look after Eleanor. Someone else might not."

"Oh. Well. I'd never figure you for a philanthropist, Mondaine. Pass the salt."

Tony passed. He also shrugged. "Figure what you like. The offer stands."

Benton carefully spread two squares of jelly on one slice of limp toast, smoothing it to all four edges. Behind him, at the counter, a tall, skinny trucker slapped a curly-brimmed Western hat on the napkin holder and began a roll call: "Hi, Charley. Hi, Bill. Mornin' Melissa. Hey there, Helen-in-the kitchen, doubles on everything but hold the cow in the coffee."

Quietly, through the noise, so Tony had to bend to hear, Benton said, "How would you look after Eleanor?"

"I'd make sure she got the shop to run. I don't want to run it, God knows. But you

204

can see plainly if anyone else was running it she'd fret her heart out. That place is her whole life."

Benton conceded that, and destroyed the toast. "How would Eleanor feel about you buying it?"

"She'd raise hell. At first."

"And then?"

"Then she'd come around. The woman's not stupid."

Benton wondered what "coming around" entailed for Eleanor. He thought he had a fair idea. "Why don't we ask her?"

Mondaine's jaw tightened. "God damn it, Bonford, no we don't ask her! I can't hang around this town forever, and surely you can't either. And Eleanor doesn't know *what* she wants—you've seen that already, today." His voice dropped, became reasonable. Persuasive. "Sell to me. Today. Tomorrow. You go back home with a thumping down payment. I tell Eleanor her life can go on as it always did."

Benton peeled open a third square of jelly, ate it with his spoon. Then he looked at Anthony Mondaine and said calmly, "Bull."

Thus was war declared.

Eleven

The one thing patently clear to Eleanor as the two men came back in the alley door was that—however much they had disliked each other an hour ago—it was nothing compared to how they felt now.

She, herself, felt not unlike a worm between two cock robins—and as everybody knew, there was very little in the situation to benefit the worm. Julia, she thought dismally, had I not loved you so much, I'd hate you for putting me in this position.

It had already been a busy and uncomfortable morning, the sort that just dances on the edge of disaster. Her part-time helper, in packing away the Depression glass, had managed to break the Adams candy jar lid—a piece more valuable than the candy jar, as it also was made to fit the sugar bowl. After three browsers departed in their Chrysler Newport, Ben found a new crack in a Satsuma vase. And she seemed to be stuck with Marvin Coles, who apparently had nothing better to do but to bug her footsteps the last half hour.

He hopped off his perch on some packing cases as Benton Bonford approached, sticking out a pudgy hand. "How y'do, sir, how y'do. My condolences about your auntie—a fine woman. She'll be missed, and not just by the little lady, here. I'm Marvin Coles; I got the shop on the north side of the square."

Benton shook hands very briefly. He hadn't needed the stiff look on Eleanor's mobile face to cultivate his own instant dislike of the pot-gutted, red-faced smiler.

Accustomed to rebuff, Coles was undeterred by it. He went on serenely, "I wonder if I could speak to you a moment in private. I have in mind a small proposition."

Oh, God, Eleanor thought, he's going to offer to buy the place. Please—not him. Anyone but him. She turned so Benton couldn't see her face.

Benton said, "No."

Coles hesitated for only a fraction. Then

207

he shrugged. "Okay. Dandy. I'll just speak right here. I'd like the opportunity to buy you out. Everything. Shop. Van. House, too, if you like. I'll make you a fair price. Not only that, I'll keep on the little lady, here."

Oh, sure, thought Eleanor. Sure you will—at least until Benton Bonford's back where he came from and you think you've picked whatever's useful from my brain. That's all you ever meant.

She was aimlessly turning pages in Julia's day book, seeing nothing, wishing she could stop her ears. A brown hand came down on hers, protectively. Tony winked at her. And she even found dismay in that. No more than Marvin's buying the shop could she bear to think of Tony's buying it.

What was she going to do? What could she do?

Tony's hand on hers was blatantly symbolic—both protective and possessive. She didn't want to be possessed like a—a docile tabby cat. Sitting there in the scarred old captain's chair at Julia's rolltop desk with the pale sun slanting across her from high, dusty narrow windows, with Thomaseen perched on one of the sills above them, preening himself, an absurd curl of pink yarn dangling from one pointed ear, with the smell of sawdust and lacquer and stripping compound in her nose—she didn't want anything the men around her were offering. All she wanted was to go on as before.

And that could not be done. So be smart, Eleanor. Play the percentages. You have to survive. Perhaps Tony is better than Marvin.

She made herself move up her own hand, return the clasp.

Benton Bonford saw. If she'd looked, she'd have seen a small muscle tighten in his jawline. She had no way of knowing that his reply to Marvin Coles was instinctively punitive. He said crisply, "Put it in writing, Mr. Coles. Then we'll see."

"Good enough. I'll do it. Ellie, m'dear," and the smile the man turned on Eleanor rolled her stomach. "You wouldn't by chance have an extra stone crock or so, would you? I have a gal drivin' me bananas for stone crocks."

With a jerk Eleanor's mind came back from assimilating—Put it in writing. Then we'll see. Couldn't the idiot just sense immediately what sort of person Marvin was?

Despite her efforts, her lips were stiff. She said, "Probably so. Ask Ben; he's in the shed."

"Right. I'll stop on the way out. Mornin', good people. Mr. Bonford, you'll hear from me shortly."

No one spoke until the slip-slop of his steps died away. Eleanor didn't know what to say, anyway. Was this Benton Bonford's idea of working things out? Couldn't he see with even half an eye what a bum Marvin Coles was? How could he possibly equate such sleaziness with the pure class of his aunt's business? For God's sake, money wasn't everything—

Unless you haven't any.

Then she had to admit that it looked pretty good. Particularly, she thought in anger, if you lived miles away and didn't have to see daily the wreck of two women's lives.

The silence above her head was ominous. Tony Mondaine's set face mirrored obvious and blatant disapproval. Benton Bonford's was absolutely a blank, graven stone. And she was the one who chickened out.

She picked up a pencil, tapped it, broke the lead, felt like an idiot, and said nervously, "Oh—phone messages. While you both were gone. I almost forgot. First—" and she looked at Benton who looked back with blank eyes in a face she'd almost started to find pleasant. "Matt's sick. Julia's lawyer. He had to go out in the storm last night—their puppy ran off. He's caught a heavy cold, but he hopes to be in the office tomorrow."

Benton shrugged. "No problem. I'll be here."

Sure he would—as long as it took to get the money and run, hey, bucko?

Trying to be expressionless, she turned to Tony, who hadn't moved from his pose against the rolltop desk above her.

"And your St. Louis shop called. The man from Sotheby's is flying TWA into Lambert Field at ten o'clock. Do you want someone else to meet him?"

"Damn," said Tony softly. Certainly not Dominic. He hit the top of the desk with a light fist. "I suppose I'd better go do it. One doesn't send a minion to meet Sotheby's, does one?"

Grinning down at Eleanor, he was weaving a circle that enclosed just the two of them, leaving Bonford outside, inferring that a hick farmer probably thought

Sotheby was a used car salesman, not the prime antique auction business on the East Coast.

Was Eleanor ignoring him, or just not playing the game?

She'd turned, looked again at her phone pad. But her voice came up casually, "I'm impressed. What do you have that Sotheby wants—the royal jewels?"

"I'm afraid not. Just some Georgian silver from an estate. I'll run into town this evening, then get back up here tomorrow. Hey—would you like to go, too? I'm sure Bonford can spare you a few hours. And getting away might do you wonders, poor child."

"Poor child" was not appreciated—it conveyed the notion that she needed "wonders" done, and that the prospect of going alone into Anthony Mondaine's special bailiwick with Anthony Mondaine, was something that she'd done before. She hadn't. She'd never been asked before— nor had there ever been any idea she might be asked—certainly not when Julia'd been alive.

Games, games, games.

She felt like a small piece of ham between two slices of bread—two heels, she thought. Survive!

She weaseled. She shrugged and said, "How nice of you to ask. Let me see how the day goes."

She knew how it was going to go, at least as far as Tony Mondaine was concerned, but Tony didn't know that, and neither did the klutz with the stony face. That Tony's putting the moves on her in St. Louis had all the appeal of stale bagels was her affair. Even if she had to sleep here in the shop, to avoid being in the same house with Benton Bonford!

The captain's chair creaked as she leaned back, and she gave Benton Bonford a perfidious smile and said, "You had a call, too. The number's here on the pad. They seemed to be quite anxious." Her polite voice wasn't meant to imply that she couldn't imagine why. She wasn't silly enough to dig her own grave. At least not yet.

How he took the information was hard to divine. All he did was nod, hoist himself erect, lean over her, look at the telephone number and dial.

The long arm in the denim jacket was six inches from her nose and smelled of diesel fuel. While he waited, his hand tapped rhythmically on the desk top. She noticed the nails were square, neat, and clean, and there was a heavy class ring on one finger. In astonishment she recognized the University of Missouri, then was immediately ashamed of her snobbery. She'd barely made it through high school, and even then she'd been two months pregnant.

Above her, in Benton's ear, a heavy voice identified the Russian embassy. It was his chance to swank a little now, he thought with no humor whatsoever, but be damned if he would. He merely gave his name and agreed to hold.

She smelled nice. It must be that stuff he'd almost grabbed for aftershave in the bathroom. Certainly not the fifty-bucks-an-ounce stuff Jill had used from the fancy bottle with the unicorn on top. This aroma was pleasant. Like daisies in a field.

Daisies don't smell at all, you idiot!

And get off it—this gal and her buddy are treating you like crabgrass, anyway—even if they don't think you know it.

Fortunately, at that point, Ivan Doganov's voice came on, full of hearty camaraderie.

The return agricultural delegation from Russia was to be in the United States in two weeks; he was the advance man. They were planning a deer hunting trip into the Dakotas, and the delegates had most strongly asked for Benton Bonford. Would he go?

Oh, Lord, Benton thought, can I get my beans out of the field in time? And this place of Aunt Julia's—what am I going to do here?

He didn't know. He honestly didn't know. Clear matters sometimes get obscure very fast, and that's what this one was doing.

But one thing his grandfather had taught him well: first things first.

None of the anxiety showed in his voice. He accepted, said the rest of the proper things and hung up, frowning. Two weeks. That was pushing it. That was really pushing it.

Eleanor saw his frown. "Bad news?"

"A hunting trip," he answered and stubbornly said no more. If Mondaine wanted to play the one-upsmanship game, let him. Damned if he'd lower himself—especially for the favors of this silver-haired female who was starting to irk him again.

As he turned away from them, Ben came in the back, wiping his hands on a wad of rags. "Want to go get that gas now?"

Benton said, "Sure. If you're ready."

Ben dropped a check on the desk before Eleanor. "Sold 'im six," he said briefly, not deigning to identify "him." No real good ones, but he doesn't care. Shall I take the van, and haul in that load from the Zimmer farm sale?"

"Can you handle it?"

Ben grinned. "I'll use the kid, here," he said, indicating Benton with a shake of his grizzled and balding head. "We ought to be back by five. If not, lock up. I got m' key."

"Fine. Is Mary Ann coming in?"

"Not today. She's baby-sitting; her daughter's got the flu. Oh—and if that woman from Quincy comes by for the tiger maple tall chest, be sure it's the one in the corner. I ain't got t' brass pulls on the other one yet."

"Is it priced?"

"Julia priced it. She said we could come down fifty. No more. Paperwork's in 'er desk, there. See you later."

He trotted out, Benton behind him, and once again Eleanor found it amazing how much larger an area became when Benton Bonford left it.

Tony seemed to feel the same thing. "What an ox," he murmured, then grinned down at her. "Alone at last."

"Not really," said Eleanor, as the front entrance brass chimes rang. She leaned around the desk and saw two ladies in large-size designer jeans advancing up the center aisle towards the Tiffany wisteria lamp on the china cupboard. "Duty calls."

Personally, she was glad. Duty, she could handle. Customers. Sales. With the rest of her life she had the strong sense of doing very badly.

Tony reached out a long, sweater-clad arm, caught her up and kissed her briefly—a smack on the cheek. "Run along, then. I'll go back to my motel and make a few calls and see you here about five. You *are* going with me tonight?"

"Tony, it's very kind, but I don't know—"

"Think of the alternative," he interjected. "Another evening with the nephew. Unless Ben will take him out for a beer or something. That might be about his speed."

"I have no idea," she answered, but damn it, there was some validity in the alternative *he* offered. Yet beyond validity it *was* some alternative. Fend off Tony or fight with Benton Bonford.

She knew they'd fight. If he so much as mentioned Marvin Coles she'd hiss like a cornered cat—knowing all the time he had the perfect right to do as he pleased.

"Miss! Oh, Miss!"

That was for her, from the oversized ladies.

She said, "I'll—think about it."

White teeth flashed in his dark face. "Chicken!"

All she answered back was, "See you later." But as she put a smile on her face and advanced to meet the customers, she could feel his eyes.

The woman in the hand-painted sweatshirt was fluffing her hair. As Eleanor approached, she giggled and said, "Oo, what a handsome man! Does he own the shop?"

Eleanor made herself smile. "No," she said, sweet but short.

"What a pity. I'd come this way more often. Wouldn't you, Pauline?"

"He's certainly better than that funny little man across the square," said Pauline. "Although he did send us here. Oh—and he said to tell you so." And she smiled, obviously expecting prices to fall at least ten percent.

Eleanor swallowed her anger at Marvin Coles's gall.

"How good of him," she murmured. "What may I show you today?"

They didn't know. They were just looking. So, it seemed, were most of the other people entering during the day. Some, obviously, were expecting sale signs after Julia's death, and Eleanor was savagely glad to disappoint them. Sale signs might well come soon enough, anyway, but it would not be her doing.

But the day's work was like a panacea, and even after a basically sleepless night she still felt the band around her head loosen, her back relax. At five o'clock, with perfect equanimity, she told Tony Mondaine that she was not going with him to St. Louis.

He didn't like it at all. That savage red star flashed behind his eyes—but only for a second. When he answered, his voice was calm though very, very controlled. "I said you were chicken."

"I'm not!" she flashed back, a little irritated. "Tony, I have to cope with this thing now—Benton Bonford, the shop, everything. I can't run off and play."

He had changed to a dark suit and white silk shirt, and was the picture of elegance. "Scram, cat," he said to Thomaseen, who was kneading his paws and purring like a water drum in Eleanor's lap. He lifted her erect—close but not touching.

"Play," he said, "was not what I had in mind." Then he closed the gap between them, but only with his mouth, putting gentle, butterfly kisses on her throat and her eyes. "I think," he murmured against the soft, fluttering lids, "that it's time we stopped playing. Don't you know you're my miracle—that you've been here all the time but I've just found you?"

Unfortunately for him, today it didn't work. Perhaps she was more rested than she realized, or had, more simply, regained a little perspective.

But no bells rang. Sorry, Tony.

And he sensed it. Couldn't believe it.

What had gone wrong? Surely not the Bonford klutz! He and Ben weren't even back, yet.

Good God. Didn't this aging Circe realize that Anthony Mondaines didn't come along every day?

He considered briefly re-mentioning that he might very well buy this shop and everything in it including her, but decided against that gambit. He wanted Eleanor on his side. Marvin Coles was a nonentity, but the Bonford hazard might be very real. That damned pseudo painting could still hang over his head. No. Play it cool, Mondaine. You need this woman, and certainly not just in bed, although she might be all right there, too. Getting women in bed was never a problem.

The main issue was that he wanted the shop, and he had to have the painting.

Okay. Back off. After all, he'd return in the morning.

"I did so want my virtue impugned," he said, and sighed an exaggerated sigh.

But she heard the sound of acceptance. Relieved, she said, "In the back of an antique shop?"

"I didn't have in mind the back of an antique shop. At least, not this one. Oh, well. Another day, perhaps."

He kissed her briefly, like a friend, and dropped his arms, which perhaps was fortunate. A grumpy and displaced Thomaseen, crouched at their feet, had been seriously contemplating removal of one small slice from a certain, conveniently placed, black-silk-stockinged shin.

"Meow!" he snarled.

Eleanor stooped swiftly, and scooped up a large bundle of cat, providing both a barrier and a surety that the man would not be attacked as was dictated by the tomcat's stance.

She said, "Hush!"

He said, "Damned cat."

Thomaseen, goal achieved, laid his furry head on Eleanor's breast and began to purr. Tony shrugged.

"You," he said to the feline, "had better shape up. I know a vet who works cheap. All right, Ellie, all right. If it's what you want."

"It is."

"This time?"

"This time."

Satisfied there was no other choice, and regarding it not as a failure but as a postponement, Tony said, "Okay. This round to the lady. So let me take you out to dinner before I go. No pressure. Promise."

"I should change." She was glancing down ruefully from his elegant attire to her sloppy sweater.

"Nonsense. You look fine since it's just

222

us pals." If he sounded a little wry he figured he was entitled to it. "Come on. Put down the furry chest protector and let's go."

Of course the pat he gave her as they went down the splintery dock steps was not particularly palsy, but she didn't mind. She had, after all—she said to herself with a certain ominous degree of complacency—handled Anthony Mondaine quite well.

Twelve

Tony, as usual, was as good as his word—which, in the world of antiques, had the reputation of being excellent. He dropped her off in the shadowy alley after dinner, shock her hand, said solemnly, "See you tomorrow, fella," and drove away.

Eleanor watched him go by the dim, gray light of the dirty streetlamp. The sleek Porsche eased into the silent street, turned left and purred away. She said, "Well!" and shrugged. So much for having to fight for her virtue—or whatever it was. The word "virtue" seemed a bit inappropriate.

Actually, although Tony would scarcely have appreciated it, she felt nothing but relief. The day had been long, and there were more long days to come. All she really wanted to do was go home and—

But there were choices to be made here—two of them foremost: Sleep on that old couch in the shop, which would either leave the cow jockey thinking she had gone with Anthony Mondaine, or offend him because she didn't show up at Julia's house, thus impugning his own character; or she could beat him home and lock her door—which also would impugn his character if he was bold enough to try and see if it *was* locked—

And she was a tired, bleary-eyed old lady standing in a cold alley thinking nonsense.

It was cold. Even in her sweater she shivered. Dry leaves were dancing along the broken concrete like tipsy gnomes. A scarf of thin clouds had flung itself before the Halloween moon, making ragged patterns on the dock. Fall weather had arrived, probably to stay.

And the van wasn't back, yet. Strange. It was well past eight o'clock.

But that was not her business.

Not any more.

Then suddenly she was caught up in a mental whirlwind of hard truth—and reality. She didn't like it, she hated it, she closed her eyes hard, fighting it—but it would not go away.

Eleanor Wright was acting like a 1940s total poop.

She had been moosing around, feeling sorry for herself, and allowing two men to toss her back and forth like a handball.

Those two guys didn't control her future. Not unless she allowed them to control it. And that's what she'd been doing. Allowing them. As though there was nothing in the world she could do for herself.

For God's sake, there definitely was. And it was about time she displayed a little common sense and did something positive—on her own.

She had a reputation in the business, too. She'd earned it during thirty years with Julia, and it was a damned good one.

So use it, you klutz.

And start now. You've been standing around like a stupid little lambie pie long enough.

Getting out her keys, she stomped up the splintery steps, went in the door, slammed it behind her, switched on the desk lamp and sat down.

The furry shadow of Thomaseen shot in behind her, barely missing the loss of about four inches of tail. But he was accustomed to that. Silently he hopped up on his usual high perch, folded neat paws, and settled down to watch. When it seemed propitious, he'd get her attention and do the poor-lonesome-kitty number. But not yet.

Eleanor pulled out her directory of antique dealers, scattering various other papers in the process, and slapped it open before her.

Okay. Grosman's Antiques. She got along fine with Rod Grosman, and Bernita was retiring at Christmas. Of course that was fifty miles away, but who the hell said she had to stay in this town, anyway?

So—Grosman's. And John Morrisey's place—John was expanding to a second shop in the Springfield suburbs. She could handle Springfield.

Pulling over a pad, she began to make a list.

After forty-five minutes, there were twenty names on it, ten scratched out, and four or so underlined, with telephone numbers added. Tomorrow morning she'd make the calls.

With a glow of genuine, self-commending virtue, Eleanor leaned back, making the old chair creak, stretched, and found herself scratching the ears of a purring fur bundle, having no idea when he'd arrived on her lap.

But Thomaseen looked out for himself.

Smiling, she stroked his compliant back, thinking that it was a hell of a note to learn from a *cat* how to survive. But he certainly had the basic tenets: be there at the right time. Use your personality. Perform.

But stay independent.

Never let anyone else own you.

It sounded to simple at nine-thirty at night—but tired as she was, she knew better than to buy the simplicity.

The next few days were going to be the hardest of her life—in a professional capacity. And that had to be number one.

It had to be.

She looked around at the dark shapes barely distinguishable beyond the circle of her lamplight—the looming old Welsh dresser with Ben's tool box by it, the perforated tin doors of an old pie safe, striped gently with violet and red as the stained glass from an ancient mantel mirror caught the lamp glow and passed it on.

Yes. This had been her place to be. She'd had years of contentment here. But Julia was gone, and everything with Julia. So it was now her time to move on.

Blinking tears, but facing reality for the first time since Julia's death, Eleanor sighed and firmly put Thomaseen on the dusty floor.

He protested with a pleading meow but she said, "Sorry, buddy. Tomorrow may be grim. I have to get some sleep."

And it was to be in her own bed, in Julia's house.

She knew that, too. The hell with Benton Bonford.

When she opened the back door again, the cold wind whirled inside, stirring the sawdust into whorls on the floor. Ben's old denim jacket hung over the back of the Amish rocker by the desk. She took the jacket, shrugged it on, not minding the faint aroma of tobacco, and was glad when she locked the door and stepped outside.

Frost glistened on the dock steps, the car seat was clammy, the engine groaned when commanded to start.

Reversing away from the shop, she noted the van still wasn't back, and thought with grim humor that Tony might have been quite accidentally on the money: Ben may have taken Benton out for a beer. They certainly weren't back at the shop, yet.

As she turned down Julia's silent, tree-lined street, she found it quiet, wind-swept. Lighted windows reflected TV screens, trikes and bikes were hauled up on the comfortable chair-dotted porches behind boxes of bright geraniums. Some householders, she noted, had covered the last of the marigolds still blooming bravely, hoping to save them for at least another day.

Well. Julia's *hosta* was on its own. She was too tired to bother, and the cow jockey wouldn't care.

She made the turn into Julia's driveway beneath the handsome bay window and boxy tower of the old Victorian house—and braked. Faster than she'd intended.

She needn't have worried about the van. It was parked right in front of her.

Kitchen lights cast bright squares of gold across the back steps, and even through the thickness of a closed door the sound of conviviality floated outward.

Good gravy, Eleanor thought in dismay, sliding from her car. They're drunk as skunks.

It was like opening the door on a brewery. She shut her eyes, grimaced, and waved her hand before her face, saying graphically, "Whooo!" at the sickening aroma of flat beer.

Ben, from a circle of empty cans, ignored her remark, merely saying cheerily, "Hi, hon! I told him you'd come. See, I tol' ya', kid—I said Ellie had more class than goin' with that drugstore gigolo."

The "kid," all two hundred pounds plus of him stretched out from the minuscule base of a kitchen chair, merely scowled. At the end of three yards of denim leg, stockinged feet used Charlie as a footwarmer. Before him on the table was a rather impressive tower of his own cans. He muttered something obscure but rude. His hair was tousled in his eyes, his shirt open to the mat of silver brillo, and his attitude was obviously in need of improvement.

But by someone else.

Not her.

She was going to bed.

She said, in a general announcement, "If you make a mess, you clean it up. I am not house mother. Ben, you'd better sleep on the couch tonight."

She went towards the door swiftly, but not fast enough. It was necessary to pass by Bluto, and he reached out a big hand, fastened it on her arm. "What about me?"

Irritated, she shook off the hand. *"What about you?"*

"Do I sleep on the couch?"

"You can sleep under the couch for all I care. Let go!" as the big hand fastened again.

He was still looking straight ahead, not at her. And he was scowling. Only the hand had reached back, taken hold. He rumbled, "You know what's the matter with you?"

"No," she answered grimly, "at least not from your point of view. What's the matter with me?"

"You're a snob."

Well. That was the last thing she'd expected.

"I'm a what?"

"A snob. The worst kind—because you don't know what you're snobby about."

"You aren't making sense. Let go."

"I'm making a lot of sense," he said, and didn't let go. "I could put on a three-piece suit. I could order from a French menu. I could, as a matter of fact, call the governor of this fair state right now and get us both invited for lunch. But I'm not going to do it. No, sir. No way."

Eleanor sighed and looked at Ben, who

was grinning at her foolishly, nodding his balding head. "What's this all about, now?"

He popped the top on a fresh can, took a deep drink, and wiped his mouth with the back of his hand.

"It's about your bein' a snob, Ellie."

She gritted her teeth. "Somehow I'd figured that part out, myself."

Benton turned his head as though his neck was glass, and was now looking back at her. "So you'll never know. Will you?"

"I guess I won't. Particularly if neither of you two soaks tell me."

"I tol' you."

"That I'm a snob."

"Yeah."

"And that I'll never know."

"Thas right."

She sighed. "I suppose I'll regret this in view of your—condition—but what am I a snob *about*?"

"Me."

"You!"

"Yeah. Present. Here."

She shook her head. "You certainly are," she said. "Very present. Undeniably here." She removed the large hand from her arm and this time he allowed it. "Now

I have some words to say. Happy sousing. Best wishes. Good night."

She went out into the hallway, and up the stairs. Her shoulders hurt. It had been another long day.

At the top of the stairs she paused and looked back down. In the square of light framed by the kitchen door she could only see the one pair of denim legs with their feet still buried in the ruff of a peacefully sleeping Saint Bernard. The legs were motionless.

She also saw one of the bentwood chairs leaned against the wall outside the kitchen, the cross-spindles pulled from their back leg sockets and drooping floorward.

Damnation—the big oaf! She might have known that would happen eventually. If those legs were splintered—

Then she stopped. Grimaced. Shrugged, trying to swallow the hurt.

It wasn't her problem, any more. Let the big oaf screw up whatever chairs he wanted. They were his chairs.

Feeling absolutely awful, she turned, peeled the shoes from her feet and padded in dispirited quiet down the dim hall.

The elation from asserting her own independence faded. She only felt tired. Aching. Old.

And lost.

All right, Eleanor Wright, get with it, she said to herself, dully. Tomorrow starts everything all over again. So take a fast shower while you have the chance, and get out of sight.

As she tossed her clothes on the bed, she remembered she still wore Ben's jacket. That was all right. He'd not even noticed. She'd return it tomorrow.

In the bathroom she turned the shower on, letting it warm while she scrubbed her teeth. Hot water in old plumbing took some time to rise to the second floor. The soaking container for Julia's dentures still sat on the sink. Blinking tears, she shoved it in a drawer, put dry towels on the john lid and stepped into the shower. It felt great. Then right when her muscles were beginning to uncurl and her nerves relax it hit her: a totally unwelcome truth. And she knew what sort of snob they'd meant. Worse, she knew also that it had probably been accurate.

Damn. All that nonsense about three-piece suits and speaking French and dining with the governor—

Had her attitude been that patently superior? The names she'd called him—cow caller, tractor jockey.

She—who prided herself on being open, on being honest—had been a closed-minded, flippant, pretentious idiot to the very man she knew held her future in his hands. And that was about as embarrassingly stupid as anyone could get.

The joy was gone from the shower. She turned it off, got out, toweled herself roughly, pulled on the warm, flannel Victorian nightie with its gathered yoke and throat ruffle, and wrapped the bathrobe around the entire ensemble. She looked, she reflected, like a badly tied bed roll.

Hanging the wet shower cap on its hook, she thrust tired fingers through tousled hair and faced herself in the foggy sink mirror. That was a real downer. On top of the bed roll was a fifty-year-old face that not only showed every year but went into extras. Thanks a lot, mirror.

She turned off the light, went out of the warm, moist bath into the cool hall, shivered, shuffled towards her room.

Halfway, she stopped.

The blue-jeaned legs were now mounting the stairs. Slowly. With a slight weave.

Accompanied by a sleepy Saint Bernard with a drooping tail.

The tail wagged as the dog saw her. His owner heavily gained the landing, held on to the pineapple finial and squinted. "Good God," he said, with only a slight slur, "What are you—the Ghost of Christmas Past?"

She ignored that. She asked crisply, "What did you do with Ben?"

He was still squinting as though seeing through a tunnel. "Didn't do nothin' with Ben. Ben did himself. He's on t' damn couch. Like you said. Now—kindly tell me which is mine."

"To your right."

He turned left.

She gave a small hiss of exasperation, took his arm, turned him properly.

He said, "Oh. Thanks."

By bending forward somewhat, he established some locomotion. He found his bed. Eleanor's impulse to clap was stopped by his turning around and falling, like a stone monument, on his back, smack in the middle of last night's rumple with his heavy boots on Julia's delicate appliqué counterpane.

She waited, and was rewarded with what

appeared to be a snore. Charlie hopped up on the yon side of the bed, gave her a sad look, and closed his eyes.

She primmed her lips, shook her head, sighed a deep sigh of exasperation. Damn both of them.

She shuffled to the bedside, pointed a finger at the dog and said severely, "Off!"

He opened one eye.

She repeated, giving him a smack.

This time he sighed, deciding she meant it, and obeyed, trundling into the hallway.

Then she reached over, and with a great deal of huffing and puffing succeeded in removing the two heavy boots, dropping them with dull *thunks* by the side of the bed.

A pleasant voice said, "Thank you, ma'am. Would you care to work your way north?"

Eleanor gritted her teeth. "No," she answered coldly, "I would not. I *would* care if Julia's lovely quilt got ruined by your damned boots!"

She turned, went decisively towards the door.

The same voice followed her. "What's that thing in the middle of the ceiling?"

She turned again, saw against the moonlit window one large arm pointing upward. Visions of clinging bats or hairy spiders vanished. In relief, she answered almost politely, "A plaster rosette."

"Oh. There was one on my bedroom ceiling at Turgenev's dacha. Did I tell you I stayed at Turgenev's dacha? Fantastic place in the country. Full of French furniture. Paintings by the row. My host had been a colonel in the Red Army during the Second World War, so I don't think it would be polite to ask where he got 'em, do you? I'm goin' huntin' with him in two weeks. The embassy plane is going to pick me up. You can put that in your fancy Italian's pipe and help him smoke it. But right now, tootsie, get out. I don't feel so good."

I am going to kill him, she thought, slamming the door shut and shuffling across the hall. Julia, I'm sorry. I love you dearly. But I am going to kill that man—I know I am.

In the welcome peace of her own shadowy room, she shucked off the heavy robe, went to the window and leaned on the sill a moment, looking out, trying to calm down.

It was a genuine Halloween night. The soughing of the pine trees reached her ears with eerie softness, but their fanning, wind-dipped branches flickered black and gray, as scudding clouds rolled across the high moon. The old, weathered garage looked like a witches' hut, and small seeps of cold air crept through the frame of her window, chilling her.

Storm windows, she thought, trying to think calmly. They should go on soon, or my heating bill will be astronomical. Not mine. His heating bill. Bluto's.

Then he can put on the damned storm windows, she thought bitterly and turned away.

The elongated shadow of the bronze stallion trailed across the carpet before her.

It was not an image she found charming in her present state of mind. But the last straw was what she saw as she reached out to turn off the shaded Lalique lamp.

In the middle of her high, tester bed a huge, furry heap of dog was gently snoring.

She hissed, clenched her fists, stomped her foot—which, in shaggy house shoes, was not a success—and raised her voice in resounding, heedless fury: "Get him out of here! Do you hear me?"

After a fractional hesitation, feet thumped across the hall. Two doors crashed open—his and hers. Benton Bonford stood in hers, holding himself upright by a grip on the frame. He snarled grumpily, "What the hell's the matter now?"

She pointed a majestic finger. "Get him out!"

"Oh for—" He stopped, sighed a huge draft of exaggerated injury. "Charlie! You are not welcome in this tootsie's bed. Neither of us, as I seem to recall, is welcome. Unless—"

He blinked, squinted at her blearily. "Unless my memory is faulty."

"It is," she answered grimly, "*not* faulty. Now, get! Both of you."

"My God, woman, hush up! I hear you."

Shirt tails trailing behind him, he advanced, thumping his feet at every step. The lamplight caught the mat on his broad chest, turning it curled silver to match the scowling bar of brow across his eyes beneath the rumpled white helmet.

He was not even looking at her. Charlie hopped off to meet him; he hooked a massive hand in the dog's collar, said, "C'mon, pal," and turned.

Then he looked. His eyes raked her. Up and down. Slowly.

Her breath quickened, and—helpless to prevent it—she held it instead. She thought murderously, shakily, hungrily, anger not dissolved in longing but burned by it, You stallion! You damned Clydesdale stallion!

His gaze fastened on the tied yoke of her gown, undid the ties, imagined the traitorous, rounding naked breasts beneath, traveled the line of her thighs, her nightgown blown tight against her by the draft from the hall, came back to her face, saw in her eyes what a man could not fail to see, dropped his hand from Charlie's collar.

Then his own face changed, and the Lalique lamp showed it faintly green. The hand went to his mouth; through it in chagrin and distress he mumbled, "Oh, God damn—" and ran in thundering leaps towards the door.

Down the hall, also. And presently there came unmistakable sounds from the bathroom.

She'd already loosed her breath when he ran.

Now she shivered, and hugged herself

against the cold of reality, of knowledge she did not care to have, and had not wanted.

Charlie walked slowly into the hall, listened, then collapsed into a dejected slump on the floor. Eleanor closed the door behind him. She didn't lock it. It wasn't necessary to lock it. There are some things a man does not do after being humiliatingly sick. At least, not immediately. Sometimes—not ever.

As for herself—she climbed into the tousled bed, lay with her knees hunched up and the covers clutched around her shoulders and faced her own humiliation.

What was the matter with her?

No excuses. No lame justifications.

She had reacted to Benton Bonford like a—a deprived hen seeing the first rooster in weeks. She'd sent out signals as rampant as throwing herself spread-eagle on the bed and saying "Hurry up!" And not just once—twice. In three days.

What must he think?

And worst of all—why was she doing it? Why was her body betraying her?

For thirty years, sex had been farther down on her list than brussels sprouts. She'd gone out a few times after Bobby died, never been certain the advances made were because of herself or because she offered access to Julia, and she found the total not worth a free meal. No man had aroused her. She'd been easily distracted by bad teeth or a fat gut or the sudden realization there was a wife he'd not bothered to mention.

So what was it with Benton Bonford?

It couldn't be the beginnings of—of love.

How could it be, when the man owned her business and her house and had declared his intention of selling both? And when he'd called her a snob—and laughed at her.

She could comprehend her weak moment with Tony. He'd been kind, gentle, sympathetic. Regardless of his motives.

But Bluto?

It made no sense. She made no sense.

But with an awful feeling that even drunk Benton Bonford had seen the response in her—and that in the morning he would remember—she closed her eyes and hugged herself, trying to generate some warmth from the covers and some practicality in her head.

When that morning came she must be calm. Distant. Detached. She must make those telephone calls and assure some tangible future for herself—the hell with him.

She must take charge of her own life.

For the first time.

Without her husband.

Without the doctors and nurses and therapists telling her what to do and what not to do.

Without Julia, setting the day's routine, making assignments, and dictating her day.

Just her. Eleanor Wright.

Learning to survive.

Thirteen

By morning, Eleanor had developed a pattern for survival. In two or three days he'd be gone—because of that hunting trip, or whatever it was. So at the end of those scant days the shop could be in the smarmy hands of Marvin Coles. Or Tony Mondaine, whose hands weren't smarmy, but certainly as smug and self-assured as the man himself. Or he might listen to Matt Logan, and put it up for sale, letting Matt deal with it.

Okay. So she'd offer to stay on, as long as she was needed. For Julia's memory. And on salary.

But that wouldn't preclude her making a deal for herself with some other business and setting a date for getting the hell out.

And finding that other business was the foremost thing she had to do.

Survival. The name of the game.

Keeping in mind that Tony would probably show up again to resume the Eleanor handball competition, she began to scrabble in the back of her untidy closet. What she wanted was a costume that looked practical, neat, businesslike and unisex. Plain slacks would do it, with a tailored shirt, and sensible shoes. No makeup. Hair in a bun.

She had to back off two of the tenets. No way would her hair go in a bun—and she had to put some makeup on or her face would dry up like a prune.

She grimaced at the frowning face in the mirror and gave her head a shake. The hair calmly slid back into its usual line, except on one side where she'd slept crooked. So who cared? And if one had to cream one's face, one might as well put on lipstick. There were customers' sensibilities to think about, too.

The slacks were a bit tighter than last year, but they did zip without wrinkling too much around the waist—if she kept her stomach sucked in. The problem was that she could only do that for about three minutes, then she turned an interesting shade of red. Drat.

The obvious solution was another sweater, pulled on over the tailored blouse, which also concealed the buttons that gaped over her boobs. Damn it—weight was so insidious; it just crept up on you.

She'd have to cut down . . . skip lunch, maybe. Not too many people would want to hire fat ladies, even in the antique business.

Grimly she made her bed, realizing as she did so that she no longer owned a single piece of furniture except the taboret, a Queen Anne dressing table and a vanity bench. Great. In finding a job, she'd also have to find a furnished apartment.

And from where was the money to come for a deposit? So far—unless Benton Bonford allowed her to write payroll, no one had been paid, this month, including herself. She'd have to make some sort of deal with Bluto for Ben and Mary Ann and everyone else besides her own current needs. Forget the last medical payments. The hospital would understand.

Or would they?

Shaking her head and saying good-bye to the dream of seeing herself solvent this month, she opened her door.

His was still closed.

Dandy. Until she had coffee she wasn't quite up to dealing with Bluto.

Quietly she went down the stairs, skirting the creaks inherent in old step risers. The couch in the parlor was empty, with only a dented pillow to mirror earlier occupancy. She fluffed it, shrugged, and entered the kitchen.

It was tidied. The only signs of previous revelry was a bulging garbage bag that rattled, and the faint odor of stale beer. Coffee had been made, and one cup had been consumed. The cup was upended in the sink.

Also, the wounded bentwood chair was gone.

Either Ben thought he could fix it, or he felt it the better part of valor to get it out of her sight.

Hoping she hadn't noticed, last night.

She'd noticed, all right. The big ox!

But she did appreciate the old man's efforts. He was a good guy. She would have to try to strike some sort of equable deal to keep both him and Mary Ann as employees, whoever took over. That would be only fair. Ben couldn't go to work just anywhere—he was too elderly. And she knew Mary Ann needed the job.

She glanced out the window. A dark stain of oil marked the drive where the van had sat.

Then she saw the note. It was scrawled on the back of a grocery store sales slip and said, "There's no fool like an old fool. Will you go to that farm auction at Crane's today? Mary Ann will mind the shop."

It was signed merely, "B." And the handwriting wasn't the steadiest. Ben must have a massive hangover. It served him right, the dummy. It served them both right.

Realizing she wasn't being particularly charitable, but caring not at all, Eleanor unfolded the sales bill that had accompanied the note. How long it seemed since that sunny Saturday afternoon when she had sat on the porch with Mrs. Crane and admired the lovely chesterfield in the living room. Was it gone by now? Had she let it slip through her fingers with Julia's death?

Eleanor reached out for the telephone. Then stopped.

It wasn't her shop, now. How did she know if the plow jockey wanted a chesterfield?

Then common sense overtook spite. Life went on. So did a business.

The number rang busy. For the interim, Eleanor poured a glass of orange juice, pulled her bentwood chair over to the one spot of sunshine on the table and unfolded the sales ad. It was a long one, annotated by Ben with a dull lead pencil.

The bill began, "Due to the death of my husband I will sell at auction the following items . . ."

She sipped her juice and scanned the columns. The livestock and farming equipment were outside her bailiwick, although Ben had put a question mark beside a horse-drawn surrey.

Eleanor started to cross it out—then stopped.

Ask Bluto, dummy.

But there were other things that would bear looking at—like a bow-front chest listed as walnut. She hadn't seen it at all. Of course, it might not be Mrs. Crane's; many times other people brought their own stuff to a sale. She'd watch for it. Chests always had a market.

An Irish squash hat suddenly skidded across the table in front of her. She glanced up and saw Benton Bonford in the hall doorway. He was rather pale, and had nicked his chin shaving.

He said, "I have a hazy recollection of making an ass of myself. If so, I apologize. I haven't drunk that much beer since we shivareed the guy on the next farm."

Quite, quite mildly, and proud of it, she answered, "It must have been a large afternoon. Would you like some orange juice?"

With difficulty he repressed a shiver, went by her to the refrigerator, took out a cold beer can, popped the top and drank it down nonstop.

Then he wiped his mouth, shook his head, and went on almost cheerfully, "I have no idea why that works on a hangover, but it always does for me, and I say God bless it. Except for a skull that feels a little crowded in content, I think I'll live."

"Coffee?"

"No. Not yet."

He lowered his frame into another bentwood chair—gingerly, she noted, and with a sheepish smile. Picking up the squash hat, he put it on his knee and ran a big hand through damp, ruffled hair. He seemed faintly embarrassed, and she was happy to allow it.

There was still a cigarette pack tossed on the table. He shook one out, put it in his mouth, and scratched a match on the back of a book that read Mike's Tavern. Then he had second thoughts, and looked across at her, his face a mask of uncertainty. "Oh, sorry."

She took pity on him. "All right. Just blow the smoke away from me."

"Thanks. You're a nice lady. I'm out of gum."

He lit. She watched him, not just inhaling the cigarette, but for any signs—clear or faint—that he recalled the one electric moment last night from which disaster only nausea had saved her.

She was firm in her resolve that such a thing would not occur again. After all, she wasn't seventeen, it wasn't prom night, and she wasn't looking for sex. She was looking for survival. This did not include going to bed with the boss. At least, in her book it didn't.

He had exhaled a blue plume. A little color was beginning to seep back into shaven cheeks. He pointed, lips tight on the cigarette. "What's that?"

That was the sale bill. She said so, adding, "For a farm auction."

"You like those affairs?"

The question was loaded. Honesty was the only answer.

"I used to hate them. I felt like a vulture. Then I learned that everyone respected Julia, and that they knew she was fair, that she wouldn't abuse their things. Also, that auctions sometimes have to happen—it's an unfortunate fact of life. Taking the two together, I stopped minding."

The cigarette apparently didn't taste good. He was squashing it out in the tray still gray from last night's ashes. He looked at Eleanor from under that tufted thicket of brow and said shortly, "Yeah. Ben thought a hell of a lot of Julia. And he thinks a hell of a lot of you. I got lectured last night." The latter was said sheepishly.

"Oh?"

"Yes, ma'am. I'll tell you about it when I—I get things a little straighter in my head."

I can hardly wait. But she didn't say that. Too much was riding on such a statement's ramifications to get smart-mouthy.

She only replied, "All right. I'll listen."

"He doesn't care much for Marvin Coles."

"I share that opinion."

"And he doesn't care much for the Mondaine guy. Do you share that, too?"

"Care" was what she used in her answer. "Anthony has an enviable record as an expert in antiques and as an entrepreneur. Julia respected him."

"I wasn't asking about my Aunt Julia. I was asking about you. And the question was personal. I am trying to get my lines straight before I make some decisions."

Now they were eye to eye—his eyes were level, narrow and searching, hers also level but a bit indignant.

She said quietly, "I've known you three days. That's hardly enough for a personal question."

"And I have only about ten days in which to condense a highly personal situation, before I have to bail out of here for a week. Look at me, Eleanor Wright. Look at me, damn it! Do you want Aunt Julia's shop to go to Mondaine?"

"NO!"

It came out like a shot, before she could think, could rationalize, could frame a properly diplomatic answer. Then she followed the negative with a horrified, "Oh, I'm sorry—I'm so sorry—it's your shop."

And unfortunately for her, she'd buried

her embarrassed face in her hands and was unable to see the relief, the gratitude mirrored in his. Also the "Hallelujah!" he mouthed silently.

Through her fingers she said, "Please—I think Tony would do marvelous things with the shop. I think he could make it a—a Mecca for antiquers."

"Couldn't my aunt have done that?"

"Oh, yes. But she didn't want to—didn't need to. She was content. Yet I realize that what Tony would promote could be only good for the town and its reputation."

She'd taken her hands away, and was facing him honestly, meeting his look. "And he has the money to work with."

"Would you work *for* him?"

"Only if I had to do it." And she was beyond the smallest idea what import those fatal words could have. But he repeated:

"Only if you had to do it."

"Yes. And I don't. I think I don't. I—" and she fudged a little, not trying to boost herself, but wanting him to think she was not still that 1940, helpless lambie-pie poop she'd been before. "I—have some job offers. I'm certain I'll be okay."

"Oh?"

But she didn't elucidate. She went on a little hesitantly, "I am worried about Ben. And Mary Ann. Especially. Then the others—part-timers. I don't know what they'd do if they lost their jobs, especially Ben. It would about break Ben's heart. And mine, too."

"You are a nice lady—as Ben said."

He heaved his mass upward, grimacing as though the motion hurt, and went for the coffee pot. He waved it at her. "Ready?" With her nodded consent he poured two cups, brought them back to the table. The pause had given her time to extract at least a few thought from the wool he'd generated with his questions about Marvin Coles and Tony.

Could she believe him? Was Marvin definitely not a choice? That was one enormous relief. Then—how about Tony?

He answered it himself, plonking his big butt gingerly back on the bentwood chair, and handing her the hot coffee. "Okay. So the Coles guy and Mondaine are both out. See what happens when you talk to me nice?" He was grinning, and the relief washing over her was so immense she could have kissed him where he sat.

All she did, though, was close her eyes,

shake her head like a puppy suddenly freed of a very short leash, and said almost inaudibly, "Oh, thank you. Thank you!"

"Don't thank me. Thank Ben—and you, for speaking up. I did come into this situation pretty cold, you know."

"I know." And she admitted it ruefully. "We were—we were just so scared."

"Better now?"

"Oh, yes. You've no idea."

"What I'll do," he went on, dumping milk and what seemed half a cup of sugar in his own coffee and stirring, "is get with this Matt—Logan, isn't it?—and put everything on hold. Business as usual. Then when I come back again, we'll—make some decisions." Now he was drinking, but the look over the brim of the heavy pottery cup was level and right at her. "You can stay on? At least, in the interim."

"Oh, yes!" Then suddenly realizing she might sound too relieved, she added, "I—I can arrange that."

"Good. Now can you arrange something else?"

"What?"

And the sudden return of caution to her face was as palpable as the sunshine, slanting in through the window and making her soft silvered hair a shining cap.

He said, "When's that auction?"

"Today."

"Are you going?"

"Yes. There are some things that—that Julia wanted."

"Can you arrange to take me?"

Was that all?

Her sudden resurgence of Bluto caution subsided like a tide. "Of course. In fact, since I might buy a chest, I could use the help. Loading it today would save Ben another trip tomorrow. Is the van empty?"

He grimaced—a very sheepish look. "Damned if I remember. I don't think so. But it won't take five minutes. Look—why don't I just go change my shirt? I sort of reached out for something this morning when I heard you going downstairs. I didn't want to miss you." He stood up, a bit incautiously again, made a face, grabbed his head and said, "Wow. Sins do catch up with old guys. How come I could party all night and plow all day ten years ago? It's not been that long, for God's sake. Anyway—be right back. Drink some more orange juice; it's good for you."

She watched through the door as he took

the stairs in not precisely gazellelike bounds.

She was glad to see him go—at least for a few moments. She needed to organize her thoughts. He had said no Marvin, and no Tony. He'd also said that everything would go on hold until he came back from whatever he had to do. And she'd agreed to stay on until then. Oh, those precious days just granted to get her own act together. With Matt to help. She knew he would.

But—she'd also said she already had another job. Why in the blue-eyed world had she done that? She was not ordinarily a liar, and saying she had another job was an outright lie.

And that was a lousy way to begin managing her own life.

Then what she'd have to do was make the statement true—as soon as she could get to a phone.

After that security, then she could take what came. Right?

She had to be her own number one. There wasn't anybody else.

She rinsed her cup and her orange juice glass in the sink, put them in the dishwasher with his and Ben's. Then she went into the front hall to telephone Matt Logan and try to set up something positive.

Charlie was in a heap at the top of the stairs, head on paws, waiting. He raised his massive, fluffy head, and looked down at her in obvious inquiry. She said politely, "Good morning, Charlie." She had, after all, no quarrel with the dog.

Charlie's ears tilted at the sound of a friendly voice. He decided to join her, and descended in a sort of awkward four-paw pavane. Grace on the staircase was not one of the dog's achievements. Laughing despite herself, she patted his large soft head, and he accompanied her across the hall floor, jewel-patterned in the shine of morning sun through leaded glass.

Matt's wife answered in a worried voice. Matt was really no better, but he still hoped to be up and around during the afternoon. Why didn't she call then?

Eleanor said she would, sent her love, and hung up, vaguely worried. Even with the definite improvement in communication with Bluto, she still wanted something concrete before Tony came back. He'd not take Benton Bonford's decision against selling to him at all well. She'd rather, in fact, not even be around when the two men clashed—because clash it would be.

The mental picture of Anthony Mondaine's face when he heard Benton's decision was not a pleasant image. No—not his face. His face would be a mask.

His eyes.

They'd tell the tale of a man unaccustomed to being balked—particularly by Benton Bonford.

Not up to being the heroine type, if she possibly could, she'd make certain she was not on the spot. Diplomatically, it was the only wise maneuver for her. Whatever job she took, good relationships with Mondaine were highly advisable.

Wondering sadly if every profession was so rife with politics, she turned as Bluto came thundering back down the stairs. He had buttoned his vast expanse into a plaid shirt, and was hauling on a jacket. He also looked somewhat more cheerful.

Unaware that the sheer movement of his mass had set the old chandelier gently swinging above his head, he fluffed Charlie's soft ears and said, "Ready?"

For what? The Apocalypse?

Because hers was coming as sure as she'd been born.

But his eyes had gone from her tense face to the hand still on the telephone. His brows went up.

"Now what? More bad news?"

"Matt. He's still not very well. His wife said maybe this afternoon."

"Okay. Cheer up. We'll get 'er done."

But the worried look didn't totally disappear, and it annoyed him. He'd seen those eyes behind the guard-dog glasses snap fire. He'd seen them smile, although not particularly for him. He'd seen them look another way, which had put a stop on his heartbeat, and a large knot in his gut. That look he wasn't quite prepared to handle, yet. But he did know, clearly, that this fixed, haunted stare was not his favorite.

A bit testily, he went on, "Hey—when are you going to learn to listen to me?"

She had turned away, reaching out for a tan windbreaker, and the hand that reached was unsteady. Over her shoulder she said, "What do you mean? I have listened to you."

Even the back of her was tense—nicely rounded, definitely mature, but as brittle as a stick. No skinny teenager here—but an uptight woman. Damnation. He answered shortly, "Horsefeathers. What did I say to you the first time we talked?"

She was putting on the windbreaker. She was not looking at him. "You called me Tootsie."

"You were being a Tootsie. And that's not the time I meant. I said the first time we *talked*. Like a little while ago. When I *thought* I made some Brownie points."

"You—you said we'd see Matt and—and put everything on hold. Until you got back."

"Bingo. And we will. So quit worrying. Believe me."

Heaven only knew, she'd like to believe him. It would buy her time, give her a chance to arrange some life-saving alternatives.

She made herself smile—a look *he* didn't believe—and shrugged. "Okay. Bear with me. I have blank flashes now and then. And we'd better go. The auction starts at eleven and I do have some chores before then."

Charlie watched them out the kitchen door, sighed enormously, then padded towards his food bowl to fortify himself for another boring day.

It was empty. But that was really no problem; the open bag sat next to it. He gave the bag a push with his nose. It fell over, and a gratifying amount of dry crunchies skidded out across the floor. All right. He wasn't proud. He ate what he wanted off the worn old tile, then left the rest for later. Lapping up two quarts of water, he then dripped back upstairs for a nap.

What should it be? The woman's, or his master's bed? The woman's was farther away from the tree with the squirrel in it. He hopped up on Eleanor's crewel-work counterpane, turned around three times, flopped, and went back to sleep.

Downstairs the telephone was ringing, echoing in the upstairs hall. But Charlie knew from long experience that it was not for him.

Well beyond earshot, Eleanor was backing out her small car, taking a sort of perverse pleasure in noting that the large man beside her had his knees practically to his chin.

He said, "You may have to use a can opener."

"Sorry. I don't drive well from the back seat."

She was pleased to see that Ben had parked the van in the shed, unloaded. She

265

was not pleased to see that the left tire was unmistakably flat.

"Damn!"

He'd freed one leg and was working on the other. "What?"

"There's a tire down on the van."

"No sweat. We can take my pickup. It's got a long bed."

He achieved automotive freedom and stood erect, peeling off his jacket. "Go on in the shop, do what you have to do. I'll take the tire off and get the spare, too. We can drop them both at the service station on the way out."

She nodded, a little startled. It had been quite a while since anyone had arranged the mechanics of her life for her. That part she could get to like, as long as she had charge of the main events.

At least, she thought, going up the dock steps, there was no sign of Tony's red Porsche. Perhaps the representative from Sotheby's had been female. She appreciated the delay granted in having to deal with that nuisance.

And what a blow to Tony's ego to know he was a nuisance. Of course he'd never believe it.

"Good morning," she said to

Thomaseen, who was chowing down and returned her greeting with a flick of his silky tail. Mary Ann called a cheerful "Hi!" from the front of the shop where she was dusting china cupboards. "Hey—help me a minute, will you? I need to clean behind the pie safe."

"Sure. Call when you're ready."

The morning mail was neatly stacked on Eleanor's desk. Obvious among the envelopes were the monthly bills—and those needed to be paid. She knew Matt would say to go ahead, but she'd probably better get Bluto's permission, anyway, if only as a diplomatic maneuver. Pay checks, too. She knew she had only fifty bucks in checking, right now.

Draping her windbreaker over the back of the old Windsor chair that had served its purpose handsomely for almost a century in the waiting room of a doctor's office, she sat down at her desk, leafing through the rest of the mail.

One envelope caught her eye: Giametti's Antiques.

John Giametti, in Jacksonville. Why hadn't she thought of him before? She'd love to work for John—he was a prince of a fellow, and just now really getting started.

She slit the envelope, scanned the sympathy note, put the letterhead within eye's view of the telephone and glanced around.

Ben was on the dock with Benton; she could hear their voices. Mary Ann was absorbed in the fretwork on a Victorian gaming table at the far end of the display room.

Hating to feel guilty, Eleanor dialed.

John Giametti was delighted. He'd made some recent contacts in St. Louis, he was hoping to expand, and had always admired Eleanor's expertise. She was to call again in a week and they'd work something out.

Eleanor leaned back in her chair, feeling a load off her shoulders. Jacksonville was only a scant thirty miles on the interstate. She could drive back and forth until she got on her feet. And working with John would be a pleasure.

The day suddenly looked immeasurably brighter—even guiding Benton Bonford through the nuances of an auction. If, she thought, I can keep him from bidding on a 1930s farm tractor with plow attached.

The idea of an old green and gold John

Deere in the midst of the elegant Queen Anne chairs did not amuse her.

But now she wouldn't have to worry about it anymore.

See what happens when you finally take charge of your own life, Eleanor?

A small niggle of concern said she probably should make those other phone calls to Grosman's Antiques at least, if not the rest of her list—just as a backstop.

But Eleanor was on a roll.

She didn't.

She did, in fact, tear up the list, and drop it happily in the wastebasket.

Ben wandered by—walking a little cautiously. He said "Mornin'. You found m' sale bill."

"Yes," she said, not adding, You old idiot, because she loved him.

He did it, himself, rubbing his bald spot gingerly.

"No fool like an old fool," he said. "I ain't done such a good 'un since the Cards won the World Series. Mary Ann's a callin'. And Bent—he's ready when you are."

It took both Eleanor and Mary Ann tugging to bring the old pierced-tin cupboard away from the wall. The sight that then rewarded them was a feline treasure trove consisting of one angora mitten, a large, brittle and defunct cricket, a blue Easter ribbon that had disappeared from Thomaseen's neck within minutes of being placed there, and a tattered pink yarn ball.

"Damned cat," Mary Ann muttered, digging with her broom. "Okay. Hand me the dust buster."

The phone began to ring. At the same time Benton appeared in the doorway, wiping his large hands on a piece of rag. Eleanor called, "Get that, will you?"

After all, it was his place. He may as well start learning now.

Mary Ann picked up the mitten, put it on, and scooted the cricket towards her dustpan, saying, "Yick!"

Eleanor was looking at the pink ball, trying to remember where she'd seen it before. She couldn't hear Benton's voice. She would hardly have recognized Matt Logan's, it was so hoarse. But what it was saying was intelligible enough for Benton to answer soberly, "Yes, sir. I don't like things dangling either. I know what I want done with the shop. If you'll draw up partnership papers, I'll stop by this afternoon and sign them."

There was no disguising both the surprise and the pleasure in the old lawyer's hoarse voice. It was his secretary's day off but he'd be happy to do the legal work, himself.

"Does Eleanor have to sign?"

"Eleanor? Well—yes, of course. But she can drop by, any time. Your signature is the one of importance; it signifies your intent."

"Very good. You are at home?"

"Yes. The stone house on the corner. My wife's out for the afternoon, but come on in. I'll leave the door on latch."

"Thank you. Just one thing—"

"Yes?"

"Don't tell Eleanor. I mean—not yet."

The old man's eyebrows went up, but he forebore comment, only agreed. The nephew rang off. Matt leaned back against his pillows, coughed, waited until the spasm in his chest relaxed, then swung pajamaed legs over the side of the bed. Martha would have a fit, but Eleanor's future was sufficiently important to justify a little exertion.

He was even humming a bit as he went down the hall to his small home office.

At the shop, Benton Bonford was not humming. He was staring into space, a deep line between heavy brows.

He was doing the right thing. He knew that. Being blessed—or cursed, depending on one's point of view—with the Bonford conscience, there was really no other course.

Just the same, Eleanor Wright was going to have to shape up a bit before he'd tell her she was finally going to get her partnership.

The ramifications of what all of that would involve were a little fuzzy in his mind. But he had no doubt that eventually it would all come clear.

Then his musings were interrupted again by the telephone. He picked it up and was astonished to hear, through a tinny long-distance connection, his nearest neighbor's voice:

"Bent? Bent, is that you?"

Benton said, "Yeah," then listened. His face twisted into a grimace of dismay. He hit the old rolltop desk softly with a doubled fist. "Damn! Damn it, Vince! Okay, listen—I'll drive in tonight. Get out the good Scotch; it sounds as if we'll both need it."

As he hung up and turned around Eleanor was coming back through the door from the shop. She said,

"Bad news?"

He nodded grimly. "That was the guy

on the place next to mine. We got a hell of a wind last night and it flattened about a hundred acres of corn. He says the fields look like jackstraws. I'll have to go home today."

"Oh." Why did she feel so curiously deflated? "Of course you do. I'm sorry about your—your corn."

He stared at her a moment thinking, She doesn't even know what she's sorry about. She can't envision those fields, the dry brown stalks with their heavy ears all lying at sixes and sevens, or having to run the picker against the rows or maybe even having to handpick before the rain soaks the husks and the corn starts to mold on the ground.

But she is sincerely sorry. She is that. This just might be a hell of a woman.

He dropped his eyes. His wristwatch was as good a place as any to focus them. He said, "I'll still go to that auction. There's no point in leaving right now; I couldn't possibly get home before nightfall and wouldn't be able to do anything constructive until tomorrow, anyway. So let's load up. Got whatever you need?"

She nodded. "If you're sure."

"I'm sure."

His red pickup truck, full of gas, was parked by the van with the two tires heaved into the back end. Eleanor went around to the right side. She felt as if she were walking in a vacuum. She thought, What is wrong with me? This morning I didn't want him to go to the auction. Then when I thought he wasn't, it was like the whole day clouding over.

You'd better watch it, sugar. Your priorities are really screwed up.

Above her, a long arm reached over, pulled up the lock, pushed open the door, then grasped her hand, giving her a hefty heave upward.

"Four-wheel drive," he grinned as she bounced onto the seat. "They're not built for short legs. Even nice ones. Unless you can handle a straight shift, you'd better let me drive."

He'd made room on the seat by casually sweeping towards him a stack of agricultural bulletins, a Snickers wrapper, two mismatched yellow leather gloves, a plastic bag of Doggie Treats and three old *Playboy* magazines. She settled herself on the space that remained, glanced out of the window at the alley concrete which looked as if it were twelve feet below, then looked at the gearshift whose knob was etched with a shifting diagram that resembled a loser's game of dot-to-dot.

She said, "Turn left out of the alley and take the first street south."

"And the service station for the tires?"

"On the edge of town."

While he started his engine, she surveyed the rest of the cab. It contained a stereo, a tape player, a CB radio and factory "air." The floor mats were worn, with two ears of corn rolling beneath her feet, the dry husks pulled back to show rows of dented, hard, gold kernels. The vinyl on the seat had been mended with a broad strip of duct tape. There were three telephone numbers written in ballpoint on the liner above his head.

Where, she wondered, are the cute giant dice swinging from the mirror, and the little plastic dog going noddy-noddy in the back window?

Then she blushed crimson. She was being snobbish again. This time it wasn't working. This time she recognized it for what it really was: a defense mechanism. A shabby means of putting herself up by putting him down.

Whatever she must do to keep her own balance, that wasn't it.

She watched with very mixed feelings as he found the service station, rolled both Fiat tires into the greasy shop, loped back and swung himself up with a draft of fresh cold air into the seat beside her.

He said, "They'll be done when we get back. Now, where to? On down the road?"

She nodded, and they got underway again.

The silence between them was not totally comfortable. Perversely, neither wanted to break it with inanities. Yet both felt the need for communication.

Benton reached out, punched the tape player, and a pleasantly nasal voice began to sing of Georgia on his mind. It also, over an interminable period of time, spoke of being on the road again and then, poignantly, of September.

That one very nearly did it good. It had always made Eleanor want to cry, and today the feeling was almost unbearable. She would not make a perfect fool of herself again. She began to say, "It's not too far, now," then discovered that Benton was already saying, "How far is it?"

They both started.

They both laughed. Sheepishly.

Benton said, "Before we get there—" He hesitated, sighed. "I guess there's no good way of putting it."

He frowned, staring straight down the ribbon of highway that was like a shelf between the browning bluff and the browner river bottom. She waited. She was conscious of her hands clasped together quietly in her lap, clasped so hard they hurt, but he couldn't know about that.

Still staring, he went on, "Unfortunately—I seem to talk a lot of nonsense when I'm drunk. If I did, I'm—I'm really sorry. I apologize."

He turned his head, then, and saw that she was the one staring straight down the road now. He saw her visibly swallow. He saw her bite her lower lip for just a moment.

Then she turned and looked at him.

She said, "I'm sorry for something, too. I'm sorry we got off on the wrong foot when we met."

He looked at the road; he had to look, but they were still going straight ahead, between the bluff and the bottom and he was able to glance back at the woman beside him.

Quietly he answered, and his words were

half laughter, half not, "I could go out and come in again."

"All right. And—and I won't yell at you if you won't yell at me."

"I won't yell."

He took a large brown hand from the wheel, held it out to her. "Shake?"

"Shake."

He didn't try to hold on. She took her own hand back, put it in her lap, covered with the other the warmth and strength he'd left lying along her palm with his— almost as though she were trying to keep it there. Which was, of course, absurd.

But suddenly it was a rather beautiful fall day. She could tell Tony Mondaine to screw off, and she could tell Marvin Coles the same—that they'd never own Julia's shop because the large man beside her had promised. And she believed him.

Who *would* own the shop was something else. But whatever happened, she had a job with John Giametti. And she'd done it on her own. No handouts.

For the first time since Julia's death, Eleanor Wright relaxed. Just a little.

Everyone makes mistakes now and then.

Fourteen

As Eleanor remembered, the road turned and unrolled its gray ribbon far across the valley between bean fields now shorn and brown. At the rise of the river bluffs a new sign had been stuck in among the tangled, dry cattails by the Crane mailbox. It read AUCTION TODAY! In smaller letters it added: Col. Rollie Carr, Auctioneer. Lunch served at 12.

Eleanor said, "That's our turn. If you haven't guessed."

"I guessed." He was already shifting gears for the climb.

The truck growled upward. It was taller than Eleanor's little Chevy, and persimmon tree branches dragged along its roof, dropping small, squashy persimmons like orange rain. The other side of the road was a leaning fence row, choked with struggling, drab cedar scrub. The center was a ridged clay, still soft from the rains, and scarred with the passage of other recent vehicles.

Benton said, "It looks as if we aren't the first." He was shifting into four-wheel drive and the truck lurched on powerfully.

Eleanor nodded. "I'm sure we aren't. The Cranes have been very well known in the area."

"Did they farm big?"

What was big to this man?

She shrugged. "A lot of bottom land. I know that. Hogs. Cattle."

They crossed the same, thin, sparkling trickle of water over layers of limestone crunched flat, climbed again, turned, and found themselves the last of a long, snaking line of pickups, stake trucks, jeeps, campers and a few modest sedans. These were parked along both sides of the road, leaving only a perilous center passageway for the daring. Far ahead, on the left, could be glimpsed the barbed-wire fence of the sagging Crane house, encompassing a milling crowd moving up and down rows of furniture.

Eleanor said, "I hope you don't mind walking."

He was already maneuvering his own truck into line beneath the drooping, tattered branches of a scaly sycamore. Then he looked at her. "Lock up?"

Her returning glance almost reflected insult. "No. Of course not."

He shrugged, reached behind the seat and extracted a smashed red tractor cap. Carefully reshaping it, he said, "If Nature abhors a vacuum, a farmer abhors a bare head. And I certainly don't want to be caught out of uniform."

From under the freshly curved brim he grinned at her. "Are you going to leave on those glasses? You look like an owl."

She said, "I thought I was going to drive," which was answer enough, if not strictly truthful. She took them off and stuck them in her bag. "Let me get out your side. Mine's in a ditch full of cockleburs."

He got out, unceremoniously swung her down. "Shall I stick with you or may I go off on my own?"

"Are you going to bid?"

"I may take a number. Just in case I see

something my little heart can't do without."

They attracted a certain amount of attention as they went through the squeaky
gate. Word does get about, Eleanor realized, and besides, Benton Bonford was a
little hard to miss.

She felt a touch on her arm; it was May
Crane. "Your thing is in the smokehouse,"
the elderly lady whispered. "Don't worry.
No one else will see it."

Smiling her thanks, Eleanor made her
way to the high auction van pulled over
beside three long tables piled high with
crocks, kitchen utensils, water buckets,
canning jars and rug beaters. An ironing
board held clothes pins, three sad-irons
and a trivet. Beneath, on the tired, trampled grass were old, galvanized tubs and
cardboard boxes piled high with other domestic flotsam.

Eleanor said, "Hi, Pat," to the auctioneer's wife, picked up a cardboard number,
and nodded to the florid-faced, Western-
hatted auctioneer. He nodded back, blew
into his microphone, was rewarded with a
resounding squawk that roused startled pi-
geons from the roof of the distant barn,
and said, "All right, folks, let's gather

around the kitchen stuff. We're going to start this little clambake in about five minutes. Five minutes, good people, get your numbers no bids without a number." Then, his beefy hand over the mike, he leaned down from his perch and said to Eleanor, "Hi, Ellie, glad to see you. Who's the Houston Oiler?"

Eleanor introduced Benton and they clasped fists briefly over her head. Benton picked up his own number, murmured "See y', kid," into her ear and sauntered off through the crowds.

Rollie Carr, watching him go from his lofty perch, bent and asked, "Does he arm wrestle?"

"What?"

"Arm wrestle. There's a contest over in Calhoun Saturday with good stakes and my boy's sprained his thumb."

"I really can't say," Eleanor answered, laughing. "You'll have to ask him. Pat, is there anything not on the handbill?"

The auctioneer's wife shuffled through her lists. "Not really. There's some peach-blow in a consignment, around by the summer kitchen. And some ruby glass turned up. Most of the unlisted stuff will be here tomorrow when they sell the livestock and farm equipment."

Eleanor nodded, not being interested in either. As she moved off, Rollie blew in his mike again and took up his chant: "All right, folks, all right, here we go. Hold up No. 1, George, so the folks can see. A fine old milk crock, and George, put in that strainer and a couple of stone jugs with them, do I hear two dolla, two dolla, will you give me three . . ."

Down the sloping, dead lawn to the smokehouse marched three uneven rows of household furniture, all their scratches, mends and other idiosyncrasies bared to the cool fall sunshine.

Halfway along the middle row, Eleanor saw the walnut chest sitting forlorn and gray beneath a cardboard box of curtain rods. She meandered casually to it, stopping on the way to inspect a Larkin chiffonier and a bow-front dresser. The veneer was splitting on the dresser but the mirror was impeccable. Putting a mental check on the mirror, she moved to the next item, a treadle sewing machine, and a fat little woman in a snagged double-knit pants suit put her hand on it possessively.

She said, "Hi, Ellie, bug off."

Eleanor laughed. "It's yours, Mabel. Go for it. How's Clyde?"

"Better. Being tail-ended doesn't really improve the human frame, but he's getting along. Who's the ox with you?"

"Julia's nephew."

"Big, ain't he?"

"Adequate," said Eleanor, and sauntered on.

Hardly pausing by the chest—Ben, after all, knew his stuff—she found herself at the end of the line by trestle tables set up in front of the smokehouse in a fine miasma of fresh coffee. She said, "Hello, girls," to the ladies of the First Baptist Church, and "Midmorning snack?" to the large mass in the red tractor cap who was attacking half a chocolate pie with a plastic fork and every indication of having just conquered starvation.

"Ambrosia," said Benton, through a mouthful of three-inch meringue. "I asked this lady to marry me but she says she's a Trappist monk in disguise. Do you believe that, or is she just putting on an outlander?"

Eleanor said to the lady, "Give me a piece, Maude, if this outlander left any."

She received another hefty chunk on a

paper plate and sat down at a picnic table. Benton followed with two styrofoam cups of coffee and sat down beside her. On the other side, a lean-faced man in bib overalls glanced up, said, "Hi, Ellie. Real sorry about Julia."

"Thank you, Jim. This is Benton Bonford, Julia's nephew."

They shook hands, eyed each other. The man went on pleasantly, "I'm Jim Crane. This is my mom's farm. Where you from, Bonford?"

Benton told him. He raised sandy eyebrows.

"Isn't that in the area where they want to put a government dam?"

"Smack in the middle."

"You farm?"

"Yeah."

"What will that do to you? If it goes through, I mean."

Benton laughed, a little grimly. "Put me forty feet under water."

"Hot dog. I hope you swim."

"I'll learn."

"Is it really going to pass the legislature?"

"Sure looks like it will."

"Hell, man. You don't look like a fish.

286

Why don't you come over in God's country and buy this place? I'm farmin' it this year for my mother, but next fall my oldest kid goes to the university and I won't be able to hack 'em both. Let me show you around."

Benton shrugged, wiped chocolate off his upper lip and chugged the rest of his coffee. "Never hurts to look," he said and stood up, rocking the table.

Jim Crane, tossing his empty cup in a bag-lined rain barrel, said, "There's a dandy new pole barn my dad put up, and a good tight machine shed. The house ain't much, but one good year of crops on the bottom land would buy you a new house."

They moved off through the crowd without a backward glance, talking animatedly. Eleanor, steadying her rocking coffee cup, said in a voice that was rather dry, "See you later."

If he remembered who she was. Or that she came with him.

She finished her own pie, and started back up the slope. On a flatbed trailer beneath some ragged mock-orange bushes was displayed, helter-skelter, a generation's collection of knickknacks. Kitsch was not Eleanor's thing, at all. More than two decades with Julia had schooled her tastes far away from jolly ceramic baker-boys with wooden spoons in their stomachs, or ashtrays in the shape of johns, or obscenities made of nondescript shell and labeled "Happy Days at Orlando, Florida." Nevertheless, smack in the middle of the trailer bed was a piece of nonsense so blatantly awful it caught her eye.

It was an enormous ceramic cow—too large to be a creamer, so it must be a jug. The tail was arched coyly into a handle. The muzzle was opened wide into a silently mooing spout. It had long eyelashes, a barrel body with the appropriate appurtenances beneath, and it was absolutely, trumpetingly purple.

"Good God," murmured Eleanor, then glanced around swiftly to be sure no one had heard. Mary Ann would love the thing. She'd have to bid on it.

Rollie had moved his rig around the house. Red-faced and sweating, even in the October air, he was starting on the furniture while his hatted helpers in their own too-tight, trim-cut Western shirts walked down the rows, indicating either the article or the lot. Eleanor made her way through the crowd and got in place.

The chest was easy. There were no other dealers, and none of the Cranes' neighbors wanted a gray old, water-stained thing that had sat on the back porch as a wash stand for thirty years. She had to buy the bow-front bureau to get the mirror, but that was all right. The mirror was worth the price.

Then if it wasn't for the awful purple cow she could collect Bluto and go home.

But she was hooked on that cow. It would be such a gorgeous Christmas gift for the faithful, hardworking Mary Ann.

Patiently she waited, fortifying herself with more coffee and a couple of excellent doughnuts.

Rollie waded through the furniture, braced himself, and hung on as his driver moved the rig across the trampled lawn. They stopped by the flatbed. Thank God for small favors. She'd been afraid she'd have to wait clear through the glassware and there was a lot of it.

She quietly moved herself into position with her number card in hand. Rollie looked down at her with surprise. Bending to fiddle with his mike cord, he asked out of the side of his mouth, "What do you want, Ellie?"

"The cow."

"You're kidding."

"No. I want it."

"Is there something I don't know?"

"Nothing."

"Okay. Hang on."

He led everyone with great good humor through two boxes of Reader's Digest books, a stack of towel calendars, and an apple basket full of Christmas tree ornaments. Then his helper picked up the cow and held it above his head.

Rollie said, "Now, folks, look at this here gorgeous creature, it's even got the tiddleys on the bottom, show 'em, George, and what am I bid, let's say one dolla, one dolla—"

He glanced at Eleanor. She moved her number card.

"One dolla it is, do I hear two dolla—"

"Two," came a timid voice from the rear.

Eleanor indicated two and a half.

The timid voice said, "Three."

Eleanor nodded.

Rollie went on, burbling, "Three dolla, three dolla, do I get three and a half?"

"Three and a half."

It went to five, just Eleanor and the timid voice, then six, then up to ten. Irritated, Eleanor dropped out, but before the mousy soprano in the back could clinch the deal, Rollie went in, "Okay, number thirty-eight, I see you, and ten and a half it is, do I hear eleven, all right, eleven, and is there eleven and a half?"

The incredible monstrosity went for twenty-five dollars before it sold to number thirty-eight—whoever that was.

Eleanor tried to see, but her view was blocked by a chunky lady clutching a hand-painted chamberpot to her polyester bosom. She shrugged, still irritated, and made her way through the crowd to settle up with Pat Carr and assemble her purchases.

On the whole, she was pleased with herself. For twenty-five dollars, Mary Ann could have two purple cows and a lamp in the shape of a Siamese dancer. Or something similar. It was a long time until Christmas. And she had got what she'd come for, plus an excellent mirror worth three times the price. Not too bad a day.

After a fair search, she found Benton and two other guys in plaid shirts and tractor caps, leaning on a fence and silently contemplating the scrub-brush covered south end of a large hog going north. She said, "Hi," and all four of them swung around and contemplated her.

She wondered, should I oink or moo? She said to Benton, "If you want to bring the truck up, we can load and go now."

Benton said, "Sure thing," and loped off. Jim Crane looked her in the eye and said, "Nice guy."

'The second man said, "Sure knows his hogs."

The hog grunted.

Eleanor laughed. "Who am I," she said, "to contest a unanimous vote?"

On the way back to town, she observed dryly, "You made a hit with the locals."

Benton's eye was on the rear-view mirror where he could glimpse the corner of a wrapping quilt whipping loose in the wind. He slowed up a little. His voice was also a little dry. "Locals. Is that another word for *redneck* or *peasant?*"

"No. Of course not."

"It sounded like it."

You want to pick a fight, Bluto?

But she didn't. Instead, trying to be light, she asked, "Did you buy the farm?" Then she was instantly sorry, the possibly

292

horrid truth suddenly exposing itself: would one farm equate to the sale of one antique shop?

Had the same thing occurred to him? His answer was short: "With what?"

Hurriedly she plunged on, "Were you serious about a dam or something flooding your land?"

"Yes, ma'am."

"Aren't there options? Do you have to sell?"

"If all around me my neighbors are selling theirs, the options get mighty slim."

"And they are?"

"They will."

"It doesn't seem fair."

What a place for a platitude about fairness. He refrained. Instead, he said, "That Crane place is a good one. A bit of timber, plenty of water, tight buildings and rich bottom land."

"And hogs."

"And hogs."

He leaned forward, lips tight on a cigarette, and punched the lighter button. Beneath that hair thicket, his witch-hazel eyes cut sideways. "You got something against hogs, lady?"

"I eat as much bacon as anyone. But I

have to admit, my speaking acquaintance with the source has been slim." Bent on self-destruction, she added, "My largest impression is that they wallow a lot."

"Not anymore. Pigs like to be as clean as anyone. They also like to be cool. You keep them cool, they don't have to wallow. Lesson for the day," he finished, and laughed, once more stubbing out his cigarette in the ashtray. "Phoo! Whatever was in that brand of beer Ben buys, I may never smoke again! My mouth tastes like a buffalo nickel!"

"It didn't seem to stop your eating pie."

"Pie, dear girl, I eat when and wherever I find a good one. My lovely wife, Jill, did not measure pastry among her accomplishments."

He was arching his tufted eyebrows at her. She answered quickly, "Nor mine. Sorry."

But the sudden mention of Jill Bonford inexplicably jarred her. Blond, pretty, and young. She'd bet money on that. And she'd left him. Flat. Like a coward, leaving while he was gone. His only reaction seemed to have been anger, yet Eleanor, herself, knew too well that anger sometimes concealed terrible hurt. Had he been hurt? Was he hurting?

Why should she care? Their connection was going to be brief, anyway. It wasn't any concern of hers.

At least she didn't think it was.

Was it?

Fifteen

Suddenly Eleanor was scared again.
Suddenly she wished she were back in
town, that he was already on his way upstate.

She felt out of her depth and flounder-
ing; she couldn't afford to be so, nor feel
that she was. She needed nice straight lines
with Tony and Marvin and this man safely
inside readable slots. She'd thought she
had them there. Now she wasn't so sure
again. And she couldn't afford not to be
sure.

He'd been saying something else. What
had it been? Good God, she had to get
herself together.

Struggling for a vestige of calm, she
said, "What? I'm sorry. I was—doing a
blank again."

He half smiled, but didn't take issue. One big hand came off the wheel, gesturing at the roadside with its tall trees reaching ragged, graceful branches to the slate blue sky, trees with their feet buried in scarlet-leaved sumac and tangled brambles, delicate grapevines and orange bittersweet, trees unnumbered, marching up the hillside to infinity. Softly, he repeated, " 'The woods are lovely, dark and deep—but I have promises to keep. And miles to go before I sleep.' Robert Frost. A good man with words. Because I have."

" 'Miles to go' before you sleep?" She was trying to smile.

"And 'promises to keep.' " He gave her a quick but level look from those heavy silvered brows. "I do keep my promises, lady. Remember that. But—damn!" Now he was looking at his watch. "I'm really going to have to move! There's still a five-hour drive ahead of me."

She'd been caught by the deep tone of his voice. What promises? To whom?

Could she really believe this man?

But all she said aloud was, "Sorry. I guess I could have hurried."

"No, no, not at all. Hell, you can't hurry at an auction. You'll lose your butt. We

297

both know that. I just thought I'd have time to buy you a Bunny Burger."

What a change from Tony's mushroom quiche and beef bourguignon. How—comfortable. Hardly thinking straight, she said quickly, "Never mind. Next time. I mean—you are coming back." Then she was appalled at what she thought she heard in her own voice: a little girl, begging for treats.

He turned his head and looked at her. The look flurried her even more. It was level. Questioning.

She rushed on, "I mean, with Matt sick and nothing settled—" then stopped. The petulant-woman image was worse than the begging little girl act. She took a firm grip on herself, and began acting adult again, not like a moonstruck teenager.

"Sorry. I have no business saying that. I can't tell you what to do."

He looked back at the road, at the bright yellow cottonwoods lining the other shoulder, at the orange sun shining through their tattered leaves as it dropped towards the distant blue line of river bottom. A little roughly, he answered, "Of course you can, damn it! You have every right; you're just as much a participant in this inheritance deal as I am. Yes, I'm coming back. As soon as I reasonably can. In the meantime you are to run my aunt's place just as though she was there, just as you always have run it! Okay? It shouldn't be long—three weeks at the most. Then when Matt what'shisname is on his feet again we'll look at the whole picture and go on from there. Okay? Got it?"

She had it—at least she had what he'd said—that she had three weeks in which to work out her own salvation because the bottom line was still what was best for him—not her.

She said, "Got it. Thanks."

"That's not enough."

Whoa, Bluto! "What's not enough?"

"Thanks."

A bit stiffly, she asked, "What else do you have in mind?" She almost said, What else do you have in mind, turkey? but she restrained herself.

Still, the hesitancy reached him. He turned in astonishment, and saw her face. Then he laughed—a big, deep ho-ho-ho from the bottom of his chest. "That, also," he grinned, "but not just now. And only maybe. If there's positive cooperation.

Quit blushing; it's my fault if I don't make things clear."

"Please," she said between clenched teeth, "make things clear."

He turned into the alley, and with one big arm along the back of the seat, and looking through the rear window he deftly maneuvered the tailgate up to the loading dock.

Then he turned the engine off but left the arm where it was. He was uncomfortably close. Eleanor put her hand on the door latch; his hand left the wheel and covered hers.

"Wait," he said. "Listen to me a minute. I'll try not to be too obnoxious. Look. I'm not certain what your personal relationship is with the Mondaine character, and I don't mean to pry. But I do want one thing understood. I don't like him. And I don't want him taking over while I'm gone. In that respect, the place *is* mine. And I'll raise hell. Okay?"

He was so close. All the smells of outdoors and smoke and man mingled in her nose, along with the shaving nick along his jaw and the brow thicket gone into a straight bar across the top of a very positive set of green, unmoving, probing eyes. She caught her breath—just a little, just softly.

Then he tore it. He said, "You've got two feet. Stand on them."

That was succinct—far more than he probably meant it to be. But it snapped her up sharply. The hand beneath his pushed the door open, she slid from his hovering mass and stood on those two feet.

She wasn't certain what he'd really meant: that he'd seen a tendency in her towards letting Tony lead her around— which she resented because it might be true; or that he simply wanted to see in the interim of his absence whether she could handle the business.

"That," she said, "I can do. Just watch me."

Perhaps her voice was a little too cool, a little too grim. He threw up both hands, sighed, slapped the wheel with them and said her own favorite barnyard word. "I told you I wasn't very good at these things. So I mucked up what I meant. I'm sorry. I think. Anyway, we'll let it stand until I can do better. Where do you want the load?"

Mary Ann's husband was cooling his heels in Julia's old captain's chair. He came out and lent his muscle; between the two men they hefted the chest and the bureau out of the truck and into the workshop. Benton came back to Eleanor who was rather mechanically folding pad quilts. He was looking at his watch again. "I'll run by and get the tires."

She started, "No, you don't have to—"

"Yes, I will," he interrupted. "Bill, here, says he'll put one on while Mary Ann closes up. Are you needed in the shop? If not, I'll meet you at Aunt Julia's."

She faced up to it: his departure was prolonged a little more, and she was glad. Realizing helplessly that she'd never blown so hot and cold since she was a gauche sixteen, she said, "Okay," and watched him one-hand the truck wheel into a sharp reverse, straighten out and drive down the alley.

Mary Ann's husband said casually, "Nice guy."

Must people keep telling her that?

She said, "Yes," briefly, told Mary Ann where she was going, got in her Chevy and left.

She didn't notice that it took him rather long to pick up and drop off two tires. She went through the fast food drive-in, picked up two Bunny Burgers and a double order of fries, got behind a Trans Am with a dead battery causing a minor traffic jam, switched off, drove three back alleys, caught four red lights in a row and he still wasn't at the house when she arrived.

But as she went up the back steps, he pulled in behind her and came scuffling through the dry leaves. He was whistling cheerfully, as he reached around her and opened the door.

"Four and a half for fixing and two for mounting," he said, of the tires. "I put the bill on the rolltop at the shop. Look out— Charlie's knocked over his dog food. My fault; I'll bet I forgot to leave him any."

She stepped around the spill. Oil based, it was slippery. "That's all right. I'll get the broom. Can I help you?"

"No thanks, I travel light." He went on by her into the hall and she called after him, "I picked up some Bunny Burgers."

"Brilliant woman. I'll be right back."

She put the bag on the table by the squash hat and began to sweep the rolling nodules into a pile. Some were shaped like little bones, some like tennis shoes. Cute. The average American pet owner was really a pushover to buy silly stuff like that.

It takes one, she thought grimly of the term "pushover," to know one.

Long after the pile was completed, she went on sweeping mechanically, her mind far away.

Benton came downstairs again. He was accompanied by a sheepish-looking and rather chastened Saint Bernard, and all six of their assorted thumping feet rattled the dishes in the cupboard.

"Out!" he said to the dog, opening the kitchen door with his knee and leaving it gapped. Then he grinned at Eleanor. "I am sorry to say," he said, putting a canvas travel bag on the table by the hat, and extracting a messy roll of shirts and jeans from beneath his arm, "that of the pair of us, my dog has been the one to sleep in your bed. I apologize for the hairs. He knows better, but I have to admit his taste is excellent. Got a grocery sack for my dirty clothes?"

"Behind you."

He wheeled, put one foot on the dog food pile, skidded, grabbed futilely at insufficient air while the shirts and jeans inscribed a fluttering parabola of disintegrating mass and crashed to the floor. Eleanor tried to help, but it was like

304

a skier attempting to stop an avalanche. She fell on top of him, a pair of blue jeans across her behind and the shrunken T-shirt on her head. They both said varying forms of "Oof!" They both began to scramble, nullifying each other's efforts. Charlie appeared in the doorway, looked fascinated, and joined the fun, lolloping whatever bare surface was available with a wet flannel tongue.

Eleanor said, "Yech," and hid her face on Benton's plaid chest. Benton said, "Damn it, get off, Dumbo!" shoving at the dog. They were both laughing. "Move, you big oaf! Cut it out! If there's any kissing to be done, I'll do it, okay? In fact," he added suddenly, "I think I will."

She felt his big hand on her sliding hair, turning her head. She had a hazy glimpse of his mouth only inches from hers before he closed the gap and stopped the laughter.

At first instant it was casual, warm, pleasant. She wasn't sure when it changed. It certainly wasn't the beat of her heart or the sudden surge of her breasts because he couldn't know that. A shirt and a heavy sweater are excellent insulation against the rising sweep of helpless want. But it did change, and she found herself cradled inside both big arms, heard him murmur, "Oh God," against her soft mouth and slid down the pulse of her bared throat into her open shirt. She clung like a mindless idiot as he struggled to his feet, wanting to feel the whole pliant length of her body against his.

Her shirttails were out. His searching hand slid up her warm, bare back, stroking its way, finding the fastening of her bra, disengaging it, catching his breath at the sudden freed burgeoning of the satin loveliness he hungered for. His other hand started to push up the sweater, the shirt; his fingers were warm—and shaking. She could feel them tremble.

She also felt him—suddenly—freeze.

Then in her ear he said, "Whoa."

Her surging heart stopped.

He said, "Whoa," again, and pulled the sweater back down. But he didn't let her go; he still held her tight, close, and she could also feel his own demanding desire pressing against her thigh.

But his mouth moved, said against her cheek, "Cease and desist. I don't know what's going to become of this. Maybe nothing. But if something does start between us, Eleanor Wright, it's going to start with class—not in the middle of my aunt's kitchen floor. Okay? Of course," he went on whispering, "I may just—kiss you again. One more time—" and he did, stopping her own words with his hungry mouth, then saying urgently, "Oh, damn. Damn, damn, damn," taking his arms away, removing her hands with his, but holding onto them and making her look at him, making her open her eyes to see the pain in his.

His brows were twisted, drawn. He said in the same husky whisper, "This can be too important. I have to know where the lines are. I've been stung, baby. I know how women can fake it out with a man because they want something else. I can't take any more faking."

Her own whisper was indignant: "You think I'm doing that—pretending?"

"I think you don't *know* what you're doing. I think we're both trying to survive. I think neither of us needs any more hurt. I think—" and his voice shifted, tried for laughter, "—that it's a damned good thing I have to leave."

"But you are coming back?"

Fake or not, the sound of pleading in

her voice fed his hungry heart. He answered thickly, "Is the Pope Catholic?" and kissed her one more time—on the top of her mussed silk-silver head.

Then he loosed her, stepping away, saying, "You get the grocery sack. That's what started this."

"Your dog started it," she said, but turned and took one from the rack. She stood quietly while he retrieved his scattered laundry and stuffed it away. She was telling herself to be calm but inside her silly head a little voice was singing tunelessly, mindlessly—a rather triumphant little voice.

He picked up his tractor cap where it had fallen to the floor, stuffed it into the sack also, and put the squash hat on his head.

"My traveling uniform," he said, and stopped smiling. "Damn. I don't understand it, but—I don't want to go."

"I don't understand it either, but I don't want you to go."

She said it quite simply, without subterfuge.

They looked at each other, wordless, because neither knew quite what to say.

He picked up his canvas bag, said to the

large dog sitting patiently by the open door, "Come on, Charlie."

They both got into the red pickup truck, the Saint Bernard arranging his mass on the passenger side with an air of being quite at home.

Eleanor said suddenly, "Oh! The Bunny Burgers!"

She ran, got the sack, held it up. He rolled his window down, leaned out, said, "Thanks. I'll call. I promise. What's the number here?"

She gave him the house number, and the one at the shop. He took a felt-tip marker from the dash, reached up, and wrote them on the ceiling.

"There," he said, replacing the cap on the felt tip. "You're even over the International Harvester repair, and the Farm-Field Service man. And believe me, Eleanor Wright, they're important. Good-bye."

"Good-bye. Drive carefully." She'd said that phrase a thousand times and never meant it so much.

"Okay. And you—don't worry. I'll get back as soon as I can."

"All right."

"Also, remember what I said about that Mondaine character."

Good God—she'd even forgotten Tony. She said quietly, "I don't think you need to worry, either."

His mouth twisted; it was a funny sort of half smile. He put the truck in gear. He drove away.

Her last glimpse was of Charlie, his fluffy ears perked, big paws on the dash. They turned right, down the street beneath the falling leaves just as the lamps above them flared to a pale, twilight glow.

Then she turned, and walked back into a very silent house.

The dog food was scattered all over the floor again. She took the broom, swept it up, put the broom away.

Then she realized: she'd given him both Bunny Burgers.

Oh, well. She really wasn't hungry, anyway.

Damn. The kitchen seemed far too large.

She left it, went across the quiet, shadowy hall and up the stairs.

His bed was made. A tidy man.

He'd also opened a window but it still smelled of smoke. She left it open, went into her room, saw the crumpled crewel-work cover, walked towards it automatically, her feet disengaged from her brain.

Then she saw something else: a ratty, cardboard box with crumpled paper sticking out of the flapping top and a note stuck on the side with a paper clip. The note was in black felt-tip pen. It said, "I can't understand why you wanted this, but since you did, I wanted you to have it."

Beneath the crumpled papers, in all its ceramic glory, was the purple cow.

Sixteen

It looked up at her coyly through long-lashed ceramic eyes, saying its silent, perpetual moo. Eleanor looked back, caught between laughing and crying.

She lifted it out very gently, put it on her Pembroke night table next to the delicate Lalique lamp. The contrast ordinarily would have made her very teeth grind. Tonight, she only sat on the side of the bed and stared at it with an April face.

"Well, Tillie," she said aloud, and the name came naturally. "I guess it's just you and me together. And I'll never tell him if you don't."

Sorry, Mary Ann. I'll find something else for you. Promise.

The sweet chime of the Neuchâtel clock rang seven times, startling her. It seemed as if it should be at least twelve—or even perhaps the next century. Accompanying the chime was the more strident ring of the telephone in the hall.

"Be right back," she said to the cow, and went to answer.

Tony's mellifluous voice said apologetically, "Hello, sweetheart; did you think I'd dropped into a hole?"

She hadn't even missed him.

She grimaced silently. "No, not really. It's been a busy day."

"Darling, are you catching cold?"

Then she heard the husky timbre of her own voice, thickened by the threatened onslaught of tears and not cleared by speaking—until now. She alibi'd: "I don't know. Perhaps."

"I'd rather think it passion at the sound of my voice, but I suppose not."

She answered that one cheerfully: "You're right."

"Thanks a lot." Then his own voice dropped. "Are you alone?"

No—Tillie's here. But she couldn't say that. "Yes."

"Where's the country's gift to agriculture?"

"He went home."

"Home!" And there was no disguising the sudden anxiety in his tone. "Damn. And I wasn't with you. What happened? Is he going to sell?"

"I don't know."

"You don't? For heaven's sake, why not?"

"Matt is ill, and Benton had some sort of domestic disaster that took him home. He'll be back."

"When?"

"When he can. Or when Matt is better."

"And in the meantime?"

"I guess the shop's on hold."

"Poor baby."

Nonetheless, there was relief in his voice and he couldn't quite hide it. Eleanor heard. She frowned, wondering at the reason. Heavens, she thought, I maybe have two men wrangling over me—and I'm not certain why either one of them is.

Except I know it's not my youth and beauty.

I hate being a handball. I resent it. Why can't I just simply be in love, with no tensions, no sense of being used, no need to hide what I feel—and not with this man. Oh God, not with this man. With Benton. With Benton, the tractor jockey, with whom I probably have no more in common than night and day.

Except that night melts into day as I could melt into Benton, like a giddy schoolgirl giving herself to the team captain, caught up in the simple, enormous scent of his male virility—because that's what it is. Isn't it?

"Eleanor. Eleanor, are you still there?"

She came back with a jolt. "Oh. Sorry. I thought I heard someone at the door." Lying again. That's what intrigue does to one's morals. All the rules go down the tube when you're trying to survive.

"Eleanor, you really don't sound well. Perhaps I'd better run down tonight."

"Oh, no, Tony, really. I'm fine. I went to an auction today and I guess the fresh air wore me out."

"Nonsense. You're reacting—that's what you're doing. Julia's death and all the other complications are finally getting to you. Why don't you drink something hot and go to bed. Alone, of course."

Why "of course"? Is that your assumption, Anthony, that you are the only man with whom I might possibly go to bed, and as a consequence of your absence I have to seek a lonely couch?

She arrested her own wild thoughts. Good God, she thought ruefully, I am wacko tonight.

She sighed, said aloud, "Not too bad an idea."

"It's an excellent idea. Inspired. I have, after all, only excellent and inspired ideas. Besides, something's come up with the Sotheby affair and I do need to stick around."

He partly turned, smiled across the living room at the lissome form only half covered in his Napoleon bed. Miranda had nothing to do with Sotheby's, but when she was in town, passing her up was like a hungry hummingbird's passing honeysuckle. And after all, as long as the clodhopper was out of it for a while, Eleanor would keep. Besides, the old geezer had said if he saw any paintings he'd let Tony know. For a price, of course.

Unaware of her staying quality, Eleanor was feeling only relief. At the moment, she did not want to have to cope with the sheer physical presence of Tony Mondaine. She said, "Tony, I'm fine. I appreciate your concern—really. But you certainly needn't come down here tonight because of me."

"Why else would I ever come down to that hick town?"

She smiled at the sound of lust in his deep voice, but it was an uncaring smile. You would come, she thought, because you want something—badly. And I can see little advantage in it's being me—to either of us. You made love to me, and you felt a genuine sensuous pleasure in my body against your body. I could tell that. Unfortunately and inexplicably I felt it, also. And we were both playing games. I'm not certain what your game is. But I don't think I have to play any more.

All she actually said aloud was, "Anyway, thanks for calling, Tony. Good night." Then she hung up and turned away.

He would return. Not tonight, but soon. She knew that. Because he did want something—probably the shop. Undoubtedly the shop. Julia had realized its potential. Julia hadn't cared. Tony cared.

But he had yet to realize one thing important to her: she didn't go with the shop, any more, so any time he wanted to do the hot-potato number on her, it would be just fine. And she wished him luck with Benton Bonford.

The long hall was quiet, shadowed. Too

quiet, and too shadowed. With the wrong shadows. The large man and his large dog had gone away. Worst of all, Julia was gone—and tonight, of all nights so far she ached for the sound of Julia's voice, the sight of her smile. She went upstairs, put on her heavy robe and fuzzy scuffs, then shuffled back down to the kitchen.

There was no one to talk to.

She stopped.

She went back up the stairs and into her room.

She picked up the purple cow, and went back downstairs again.

She put the cow on the table where she could see her from the stove.

"Tillie," she said, "it may as well be you. Someone has to listen to me."

She broke eggs, got out a whip, made a small, frothy omelet and cooked it recklessly in the last of the butter. Then she sat down at the table with it, and looked Tillie Cow right in her long-lashed, ceramic eye.

"So I want him to come back," she said. "So I am a giddy school girl. So what? I'm also almost fifty-nine years old, and a great deal of the world can go ahead and pass me right on by—I won't mind. But I *would* mind never seeing Benton Bonford again. I can't explain. But it's true."

And further, the next time I see him, sight is not going to be enough.

Not if I can arrange it.

So there you are, Tillie. Put that in your spout and moo it. I've found my parade, and I'm marching.

She ate her omelet, shoved the utensils into the dishwasher, tucked the purple cow beneath her arm, and started back upstairs. As she reached the wax-rubbed patina of the pineapple newelpost, the telephone rang.

She debated not answering. She had no wish to talk to Tony again. Then the sudden, unreasoning hope that it might be Benton took her across the cold marble floor, through the jeweled reflections from the stained glass transom, and to the phone on its small taboret in the hallway.

She picked up the receiver, saying a little crossly, "Hello."

It was Ben. She should have been warned when he said, "Hi, hon." Ben did not show affection except under stress.

As it was, she merely replied, "Hi, Benjamin," and waited.

He said, "I got to tell you. Damn it."

"Tell me what?"

"Matt's dead. Heart attack. His wife found him layin' in the hallway."

It took a moment for it to sink in. Then her reaction was sheer, unreasoning anger. This had to stop! Two deaths. And she was not made of iron.

"Ellie? Ellie, are you okay?"

No, she was not okay. But she choked it back. "Where's Martha?"

"She's home, now. But their daughter can't get here for a couple of hours."

"I'll go right over. Thanks, Ben."

It was only two blocks away. Eleanor struggled into a sweater and slacks, grabbed her bag and ran across lots. Her feet pounded on dry leaves, the wind billowed the tails of her unfastened coat behind her and streamed her hair into witch tresses. There were two cars in the drive, but when she opened the door, it was into her arms that a white-faced and stunned Martha came running.

Over her tousled gray head, Eleanor asked the tight-faced neighbor, "What happened?"

He shook his head. "We think he had a client because there were papers laid out on his desk. Anyway, when the client left, apparently Matt locked the door and started back for his bedroom. Then it hit him."

Eleanor glanced down the hall to the small office where the neighbor's wife was aimlessly tidying, sticking things into drawers and pigeonholes. In her arms, Matt's wife moved restlessly, said in a despairing voice, "I shouldn't have left him. But he said, Go on. It's just a cold, he said."

"Martha, you couldn't have known. You had no way of knowing." Eleanor stroked the bent gray head. "Come on, let's put you to bed. I'll wake you when your daughter comes."

Between the two of them, she and the neighbor's wife succeeded in tucking the distraught woman into the guest-room bed and giving her one of the doctor's Valium tablets in warm milk.

Closing the door gently behind her, the neighbor's wife said, "He did have a client. I saw a truck pulling away and Matt waving. But he was all right, then. I suppose it's—just one of those things."

Eleanor nodded. Her eyes were gritty and her entire body ached. Not Matt. It couldn't be Matt. Not so soon after Julia.

Then she realized that was an asinine thought. Julia had nothing to do with this. She'd better get her act together or she'd be worse than Martha.

They went into the neat, green and white kitchen where two other neighbors were drinking coffee, poured their own, and made constrained conversation. They all listened, unconsciously, for the sound of another car in the drive.

It came about ten-thirty. Matt's daughter hurried in with her husband, two grandchildren and Matt's minister. Eleanor made a tactful departure.

But, alone again, in the cold and moonless dark, she scuffled slowly around the proper sidewalks, this time, buttoning her coat against the chill, and walking with her hands thrust deep into patch pockets.

Awful, how life could go on so evenly, so unchangingly, for years and years—then in a moment's notice go skewing off at a hundred and eighty degrees into total misalignment. Worse than awful—it was scary.

She stopped on the walk before Julia's house—a chalky, towering glimmer in the dark. No lights gleamed except the chandelier, turning the stained glass transom into a glittering jeweled brooch on the pale breast of the verandah.

For a serene, comfortable time the place had been her home. Her only home. Now what was it? And—whatever it was—for how long?

Wearily, she went around to the back, loose loafers making staccato clopping noises on the broken cement, climbed the steps, and entered the warm kitchen. The furnace was thrumming away in the basement, always before a cozy noise, now sounding like the distant, unremitting beat of an alien drummer.

This was nonsense. She had to get hold of herself.

She certainly wanted no more coffee; she was sloshing.

The purple cow sat where she'd been abandoned by the phone, a homely travesty, exquisitely monstrous.

Eleanor picked her up, muttered, "You and me, kid," and went to bed.

As projected during that sleepless night, the next day was no better and extended its misery into the continuing week.

The obligations of Matt's funereal rites were endless. Tony sent his regrets and a mass of flowers but stayed away.

Benton didn't call.

Five days later he still hadn't called.

On the tenth day, when she'd drearily given up everything, and was merely plodding along her course, a scrawled letter arrived, complaining, "Where the hell are you? I've phoned four times with no answer anywhere; and I don't talk to damned machines! The coming weekend is my hunting trip, then look out. Expect to be severely beaten about the face and body for not staying home."

The sun inexplicably brightened and stayed bright until Monday morning. That day, humming to herself, pouring fresh coffee into her footed cup, and sitting down in the pale warmth of a frosty November morning to read the paper, she unfolded it, sipped, leaned on her elbows because her glasses were lost again, and focused on the headlines.

There had been an unexpected blizzard in the mountains. A plane had gone down. Passengers had included a Russian agricultural delegation and two Americans. The nature of the crash indicated no one had survived.

One of the Americans had been Benton Bonford.

Seventeen

Eleanor remembered vaguely slipping to the floor because she thought through gathering fog, Oh, my blood pressure pills. When did I last take them? Could this be a stroke?

That was all she did remember—not the gust of wind opening the kitchen door, nor the cold air pouring over her, blowing fine, saltlike granules of snow across the worn tile—nor Ben, entering hours later, saying, hoarsely, "Oh my God—not you too."

With great surprise, she awoke to find herself hospitalized inside an oxygen tent. Blearily she checked her surroundings, decided she really didn't care for them, and sank back into beautiful, unfeeling oblivion.

During the course of a long week she was briefly aware of Ben and Mary Ann tiptoeing in and out with worried faces, and that of Tony Mondaine behind a great, velvet cluster of pink roses. But she dreamed—she dreamed of Bobby smiling at her, saying as he had so often, "Hang in there, Mom." She dreamed of Julia frowning, muttering, "It's not as I do but as I say. Take your damned pills, child." And she dreamed of Benton Bonford, heard his voice saying, " 'The woods are lovely, dark and deep. But I have promises to keep . . .' "

It was lovely to listen to them, to turtle down inside the covers, eyes closed, the world shut out.

Unfortunately, with modern medicine, the infection began to subside, the pulmonary process improved, and the tight pain in her chest eased. Her strength crept back. And with it came a wearisome sense of responsibility to those around her bed.

She didn't want that sense. She didn't want it at all, and for a while she fought it, clinging to her white shadows and languorous apathy like a child to its security blanket.

But in the end the sense of obligation

won out. She opened her tired eyes on a crisp, snowy November day, saw Ben's old and worried face, sighed, and surrendered to the inevitable.

Julia and Matt and Benton were dead. She was not. No matter how she felt or how she might rant and rave and hold her breath like a spoiled baby, she was not.

By Saturday she was sitting in a chair, and forcing herself to listen to Ben tell what he knew about Benton—which, actually, was little more than what she'd read in the papers.

The weather in the mountains had stayed bad. There had not even yet been any sort of successful effort to get a copter in and bring out the dead. But before the snow had gently covered them over, there'd been a number of bodies strewn motionless on the mountain slope. The United States and Russia had exchanged condolences over the loss of the agricultural delegation. Then, almost on the next day, the entire affair had been relegated to page two by a gas line rupture in a populated area.

And that, pretty much, had been that.

But not for me, Eleanor thought painfully. Not for me.

I've lost Benton Bonford.

I never realized that one could lose what one really never had. But it's possible. I've lost him. And now I know I could have loved him—more, far more, than any other man I've ever known, and—perhaps—shall ever know again.

But life does go on. Doesn't it?

So, now. Some strange dictum decided I should live, and he should not. There must be a purpose. How can I find it?

The answer came, inside her weary head: by keeping his promises. As he would have kept them.

But how, O Lord? I don't even know at this point who owns the shop.

I shall have to call Matt's junior partner, she thought and swung white feet to the cold floor. Peter what'shisname. But—today? It's Sunday. Ben's coming to drive me home at two o'clock.

Wherever home is. I don't even really know that.

Tears began to well—self-pitying tears— and she blinked them back fiercely. For heaven's sake, Eleanor Wright. Don't turn into a 1940s clinging vine again. Grit your teeth. Deal with today, damn it. Hope you've got enough insurance to cover this hospital disaster without going further in the hole. Hope John Giametti hasn't changed his mind and will still give you a job. Hope whoever does own the shop will either keep Ben and Mary Ann on or will sell to someone else who'll keep them.

In short, enough lollygagging around. Get back on the damned stick.

She stood up, grabbed for the bed as the world began to swing in circles, and realized that saying was simpler than doing.

But the dizziness subsided after a few moments. Still holding on cautiously, she moved to the chair between her bed and the empty one, decided that was far enough for the moment and sat down. The door to the hallway was open, and a bright, strutting paper turkey pinned to the hall wall caught her eye.

Tony Mondaine, she thought acidly— then the reason for the turkey caught at her turgid mind.

Thanksgiving? It couldn't be Thanksgiving—she couldn't have been in this place *that* long.

She had. Two weeks had gone out of her life without memory. Two weeks without Benton. Three without Matt. More than four without Julia.

Ben better be careful; he's probably next on my hit list, she thought, and realized it wasn't a funny thought at all. In fact, it was not a healthy thought, either—and her mind began to scrabble like a burrowing mole for something solid and hopeful.

Like what?

Her frantic eyes caught sight of her image in the small, vanity mirror, and that certainly wasn't it. There were lines beneath those searching orbs a gallon of cream would not erase. She seemed almost lipless, and the color of wax. More than her real years, she looked seventy. Or a hundred. In fact, with her ashy, limp hair around her face she could do just dandy as one of *Macbeth*'s witches, stirring the cauldron, muttering, "Bubble, bubble, toil and trouble . . ."

Well. There was one positive thing. The plaid skirt would fit, now. When they'd hauled her in here they'd probably had to rip the seams to get her out.

Did she have anything to wear home? She might have to call Mary Ann and have her pick up some stuff from the house.

Cautiously, she got upright again, moved step by step, and opened the closet door. Okay. She'd get by with the things there.

Who the hell was there for her to be a fashionplate for anyway? Tony Mondaine?

Hardly. But still, the name caught at her ragged mind. Involuntarily she looked over at the lovely roses in their vase on the windowsill, drooping a bit now, past their prime—like her—but there, a token of Tony's what?

What was now motivating Tony Mondaine?

That was another item to be ascertained when she got back into the real world.

It could be an interesting week.

There was a rattle of wheels in the hall, and the chubby little candy-striper appeared, carrying a tray.

"Well, hi there, Mrs. Wright! You must be better, today. Shall I pull the chair over to the window? And look—real food for you. Not even any Jell-O."

Eleanor sat down again, realizing that she was quite ready to sit, and let the tray be arranged on her lap. She declined television, feeling the "World" had been "Turning" quite successfully without her support—besides, if she wanted to catch up on any plot, it would be the one set in the shop on the south side of the square, not beamed from a major network.

When Ben came in at two o'clock, she was back in the chair again, but this time dressed and waiting. The candy-striper had lent her some makeup, and her morale was a little higher with the application of blusher and lipstick. But the plaid skirt was now rolled over at the waist to keep it a proper length, the pantyhose had obvious runs, and the only shoes that accompanied her to the hospital had been the shabby old lambswool house slippers. A fashion plate she was not.

Because it was cold outside, Ben had grabbed up from the shop her old, tatty, Sherpa-lined car coat with the varnish stains on the elbow; also one of his own thick, sick-green stocking caps, inherited from an army nephew.

Eleanor added those to her initial garb, pulled the cap down around her ears, and everyone started laughing.

The nurse who brought her wheelchair asked, giggling, "Do you want a tin cup?"

Eleanor seated herself carefully, saying, "Oh, thanks a lot, Irene. I hope there's a back way out of this place."

"Oh—you don't look that bad. Besides, everybody knows you. They'll just laugh, too. What about the roses?"

"Leave them. They don't go with a rag bag, anyway. Do I sign anything?"

"It's done. You just go. Take care, now. See your doctor Thursday. Okay?"

"Okay. Thanks for everything."

"Any time. And if you see the lid to an American Beauty sugar bowl, call me."

"I will."

Ben had backed the old van up to the side entrance, where it sat quietly with Bonford Antiques showing a faded gold beneath the sun. A hiss of steam came from the exhaust.

"She's been runnin' a mite tetchy," he said, carefully handing Eleanor inside. "Bent, he said 'twas the carb or something. I ain't looked into 't, yet."

Before he slammed the door Eleanor saw from his face that someone *else* was also mourning Benton Bonford. Inexplicably, it made her feel better.

The old man heaved himself up beside her, poking the heater fan on full blast, and began backing into the street.

"Where to, Ellie? I know Mary Ann laid in a few groceries for you at Julia's—she said she'd be by this evenin'."

"Oh, that's kind." Despite herself, Eleanor's eyes welled, and she realized a classic truth: illness leaves one with little defense against emotion.

Trying for steadiness, she said, "Take me by the shop a minute. Then I'll go home."

The air was crisp and biting, the sky a cold blue as he helped her out of the van in the alley. Eleanor saw each frozen weed on the broken concrete was bent beneath a cap of snow, and small rows of white waved across the loading dock before the gusting wind like breakers on a shore. Their neighbor, the hardware man, was out burning packing cartons in his wire container. The flames were a startling orange against the bleak grays and tans of the old buildings, and the smoke floated like a plume in the icy atmosphere. He waved, said something vague about it being nice to see her back. They nodded, waved in reply. Ben unlocked the rear door and bundled Eleanor inside.

It smelled warm, musty. He turned on the lights and each shadow sprang into familiar objects. The old rolltop was open, mail strewn across its scarred surface. From his curl on the hollowed nest of the captain's chair, Thomaseen arose languidly, stretching furry hindquarters, tail a spike in the air. His greeting was a yowling request for immediate sustenance.

It was hard to realize she'd even been gone.

Yet, to Ben, her face was so pale, so sad. He thought of the bright Picasso tucked away waiting, and was sorely tempted to give it to her right then, and not wait until her birthday.

Then he forebore.

Birthday, Julia had said, and birthday it would be. Surely some things could be made not to change in this damn world. And his word was one of the things.

Instead, he poured cat food into the margarine bowl. Thomaseen, who had leaped up to Eleanor's arms to tell his woeful tale of starving cat in her ear, immediately shot from her Sherpa embrace like oil from a tube, crouched over it, and began to dine with lashing tail and various growls of self-indulgence.

Eleanor sat in the Windsor chair, unbuttoning her old coat. Ben leaned against the doorway to the shop, arms folded.

"That fat gal—for the Queen Anne chairs, saw the Belter set—she ain't never come back. So far."

"Good."

"There's a pressed glass seminar over t' Quincy. They want you to come. The letter's there on the pile."

"I'll get to it. When?"

"I disremember. Before Thanksgiving, I think. Oh—and we can sell that bureau. From the Cranes. To John Giametti. If you like."

"As is?"

"As is. He's got a good boy, doin' that stuff for him. We'd make a little profit. Not much. John's pretty close."

John Giametti.

It might be to her advantage if she let him have it. If she was going to work for John. If. So many "ifs."

Something hit her: "Good lord, Ben! Did you guys get paid? I'd not written any salaries."

"No sweat. Matt's partner did 'em—and your insurance papers for the hospital. That crap. He seems like a nice guy. Ellie—"

She looked up. He was squinting his eyes, running a nervous hand through what grizzle was left around his bald spot. He grimaced, went on,

"What's going to happen to this place, now? To us?"

She answered slowly, "I don't know. I suppose that it goes to—to Benton's nearest kin—whoever that may be."

"What if there ain't anybody?"

"Oh, there'll be someone." She was picking idly at the seam on her sweater, not even knowing what she did. "Even if they have to go back to a great-great, or down to a cousin thirty times removed. There will be someone. I guess all we can do is wait. Again."

"But they can't sell?"

"Not without legal authorization."

"So we just keep on runnin' it."

"Until someone tells us to stop. Or takes over."

"That could go on for years."

"Not likely."

"Maybe if someone does turn up, they'll let us go on runnin' it. It'd be okay with me. You do a fine job, Ellie."

It was the biggest compliment Ben could give, and Eleanor knew it was. She gave him a rather bleary smile, saying, "But you're the one hard to replace. Julia always said so."

He shuffled his feet in their splayed-out workboots, grinning. "Whatever. I guess we just do good together."

Not if I go to John Giametti's.

She couldn't tell him about that. Not yet. One thing at a time.

He was going on thoughtfully, "But most likely—whoever—they'll want to sell. You reckon?"

She nodded. "Most likely."

"Then who to? We ain't got the money—you and me. Damn. You ain't had nothin' but hard luck, and me—I jis' ain't the saving kind—being by m'self, and all."

He was rubbing his bald head; the hand came down his thin old nose and cupped his mouth and chin. Above it, his eyes were squinted shut. "I've been thinkin' and thinkin'. I reckon we could work for Mondaine. At least, I could—if he'd let me alone to do what I know to do. But—I'm sorry Ellie—I jis' don't like the guy. Bent, he didn't, neither."

How well she knew that. She swallowed, said, "I know. I know he didn't."

"Yet—he might be better 'n Marvin Coles."

"Anyone would be better than Marvin Coles."

"Amen. It's a helluva choice, but if'n it comes to that, I would go with Mondaine.

At least he takes a bath without waitin' for the creeks to rise."

He reached out a scuffed toe, ran it down the length of Thomaseen's satin back. "And I do think Mondaine wants it. At least he's sure been nosin' around here a lot lately. Checkin' the place out, I reckon. So—I s'pose we best be prepared for a sale. To somebody."

He looked down at her hard. "Can you think of any way the damn banks would even look at financin' you and me?"

She shook her head, smiling ruefully. "I own the clothes in my closet, three-fourths of a car, and about four good antiques. I owe about two more good, thumping payments on Bobby's medical bills. No way, Ben. I'm afraid we're up the creek."

"So we best be prepared."

"You got it."

The sound of salt peppering the dusty windows made them both jump. The sky was loosing snow granules again. Eleanor shivered. Ben asked quickly, "You warm enough?"

"I'm fine." She shifted in her chair, leaning one elbow on the arm. "Tomorrow I'll call Peter—Matt's partner. Maybe he can get us out of this limbo."

"Go ahead. But if he knows anything it's more than he knew yesterday when I talked to 'em. He's started what he called proper procedure—"

"Trying to trace heirs."

"That's it. He says it could take time. So for now we jist keep on—goin' on."

But, Eleanor was saying to herself, can I do that? Will John Giametti understand? Suddenly he caught what Ben had said further: "Mondaine, he's been on 'm, too—Matt's partner, I mean. Peter Who-ever. I mean—really on 'm. Out to dinner, and that stuff. We may end up workin' for Mondaine yet, Muffin, like it or not. He's slick."

He was watching the wan face before him very closely. *Slick* wasn't all Tony Mondaine was, in his book. But he saw nothing in Ellie's eyes but displeasure and felt vaguely relieved. Ellie wasn't so dumb, after all.

"One day at a time, Ben," she said. "Protect our own selves as best we can—you and me and Mary Ann. That's about all we can do right now."

He nodded.

Thomaseen was through with his dining. He leaped back up on Eleanor's lap, gave her a forgiving kiss with a rough tongue, wrapped himself in his ginger tail and began to purr. She put a hand on his silky back, stroking him automatically. The outer door opened, letting in a whirl of fine snow. The hardware man said,

"Feeling better, Ellie?"

"Oh, yes. Yes, thank you."

"Good. I'll tell my wife you're back. And say—I have a fine fire, out there, and I'm through with it—at least through with what I can legally burn." He grinned. "Anything you guys want to put on it?"

Ben hauled himself erect. "Reckon there's some cartons in the shed."

Both the men went out, leaving a knife-blade of cold air behind them. Eleanor sat where she was, huddled deeper into her shabby old coat, grateful for the cat's warmth against her stomach.

The shop was quiet. The two men's voices came dimly. The half-stripped Dutch kas cast an enormous shadow across the floor. And another enormous shadow stood before her tear-sparkled eyes, leaning against it, big arms crossed, gray brows drawn.

"Benton," she said aloud, in anguish, "Oh, Benton—Benton—why?"

341

It was too much to bear, too much to stay there huddled in her chair, looking, remembering.

She stood up, lumping Thomaseen into a limp, acquiescent fur scarf over one shoulder, and went past the shadows into the shop.

But he was there, too. Bent was there, in the stillness, looking in amazement at the Venetian cruet, replacing the peacock sidechairs in the window, roaring at her from beneath that awful squash hat and calling her a "tootsie."

He was everywhere! How, in four short days could one man so interweave himself into the fabric of her life?

Her impulse was to run. But she couldn't run. 1940 lambie-pies ran. She had to stand and deal with it.

The persistent banging and rattling on the street doors finally penetrated the aching void in her head, and the noise was almost welcome. Anything to chase the terrible ghosts.

She threaded her way across the soft old carpet, fumbled with the chain, released the brass lock, opened the door part way.

"I'm sorry," she began politely, "but we

are closed on Sunday. Won't you come back tomorrow?"

"Yes," said the tall, blond woman in the smart leather coat, the Hessian hat, and the boots. "I'll come back tomorrow. But I'll also come in, today. Who are you—the cleaning woman?"

Eleanor should have found that funny, but she didn't.

She replied stiffly, "I'm Eleanor Wright. I manage the shop."

"Oh. Really."

Eleanor was brutally conscious of crisp brown eyes that raked her up and down in one swift glance. Her own voice took on an automatic chill. "And we are closed."

She started to shut the door. A hand in an elegant leather glove flashed out, stopping her.

"You don't understand," said the woman, in a tone equally chilly. "I own this place."

"I beg your pardon?"

"I own this place."

The obscure man standing behind her suddenly stepped up another step, became as tall, and also recognizable. It was Matt's partner.

Quietly he said, "We've been looking for

343

you, Ellie. You weren't at home, and I finally thought to try here."

He gave her a bleak smile. Hers was frozen, and she was too immobile to reply, barely managing to step backward as the tall woman breezed by, stripping off her gloves and stamping wet snow from her custom-made boots on the old Aubusson. She also was glancing about swiftly, like a bird, the silky blond hair swinging from beneath the smart hat and spraying against a peachbloom cheek.

"I always find it so amazing," she said to no one in particular, "what people are willing to pay for this incredible junk. Oh— by the way—" and now her eyes came to rest again on Eleanor. "My name is Mrs. Benton Bonford."

Eighteen

Eleanor was helpless to stop the gasp that tore from her, the stiffening of her body that brought Thomaseen's head up in surprise. She blurted out, "But—you were divorced."

"Did Bent tell you that?"

Jill Bonford contrived to look amused, indulgent, but her eyes sharpened warily. Once more she flicked them over the vaguely female figure in the shabby, stained coat, the droopy-skirted plaid something-or-other, and the faded stocking cap jammed around a pale face on which now patches of blusher shown too sharply. She laughed. "Of course. I suppose he did."

"Yes."

"Dear Bent. Always so—painfully honest. Well, Miss Wright—it is Miss, isn't it, Peter—or did you say Ms.?" She made the title sound like *Mizz*.

Eleanor ignored the word anyway. She said coolly, "Mrs.," and saw a brief flicker of uncertainty. But it was gone in an instant.

"Well—to be truthful—I did file. But I also had second thoughts which—now—seem rather fortunate. Wouldn't you say so?"

"It is all," answered Eleanor coldly, "in one's point of view."

At once she knew the total lack of economic wisdom in having said such a thing but was fiercely unable to regret the saying.

From behind Jill Bonford, Matt's partner rolled his eyes upward and made caution gestures. Please! he mouthed silently. Please!

Jill had put a slender hand, palm up, out to Thomaseen, who sniffed it, then consented to have his ears scratched. She said casually, "I get along well with most cats."

You probably have a great deal in common.

But this time Eleanor didn't say it aloud.

Instead, she merely handed him over. The big tom settled amiably against the smart leather coat. Over his battered head, Benton Bonford's wife went on calmly, "You're quite right about the point of view. I didn't expect it to be a pleasant surprise—but I really don't have to be a nasty one. I don't particularly want to rattle your cage—as long as I can feather mine. If you'll accept that, then we'll work together handsomely."

Whatever else Benton's wife might be, she was forthright.

Hardly the fluffy-headed blond pompom girl Eleanor had envisioned.

I've been wrong before, Eleanor thought soberly, but this one can be a lulu.

She managed a noncommittal shrug and answered, "Then let's sit down. It's more comfortable in the back where the heat's turned higher."

She led the way, trying to reason herself out of the enormous psychological handicap of looking like a ragpicker's daughter, trying to stem her wild jealous anger of this beautiful, self-possessed woman's having been Benton Bonford's wife and having left him, hurt him and not cared. That was evident. She hadn't cared. There had been no word of grieving widowhood.

In an indulgent tide of self-pity, Eleanor envisioned herself in Bent's bed, against his warm, satisfying body, being held by him, loved by him—and, she thought furiously, I never could have gone.

Behind her, she could hear Jill's voice, and wished the tones were chattery, wished they were shrill—anything to hang a fault on, to give her some superior satisfaction. But they were not. They were well-modulated, almost husky. She was saying, "See those lamps—Tiffany, aren't they? God! I wouldn't have them on my trashheap. There's a china cupboard like the one my mother junked when I was six. And will you look at that awful suite with the over-dose of knobbies! What is that, Mrs. Wright—just Victorian?"

Eleanor paused. She answered briefly, "John Belter."

"How much?"

Eleanor told her.

Jill said. "You are kidding me! Will you get it?"

Eleanor thought of the fat lady and her husband, Calder. "Yes. If we want it."

"What do you mean—if you want it?

Good God! I'd unload the stuff before someone got a sudden case of good taste and queered the deal."

"Once again," said Eleanor, and tried to smile, "It's all in your point of view."

She guided them through the door, installed Jill in the captain's chair, the lawyer—obviously looking and feeling vastly uncomfortable—received a Stickley rocker, and she sat herself on a Chinese garden stool, leaning gratefully against the end of the kas.

Thomaseen, on Jill Bonford's knees, was kneading his paws and rumbling in his furry chest.

Traitor, Eleanor thought. She said, "Will you drink coffee? Ben will be here in a moment—he's our restoring and evaluating expert"—Ben would be surprised to hear that that's what he was—"and also the only one who totally understands the vagaries of the resident percolator." You're not sounding relaxed, Eleanor, you're sounding pretentious.

Jill Bonford was saying thoughtfully, "No—I think not. Thank you. Peter bought me an excellent breakfast—" and she shot Peter a dazzling smile. "Besides, I'd rather get myself installed in the house. There is a house, I understand—a rather nice one, Peter says, and I'd much prefer it to the motel I stayed in last night." Now the bright smile was directed to Eleanor. "May we do that, do you think?"

Eleanor could be forthright also—when she had to be.

She said, "Yes. Of course. I live there."

"Oh," said Jill. "Indeed. Well, I'm sure we can work out something."

"There are five bedrooms," said Eleanor a little grimly.

Jill answered, "No, no—you misunderstand. I mean when the house is sold."

She took a deep breath, pulled off the Hessian hat, and ran one hand through her blond hair, restoring it to perfect, feather-cut, and pale golden order. She looked at the lawyer, then back at Eleanor and shrugged. "Right now," she said, "right off the bat. Let's get one thing straight. Okay? I am here to sell. The shop. The house. Whatever. I don't want it. I hate small towns. I love money. I can be no more honest than that—now can I?"

"No," said Eleanor, "indeed."

Well. The wondering is over. Now she knew.

Desperately, she said, "Will you sell to me—to Ben and me?"

"Of course. In a moment. But it has to be cash. I'm sorry—I'm sorry to sound hardnosed, but I don't want something down then dribbles for the next century. When I sell, I'm through and never really want to see this place again. Can you manage cash?"

"I don't know. I'd have to consult."

But I do know, Eleanor thought in anguish. I do know. I can't do it.

She got up, a little unsteadily, said, "Excuse me," dialed the phone, and asked Mary Ann to run over to the house and open the bedroom with the Empire furniture. She would not let this blond woman with her beautiful skin and lithe, shapely body lie in the same bed that had held Benton Bonford. It might be petty, it might be totally beyond reason but Eleanor didn't care if it was.

As she hung up, Ben came inside, shaking snow from his denim jacket. "Sorry I was so long, Ellie. Let's get you home to bed."

Then he saw the lawyer, said, "Oh. Hi, Pete. What's new?"

"I am," said Jill Bonford, and held out her hand. "Jill Bonford. And you're Ben."

Ben took the hand, looked at her appreciatively from beneath shaggy brows. "Who the hell's Jill Bonford? Did Bent have a sister?"

"No. He had a wife," smiled Jill.

"The hell. Well, the boy finally showed some good taste."

"Ben, you're my kind of man," she laughed.

"He was my kind of man," Ben answered quietly. The look he shot Eleanor covertly was puzzled, but Eleanor, with perverse and self-acknowledged jealousy, refused to bail him out. She was suffering a double dose of the same obtuseness that kept her from pulling off *her* hat and fluffing *her* hair. She knew she was. She hated it. But neither could she seem to stop. Perhaps she'd self-destruct in ten minutes, and it would be better for them all.

There followed a moment of ill ease. Peter-the-lawyer broke it by saying brightly, "Look—it's after three o'clock. Why don't we all go by my apartment for a little wine and cheese and some useful dialogue?"

To Eleanor the idea had the appeal of the Black Plague. She'd much prefer her bedroom with a hot pad on her aching back and some useful sleep—sleep that would bring oblivion, that would end the necessity of coping with this gorgeous broad who now owned her shop and her house and everything else she valued.

It was Ben, wise Ben, bless his heart, who took it out of her hands, saying firmly, "Thank you. But Ellie ought to go home and rest. She just got out of the hospital an hour ago."

"Really?" said Jill. "Well, in that case, do run along. May we stay here a while. I want to look at more of the funny old things."

Eleanor said in a voice devoid of expression. "Of course," reached up on a nail behind her and handed Jill a key. "That's back door only. I'll see you later at the house. Peter knows the way."

"Thank you. And please don't wait up. I'm not fond of house mothers."

"I'm not fond of being one," said Ellie, and followed Ben out to the van.

"Holy Christ," he said, as he backed it around and headed west off the town square. "She's a looker, all right. But what in hell are we in for, Ellie?"

Grimly Eleanor told him. "She's going to sell. For cash."

He whistled soundlessly. "I wish her luck. Not even Marvin's got cash."

"Tony has."

The looming portent of that fact hung between them. Finally Ben shook his head ominously. "God. Talk about bein' between a rock and a hard spot." He drove into the snowy driveway, tires crunching on cold gravel. "But Tony won't go overboard—I mean, he'll know what's reasonable, and I doubt if he makes many mistakes. They'll probably advertise—and that will take a while. Give us some breathing room, maybe."

"While we look for a miracle?"

"That's about it."

He helped her into the kitchen, and she refused to let him bother any more than that, bundling him back out the door under protest. "Go get your wine and cheese."

"Oh, hell—that's out of my class. I'm a brew man. Besides Pete Wilson's a bachelor, and he ain't really looking forward to my showing up."

Wilson. That was Matt's partner's name. Peter Wilson.

She put it in a mental file, hoping she'd remember the next time, then kissed the old man's cheek affectionately. "Then go get your brew. I'll see you tomorrow. Perhaps it will look better than today."

Ben said grimly, "Don't count on it. I suppose this house goes on the market, too."

"She says so."

"Do you know what you own in it?"

"I know. Yes. But she doesn't. And I somehow think she isn't much of a believer."

He said, "Christ!" and spat out the van window. "Maybe you'd better start moving your stuff into my back shed."

"Is there room?"

"Sure. And it'll be fine there until you get your own place. But don't dilly-dally. Make yourself a list in the morning; I'll open up. Okay?"

"Okay."

"And take it easy. Right now you look like something the cat dragged in."

She said wryly, "Thanks a bunch."

She had to allow that not only did she look like what he'd said, she felt like it, also. Her knees were shaky, and she had to sit down in one of the old bentwood chairs a moment to get her breath.

There was a note stuck on the fridge in Mary Ann's handwriting. It said succinctly, "Three TV dinners and some soup to warm up. Eat!"

Eleanor had to smile, but nonetheless eating had all the momentary appeal of walking a high wire. Over a bottomless pit.

Sitting was what she wanted. Slowing her heart rate from gallop.

A chance to make some sense of her world.

Again.

Bottom line time: Jill Bonford was going to sell—as soon as she could, and to anyone who had her price. In cash. The cash stipulation probably eliminated Marvin Coles, but it did not eliminate Tony Mondaine.

Benton Bonford would not have sold to Tony Mondaine.

Benton was gone.

If Tony bought the shop there wasn't a damned thing Eleanor Wright could do about it—except try to protect Ben and Mary Ann—and make certain she had a job somewhere else.

Get on the phone, Eleanor Wright.

John Giametti was not in—he was, in

fact, on some business in St. Louis. But his son was glad to hear Eleanor had been released from the hospital. He'd tell his father. And yes, indeed, they were looking forward to Eleanor's joining their staff any time after the first of the year. If that was convenient to her.

Hanging up, Eleanor felt as if at least one enormous load had been lifted off her chest. So next on the agenda: Ben and Mary Ann.

What could she do? Instinctively she knew Jill Bonford wouldn't care less. If only the person buying was someone she knew, someone with whom she could personally use any influence she might have. That was really their only hope.

One of the bulbs had burned out in the overhead light. Illumination was reduced to a dim pool beneath which she sat, breathing like a winded runner. Suddenly she was painfully aware—of the enormous silence of the big old house around her. It was a dusky, breath-caught, waiting silence. A hovering silence.

Where were the familiar sounds of yesterday—the stairs that creaked as the day cooled, making ghostly footsteps on the risers, the tap-tap of dry vines on the dining room window, the hitching catch as the furnace went on and off, the distant chime of the Neuchâtel clock, the clapping of the wind through bamboo sticks on the side porch.

There was nothing. It was almost as though the house knew, too, that things were wrong. That things were going to change again.

The king is dead—long live the king!

Oh for heaven's sake, she thought crossly, and made herself get up, move, go towards the stairs. No king died and no king lives. Exactly. You're letting yourself get a prime case of the weirdos and cut it out.

Leaving the light burning in the kitchen, she also turned on two of the chandelier bulbs and stuck a note on the newel pineapple which said, "Upstairs, third door on the left, bathroom at hall end. Latch the kitchen lock."

Not, she thought, eyeing it critically, terribly loving, but succinct.

The new door locks were post-Charlie and Ben-installed. She'd never figured out yet who Benton thought had been in the house, but now that she was mostly alone, it had seemed a reasonable installation.

Slowly, hanging to the solid baluster, she

went up the stairs, and now the risers creaked beneath her feet as they properly should. Of course. Of all things, she certainly needn't let her imagination get ahead of her.

Mary Ann had left the hall light on. In its dim glow she went on down, opened the door of the room with the Empire furniture, peered inside. The ebony-based lamp was on by the smooth sweep of bed, turning the puff satin counterpane into iridescent emerald, and striking peacock colors from the hard cylinder pillows on the elegant, curve-backed chaise. Beyond, one of the tall windows behind dark green drapery was cracked upward, sifting a light fluff of snow across the sill onto the floor. Eleanor trudged across and closed the window. The snow felt good, and she realized her hands were hot.

"Lots of luck with the new kid in town," she said aloud to the two pure white Houdon busts on their slender ebony stands, pulled a brown leaf from the luxuriant green dieffenbachia and went on to the bathroom.

Mary Ann had been there, too, bless her heart, putting out fresh, fluffy guest towels and a new bar of soap. Eleanor used a scroungy one to clean cream from her face, avoiding the pale image in the mirror. Her self-esteem was low enough already. Then she knelt by the tub, waited for the whizzing to subside in her brain, and shampooed her filthy, stringy hair.

Blowing it dry, she was amazed at how much better she felt—at the feminine mystique that may be improved by one single, beautifying action. She also found herself actually smiling at the picture in Jill Bonford's mind: Eleanor Wright, tacky, ragged, sloppy, aging broad.

Well. Tomorrow, by all that was holy, Jill Bonford was going to get some sort of a surprise.

A raving beauty Eleanor Wright was not—but she did have class and she did have connections and Benton Bonford's "widow" was going to get hit with them all.

The exertion, however, had fatigued her terribly, and she tottered back into her own bedroom and literally fell into bed.

Tillie, on her flanking table, seemed to give a sympathetic moo. From the pillows, Eleanor reached out and touched her gently.

Where I go, you go, Tillie. It's you and I.

It would also be nice if I knew where I was going. At least in the next few days.

Oh, God, Benton—I want to keep your promises. I desperately want to keep your promises. For you.

But you're the one who married that broad.

On that acid note, she drifted to sleep, tossing restlessly, envisioning Bent's accusing eyes on her, calling out in useless protest, "But what can I do, what can I do?"

Waking some time later with a vague sense of disorientation, of hearing strange voices, thinking fretfully how noisy the nurses were tonight, she opened her eyes and found herself, of course, in her own room.

But she did hear voices. She was hearing them again—a masculine voice, and against it a woman's, clear as a bell and bright as crystal drifting up from downstairs.

It must be Peter Wilson, bringing Jill Bonford home. It had to be, as there was Peter now saying, "Then I'll call you tomorrow after I've contacted some of the possible buyers," and Jill responding clearly, "No, my dear, I'll call you. Go ahead and do all those legal things—whatever it will take to get this affair going. I am going to sleep as late as I please. That was one of the things I absolutely loathed about Bent's precious farm—the getting-up-in-the-morning syndrome. You have no idea how glad I shall be to see all those grunting hogs and mooing cows under eighty feet of water—well, not them, but where they were. I shall be sunning in Bermuda, happily—no, no—rapturously taking my revenge."

Good God, thought Eleanor, she's already sold Benton's farm.

The voices dropped to a murmur, a door slammed. Shortly thereafter a car started in the drive and drove away. Light feet and a humming voice came up the stairs.

With one swift movement, Eleanor switched off her lamp and lay stiff and motionless in the dark.

And she made a sober resolution: she'd play Jill Bonford's game however she absolutely had to play it. But no way in hell was she going to give an inch of anything she didn't have to give.

If that dreadful woman wanted a fight, she'd get it.

Nineteen

She slept only fitfully during the rest of the night. She was too hot, too cold, too hot, too cold, her brain whirring with wild schemes underlined by a self-pitying sense of personal injury—and even her more lucid moments were badgered by the barrel-thumping, echo-chambered wailing of some overpaid rap group on a cranked up radio in the Empire bedroom.

What she finally realized at five in the morning as she cowered beneath her pillow with both ends over her ears was quite simple: the only real hope for the shop was Anthony Mondaine.

It had been easy for Jill Bonford to say airily, "Do all those legal things" to line up potential buyers for the estate. But what Eleanor knew, and what Peter Wilson would shortly discover, was the king-sized hang-up embodied in one simple word: cash. Eleanor would think of at least six outfits who would love to own Bonford Antiques, and who could easily come up with banking arrangements on a contract sale.

But Tony Mondaine was the only one who could produce cash.

Woefully she thought to herself, I'm sorry, Benton, I'm sorry—but I said I could work with Tony if I had to do it.

And I have to do it.

I have to locate Tony, let him know what's going on, let him be ready—or God knows what will happen. Jill Bonford is capable of anything from putting Julia's whole life down the tube in pieces, to hiring an arsonist to burn the place to cinders so she can collect the fire insurance.

Eleanor sat up, waited a moment for the bedroom to stop whirling, then shoved white, cold feet into the fuzzy house shoes. They were damp, and she was also a bit dizzy again when she stood up in them, but that faded fast. Pulling on the shapeless old bathrobe for its warmth, she shuffled quickly down the hall.

She could not resist a fast glance through the open door of the Empire room. All that was visible was a silent lump beneath the puff terminating in a wisp of blond hair and a slender white arm curved gracefully above the silky wisp. The radio sat on the night table, still pumping out its musical travesties, but in a more muted tone.

Eleanor would have loved seeing clothes strung untidily about the room. They were folded nicely on a chair. Drat.

She wanted to be petty; ergo, she needed things to be petty about, lots of things, so she could positively wallow in pettiness. She wanted to like nothing about Jill Bonford, nothing that could distract her from the main point: an enemy, to be disposed of in the manner most conducive to Eleanor Wright's own satisfaction.

On her return from the bathroom the lump had not stirred.

Dandy. She preferred it not stirring. She wanted no contact—merely a chance to get down to the shop and locate Tony before more hell broke loose.

She did, however, take an inordinate amount of time on hair and makeup, and spent five precious minutes debating between the Chanel suit and a ruby-red wool dress. The dress won, topped with her pearls. The suit, being gray, did nothing at all for a wan-looking broad just out of the hospital. The dress was smart, with simple lines. If Jill Bonford wanted to look down the back of her neck to see the K-mart label, then she was welcome.

It was also warm—a fact she appreciated as she sat on a cold seat, trying to warm up a reluctant Chevy engine.

The early morning sparkled with frost in the pale sunshine and even the power lines were loops of diamond sheathing, shining filigree necklaces, strung from corner to corner. When a slight breeze swept by, the world was filled with the sound of fairy tinkling, as glassy bits broke free and fell.

A neighborhood dog ambled by, nose to the ground, glanced up and gave her a waggy greeting. It reminded her painfully of Charlie, and all of a sudden she wondered where he was, who had him, if it had struck him yet that his master was not coming back.

She didn't want to think about those things; they blurred her resolve. Grimly she put the car in gear, heard it shift stiffly, and drove out into the street.

The van was parked at the fast-food

place on the next corner; Ben was eating breakfast. Good. She'd rather not have Ben around when she talked to Tony. Desperate situations sometimes called for desperate measures—and if they did, this morning, she'd much prefer them to be private.

Thomaseen came to greet her in the blessed surge of warmth as she unlocked the alley door—that is, his front quarters came forward while his hind quarters remained, an amazing stretch of ginger fur. "Meow," he said, pleasantly, while in this elongated position, then snapped back to ordinary cat size and began to cleanse himself, with one hind leg hoisted like an exclamation point.

Eleanor put her bag on the desk, loosened her coat, and sat down in the captain's chair. The world was spinning again—just a bit, and it passed. Then she reached for the telephone.

Behind her, in the shadows of the kas, Tony Mondaine cursed silently to himself. He'd hoped to have another entire hour of uninterrupted searching for that damned Picasso. It was more vitally important than ever, now, to recover it. One faint whiff of chicanery, and his once-in-a-lifetime chance at being numbered among the exalted employees of Sotheby's would be down the tube forever.

He had to find it and he had to destroy it—whatever the effort might take. He could not live the next few months jumping at shadows that might besmirch his reputation.

Eleanor was moving slowly, as though the burden of the world were on her shoulders. She had lost weight, but the curve of her breast was still nice as she reached for the phone. There was a little sag around her cheekbone. How would she feel about cosmetic surgery, he wondered—then almost physically shook himself in anger. You randy idiot. What the hell does it matter? What the hell does anything matter in that category? You need this woman, she's sharp, she's good at what she does, and you want her on your side. Whatever it takes, you have to get her on your side. Smart up.

She was dialing the phone. Softly, softly, he wove his way around behind her, buttoned his trench coat, opened the door and shut it again, stamping imaginary snow from his feet.

"Eleanor, what a nice surprise!"

She turned around, her eyes wide. She smiled, and he did so too, inside, because she was obviously glad to see him.

"Tony, I was just going to call you!"

"Excellent. You missed me, you needed me, you wanted me—all, I hope, of the above. How fantastic to find you up and around."

He was calmly reaching out, pulling her upward into his arms, possessing her mouth with his—and it was not the same, not the same, dear God—not the same as Bent's arms, Bent's mouth she'd known so briefly. She had to steel herself to play the game, to respond, because he was right in one respect: she needed him.

Not precisely in the way he expected. Or assumed. With Tony's ego, he'd find response in a rock.

And she was right. Tony was satisfied in her answering lips—and had expected himself to be smugly amused. He wasn't. Eleanor was a pleasure to hold; her hair was soft and silky beneath his cheek, not a stiffened over-sprayed mess like the woman in the bar last night, and her body was warm, curved to fit his own.

Whoa, Mondaine. This is nonsense.

Alarmed at the bells ringing inside his

369

own body, he turned the embrace into a hug, the kiss into a smack, plopping her back down into the chair, grinning at her.

"You look great. I thought I'd find a hollow-eyed wraith."

"I may be when this day is over," she replied grimly. "Tony, I'm in terrible trouble."

His dark eyes suddenly seemed to bore. "Oh?"

"Jill Bonford has turned up."

"Who the hell is Jill Bonford?"

"Benton Bonford's wife."

She saw him start. His breath stopped. "And?"

"And she's Benton's heir. This place is hers. The house is hers, the van is hers—everything you see."

"Ah." His hard lips were barely moving. But she could almost literally hear the tick-tick-tick in his mind.

"And she wants to sell. Everything in one package. Now."

"To whom?"

"Anyone she can find."

"Has she found anyone?"

"Not yet. She just came yesterday afternoon."

"Then there's no problem."

So he did intend to buy.

Oh Benton, she thought painfully, please forgive me. Please, wherever you are, understand.

"Cash, Tony. Only cash."

"Damnation," he answered softly, and shut his eyes, concealing his thoughts from her—his racing, whirling thoughts. Don't panic, Mondaine. You've been through worse. There will be a way.

But cash, Christ! Now of all times, with the kickback to Dominic's connections due, and property taxes, and the looming threat of some very expensive entertaining.

His credit line was impeccable. But at this point the last thing he wanted was some bank loan officer inspecting his affairs. Later. After the first of the year. But not now.

His eyes still shut, he shook his handsome head, moving it slowly, almost ritually. "Cash will be—tough. Won't she accept a contract?"

"She says not."

"Who's her lawyer?"

"Matt's junior partner. Peter Wilson."

A break. A small one. But to this point Wilson had been very cooperative—knowing about his little thing on the side in St. Louis hadn't hurt.

He said, "Get him on the phone."

"He's not at the office yet. It's not nine."

"He has to be somewhere. Let's find him."

He reached over her and picked up the telephone book by its tatty shoelace. "Say we'll buy his breakfast," he directed and handed the phone to her. "You probably know him better than I." Wilson's penchant for high-class whore houses was not shared by Tony Mondaine. His sole interest had been exclusively in furnishing the excellent Sheraton decor. Well—more or less. He'd known the madam since she'd been ragged, fiercely motivated Madelena Todara.

Eleanor dialed the number he gave her from the book. It began to ring.

Tony walked to the door, turned, walked back, bent, stroked Thomaseen's ginger ears. The cat paused in his intensive ablutions to tolerate this as part of his duty roster, then resumed his cleansing.

A receiver lifted. A sleepy voice answered, "Yes?"

Peter Wilson could not, it evolved, tolerate the idea of food, but would meet them

372

at his office in an hour. Accepting this, Eleanor hung up and looked over at Tony, who was still pacing, his trench coat swinging behind him, his brows drawn down.

"Eight-thirty."

He glanced at his handsome Rolex watch. "All right. Then there's time for us to go get something. I could use a little fortification and not Ben's usual coffee."

She nodded and rose, steadying herself against the momentary whirl. "I have the Chevy."

"Fine. I walked from the motel."

At her raised brows, he covered smoothly, "The Porsche was meant for warmer climes and non-salted streets."

"Oh—of course." Still, vaguely aware suddenly that something, somewhere, didn't quite jibe since Tony had come in, Eleanor turned, picked up her coat. She allowed him to put her in it, kissing her cheek briefly in the process.

His lips were warm.

Warm. That was the problem. When he'd first kissed her, how could his lips, his coat, his hands have been so warm when he'd just come in from outside—and from walking four blocks in the cold, November wind?

Something was not quite kosher here.

He saw her hesitation. What had he said wrong?

"What is it?"

And she covered swiftly, smiling up at him, "Oh, nothing! I was trying to remember if I'd forgotten anything."

But it stuck in her mind like a burr, a tiny bit of fiberglass in her mental finger. Tony had lied. Why? And about something totally inconsequential, like walking from the motel. So—why was walking from the motel not inconsequential?

She couldn't care less if he'd had female companionship—although he probably thought she'd care, the idiot.

The hour being early, she drove to Bunny Burger, and they settled into a booth behind elderly Wilma Williamson and two white-haired buddies. Wilma waved, and said, *"Buon giorno!"*

Tony replied, *"Buon giorno, Mamacita,"* as he seated himself with his back to her. Behind him, Wilma's hand came over the top of the booth to Eleanor; it was making the "Okay" sign.

Eleanor laughed. "Wilma likes you."

"It's my Sicilian charm."

He'd turned to the pony-tailed waitress

with the lop-eared bunny hat. "Does it work on you?"

"No," the waitress answered calmly. "I have one little kid to show for Sicilian charm, and I don't need another. I can send over the waitress with the red frizz."

"That's all right. You'll do. Two orders of breakfast quiche with everything, and black coffee."

She was already pouring the coffee, smiling down at Eleanor. "Good to see you around, Ellie. Hard lines, huh?"

"Things happen."

"I'll tell the world. Two quiche with everything, coming up."

"Now," Tony said, as the waitress departed, "tell me about this Jill Bonford."

Eleanor found herself giving noticeably cautious answers, not protecting Jill so much as she was protecting herself. She certainly wasn't going to say what a gorgeous creature Jill was; he'd find out soon enough. Also, it would scarcely be diplomatic to admit that her resentment of Benton's wife had its feet as firmly implanted in Jill's shabby treatment of Benton as much as in her own personal problems. This was not the time to lay that piece of information on Tony Mondaine—if the time ever came.

The focus was entirely to be on Jill's selling the shop, and Tony's buying it.

Yet, on the way to Peter Wilson's office, she kept seeing Benton's face when he so much as said Tony's name, and the image was forming a lump in the quiche.

Damn. Just what she needed—heartburn.

When they got out of the Chevy, she quietly fished for antacid tablets in her bag, found none, took a deep breath. Tony was holding the door open for her, saying "Good morning," to Peter. She'd just have to bear with it.

Peter Wilson seated them with a simple statement of helplessness.

"I am sorry," he said, looking at them across his morning-tidy desk. "Sorry as hell that it's turning out like this. But Julia left no instructions, and Matt left no instructions, and Bonford left no instructions. Ergo: Mrs. Bonford is the heir. The sole heir, as far as I can ascertain."

He sighed, looked out his window at the water dripping from ice-rimmed eaves, then back at Eleanor sitting very straight and tense in her chair. "And Mrs. Bonford is, as she told you, Eleanor, very forth-right. Simplistically so—although do be aware she is not a simplistic person. Far from that. Perhaps a better term is—direct."

"How direct?" This was from Tony, leaning easily back in his chair, the sun striking soft frosty silver waves from the hair brushed across his ears.

Peter, who had been momentarily distracted by wishing he could, on a small-town income, afford sixty-dollar shirts and platinum chains, snapped back to business.

"A quick sale," he said. "On a cash basis. She has other imminent plans. She does not like small towns—I gather that life as a farmer's wife was not to her taste."

"And what is to her taste?"

Tony asked the question while trying to disguise the importance of his words with pseudo-humor. He needed a handle on this broad, and fast.

Peter grinned. "City," he replied, "as large as you can get. Where water comes from a tap, and rings from Cartier, not hog noses."

Tony grinned back. "I can't fault that,"

he said. Then he sobered. "Has she a price?"

Peter shuffled papers. "Fortunately, Julia had her properties reevaluated about a year ago for tax purposes. Remember, Eleanor? Mrs. Bonford will accept that, so we needn't call in appraisers unless the buyer requests that we do so. But she is hung up on cash—and that's the sticker. I called a few places last night. Torwald's—isn't that right, Ellie?"

"From Kansas City? Yes. Torwald's." And Eleanor's heart had jumped. Mason Torwald she could deal with.

But Peter was shaking his head again, ruffling its smooth brown, and impeccable sheen. "No soap. Ditto, Swanson's place in Springfield. Also, John Giametti. John says he's not interested, either."

Tony said, "John's pretty tied up right now."

But Eleanor hadn't sense enough to wonder how Tony knew that. She felt sick with disappointment. How great it would have been for John Giametti to buy the shop. She might not even have had to move. He might have let her just stay here while working for him.

She took a deep breath, trying to settle

the bubbling quiche. Both men glanced at her, both misunderstanding. Peter asked, "Hey—are you okay?"

She nodded. Somehow it didn't seem too cool to ask either of those two if they possessed any antacid tablets.

Tony switched his sharp gaze back to Peter. "So she's hung up on cash. Can we un-hang her?"

Peter shrugged. "I haven't been able to do it," he said. "Perhaps you could." He leaned across his polished desk, clasping his hands. "Are you a buyer?"

Tony answered smoothly, "I have always been a buyer. What I have needed is a seller. Mr. Bonford and I failed to come to terms. I'd like to think I'd have better luck with Mrs. Bonford."

Peter shrugged again. "Have a shot," he said. "I'm willing—and I'm sure Eleanor would be happier with you than Marvin Coles, or that Torwald guy."

He was looking at Eleanor. What could she do but nod?

He went on, "Of course, there's the house, too—but it shouldn't be too hard to unload independently. The market's up a little on old Victorians, and it is in pretty good shape, isn't it, Eleanor?"

Eleanor jumped. Her mind had just done another miserable backup, and snagged on what Tony had said: "Mr. Bonford and I failed to come to terms." And she had remembered again Benton saying of Tony, "And I don't want him taking over while I'm gone!" Oh, God. God, please—how can I keep Benton's promises?

There was just no way.

To Peter, she answered, sighing, "Yes. It's in good shape. There's some eaves-troughing, and a pine limb on the garage. Minor stuff."

To herself she was saying, to her wounded and grieving conscience, There's nothing else to do. I have only Tony now. I must make the best of it—if only for Ben and Mary Ann. Benton would understand. Benton would surely understand.

Tony was standing up with that lithe, catlike movement, and holding out his hand to her. He said to Wilson,

"Then that's it. Thanks for your time. If you have any influence with the lady, I'd appreciate having it on my side. Eleanor's side, really. This thing is pretty unfair to her."

"It is. I know it is. I remember how upset Matt was. And I don't want to see Julia

380

Bonford's whole reputation going down the tube; Julia was good for the economy of this town."

"I'd hope to be so, also."

"I'm sure you would. I'll be glad to do what I can."

He escorted them out, and Eleanor averted her head from the familiar sight of the door to Matt Logan's office. It still bore his name. And she'd already had one batch of poignant remembering; she didn't want another. There was just no way out but Tony's way. She'd have to make the best of it.

They got back into Eleanor's car. Tony sat still a moment while she fumbled for her keys. He was frowning, looking straight ahead into some sort of infinity. Eleanor sat still also, but from discouragement, from weariness, putting her mind into a mental block, allowing it only one step at a time. She dare not look too far ahead.

"Eleanor."

He had reached across, loosed one tense hand from the wheel, and gently kissed the palm.

His eyes were looking at her, challenging her.

Wearily she answered, "What?" and tried to smile.

"If I buy the shop—it's yours. As it has always been. You do understand that."

The statement, meant to be reassuring, was like an iceberg to Eleanor: one-third apparent; two-thirds under water.

The shop would be hers—if she would be what to Tony?

And she wanted to be nothing to Tony except a peer. She did not want to be obliged. The water around the iceberg was deep.

He was going on, "Whatever else—between us—we'll work out. Okay?"

"Okay." What else could she say at that point?

But now he was not looking at her. He was staring straight ahead down the morning street, with its few early passersby bundled against the chill, and the bright sun beginning to blur the shining glass of water frozen in the gutters.

Could she only have known, could she have possibly visualized, she would have imagined an astonished Anthony Mondaine standing detached, looking at the Anthony Mondaine sitting in an old Chevy, sitting next to a woman he'd ignored for at least ten years—looking with disbelief.

Yet what the Anthony Mondaine in the Chevy said next was with absolute if incredible necessity: "There is—something between us. Isn't there?"

She couldn't lie. She had to hedge. Hating herself, she answered with tight-shut eyes and shaking head, "Tony, I don't know. Don't ask me."

But even that half answer was enough for Anthony Mondaine—both of them: himself, and his ego. He said, "Cautious woman. Perfidious woman. I'll challenge that coolness—later. Not now." And there was laughter in his voice. But it faded as quickly as it had come. He went on calmly, "I want the shop. I want you. Therefore, please—please, Eleanor. I must have you understand one thing plainly, with no question about my feelings. If to get what I want I have to seduce Mrs. Jill Bonford, I shall do so."

He had still been holding her hand. He felt it tighten convulsively. He said, "Don't go middle class moral on me, Eleanor. It's a tough world. I fight tough."

All she could say was, "Tony, you've never even met the woman."

"But she's a woman."

"Is that your standard approach?"

"Many times. Now don't say I've shocked you."

"No," she answered soberly, "I've just never heard it put so—so blatantly before."

"I've never put it so—so blatantly before. I never felt impelled. I am doing it now because I want you to understand why I'd be doing it. Because I—I care about your understanding."

Now he was looking at her directly, meeting her eyes with his, holding them with an inner force. His voice was as gentle as the fingers clasping her fingers. "I really," he said, "care about very few things—but when I do—God help the people who try to take them from me."

The passion was there, barely leashed, burning from his eyes. She realized truly for the first time how deep were the waters in which she was trying to swim. Someone could get hurt. It easily—even inadvertently—could be her.

Twenty

From its regal limestone tower on the corner, the First Church bells began to cascade into the crystal air, sounding nine o'clock.

Tony released Eleanor's hand and said soberly, "Darling, you need something more potent than coffee. Let's go by my motel. I'll see if the Porsche will start now, and also pour a little cognac on your starter. I'll be a good boy. I promise. Scout's honor."

"What scout?"

"Probably Custer's."

But she laughed, started the Chevy, backed out and turned west. Getting him into his own car didn't seem to be too bad a suggestion.

She parked by the wet and shining Porsche. Handing her his key, he said, "Go in where it's warmer. I'll have to let the engine run a bit."

The room had the tidiness of any motel, with rake marks on the shag rug and Naugahyde on the two chairs by the window. Eleanor took one of the chairs, dug into her purse again, found a blessed antacid tablet at last. Crunching it, she watched as the Porsche jetted an obedient plume of blue-white exhaust.

She was tired already. The hospital seemed to have removed her starch and substituted Jell-O.

Wearily she took her eyes from the static display of Tony running his car engine, and let them roam the room. The bed was rumpled, with a dent on the pillow where his head had lain—presumably Tony's head, she amended with no pain, just recognition. A handsome cordovan leather suitcase lay unopened on the luggage rack, and another smaller one crowded the standard lamp on the standard desk top. Beyond it she caught a shadowy glimpse of her own face in the mirror—all eyes, cheekbones and gray hair. Every year showing.

Well, why not? Her birthday was only three days off.

She sighed. Perhaps one's birthday was a good time to bug out, start over clean, no ties, no memories.

If a woman could ever do that—even when young. Women always have memories. Regrets. They're probably built-in when she's born: sorry I hurt you, Mom; sorry I wasn't a boy, Dad; sorry I came here, Uncle Jack, but there was noplace else to go; sorry we didn't go to Disney World, Bobby—we could have found the money somewhere—

No. Women carried their regrets forever. She may as well make up her mind to that.

The opening door, however, brought in only Tony on a crisp snap of cold air, rubbing his chilly hands, stooping to kiss her with a cheery smack of icy lips.

"A drink is what we both need—myself, and milady," he said, turning to the leather case by the lamp, unaware of her thinking, Now that was right. He was cold. He was not cold before, in the shop when I came—and why did he lie about it? He well may have a key by now and I certainly wouldn't be upset if he did. Why didn't he say he had a key?

Dear God, just when I need certainties so badly why must I only get uncertainties?

He'd taken two balloon glasses and a flat bottle from the beautifully fitted case, poured golden liquid into the glasses and handed one to Eleanor, gently swirling it as he did so.

"Sip," he said. "It's far, far older than we are, my love, and guaranteed to warm the cockles—also all the other nice things about you I so admire."

He wasn't even telling Eleanor about Sotheby's offer. He wasn't going to tell her for a while; there was no good reason to activate a new set of thoughts, start her reading possibly damaging motivations into whatever he had to do in the next few days. He hadn't, as a matter of fact, even told Dominic. He was holding it greedily to his chest, thinking, Me—Tony, from the streets—I'm making it big.

It was to that, he sipped his own mellow cognac. To Mondaine's—an associate of Sotheby's.

God help whoever even tried to stand in his way.

He reached down to the half-smiling

woman curled in the plastic chair, took her free hand and kissed it.

Amazed at his own thoughts, he was thinking again that he might even marry her. Sotheby's approved of the married state. Eleanor had class. She had professional reputation. It could be a good deal for both of them.

All right. He admitted that at the moment she was turning him on. Why, he could not precisely explain—particularly after five nights of super-charged sex with Miranda, the girl with the golden boobs and the satin, super-charged body of a Titian bathing beauty. But Miranda had gone back to Dallas, his own chargers were full bore again, and Eleanor was just sitting there not realizing he remembered the succulent velvet warmth that could be released with only two unbuttonings.

She had responded once. Certainly the Bonford klutz hadn't got to her. And hospital beds were scarcely sex pits.

Perhaps she was ready, too. Perhaps she was just waiting for his other hand to reach out, touch the curve of those nice breasts, undo those buttons.

Eleanor was not certain whether she saw the sudden flash of dangerous fire, or felt it in his fingers. But she knew it was there. Adrenaline poured. She stood up oh so casually, draining the last dregs of the cognac, holding on to a chair arm so inadvertent dizziness wouldn't pitch her forward into disaster.

She had no idea of the upward movement, the simple motion of the raised arm brought up the tempting line of her breasts, the plunging curve of her throat into warm red wool and he felt his loins tighten.

But she was smiling, saying gently, "No, Tony," putting the balloon glass on the desk and going to the door. "What happened to that scout's honor?"

"It fell among thieves."

"You're mixing metaphors, and I need to get back to the shop. Ben probably thinks Mrs. Bonford and I have killed each other like the gingham dog and the calico cat. A good and proper allegory. Come along."

"I accept second thoughts. There's no recognized time frame on making love."

"But there is a comfort frame—and it's not an anonymous motel room during a coffee break."

He shrugged, accepted the situation

gracefully—Tony was damned graceful, these days—locked the door behind him, and helped her into her own Chevy. The trip back to the shop was a dual exercise in regaining control—until they turned into the alley.

There, Tony found his way blocked by a huge covered truck backed to the loading dock. On the dock stood a vaguely familiar fat lady in extra-large Calvin Klein jeans. Beside her stood a tall, lissome blonde in molded Jordaches. They were mutually directing the loading into the truck of the John Belter divan.

Eleanor saw it first—and almost hit the van. Managing to stop, she said a piteous, "Oh dear God!"

She knew what was going on—and there was nothing she could do to prevent it.

Hardly aware of the Porsche sliding alongside, she could only watch numbly as Jill Bonford jumped from the tall dock—a movement graceful as a dancer's—and came to Eleanor's car.

Above a trim waist she wore a satin-striped tissue blouse, half unbuttoned, and beneath it the merest wisp of a bra that cupped rather than clothed whipped-cream breasts. Her silky hair sprayed in the air as she walked, then settled into perfection. Rose-enameled toes in high-heeled clogs clicked a swaying poem of motion. Stopping, she pulled around her a heavy-knit sweater that merely provided a frame for her inherent beauties as she bent, tapped on the car window. Her eyes were sparkling, clear as cider.

"You were right!" she chortled as Eleanor numbly rolled the window down. "I even added a thousand and she bought! Now she wants those Queen somebody chairs with the birds on the seat. The old man's getting them out of storage for her. Think—what else might the old broad buy?"

Eleanor was voiceless. Tony had suddenly appeared at the window, also, and was saying, "It sounds as if you've already done quite well."

"I can hardly believe it. Twenty-five thousand dollars and still going—in half an hour's work. I may not offer this joint for sale—I may just hang on and sell it to the floorboards."

Gently Tony answered, "It isn't always that easy."

He held out his hand, trying not to look at a stunned Eleanor whose blusher was standing out in patches on her cheeks. "Anthony Mondaine."

"Jill Bonford." She put her hand in his; her eyes were already tabulating the handsome face, the urbane voice, the strong-columned throat above the silk shirt, the Sulka tie. "Do you work here?"

He laughed. "No. My place is in St. Louis."

"Do you sell like this? Thousands at a crack? My God, I can't believe her—she came trotting in with that sheep of a husband and said, 'I want that, and that, and that—' and he just—nodded. And started writing a check. Oh Christ—the check is good, isn't it?"

"Eminently. I think I know the fellow."

"Wow." She put a hand on her breasts, exhaled in relief. "I never thought of bad checks—until now. I was so excited. Beginner's luck, I suppose."

Then she suddenly glanced down at Eleanor's frozen face. "I didn't really believe you yesterday, you know."

Eleanor nodded painfully. She'd never felt so utterly helpless in her life. Behind them on the dock, a sharp voice called, "Good morning, Mrs. Wright. I said I'd be back."

"You did," said Eleanor with the calmness of resignation, "indeed."

Tony opened her door and she stood up unsteadily, holding covertly to the car for balance. Bite the bullet, Eleanor. It was hers to sell.

Jill Bonford was also suddenly tabulating the smart red wool dress, the well-cut, ashy hair—and reevaluating yesterday's opinion. Her eyes went to Anthony Mondaine, back to Eleanor again, and turned lidded. Cautious.

"Let's not stand here. It's cold. Come inside."

The steps were blocked off. She waited until Anthony had swung Eleanor up to the dock floor, then allowed him to boost her, making certain his hand found her round, succulent derrière.

Above them, Eleanor was rigid with the effort of facing Emily Smith's smug smile. Seeing it, Tony made himself move away, take Eleanor's arm.

Good God—this Jill Bonford was like Miranda when he'd first met her years ago—all peach bloom and velvet.

Watch it, you randy fool. She's going to be as open as a blossom—you've already got the signals. How much will the traffic bear? Which side of the fence will be better first?

He turned to give Eleanor a supportive smile but he was also watching the lovely bobble of the Bonford boobs as she pushed at her blowing silken hair.

Perhaps if he worked it right—he could have both sides. After all—it wouldn't be the first time.

At that moment his Porsche horn beeped. It was a polite beep, but it was an attention-getter.

Tony patted Eleanor's arm and let go. "Excuse me," he said. "My car phone."

He jumped lightly off the dock, grateful for the hours on the jogging track that allowed him to do so, and went over to open the door and lean inside. Jill Bonford's eyes followed him.

"My, he's a knock-out," she said to Eleanor. "Yours?"

Well—whatever else Benton's wife might be, evasion was not a trait.

"No," Eleanor answered shortly, swallowing the temptation to add, —he's anybody's if they play it right. She had no reason to be nasty—at least about Tony.

Ben was going by her, lugging a Queen Anne chair. She saw the look of complete misery on his face and patted his shoulder in passing. The creaking of the loading doors prevented her from hearing as Anthony Mondaine said, "Well, good morning, Giametti. How's it going with your nouveau riche customer?"

The words would have meant nothing, anyway. And she wasn't interested in Tony's world—except where it touched hers.

Jill's arched brows had gone up at Eleanor's brief reply. "Okay," she said, following her into the shop. "I put the check on that desk, there. I suppose it has to be deposited. Can you think of anything else we might unload on this fat idiot?"

With great difficulty Eleanor kept her voice calm—and sane. "Is she buying for herself?"

"Lord, I don't know! Who the hell cares as long as she buys? She doesn't like the stuff with the claws on their legs—I tried those, and God knows, I wouldn't either. They look real enough to reach out and scratch you while you were just sitting there. And she doesn't want pictures, either. Or any of that silver in the other room. Hey, how about rugs?"

Eleanor was sitting wearily down at her desk.

"Ask her," she said, and Jill was back out the door like a shot. As she left, Thomaseen descended from his perch on the shelf and indicated that his bowl was empty. Eleanor informed him rather shortly that the condition was going to exist for a little while longer; she wasn't getting up again. Always insouciant, he plopped his furry self on her lap and nuzzled her arm.

From outside came the sounds of departure; apparently Emily Smith wasn't into rugs. Ben, Jill and Tony came back in together, Ben closing the door against the cold and going to the glowing heater to warm his old hands. Tony said to Eleanor, smiling, "I'm going to take this *enfant terrible* out for coffee and try to teach her a few rudimentary facts. And give you a breather," he added quietly, as Jill went to retrieve her coat from where she'd tossed it on the Stickley rocker.

"You mean, 'hide the family jewels,'" Eleanor answered in a grim voice. "But I'm afraid it's a little late for that."

"Perhaps not. If I can work a deal, I will, Ellie. I promise. And whatever else about me, Eleanor Wright—I do not make promises lightly."

His black eyes were on her face now, and in their depth was that burning coal of fire.

She nodded, trying to smile, trying not to remember another man's promises. "I know. Thank you, Tony."

"I shall expect a bit more than thanks."

"I'm sure you will."

"Good girl. You're learning."

And so am I, he was saying to himself, standing indolently erect as Jill Bonford came back towards him, wrapping herself in a handsome leather coat. In five minutes I've learned four vital facts. Three of them I knew already—that I must have the shop, with Eleanor in it, and the house, in case Julia hid that damned painting there somewhere. I now know from John Giametti that Eleanor meant to go to work for him, which I cannot have. Hopefully I've taken care of that situation. But it's not enough. I need a hold over Eleanor—some sort of insurance. And what is that going to be?

Most women fall on their ass when I look at them. Why the hell doesn't she?

As he shepherded Jill out the door, he

glanced back over his shoulder. Eleanor was watching. A hopeful sign? He winked at her broadly before he shut the door.

In the sudden silence, Ben turned from the heater, looked at Eleanor and shook his balding old head.

"God, Muffin," he said. "What are we goin' t' do?"

She took a deep breath, and tried to smile. "Tony's going to try to buy it from her."

"He said so?"

"Yes."

"Cash?"

"I don't know. That's his deal. Peter said this morning that he can't find anyone else. Not for cash."

He was fishing an enormous tobacco chew from his pocket, poking it into his lean old cheek. "At least that'll get her out of here. She—she's somethin' else, Ellie."

Stiffly he went over to the storage loft steps, began to mount. "Never thought I'd be rootin' for the Mondaine feller," he mumbled, and went up out of sight.

"Nor," said Eleanor to herself, "I—welcome to the club, Ben."

She was already there; she may as well tackle the stack of mail that had accrued to a basketful during her hospital stay. Ben and Mary Ann did not do bills or correspondence. That had been her particular province for years.

It was clear at the bottom of the mess that Eleanor had found her next crisis. It was from a legal firm. It was very crisp, and quite succinct. In regard to Robert Wright's outstanding medical bills, since Eleanor Wright had neither answered their telephone calls, nor letters, and was two months remiss, they had no other course but to seek compensation via the courts.

The bottom line: Eleanor Wright was being sued.

The information was not quite what she needed to make a perfect day.

Twenty-one

The next few days weren't so great, either.

If Tony was making progress with Jill on a business deal, he wasn't discussing it. On a social basis—"social" being an all-purpose term—he seemed to be doing handsomely. He was, in fact, and in Ben's words, dancing attendance like a suave monkey on a stick.

However, even Tony couldn't spend twenty-four hours in this endeavor no matter how meritorious it seemed to those so vitally involved. And in the unfortunate interims she haunted the shop. Her motto was Sell! Each time the brass bells on the front door rang their flat chime she popped out of the back like a bird from a cuckoo clock.

Unfortunately—or fortunately, from a harried Eleanor's point of view—she tended to rate the customer by his mode of attire and left the shabbier ones to Eleanor and Mary Ann. This was in the category of "Thank God for small favors," since genuine antiquers, by and large, eschew the show of wealth while pursuing their favorite pastime. Eleanor, thereby, was able to rescue her most rewarding customers from a beautiful young lady in tight jeans blindly shoving mission oak at them and calling it "Gus Stickers."

The total situation, however, had little merit.

"Oh well," Ben said philosophically, "at least she's cleanin' out the attic." He was doing a lot of fiddling with the Welsh dresser to keep it from being moved into one of the empty spaces on the showroom floor, and noticeably putting no time in at all on the Dutch kas.

Truthfully, it was a moot point whether Jill was losing them money or not. She refused to dicker—the antiquer's favorite indoor sport. Totally sold on the sticker price system by Emily Smith's instant purchase of the Belter set, she quoted it to a customer; if he murmured something about

402

the price being too high, she lost interest immediately and wrote him off. Her absorption with cash was almost an obsession.

However, Eleanor could relate to that. Local banks were showing no interest whatever in lending money on a collateral of one elderly Chevrolet and three antiques, the lawyers were becoming more and more adamant in their fixed demand beyond granting thirty days, and John Giametti, to whom she hoped to sell the three antiques, was not answering her calls.

He was working hard on an important deal, his son said, half apologetically. They had a newly rich client who wished to furnish his recently purchased mansion with only seventeenth-century furniture and John was traveling thither and yon trying to buy him what he wanted. Unfortunately, the major portion of furnishings of that time period were either in museums or private and inviolable collections.

Hanging up for the fourth time, Eleanor thought wearily, Why doesn't he consult Tony? I certainly would. But then, perhaps he has.

What am I to do?

Abruptly her eye was caught by Mary

Ann signaling wildly from the front of the shop. But it was already too late to retrieve the transient but potential customer in a rusty pickup truck. His knowing hands had felt the modern saw cut on the wide-boarded back of a bureau; he'd given Jill a look of pure disgust, heeled about and left.

"Oh, well." Jill said cheerfully, sitting in a Federal chair to resume painting her nails. "He'd probably want to pay ten bucks down and five a week forever. And I'm not interested in that. Hey—I meant to ask—who the hell is Torwald?"

Eleanor paused in her trek back to her desk, and automatically blew dust off the shining surface of a William Lloyd, D-shaped card table. "Torwald? The only one I know is the largest dealer of antiques in Kansas City."

Jill splayed long fingers to admire the bright red polish. "No shit? Pete Wilson had tried them—to sell, you know—and got nothing, so I thought I'd go the personal call—I have a real sexy voice on the phone; I used to do solicitations—for insurance policies and medical plans and that crap. But the guy I got never even seemed to have heard of this place. I thought Julia Bonford was well known."

"She was," Eleanor said a little stiffly.

"Not with that Joe. He practically hung up on me. And another place, too. Grosman's, I think it was."

Suddenly Eleanor didn't want to hear any more.

"Money's tight," she said with grim, personal truth, and went back to her desk.

As she sat down, her back twinged. She shouldn't have tried to help Mary Ann shift that black-lacquered Chinese cabinet last night, but Ben was gone and they'd needed something to fill in where the big armoire's sale had left a shabby hole showing in the Aubusson.

At least, she thought wryly, Julia would have been happy about the sales.

Except the Belter set.

Suddenly she was distracted by a sweep of cold air from the alley, a smell of expensive cologne, and a swift hug from behind.

Anthony Mondaine was back.

"Of course you missed me," he was saying cheerfully, taking off leather gloves and holding his hands out to the heater. "It's been eight entire hours. But I have learned to shave at least fifteen minutes off the travel time on Highway 70 by going through St. Ann. How about that? Well— what's she done while I was gone—try to sell your depression glass for Venetian? Play a tune on the Willard banjo clock?"

He was obviously in a good mood. Hooray for him. Eleanor was glad something was going well for somebody.

She was saved from replying by a second blast of cold. Turning, she saw the local deputy sheriff coming inside, dusting frost off his blue coat. She said, "Well, hi, Don. I hope this's a social call."

"Just passing through."

He nodded at Tony, and went on, "Have you got a—a Mrs. Benton Bonford?"

Now, Eleanor thought with a tiny bit of amusement, perhaps Mrs. Benton Bonford will stop parking her rental car in that yellow loading zone. "Sure. Up front. That's Jill in the big red chair."

She almost added, Take her; she's yours, but thought better of it. She was not in the proper position to see Jill's suddenly paling face and furtive glance around as the deputy handed her, in his guise as process server, an envelope of very official appearance.

Tony was watching, from the corner of his eye. It was in his best interest to know whatever he could about Jill Bonford. And what he saw he found curious.

Okay. Whatever she'd just received, she didn't like it. Not one bit. Perhaps she'd back off on the "cash only" hang-up a little now. It would help. Those four 1700 Hepplewhite pieces going to John Giametti had given him a good chunk, but he'd had to back off a few thousand to get John to agree not to hire Eleanor. The cash was not in his hand, but it would be there tomorrow. He was ready to deal, so by God, blondie better be.

"Be tolerant," he said to the attractive wench tickling her ginger cat's ears as he purred his consent from the desktop. "She had a deprived childhood."

"Welcome to the club."

"She grew up with eleven brothers and sisters in a two-bedroom apartment in Rolla. The only thing she's had going for her has been her looks. She quit high school and got on with an ad agency sending strings of girls to convention centers."

That caught Eleanor's attention. She arched her brows, and said, "Oh?"

"No, no, no. Don't let your mind be such

a sewer, darling; it doesn't become you. Corporations showing their products need girls to hand out freebies—you know—key chains, combs, that stuff—or to talk you into tasting fudge made out of bluegrass."

"Try soybeans."

He shrugged. "Whatever. Anyway, that's where she met Bonford."

"At a convention?"

"At a convention."

Her eyes were on Thomaseen's ginger silk fur, but her heart was hearing Benton's voice saying from far, far away, "She thought I was rich, and I thought she'd like the farm." And she could envision Benton, well-dressed, ready to party with a pretty girl. And Jill, giving him the business with those lashy shining eyes.

The front door bells jangled. She glanced around the bend of Tony's knee, but it was only the deputy going out, and Jill still in the Federal chair just sitting. Like a spider waiting on more flies, she thought darkly.

But there was a pathetic droop to Eleanor's soft mouth, and she looked suddenly tired.

Tony thought, Okay—now, while Jill is otherwise occupied, let's make a move on

Eleanor. Damn, it's a good thing I'm an expert chess player.

Because I can't make a mistake. I can't afford to make a mistake. Even after I find that stupid Picasso, I want Eleanor. I need Eleanor. How I need her I'm not sure. I don't even want to think about it now. I can't handle any more complications.

He said softly, "Hey."

She raised her eyes, looked at him. "Hey what?"

"Stop worrying. Things are getting under control."

"Speak for yourself. Ben, Mary Ann and I are still treading water."

"Idiot child, I am going to buy this place. And all three of you will stay on. Relax."

Tony, if you only knew—

She took a deep breath. He didn't. He didn't know. She said, "Have you told Little Red Riding Hood, in there?"

"No. But I will. And today. Later."

"She still wants cash."

"I have cash. At least, I will tomorrow. Can you hang on that long, poor baby?"

What was an honest answer? That he thought he was giving her a step forward, but what she really had was two steps back?

So she merely nodded. He patted her hand paternally and said,

"Let's go get some lunch."

"What about Little Miss Muffet?"

"I'll take care of it. Sit tight."

She watched him slide off the desk with that catlike grace, go down the aisle of the shop. He belonged there, he fitted in among the cabriole legs and the curved chair splats with his lean good looks, his understated elegance.

Tony bent over Jill, said softly, "I'm taking Eleanor to lunch; she's feeling abused."

Jill upturned eyes that were startled—that seemed to come back from a far distance and be surprised to see him there—that for a moment failed to recognize who he was.

Then reality clicked back like a slide on a screen, but not before he'd caught one knife-edged glimpse of guilty fright. It startled him. What had this girl to be scared about? Good God, it appeared to him she was holding her world by its tail.

Now she was nodding, smiling an intimate smile that Eleanor would not have cared for at all. "Poor thing," she said. "Be nice to her."

"Oh, I will indeed," Tony answered, winked, and went back to Eleanor.

Jill's hand fastened on the long envelope, thrust down between the cushion and the chair back. She hadn't opened it. She hadn't needed to open it. She knew what it was. The long arm of the law had finally caught up with her.

She *was* divorced.

She'd known Benton had filed a counter-suit charging desertion long before he'd gone on that fatal hunting trip. She'd hoped to avoid the final papers, hoped desperately, until everything she could lay her hands on had been turned to ready money and she could run with it, disappear, never be heard of again—and never be poor again.

Her rosy mouth hardened.

They still didn't know—Tony and that aging ingenue, Eleanor. There was time, yet. A little.

Not enough to keep waiting on a cash offer. She'd have to take whatever Tony Mondaine could come up with now—and write off her losses. She'd tell him tonight. She'd make a good story of it. In the meantime . . .

Her eyes darted about the shop, assessing the softly shining row of sidechairs, the crystal gleam of glassware, spraying amethyst and sapphire in the winter sun. She willed customers to come in the door.

A sale, she thought. That's what I'll have. A sale.

In the cold Porsche, as the engine purred its stiff oil into liquidity, Tony pulled Eleanor over into his arms, down coat and all, and kissed her chilly cheek, her warm throat. "God, I miss you," he murmured huskily, and there was, surprising him even yet, more than a grain of truth in his voice. Jill Bonford had not yet learned the rewarding passion of elegant restraint in her lovemaking. And he had the strange but undeniable sense that the same act with Eleanor would be—pure class.

Further, he was going to find out. And soon.

Anthony Mondaine, looking forward to making a gray-haired broad.

And—not as just another conquest. Which was a little disturbing. But he'd deal with that, soon.

Eleanor had given his lean cheek a friendly smack and neatly removed herself from his arms. It wasn't embarrassment.

The row of chirping sparrows along the sagging power line couldn't give a damn. It was indifference. However, as he put the Porsche in reverse and backed away—the line of his handsome face in sharp profile—she couldn't help but think, God, what would I do if I really cared about this man? Watching him with Jill Bonford, I'd go absolutely mad.

But she didn't care. Sometime in her life she might love a man again. But just now her entire body and soul still cried out piteously like a lost child for Benton Bonford.

Not a child's cry. A woman's.

For what she might have had.

Tony took her to the busy restaurant on the west side of the city square. They dined on soup, an excellent salad, and a large order of fries on the side.

"Jill's plebeian tastes have done this to me," Tony said, grinning, as he mopped catsup with a long crisp potato strip. "I love 'em. Couldn't afford them when I was growing up—like other kids. We ate pasta and liked it. But every now and then I go on a binge." Then he paused, and looked across at her sharply with a peculiar sensation that she'd not even been listening.

Her eyes were on the handsome green ferns banking the restaurant windows, and her fingers about the coffee cup were lax, not lifting, just feeling its heat.

Smiling, he snapped his fingers beneath her nose. "Hey—Earth to Mars!"

"Oh, sorry."

And she did smile back. A little. But sensing something deeply amiss, about which perhaps he should know, he persisted.

"All right, Circe. I've told you I'm buying the business. And that your jobs are safe. What the hell is it, now?"

He was pushing—the great male commander, master of all he surveyed, including the women in his life.

She pushed, also—the chair back from the table.

"Nothing, Tony. Nothing that concerns you. Take me by the house, will you? I need to pick up the mail."

He let it pass, but he didn't like it. Biding his time, he did as she asked, waiting in the warm, idling Porsche as she disappeared inside the tall, elegant double doors with their nice, stained glass transom.

It's not a bad old place, he thought disinterestedly, letting his eyes roam the tall Victorian tower, and the triple windows showing their hint of lace behind streaked old glass. What would he do with it? Sell? Let Eleanor go on living there? Perhaps move the main showroom off the city square, and make this house a living display of those good eighteenth-century pieces?

His brows knit, speculating on that possibility, he didn't realize Eleanor was taking an unusually long time just to pick up mail. But Eleanor, standing just inside the tall doors, was too dismayed at the letter in her hand to move.

It was from John Giametti. It said that due to circumstances beyond his control he regretted being unable to employ her. He was truly sorry, and perhaps further down the road—et cetera.

"Damn!" said Eleanor wretchedly, crumpling the letter in one fist as she made an eyes-shut grimace and tried to marshall practical thoughts.

So much for her bid for independence.

Of course there were other places. Of course there were. And surely her reputation was good enough to work for someone else besides Marvin Coles.

But right now—it appeared she was stuck with Tony Mondaine's job. And whatever else he had in mind.

A woman being pressed for medical bills certainly could not be jobless.

Turning blindly, she stumbled over a pair of Jill Bonford's abandoned high heels and kicked them halfway up the silent staircase.

Then she paused, tears in her eyes, desperately, fruitlessly longing to see a huge furry dog couchant at their head, with a huge, arms-akimbo Bluto standing behind him.

There was nothing in the shadows. There would never be again.

She stuffed the letter in her bag, left the junk mail on the demi-lune table in the entry, and went back out to the purring Porsche, avoiding last night's white snow still in windblown rows along the cracking sidewalk.

Tony's eyes were on her face. As she slid inside, he'd seen the letter sticking out of her bag, glimpsed the Giametti return sticker, realized what it had been. He thought, Oh boy—now she knows. Make your pitch before she gets organized.

John's turning her down has been a blow. Capitalize on it.

Go as far as you please—the further she's in your pocket the safer you are.

She was just sitting there, staring—not even aware he hadn't put the car in gear, that they weren't moving.

He asked the question, curious about what she'd respond: "Bad news?"

She shrugged, sighed. "I guess it's all relevant to what was bad yesterday. And the day before. By now you'd think I'd have a callus an inch thick."

"Then damn it—let me help!"

"Then damn it—find me five thousand dollars!"

"Lend me your pen and I'll write a check."

They stared at each other—Eleanor aghast as what she'd said, the temerity of what she'd said—and Tony Mondaine hoping madly that what he'd replied had been the right thing. There went much of the skinny, almost minuscule profit from what he'd make in the Giametti deal—and his brother would scream like a stuck pig. But sometimes the long view is the only one. Dominic had yet to learn that—And Dominic had screwed up on the Picasso.

Eleanor's eyes were white with luminous centers. Her hands were fluttering. She was saying, "Oh, Tony, thank you—but I can't—it's my problem—"

"Let it be mine, also."

His own hand had gone out, captured the flutters, brought them up to his cheek, holding them there.

"But—"

All the way, Mondaine.

He gave her back her hands, only to reach inside his vest to his shirt pocket. The flat velvet case was there, had been there for days because of its enormous value. He shook off the nagging knowledge that the ring therein was not precisely paid for. After all, if Eleanor was his, then the ring was his, also, handily retrievable.

He held the case towards her, opening the lid, cupping the sight with his hand from inadvertent passersby. He said to her very softly,

"Mrs. Anthony Mondaine, I presume."

He'd never said it before. It came out easier than he'd expected. Its effect on Eleanor was satisfactory.

Startled, she first looked at him, then downward. She caught her breath. She said, in a choked voice, "My God—Tony!"

The ring was the perfect example of Renaissance art—delicately filagreed by a master craftsman, the center stone a perfect diamond, faceted to catch every crystal beam, surrounded by a wreath of sapphires.

He took it from its velvet bed, held it a moment so that beneath the winter sunlight the sapphires turned from ocean blue to the blue of summer skies and the diamond flashed a single point of flame. Then he gently slid it on her nerveless finger.

"Congratulations, Tony," he said to himself aloud, grinning at her. "Thank you—we are both eminently deserving of each other."

Her mouth moved, said nothing, tried again. She swallowed, whispered, "Tony, you idiot."

"No, no. Try 'Tony, my love,' or 'Tony, my affianced.' "

"Tony, I don't—"

"But you do." His hands covered hers, covered the sparkling band on her cold finger. "Trust me. You do. I just didn't want to wait any longer unless you started really believing my gamboling in the clover with la Bonford was genuine."

But she couldn't say, I haven't cared at all. Dear God, what could she say? She needed the job, she desperately needed the money.

Tony took care of that situation also. Murmuring, "The Lord giveth and the Lord taketh away, blessed be the name of the Lord,' " he deftly removed the ring, replaced it in its flat velvet box and dropped the box into her open bag.

And he added, "For God's sake, don't lose it. I just don't think wearing my ring in front of Jill would be particularly smart at the moment."

She was still making unintelligible noises. Over them, in a voice she'd never heard before, he went on, "I want to kiss you. But approaching in a crocodile seems to be the entire enrollment of some grade school, and I really don't feel up to amusing the younger generation. Later, darling. I promise. Do I promise, indeed!"

Blindly she looked around and saw a hundred, coat-swathed children approaching two by two, hitting every melting puddle in the block on their weekly trip to the public library.

Anthony put the car in reverse, backed out ahead of them, and drove down the street, frowning—not at the children—but at the spray of dirty snow on his immaculate car sides.

One of the kids, in a scruffy storm coat, yelled, "Later, dude!"

And he laughed. "Precisely," he said to the silent woman beside him. "I couldn't have said it better."

The fact that her answering smile was a conditioned response escaped him. In his book of necessities there was now one down, one to go. And really go. Jill Bonford now had to be out of town, out of sight, and gone forever.

The fact that he was possibly a bit late was not apparent until they were almost to the alley. Then they saw the flurry of activity, cars parked, and people on the sidewalk.

Tony said, "What the hell is going on?" at the same time Eleanor said, "Oh my God!"

Then he saw what she saw: one window of the shop carried a banner emblazoned in red, "SALE! SALE!"

The second window proclaimed, "Ten to fifty percent OFF on EVERYTHING IN THE STORE!"

Twenty-two

Tony slammed on his brakes, parked.

Both Tony and Eleanor hit the sidewalk running. They converged with Ben and Mary Ann, pelting from the opposite direction, Mary Ann panting, "Oh my!" and Ben saying, "God damn woman!"

To Eleanor he said bitterly, "No wonder she told us both to go to lunch."

Jill Bonford was standing just inside the door. At their noisy entrance, she swung from an excited customer, looked at them with patently defiant eyes and said, "Hi."

Eleanor cried out angrily, "You can't do this—Jill."

Jill said as angrily, "I've done it!"

"No you haven't," said Tony his calm voice concealing his molten rage. With one long arm he reached up, tore off one of the amateur banners.

She was at him almost like an angry kitten. The other arm trapped her, helpless. He said, "Sorry, folks, a mistake. No sale today." To her furious mouthings, he countered, "Come on, enfant terrible—back into the workshop where I tell you some facts of life in the business of being an antiquarian."

He hauled her off bodily.

An elderly lady in an enormous striped muffler said anxiously, "I've already paid my money; it's mine, isn't it?"

Eleanor glanced at the depression glass cakeplate in her hand, gritted her teeth, wrote it off, and said, "Of course. We're sorry. Mrs. Bonford isn't—" She hesitated at the inevitable charity of her phrase, forced it out, "—isn't quite into the—the swing of things yet."

Another customer laid a Victorian toilet stand back down, said a succinct word between his teeth and stalked out the door. The pattern established, the half-dozen others followed suit, and in the final count, only a Federal knife-holder and a good marble-topped demi-lune table had been lost.

Seeing the last disgruntled buyer out the door, Eleanor noted with only half an eye that snow was beginning to fall softly, dotting the sidewalk with silent wet splats of white.

She felt totally limp, wrung out. After the initial jet of adrenaline, her knees were shaking. She collapsed in the rattan rocker and looked wearily across at Ben and Mary Ann who also sank down, facing her, on the matching rattan couch. From the rear came total silence. Whatever Tony was managing to do, he was doing it without audible vituperation.

Leave it to Tony, she thought, and knew she was glad to do so.

Mary Ann voiced it for them all.

"What a twit!" she said, pushing back untidy, graying hair.

Ben nodded.

Eleanor shrugged. She said, "We stopped her. At least for the moment."

They stared at each other, realizing the impotence of that phrase. Then Ben rose, and with studied deliberation, stripped down the second banner, balled it and threw against the storeroom door as hard as he could. The paper bounced off, rolled beneath a country commode and stopped.

"Good place for it," he said shortly.

Still there were no noises from the shop room.

Perhaps they'd gone.

Perhaps, on the other hand, they hadn't. Tony Mondaine had his methods, after all—some of which one of them knew well, and the other two guessed.

Their mutual ideas were confirmed when quite soon thereafter, Tony reappeared in the door to the workroom, his arm firmly around the shoulders of a Jill Bonford not precisely chastened, but definitely under restraint.

"Bulletin," he said in a cheerful voice to the three pairs of steady eyes that swung on him. "Mrs. Bonford has agreed to sell to me, the terms of which are none of your damn business at the moment." He winked. They did not wink back. "Effective as soon as the papers can be made out and payment made. Like tomorrow. In the meantime, my children, business back to normal. Mrs. Bonford and I are going out to celebrate quite largely, and I promise you'll see no more of us, today. You may now applaud."

They applauded. If Tony was going to own the shop, Ben and Mary Ann gave not one classic tinker's damn about what Jill Bonford thought. Eleanor was still too angry to be cautious.

Jill smiled, hating all three equally, but playing her own game. If she could get away with it she'd fire them right now and stipulate no sale if Tony tried rehiring. But that was taking too much of a chance. She just had to swallow those smug looks.

Yet, she'd get back at them—somehow. Especially Eleanor Wright. Especially. Look at her, sitting there in her red wool designer dress, and that clever color to her hair that won't say whether it's fashionable ash or old-age gray, so self-contained, so—so pussycat, unmarked by fear, or hard times or never knowing from one day to the next whether you'd survive or not. Always had it good, Eleanor Wright. Obviously. Always had it good.

She hated women like that.

"Bye-bye," said Jill Bonford.

When at last the three of them walked into the back, the smell of Jill's expensive perfume still lingered. Without a word, Mary Ann reached into the tiny bathroom, got the Lysol and sprayed.

The telephone rang.

Eleanor, smiling, sat in the captain's

chair and picked it up. "Bonford Antiques, Eleanor Wright."

The answering voice was Martha, Matt's wife. She said, "Eleanor dear, I'm finally getting up enough courage to clean out Matt's desk and there are some papers here that seem to be about you. I'm so dim on those things, but I see your name, and the shop's and Mr. Benton's. No—Mr. Benton Bonford's—that's it. Peter's out of town. Would you like to pick them up? Perhaps we could have a cup of coffee together. I've not seen you since you've been ill."

Eleanor glanced down at her appointment pad. She had nothing pressing for the afternoon except a call at a farmhouse just outside of town to appraise a dining-room set. And she had, perhaps, neglected Martha, who was a dear.

She agreed, fixed a time, and—hanging up—swung around. Thomaseen hopped from Mary Ann's lap to hers, gave her a quick lick with a rough tongue and settled to knead furry doubled paws against her stomach.

Taking that as a signal, Mary Ann went back to the eternal task of cleaning china on its shelves in the shop. Ben leaned against his Welsh dresser with arms

akimbo in a gesture painfully like Benton's, and asked meaningfully,

"Well, Muffin?"

She knew what he meant. She shrugged,
sighed. "We'll take it as it comes, Ben."

She couldn't bear the idea of telling him
about the ring that lay hidden in her bag.
She could imagine the shock in his old
eyes. The disillusion. He'd not understand—even if she told him of her medical
bills that had to be paid.

Ben was of a generation almost gone—
one of immutable double standards,
where what was right for a man was absolute sin and hell-fire for a woman. Selling
herself for gain was something a good
woman did not do.

He was inspecting his short nails above
cracked knuckles. "Y' don't think he'll
back out?"

"Of buying the shop? No. He really
wants it, Ben."

"But—her. She'll be outta here?"

"I—I think so. I think she will."

"Leastways, that's one good thing."

She felt impelled to be honest: "Tony is
very good at what he does, Ben."

Anger boiled out. "Then I wish t' hell
he do it in St. Louis, and leave us alone!"

Then he stopped, sighed, and shook his head. "I'm too old for all this change," he said. "But I guess there ain't no choice. A job's a job."

"Especially when we're our age." She said it dryly. But he shot back at her, "Age, hell! Me, maybe—but you're a damn good-lookin' woman. Besides, your reputation in this business is as good as Julia's. Things get tough around here, Muffin, you think about goin' somewheres else—and remember it's with my blessing."

She was completely caught by surprise. And touched. She said, "Why—Ben . . . thank you."

"S'all right," he mumbled. "Jis' don't forget it."

He scraped a match across his denim seat, lit a bent cigarette and opened the alley door. "Lord, look at it snow."

In surprise, Eleanor looked, and saw the broken concrete already covered and the floating feathers of lazy snowfall melting in the puddles that still lined the alley sides. "When did that happen? The sun was shining half an hour ago."

He shrugged, inhaling, and blowing the smoke outside.

"Durin' the hoo-hah in here, I guess.

Well. Back to work. While I know what I'm doin'. There's a stack of checks on your desk. Why don't you go to the bank afore blondie decides to finagle a few and leave with 'em in her pocket? Tony won't be back for a while; he'll have 'er in the hay before her lunch settles, or I'll miss my bet. And are you still goin' out to Martin's place?"

"I'm supposed to go."

"Git movin', then. Banks close in half an hour. When did you tell Martha you'd see her?"

"About four. And I think I'll take my Chevy—the snow tires are better than on the van."

He nodded, scrunched out the remainder of his cigarette, and picked Thomaseen from her lap, turning him belly up and blowing on the fat beneath the fur to the waking cat's indignation. "Okay. Get yourself back here about six."

"Me—why?"

"Mary Ann and I have a surprise for you. It's your *birthday*, Muffin! It probably ain't been much yet, but we'll try to improve on it."

Eleanor said slowly, "You're right on both counts. It is my birthday. And it hasn't

430

been much, yet. But I had forgotten—I guess I was just trying to block it out."

"Well, we ain't forgot," he said gruffly, and smacked her towards the hook with her coat on it. "So get goin'. Take care on the highway. Come back here on six, pronto—and don't let Martha Logan stuff you full of cookies and truck. Mary Ann's bringing fried chicken and a cake."

I spoke the truth, she thought dismally, as she backed her Chevy out, the wipers laboring through snow, making triangles on the windshield. I have been blocking it out. That's the problem with being grown. Birthdays are a pain. A nuisance. And I've had more important things going on.

Such as repairing my life—which I've botched pretty well so far. The deaths I couldn't help—Bobby's, Julia's, Matt's, Benton's. That's a sign of age. When people around you start dying. You learn to deal with that—as best you can, because there's no choice unless you want to become a raving idiot.

But surviving those deaths by managing your own life—that's where I'm screwing up. Royally.

I didn't let Tony buy the shop. That was out of my hands.

I did let him put the damned ring on my finger—without even asking questions. Now that was stupid—there's no valid excuse for that.

I should be complimented. I suppose I am. To my knowledge Tony's never been married before. He hasn't found it—necessary—advantageous? Why does it seem advantageous to Tony to marry me?

He's buying my shop. He's employing me, which makes him privy to my knowledge, my expertise, my reputation—whatever it is.

Why go to the trouble of marrying me?

Well. The bottom line is, she said to herself grimly, heading across the south side of the almost deserted square towards the highway intersection, that we need to have a chat.

I've been reacting like a 1940 poop again. When the hell am I going to learn?

The kids were wending their way back across the street from the library, two by two, swinging bookbags laden with books, and surreptitiously snowballing each other. A faint, raucous singing drifted in through her window, "Over the river and through the woods, to grandmother's house we go . . ." She was smiling until she caught the next words, "The gang is all here, we're loaded with beer—"

Times do change.

Musing on this, she was well into the country between the white fields and the black and white bluffs before she noticed that she was close to being out of gas.

Drat—double drat. All the gas stations were in the opposite direction.

Oh, well. Didn't they say you had at least a couple of gallons left when the gauge said empty?

She'd make it.

The plows were out, already, so the highway was no problem, and Idetta Martin's home was only a mile out into the countryside, just before the bluffs descended to flat river bottom. A peak-roofed old farm house, it had two other cars parked at its gate when Eleanor pulled in. The reason was apparent when chubby little Idetta answered the door and Eleanor could see two card tables, occupied, beyond her in the warm living room.

"Canasta," said Idetta of the card players, ushering her inside. "Don't worry about your shoes. A little clean snow won't hurt this old carpet. Come on in the dining room, and I'll show you what I have in mind."

As Eleanor passed by, the players waved, one of them Wilma Williamson. Beyond, in the old fashioned eating area, a heavy claw-footed table adorned the center of the room, surrounded by six chairs, all showing loose spindles and worn seats.

"My tarnal boys!" said Idetta, shrugging. "I told Floyd, next time I was going to marry a midget. He said it might be simpler to sell the old stuff and buy something in industrial steel. So that's what I think I will do."

Eleanor nodded. She'd had experience, also, with oversized men leaning hard on chair legs, and didn't care to think about it. She bent, looked underneath. From that position she asked. "The sideboard, too?"

"Sure. And there is a china cupboard but my daughter has it. I think she'd sell if the price was right."

"It's solid walnut."

"That's what my mama always said. She bought the whole set from an old lady in town for twenty dollars. Of course, that was in 1937."

Eleanor straightened, rubbing her back absently. "You can do better than that!"

"I'd hope. With two boys in college and one graduating from high school in the spring, I need to do better than that. Can you handle it for me, hon? There's no one else I'd rather."

Eleanor hesitated. "I—I think so. With Julia gone, we will have a new owner—but I don't see any problem."

"A new owner? Not you? But I thought—" Then the lady colored, and went on, abashed, "I'm sorry. It's not my business. You are—staying around, aren't you?"

Eleanor smiled, a look she didn't feel. "At least long enough to sell your dining set. Let us know when you're ready. Hi, Wilma. It looks as if you're doing all right."

Wilma Williamson had laid down her cards and was rising from her chair. "Only lost three cents," she said cheerfully. "So far. Here, Idetta, I'm out. Go play your hand. I'll see Ellie to the door."

"Well—coffee, Ellie?"

"No, thanks. I'm sort of in a rush. We'll be in touch."

If she hadn't been, Wilma was, covertly edging her towards the living room entrance. When they were beyond earshot of the cheerful chatter, the older lady said

435

quietly, "I'm interfering. Be prepared if it's none of my business."

Eleanor shrugged, buttoning her coat back up, and prepared for some bit of gossip about Jill Bonford.

It was not that. It was not that, at all. Her seamed face turned carefully away from her card buddies, Wilma said, "That good-looking Italian friend of yours. Mondaine. Anthony Mondaine—Monetavich, if you want the truth, and a perfectly good name but not fancy enough I suppose. Anyway. Him."

Eleanor's throat tightened. "Okay."

"I—I'm almost ashamed, but I got to tell you. I overheard a phone conversation between him and somebody else. In Sicilian. That's why it caught my ear. In the cafe."

She was hesitating, twisting the paisley scarf around her neck.

Eleanor said quietly, "Okay. Go on."

"There was a lot of stuff. But the bottom line was—was that the person on the other end—John, I think your friend called him—"

Eleanor's face went rigid. "It could be John." She was the one twisting, now—her gloves, around and around her fingers. "Go on."

"This John—he was not to hire you under any circumstances—or he'd lose some deal he had to have. I'm not wrong. It was repeated. Twice. And, hon—I just thought maybe you ought to know. I've called twice, but you were always out, or something."

Wilma's lined face, her faded eyes behind the plastic-rimmed glasses were anxious. Concerned.

Almost blindly, Eleanor reached over and squeezed the old hand.

"You're right," she said. "I had been wondering. Now I know. Thanks, Wilma."

"It's okay. As long as I didn't do harm. I do hate gossiping for pleasure."

"No, no. I appreciate this. Was—was there anything else?"

"I don't know that. My girlfriend came out of the rest room and I had to go. He didn't see me. I do know he didn't. Up to now I'd—I'd kind of liked the man."

Eleanor was impelled to say it: "Tony has his good side."

"Doesn't sound like this was one of 'em."

"Except—he probably thinks so. Tony tends towards playing Jesus Christ some times."

"Or Julius Caesar."

That was astute. Never underrate an old lady, especially in her appraisal of the human race. Eleanor smiled again, holding back whatever she was feeling because she wasn't certain what it was—and opened the door. "Thanks, Wilma. I owe you one."

"I hope so. Tell that old rascal Ben hello for me."

"Will do. Bye, now."

"Bye."

The door closed. Eleanor plodded back across her own previous tracks in the snow, slid onto the cold car seat and started the engine. The act was blind.

Well. Now she knew. Tony had gotten to John Giametti. And God only knew who else.

Why was she suddenly so damned important to him?

He was not that damned important to her.

Nosing back out on to the highway, she waited for two trucks and a UPS van, then bumped across the drift of plowed snow into the proper lane, heading back into town.

Should everything come out in the open

when Jill was gone? Or should she hold this new piece to her chest—and wait?

For what? The axe to fall again?

He'd said she had a job, he'd say he'd pay her bills—and at this point in time the bastard was even figuring she'd marry him.

What the hell was going on?

She glanced up in the mirror and saw she hadn't turned into Elizabeth Taylor. Neither had she inherited money. Nor caught the man in any shady deal—least of all, that. Anthony Mondaine's reputation was as ethically correct as that of anyone in the business.

She just—didn't understand.

Oh, well. She'd have to think about it later. Next on the agenda was Martha Logan.

After two cups of coffee and a cascade of conversation from Martha, Eleanor stuffed into her bag, without looking at them, the packet of papers Matt's widow handed her. She edged her way toward the door. It was nearly six. Promising to visit again, and soon, she got into her car, waved at Martha peering out of a half-obscured window and let the engine warm a few moments. It was snowing harder and harder. What had been skiffs barely caught by the fir tree branches had turned to a burden of white, weighing them down.

Nosing the car into the street, she moved on around the corner and a half a block away.

Then she remembered about the gas, because the Chevy ran out of it.

"Damn!" she said in irritation. It was her fault. She knew it was her fault. She'd forgotten. Oh, well, she was only three houses away from home, where there were more sensible snow shoes and a telephone.

Able to bring the Chevy against the snow-choked curb, she pulled the keys, locked the doors and started on with huddled collar and thinly clad feet. Five minutes later, after stumbling across a plowed and frozen garden plot, penetrating two prickly hedges, falling over a buried trash can and almost losing one silly shoe in a swirling snowdrift, she arrived puffing at her own kitchen door.

Or Tony's. Whoever. At that moment, she didn't care about semantics, only the chance to sit down.

The surge of heat as she opened the door was as welcome as a benediction. Her feet and ears felt frozen. Her heart was thumping painfully against her ribcage.

Old ladies can't hack that sort of travel, she thought grimly, and sat down on a bentwood chair to get her breath back. She was panting in harsh gasps and the melting snow began to run down her nose from her wet hair. Sticking soaked shoes straight out in front, she eyed them in dismay. Opera pumps were dandy for chic, but not worth a damn for warmth. She should have come home first and changed—but when recently had she done anything logical?

Shucking off the shoes, she massaged her cold, saturated feet with a chilly hand— a sort of draw, and not really advancing the cause of warmth. She'd better go upstairs and get dry stuff on, then call the shop. Ben would be worrying.

She padded wearily across to the hall, expecting to find it wrapped in winter gloom as snow obscured the windows.

To her surprise the chandelier was shining brightly.

Well. Jill, probably, not bothering to turn it off.

Well, again. She had words for Jill. Hopefully, they were "Bye-bye."

441

Dripping on the cold tile, she dialed the shop.

She was rewarded by silence.

She dialed again.

Zip.

Damn. The lines were down.

She should have remembered: they always went down in a deep snow, clear to the edge of the county where the new ones were underground.

She'd have to walk, and she'd better hurry, or Ben would have out the county cops looking for her in every snowdrift.

She squished up the stairs, turned on the lamp in her room, pulled the drapery against the gloom of the spectral pine trees changed into ghost dancers by the wind and the fuzzy glow of the alley pole light. Sitting on the edge of the bed, she eased off the wet pantyhose and tugged on thick ski socks. This was not going to be a night for glamour; it was going to be a night for warmth.

She discarded the red wool number for slacks and a thick, heavy-knit pullover, tugged on winter boots and thought, I'd better pack a bag. I may not get back here tonight.

That was not uncommon. Everyone had

stayed the night at the shop for one reason or another—varnish that had to be reapplied every three hours, bad weather making the heat fluctuate—hard on old furniture—too much company in the beds at home. There was a fairly comfortable cot in the storeroom, and plenty of quilts.

Her breath back, and warm again, Eleanor laid her down coat near the heat to dry and pulled a heavy, hooded windbreaker from her closet. That should do it—except she'd left her nightie in the bathroom when she'd showered that morning.

As she went out into the hall, it occurred to her that the hall light had been on, also. And burning all day, of course. Drat.

Putting her bag by the door, she thought, What else am I forgetting?

She ran her eye over her bedroom, tabulating articles in her mind—mundane things, like clean lingerie, clothes for tomorrow, makeup case—an "old lady" better have her makeup case—extra shoes, robe—

All there. But—something was amiss. Something was just touching her consciousness, lightly, like a blowing web. What was it?

She stared, retabulating.

Tillie!

The space on her night table was empty.

Who in the world—and to be just, who in their right mind—would take a purple cow?

And she knew—Jill.

Jill—who disdained a Queen Anne chair, who didn't understand the appeal of a Belter suite, who laughed at Louis Tiffany—Jill would like a purple cow.

But it wasn't her purple cow, although she might have had at one time a reason to think so.

It was Eleanor's purple cow.

They had better get that straight immediately.

In the meantime, where would Jill be likely to have absconded with poor Tillie?

Logically—Jill's room.

Then we'll see, said Eleanor righteously to herself, as she clomped down the hall and majestically threw open the door.

It was a mistake. She should have thought it through.

Too late.

As the light from the hall poured across the Empire bed, it became patently obvious that the room was occupied. When Tony Mondaine had said that he and Jill were going to celebrate largely, he hadn't specified in what mode.

Specification was no longer necessity.

Two very naked bodies, attempting simultaneously to sit upright resulted in a wild thrashing tangle of arms and legs. Jill squeaked in fright. Tony thundered, "What the hell—"

The light, while laving lovingly each curve, muscle, and hollow of two bare forms, also shone on the glazed purple flank of a ceramic cow.

"Mine, I believe," said Eleanor pleasantly.

Tucking Tillie beneath one arm, she went back out, pausing to close the door gently behind her.

Her last glimpse was of Jill's mouth open like that of a fish, and a look of total consternation on Tony Mondaine's face.

I didn't even say excuse me, she thought, going back down the stairs. Where *are* my manners?

She was laughing all the way out the kitchen door.

She had slogged, huffing and puffing, halfway to the shop before she realized she'd never retrieved her nightie.

Oh, well. She'd find something.

Twenty-three

It was after six, and traffic had virtually stopped on the small city square. The streetlights were snow-laden lollipops, and the face of the courthouse clock, high overhead, shone like a fuzzy moon through the unceasing, silent white curtain.

Leaving a trail behind her like an intrepid Arctic explorer, Eleanor slogged along doggedly, her head down, carrying her small bag in one hand, Tillie in the other.

A slow crunching behind her turned out to be a police car; Don stuck his head out, called, "Hey—need a ride?"

She shook her head, dislodging a tiny avalanche of snow. "No, thanks. I'm just going to the shop. Then I'm going to stay there."

"I would. Everything seems to be drifting in."

"Are all the phone lines down?"

"Pretty much. Expecting a call?"

"No, it's just a nuisance."

"Tell me," he answered grimly, withdrew his head, and drove on ahead slowly.

Eleanor decided against the windy deepfreeze of the drifting alley, used her key, opened the front door and stepped inside over a twelve-inch drift of snow.

There were lights in the back, casting mellow shadows on the rattan set that had replaced the Belter. She called, cheerfully, "Here I am!" and as she pulled off her boots, shaking them out on the rope mat, her warming nose smelled fried chicken and fresh coffee.

Ben appeared, a black silhouette against the light.

"Where the hell you been?"

"Walking."

"Walking!"

"Have you been out recently? Driving is not too swift just now. Also the lines are down."

"I know that; I've been trying to find you."

He met her halfway, took her bag and

wet boots, glanced at the purple thing beneath her arm. "What's that?"

"Not what—who," said Eleanor. As they entered the warm, cozy untidiness of the workroom, she held up the ceramic creation. "This is Tillie. Tillie, meet Ben. And Mary Ann. And Mary Ann's husband, over there behind the chicken leg, Leonard."

Leonard waved the chicken leg, mumbled, "Hi."

"Just like a kid," said Mary Ann, of her husband. She was opening a package of paper napkins with party hats printed on them. "Couldn't wait. Starving to death. My good land. Hi, Tillie. You're cute."

"What she does," said Eleanor, "is grow on you."

"I hope not," said Ben, pulling the captain's chair around to the makeshift table. Ben's tastes, after thirty years with Julia Bonford, were pretty pristine. "Let's eat. It's past my suppertime."

The food was picnic style, topped by a three-layer German chocolate cake, and very good champagne.

"Of course you know," Eleanor said, wiping crumbs from her sweater, "that I am going to gain back all the fat I lost in the hospital."

"Do you good," answered Mary Ann crisply. "Men only like chicken bones on a chicken. Are you set on staying here, Ellie? Len and I can get you home."

"I'm set," said Eleanor. "And you'd better go. It's really deep out there. Thank you for the dinner and the presents."

Mary Ann nodded approvingly at the Avon scent bottle on the paisley scarf. Her mom had always said that a good scarf was always welcome. "You'd better come, too, Ben. We'll drop you off."

"Go warm up the car," said Ben crisply. "I got something to give Ellie in private."

After they'd gone on a chill blast of air, he reached deep under a drawer in his Welsh dresser. Eleanor, sitting on the Chinese garden stool, saw him carefully draw out a flat package smaller than a poster and wrapped in brown paper.

"Had 'er taped up there," he said, grunting. "There we go. She's clear."

In puzzlement, Eleanor said, "Taped up there? Hidden? Why, Ben?"

Ben shrugged. It was of no consequence, now. "Too damned many nosy people," he said and didn't specify. "Here. Open." Then he added, almost shyly, "It's from Julia and me."

449

Her fingers faltered on the knotted cord. Silently he got out his big old clasp knife, cut the knots for her. She said, "Julia?"

"Before she died. Got it from Mondaine's place. Meant to give it on your birthday. I couldn't ruin that. Don't cry, damn it, or I will."

Brushing off the wet with the back of her hand, Eleanor gently removed the brown wrapping. Inside was a painting simply framed in dark wood. It showed a woman and a cat curled on a window seat. It was mostly in blue. It was signed in the corner: "Picasso."

Eleanor sucked in her breath, tears dried in wonder. She started, "But where—"

Ben cut her off. "Don't ask," he said brusquely. "Just know she wanted it for you."

"It's—beautiful. I love it. I'll keep it forever."

She stood the painting up on the rolltop desk, leaning against the cluttered pigeonholes, went back to her porcelain garden seat, looked at it with misty eyes.

There was a minimum of brushstrokes. It was more illusion than depiction. Yet there came from it a sense of serenity, of somnolent repose.

Eleanor laughed, said softly, "It might even be Thomaseen," she said. There was just a hint of stripe down the feline spine.

"Not likely," said Ben. He was shrugging into his heavy old brush coat.

She got up, went to the old man, put her arms around his neck and kissed him. "Thank you."

He hugged her, kissing her cheek in return. "You're like mine, you know," he said in a rare moment of affection, "although I never had none. Her and me—we both like to see you happy."

Eleanor answered gently. "And you're like mine. I love you. Good night."

She locked the door behind him, heard the scrunching of tires as they drove away. Thomaseen appeared, and wove a sinuous rope about her ankles. She picked him up, and buried wet eyes in his fur.

But it was a momentary lapse. After a minute, she released him per request, and he disappeared into the showroom, tail high, bound for some secret place of repose.

It was, in fact, time for her to seek her own.

She sighed, rubbing the back of her neck, and knowing she was very tired. It had been quite a day, all in all.

She turned down the blanket on the cot in the small storeroom, put her bag on a handy packing crate, the overnight case beside it. Hauling out toothbrush, paste, and cleansing cream, she headed for the minuscule bathroom.

Eyeing the face in the mirror through toothpaste flecks she said soberly, "Happy birthday. Shall we try for a few more? Or should we be satisfied with just getting some sleep tonight?"

The wind had started to whistle around the corners of the building, hitting the south wall in gusts, and banging at a loose windowframe. Eleanor shivered, turned out the light and padded on cold, stockinged feet back through the workroom. She stopped, looked at the Picasso, touched it gently with one hand. Bless Julia. Bless Ben.

She turned that light off, and guided by the square of illumination through the doorway went back into the storeroom. It was an interior cubbyhole and quite warm, but she shivered again as she stripped down, reached into her bag, then stopped.

Damn. She'd forgotten. What was there to wear?

It was a bit too much of a public place for sleeping in the altogether.

She turned, surveyed the packing crates, the shelves, full of unregenerated artifacts and ancient kitchen things, the end wall nail-studded and hung with elderly farm tools, Ben's varnish-stiffened shopcoat, her own painty Sherpa, a frayed sweater of Julia's—and a blue shirt. There we go, she thought, that will do nicely. I do thank you, Ben for leaving me a shirt.

But when she put it on, she knew: it wasn't Ben's. The tails came below her knees, the shirtsleeves hung far below her fingertips, and the collar was for her an abyss.

Oh God. Benton's. Benton's blue shirt.

She could not take it off. She could not physically take it off; the soft, well-washed cotton clung to her bare skin, wrapping it, and as she buried her nose in the collar, the smell of him, real or not, came up to her in waves of pain and joy. Surely—surely an unhappy woman, on her birthday was entitled to one fantasy.

No, she wasn't. She couldn't afford a fantasy. Things were too critical; she needed all her wits bright and sharp, not lulled by sweet, betraying dreams about a dead man. Say it, Eleanor: dead.

She needn't take off the shirt. She could simply administer to herself a counterdrug, an antidote to the stultifying lure of pretense. And further, she knew just the one.

She turned to the packing crate by her bed, pawed with incurious eyes passed the legal envelope Martha had given her, and found the flat velvet box. She opened it. She put the magnificent ring from Tony on her finger.

That should do it.

She slid into bed, pulling the covers up, saying, This is just a shirt, any shirt, keeping me warm. She thrust beyond the covers a bare arm, emerging from six inches of accordioned sleeve, moved the fingers, made the ring flash and sparkle in the light from the overhead fixture.

A beautiful ring.

Promising what?

More sham, more pretense. You hypocrite! What's the difference between dreaming about Benton and accepting a ring from a man you don't even trust?

Cold, hard sense, you loony.

Survival. Until you learn the new rules. And—perhaps—get even. Nonetheless, she pulled the bare arm back beneath the blankets, forced herself to shut her eyes. Sleep, damn you. Morning will come fast enough, and an old lady needs her rest.

Miraculously, she did sleep. Perhaps the champagne did it, or the fatigue of slogging block after block through heavy snow, or a combination of both. But she drifted away and sank deeper and deeper through black velvet clouds.

Yet, human reason cannot always control human longing. She did dream. She dreamed of Benton—Benton in his pig jacket and tractor cap, coming in through the door, stamping snow from his boots, Benton saying, "Charlie, damn it, I'm tired, too. Move over!"

Charlie.

Charlie? Why was he calling her "Charlie"?

Her eyes popped open. And of course, it was a dream. She was in the little storeroom, covered with blankets to her ears, the wind whining a cold song outside, and the light from the workshop putting a glassy shine on Ben's varnishing coat.

With a small, choked sound of utter

desolation, she shut her eyes again, and burrowed like a mole, seeking total forget-fulness. Tears began to trickle, wetting the shirt, making small damp spots on the pillow.

Damn.

One persistent needle pricked her mind, got her sodden attention: I thought I turned off the workshop light.

Well, you didn't, you dipstick. You're such a disgusting puddle of self-pity you don't know what you did.

But she had turned it off. She remembered being guided into this room by the light shining through the door.

Yet it was on, again.

Hazily, she forced herself to repeat the phrase, trying for rationale—and the truth hit.

Someone else was in the workshop!

Ben. Of course. He hadn't been able to make it home.

She started to call out. Then she stopped.

What if it wasn't Ben? What if it was Tony? Tony, looking for her?

He had a key. She knew from the morning's experience that he must have a key. Okay. All right.

But the last thing she wanted was to have Tony find her. Here. In bed.

Yet, he could have come looking. Her finding him in bed with Jill might have worried him—although probably it was not the discovery but her calm reaction that would have concerned Tony Mondaine, or pricked his vanity—which with Tony was possibly synonymous with heart.

Still, there was no noise from the workshop, nothing but the chilly sign of the wind, and that banging windowframe.

Yes there was.

She'd just heard something—a rustling, a movement.

Thomaseen. Of course. It was Thomaseen.

But Thomaseen does not turn on lights.

Then it happened. Something large came between her rigid gaze and the light in the workroom door. Something large, but rather low to the floor. It had furry ears and sad, brown velvet eyes. It looked at her and said wuff! in recognition, and came padding silently across the room.

It was a dream, after all.

In her dream she whispered, "Charlie." She put her arms around the white fur ruff, buried her wet face in the soft dog shoulder, felt a rough tongue lick the salty tears.

Then a thought hit her, like a bolt of lightning, a shaft of fire: Benton was dead—but no one had said Charlie was.

If this was real—if this was not a dream—where had Charlie come from?

Slowly, slowly, her heart pounding against her ribs like a wild thing in a cage, beating its wings, she swung her bare feet to the cold floor. She stood up, loosing herself from the dog, who looked at her questioningly. She walked as if in a trance towards the workroom.

Behind her, the Saint Bernard said, again, wuff. This time it was not recognition but resignation.

She stopped, looked around.

Charlie had already hopped up on her bed, was turning in a circle. As she stared, he flopped, put his head on his paws, closed his eyes.

Charlie the opportunist.

It was no dream. He was real.

Then—if Charlie was real—

Oh dear God, she said, and ran towards the door.

This time it was not slowly. This time her feet had wings.

Twenty-four

Between the rolltop desk and the dresser, a plaid sleeping bag was laid on the floor. On that was another sleeping bag, spread for a blanket. Between those was a very large, wide lump. On the back of the captain's chair were hung a wool shirt and a canvas hunting coat, melting snow into a puddle beneath the rungs. Heavy, wet, unlaced boots stood like tired soldiers by the door.

But Eleanor saw little of that—only the lump, with one bare, enormous, Bluto arm outside the cover, pillowing a heap of thick, white hair.

She fell to her knees, reaching out gently, so gently, unwilling to tear the fabric of this moment lest it not be true. Tears were running silently down her cheeks; they fell on the bared shoulder and with that shaking hand she wiped them away, not wanting to wake him yet, only to fill her soul with the ecstasy of seeing, of feeling, of watching him breathe, of thinking, dear God, the miracle of breathing, of life—

But he felt her touch. His eyes flashed open, he turned, rearing up on one elbow, he knew her and he said in harsh anger, "Where the hell have you been?"

She gasped—yet, all his anxiety, his tearing concern, his hungry longing were vented in that furious outburst. He reached out, clutched her to him, rocking her against his chest, saying brokenly against her warm throat, "I couldn't find you—your car wasn't at the house and it wasn't here and I didn't know where else to look, where else to go—damn it, woman, why can't you stay put?"

If he only knew, she was "put," she would stay, for ever and ever, here inside his arms, burrowing down under the spread sleeping bag to thrust herself against his long body, clinging like a vine to a tree.

He was saying between kisses, between hungry sweeps of his mouth, "Oh, my darling, my darling, I love you, I've missed you, I've been going through hellfire, not knowing—"

Now wasn't the time for her to ask questions, to recriminate—only to accept the love that he was pouring out through his husky voice, his mouth, the hungry press of his body against her body, to take that love, to give it back.

Neither was he thinking now of anything else but that they were together, a pair, a union. Against the bare velvet of her throat he said thickly, "We must have a thing about floors," and she answered softly, "Floors are not so bad," at the same time moving to twine their seeking bodies, raising to put her mouth against his hair and his mouth against the soft, swelling desire of her breasts, offering their sweetness to his kisses. They came, and she caught her breath at the loveliness, felt more than heard the tear of buttonholes as he ripped open the shirt, his own breath catching convulsively at the bare, warm surge of her satin thighs against his. Her one cogent thought was, How different it is with love, how sweet, before she was swept into the thrusting kingdom of paradise, then slipped gently down, down, all too soon into the warm, lapping waters of repletion.

He had not loosed her, had not let her go, was holding her as closely to his long, hard body as he had in his undeniable, unwavering passion. Had she wanted to deny, to divert, she could have not, so totally had been the sweep of her own passion to meet him. She was content to lie along the warm length of him, feel the silk mat of his chest beneath her cheek, hear the buried thudding of his heart as it slowed, feel his hand still stroking her breasts but now with gentle love, with caring.

In her ear, so softly she almost didn't hear, he said, "I'm sorry."

Languorously, she murmured, "I'm not. Why should you be?"

He kissed her ear, and went on into it, "No, no—not sorry we made love—never sorry for that, you precious idiot—but I'm a conservative guy, I wanted to work slowly, in a proper bed, enjoying every inch of you, every minute—and now look at us—"

She raised her head, said to his chin, "Is it all over? Can't we improve the pace with practice?"

And he laughed. He said, muffled against her hair, "You'd better believe it." He also said, "God, I love you. I can't believe how I love you. Me, the unbeliever."

She clung, and in the very, precious feel of him alive and breathing against her, she remembered. She said, "They told us you were dead."

"I know that now. But I didn't, then. I had no idea—and couldn't have done anything if I'd had, we were so isolated."

"In the plane?"

"I was never in the plane. Those poor guys are dead—no question. You see—" Above her head he squinted his eyes painfully, trying to put it in proper order. "You see, babe, our two guides ate their own chow, not ours. They came down with food poisoning. So Ivan and I—he's the delegation secretary—we put the guides on the plane in our seats, and sat tight, waiting for them to come back for us. But they didn't. They didn't come. And it began to snow—God, it snowed. To make things worse, we were running out of supplies. So we decided to walk out. We did, too. I'm not too bad on a trek, and Ivan's no softie—he's from the steppes where it snows like hell. We didn't hurry—we had enough food for the trip, and hurrying can be as fatal as anything else. But—but, sweetheart, we had no idea we were supposed to be dead."

He shifted her on his arm, kissed her ear. Softly he added, "Every night, bedded down on the trail, I thought of you. I planned—God, I planned—like I said, a bed, warm sheets, soft music—"

She kissed his chin. "We've covered that. Go on."

"I planned what I was going to do—take that option from the government, put the money down on the Crane farm, build a house up there, let you have your antique shop—"

Then he felt her stiffen. He said, "What? What is it? Did I say something wrong?"

She swallowed, back on earth, remembering. She said in a small, painful voice, "Jill's here."

"Jill? My ex-wife? Here?"

"She's not your ex-wife."

He growled, "The hell she isn't," but Eleanor didn't hear she was so full of remembering.

"Bent, it's been awful. She's been running the shop into the ground, she's sold the Belter and tried to have a sale and demanding cash for everything and losing us customers and being a total bitch—"

"That, she does well," he interspersed calmly. "For the rest, back up. Number one: she *is* my ex. I don't care what bill of goods she's sold you. I filed before I ever came here. The final papers were at my lawyer's office—I saw them before I found the lines down and plowed snow to my kazoo getting over here. So if I saw them, she's seen them."

Eleanor caught her breath, remembering the deputy sheriff asked for Jill. Good God. He was right. She had seen them. She'd known. That was the mad push for cash—to rip them off and be gone before they found out.

He was saying, "And as for the shop— that I don't understand. What had she to say about the shop?"

"She was your heir. She owned it."

"In a pig's eye. With apologies to my livelihood. What the hell has Matt Logan been doing, letting such nonsense go on. You need a new lawyer, babe."

It was her turn to twist, rise up on one elbow, creating a very pretty view of rounded lovelies almost inside a torn shirt. He bent his head, to kiss them, and was annoyed at having one hand in his hair twisting, raising his face to hers.

Her eyes were dark blue, her brows

drawn. And she was thinner; he'd been too busy to notice that, before.

Eleanor said to him, "Matt's dead. He's been dead for weeks. He had a heart attack the night you left."

Benton answered, deep in his chest, "Oh Christ. Then I suppose you didn't know that, either. But—I filled out the papers, signed them, had them notarized and took them back to him. He stood right there in his pajamas and put them on his desk to give to his partner next day. What happened? Doesn't anyone in this town read, don't they look?"

Through his angry spate of words she thrust her own: "What didn't I know?"

"That I'd stopped by his house—that we'd made out the papers saying you were my full partner, that in case of my death, you owned the place!"

Her face was stony, a mask of anguish.

He sat up, catching her back into his arms, rocking her, saying, "Poor darling, poor baby, what a mess, what hell you have been through. The shop is yours, Eleanor, it's always been yours—I couldn't go off and leave you hanging—"

"Then why didn't you tell me?"

"Because I—"

Then he stopped. Why hadn't he?

No good reasons—only selfish ones, childish ones.

"I don't know," he said painfully. "I doubted, I guess. You. Me. I'd fallen for you so fast—I guess I couldn't believe it was all right—I had to have an ace, hold something back."

And no one—no one in his right mind—could have ever thought of Matt dying, of Benton being reported dead, of Jill Bonford coming, trying to work a quick scam of her own.

And my God, Eleanor thought, Benton's alive, he's here, I'm in his arms and he loves me. What is anger against that? Nothing in this world can hurt me, now.

She said softly, "It will be all right, now. It has to be."

He kissed her then—differently, softly, and turned her face against his chest, put his chin on her soft ashy hair, and they sat in silence for a few moments, content. Together.

"Where's Charlie?"

"In my bed."

Benton laughed. "You'll have to admit he has the right idea."

Rubbing his cheek against her hair, his

eyes slowly circled the workroom. "I see the Welsh dresser isn't finished."

"Yes, it is. Ben just didn't want Jill to sell it."

"Ouch. Where did the painting come from?"

"From Ben and Julia. Before she died, but I just got it. It's a Picasso."

"I've seen it before. Recently."

"You couldn't have seen it. I said—I just got it. Before that, it was hidden under Ben's dresser since before Julia died. And they bought it from Tony—and I doubt very much, darling, that you've been in Tony's shop."

"You're right." But the crease stayed between thick brows. "A genuine Picasso?"

"Of course." She twisted, looked up at him, a little wounded, and found him scowling. "Whatever you may think of Tony, Bent, he doesn't deal in reproductions."

Benton moved his jaw from side to side and answered thoughtfully, "Would you like to bet?"

"Benton—don't be petty."

"Petty, hell, my pretty chick. Do you remember my saying that in Russia I stayed at this guy's dacha in the country? And that he had a trove of paintings swiped during the last days of World War II?"

"Yes, but—"

"No buts. Facts. Your Picasso, baby, hung on the wall at the foot of my bed and I looked at it for three days." He turned his head, shut his eyes. "Check me out. There are seven stripes on the cat. Right? And a blur in the upper corner that might be drapery? And just to the left of his signature three tiny straight lines like—like whiskers on a mouse."

She didn't answer. He pursued it: "Right?"

Her lips were stiff. She made herself answer, "Right."

He opened his eyes, looked at her. Her face was such a mask of pain that he was swept with remorse and he said, "Oh Eleanor, oh baby—I'm sorry. I'm an idiot. I should have kept my damned mouth shut."

She made herself shake her head—so hard the ashy hair swung against her pale cheek.

She said in a strangled voice, "No. No, you shouldn't have. It's just that—that in things like this I trusted him. Everyone trusted him. His entire enormous reputation as an antiquarian is built on people's absolute trust. I—I just don't understand."

He sighed, gritted his teeth. "I'm not wrong. I almost wish I could say I was. I'm not."

"But—why?"

She was so distressed, so appalled. Gently he said, "They say every man has his price."

"Not Tony—I mean—it's so needless. Risking his entire career on a fake. Benton, if this is true, it could ruin him. I could ruin him—right now!"

Then it hit her. He saw it hit her; she started backward as though from a physical blow and her face went white.

And she whispered from an almost paralyzed throat, "Oh God, that's it!"

That's why he'd needed her. That was why he'd turned up at odd hours, made friends with people he'd heretofore disdained, kissed her with warm lips that should have been cold because he hadn't just come inside—he'd been here, searching the shop when she came in. That was why he'd talked Picasso, knowing her favorite painter was Winslow Homer. That's why he was buying the shop—and trying to buy her.

Torn savagely between pity and anger, Eleanor shut her eyes against the horror, putting both hands up to hide her shocked face.

Then she heard Benton's voice—heard it thick with fury, heavy with black rage.

He was saying, "What the hell is that ring?"

Twenty-five

There was guilt in the very way she snatched the hand out of sight. It was a primitive response—but also the wrong one.

His eyes were like amber coals. His mouth was grim. "It's Mondaine's ring, isn't it?"

She had to answer. She had to answer truthfully. She put the hand back out. "Yes, it is. But please—so many things have gone on since you left—"

"I'll tell the world."

"Benton, listen!"

"Listen, hell! You knew I didn't like that bastard. You knew how I felt about him."

"But you were dead. And you have no idea how it has been. Be fair."

"Fair, hell! I'm not feeling fair. I suppose you've been going to bed with him, too."

The blood drained from her face again, leaving it waxy. Slowly she got to her knees, then to her feet, clutching the tattered front of the blue shirt about her against the cool air.

She said in a deathly quiet voice, "I'll not even dignify that with an answer. Good night, Benton."

There was nowhere for her to go but the showroom. That damned dog was on her cot, and she certainly wasn't going to curl up in the captain's chair with a shirt that no longer buttoned. Not in front of—of Bluto. She'd been seduced; she had no wish to be raped.

Burned in her mind was the picture of Benton, half out of the covers, the muscles bulging on one arm from supporting his huge frame, his eyes like green stones in a basilisk's face.

Some primordial part of her brain repeated shakily, "Basilisk: a huge, mythical lizard whose gaze was fatal."

Bingo.

Her cold bare feet took her into the dark of the silent showroom. Far at the front, street lights, filtering in the windows through falling snow made the place a gnome cave, the still shadows long and strange. Her feet blundered on the exquisite softness of an Oriental runner placed where it hadn't been before. She stumbled, caught at the reedy arm of the rattan sofa, and, recognizing it, thought drearily, That will do.

Fumbling, she found one of the folded quilts displayed on a blanket rack, wrapped it around her, and lay down on the cold chintz of the sofa, bare arm beneath her head, and knees bent for the hope of warmth against her body. Her teeth were chattering; she gritted them against the chatter, squeezed her eyes shut. Not that there were tears. There were no tears. There are hurts too deep for crying.

The coverlet smelled faintly of mothballs, and the tiny stitches ridged the pattern against her cheek. She wondered painfully if, a hundred years ago, the Amish quiltmaker had sewn her own woman's agonies into her work because times change—but a woman's heart does not. It was the same hurt, century after century, and the name of the hurt was *man*.

It's a cheap shot, God. I hope You're listening. Not that you'll change anything because I understand that it's part of Your Plan. But it's still a cheap shot, and I'd like to think You're a little ashamed, that You might see fit to help us change it just even a fraction.

But I suppose not. Since after all, You're a Man.

There was no sound from the workroom. Not even a rustle. Desperately she tried to set her mind ahead, on the morning, on what she would have to deal with in the cold light of day.

Those papers from Matt he'd talked about—that must be the envelope Martha had handed her, that were stuck right now inside her handbag. Why hadn't she looked at them?

But—what good would it have done if she had looked? The shop wouldn't be Jill's, but it wouldn't be hers, either.

The shop was not Jill Bonford's. That was a positive. There was no question about Benton's attitude towards Jill. So Tony had been wasting his charm—although she was certain he hadn't minded too much.

But—neither was it going to be Tony's—which was going to come as an unpleasant surprise to him. Among other unpleasant surprises.

And now she was really out of a job.

Again.

Like it or lump it, Marvin Coles, here I come.

Then there was the pseudo Picasso. She couldn't see herself using it against Tony just for a job. Julia had taught her more class than that. No, the Picasso was strictly Tony's problem.

As it had been for some time, she thought, but with very little sympathy.

And the memory of Tony in bed with Jill caught her achingly in the memory of Benton's warm, hungry body against hers and she had to shut that feeling off, crush it, smother it, dirty it if need be—or she knew without a doubt, that she'd find herself running back into that workroom, saying whatever he wished, anything to be in his arms again.

She wouldn't.

She was shaking—shaking from the cold, and from anguish. The rattan couch creaked in a tiny rhythm, and her jaws ached with the effort of clamping them shut, making no noise.

Suddenly, delicate paws lit on her feet,

as Thomaseen descended with light precision from somewhere above. He paced the ridge of her curved body, put his furry, whiskered face against her cheek and made a questioning meow.

She opened the quilt, let him inside. He snuggled against her casually and she wrapped her cold arms around his lovely, rumbling, warm substance.

Dimly, as from a far country, the courthouse clock struck three.

An eternity until morning. If morning ever came. If she survived until morning without relapsing again into double pneumonia. She realized the mortality chart on broken hearts was very low.

A sudden, familiar smell touched her nose: smoke.

Benton was smoking.

So he was awake, too.

Helplessly she remembered another time, in another place when he'd appeared before her, when he'd said, "We have to talk. Put on a lot of clothes."

But not this time. This time he wouldn't come. This time was different. He was too obtuse to know he'd been wrong. And she was too proud to tell him.

She had to be proud. There was nothing else left.

Footsteps.

He was pacing.

Garbled words, impatient words. Charlie had appeared and requested to be let out.

She felt the cold draft, even in the darkened showroom. She distinctly heard the roar, "Hurry up, damn it!"

More pacing.

Then, silence again.

Her very ears hurt with listening.

With sudden anger, she put her head beneath the covers, against Thomaseen's warm fur. Good God. She was acting like a little kid waiting for Santa Claus.

A hurt little kid—hoping there was one, after all.

Well, sorry, kid. There isn't.

Despite the covers, she could hear other noises now—boots clumping. Clothes rustling.

He was getting dressed. Why?

When the door opened and shut for the second time, then she knew why. He was going.

He was, in fact, gone.

She thought she heard the sound of a

478

pickup truck starting. She wasn't certain. It didn't matter. Not any more.

She was alone again. That's what mattered.

The clock struck four. Then five.

Outside, the wind had dropped, the snow was noiseless, and the shop seemed wrapped in a thick, smothering downlike shell. She was in a complete isolation, cut off from the rest of the world, from the people in it snug in their own homes with the warm bodies of their loved ones beside them.

She was huddled on a hard rattan couch in a shadowy showroom with a twenty-pound tomcat who snored.

She didn't deserve this. She really didn't. She'd done nothing wrong. So where the hell was her own sense of worth, her own fierce spirit of independence?

Damn it to hell! She'd survived Bobby's death and Julia's death—and she did have something left—the rest of her life.

So she might as well get on with it.

She swung her bare feet to the chill softness of the Kirman runner, stood up. With the old quilt wrapped about her and Thomaseen held, a furry muff, beneath her chin, she padded back into the warmer, still brightly lighted workshop.

The sleeping bags were gone. The rough old wooden floor was wet where the boots had stood. There was a smell of smoke in the air, and the ashtray was jammed with butts half-smoked, squashed, bent out of shape.

All right. She had known he was gone— gone in the total sense of the term this time. Even though he might again stand before her, thought they might speak civilized words in a businesslike manner.

What *hell* life would be with a man who could not listen. She didn't need that.

She already had problems enough.

So let him tidy up his own affairs. He might even—and an ironic smile touched her lips—still sell to Tony. If Tony still wanted the place.

As for her part in it, she reached for her bag and scrabbled inside for what she knew now were partnership papers. She'd leave them on the desk, take him off the hook.

It was then she noticed the envelope propped against the glowing blues of the fake Picasso. She picked it up, helpless to stop the beating of her stupid heart. She read the scrawl: "Tell your boyfriend that whoever did this copy for him forgot the line under the signature. On the painting in the dacha the line was there."

A sound very like a sob escaped her helpless lips. Thomaseen raised his head from her shoulder and crossly said, meow.

Realizing she'd squeezed him, she forced herself to relax.

Coffee. She'd make some coffee, then get dressed. Ben would come in about six-thirty. She'd tell him Benton was back. He'd be delighted. Life did go on.

In some form, or other.

The blast of cold air struck her like a physical blow. She swung around, clutching the quilt.

The door had opened with a crunch of snow. Benton stood in it, behind his knees a sad-eyed Saint Bernard.

Instantly Thomaseen turned from being sleepy cat to posing in armed defense. With one bunching of velvet-clad muscle he scrambled from Eleanor's arms to the desk, and from there in an elegant parabola to the top of the dresser where he crouched, glow-eyed, and hissing like a deflating balloon.

Charlie glanced behind him at the black

and white cold of early dawn, chose the lesser of two evils. Keeping to the opposite wall, with a wary eye upward, he padded around to the small storeroom door and disappeared. There came the sound of the cot creaking, and a canine sigh. On the dresser top Thomaseen relaxed also, wrapped himself into a tidy package by his tail and went back to sleep.

Below him, neither of the two humans had paid any attention.

A statue with tousled, ashy hair, clutched in an old double-wedding-ring quilt—Eleanor could not move, only look.

Benton kicked the snow-blocked door shut again, and turned, leaning against it with arms locked across his chest in his most Bluto-like stance.

For at least thirty seconds—a century, an eon—no one said a word.

Benton was, himself, a snowman. His heavy pants were caked to the knees, the laces of his boots impacted. Snow ridged his shoulders and domed his red tractor cap where already it was melting and dripping in silent runnels down his hair and his back to the floor. There was the glint of a morning beard on a very tired and very sober face.

Quietly he said, "I've been out trying to bring myself into the twentieth century."

She didn't answer and didn't move. Clutching the finely stitched old quilt about her, she only looked; and her blue eyes were almost black with a nameless something—something she couldn't define, something he did not yet hope to see.

He took an enormous breath, his chest rising and falling, and the big arms with it. Drip, drip went the melting snow into pools around his boots.

In the same careful voice he went on, "You were right, you know. What I had the—the brass to ask should not have been dignified with an answer."

She opened her mouth. He shook his head, making cold water droplets fly, cutting her off. "No. Hear me out. Listen, while I have it all straight in my mind. Okay?"

Hardly waiting for her nod, he went on in the same painful, almost husky voice, "Eleanor, I'm a country man. A farmer. That won't change. It can't. It's too much a part of me. But what can change—what, blessed God, I will try so very hard to change—is my country attitude. I was raised on the old double standard that no

483

matter what howling around a man does, he's still entitled to—to exclusive rights from his woman. I know that's not fair. I accept that it's not fair. I apologize."

"Benton—"

"Wait, damn it! I'm not finished. I spent two hours tramping around in snow, working this thing out, and I'm going to say it!"

He was almost roaring at her. But suddenly she didn't care if he was roaring.

He went on, "I'll make you a promise, Eleanor Wright. If tonight was the beginning of something good for you and me— no matter what comes of it—it's a new book. Page one. But not just for me. For both of us. Can you promise that?"

She barely made her lips move they were shaking so. But he heard the whisper. "I promise."

"I think I love you."

"I think I love you."

He made a soft sound, deep in his chest. He said, "If you are not sure, then you'd better hang on to that damned quilt."

She dropped the quilt.

He caught his breath sharply, looking at her standing beneath the overhead light, the quilt in a puddle at her feet, his tattered shirt barely on her white shoulders, fastened by one lonely button between the lovely pointed balls of her breasts. She came towards him, and the shirt flowed back, baring beauty so sweet it made him dizzy.

His coat joined the quilt on the floor, his cap sailed damply into a corner. He picked her up totally in his arms, kissing her throat, the breasts that came against his chest as she put her arms around him, stroking his hair, guiding his hungry mouth. "Oh damn!" he murmured against the warm scent of her body, "Still no proper bed, no music, just fire, sweetheart, fire—stop moving like that against me unless you're prepared for the consequences."

"The consequences," she whispered in his ear, "Please, please, the consequences . . ." and clung, drowning, wanting to drown in the strong, moving honey of his body joined to hers, thrusting with him, gasping with the pleasure of being his.

When at last his big pressing hands slid from her hips to the curve of her knees, he picked her up again, carried her to the captain's chair, sat down with his warm lissome burden snuggled to his chest.

"God," he said in awe. "Just think what we'll be when we do have a proper bed. I'm an old man. I may not be able to stand it."

"That being the case," she said severely into his rumpled white head, "stop what you are doing or we'll both probably die right here. And what would Ben think when he comes in this morning?"

"That we died happy."

She laughed softly, kissed the top of his head, but nonetheless slid to her feet, away from the insidious stroke of his hands. "I'd better get dressed. He sometimes comes in at six. Benton—"

"Eleanor."

"It's not going to be easy. Any of it."

"If you will learn about farming, I'll learn about antiques."

"Not that. I wish it was so simple. I mean about Tony. And Jill."

Soberly he answered, "Jill has no power over me. Has Tony power with you?"

She considered it. "No. Not now. Had he bought the shop—yes. He would have had power. Also—he—he was being very kind. I have some—some pressing medical bills. He was offering to pay them."

"And he'd asked you to marry him?"

There it was.

She tried to answer honestly: "Well—in a way."

He was roaring again, "How the hell can a guy ask a girl to marry him—in a way?"

"Hush. Listen."

"Yes, ma'am."

"He didn't want me wearing the ring. He didn't want Jill to know. Or—maybe anyone else. I wasn't wearing it, either—until—until tonight. For a—a reason. I think," she went on hastily, "the whole thing is tied up with the Picasso. Looking back, I can see a lot of things. Tony's been—" and she could see it now clearly, "—scared. I'll bet someone else in his shop screwed up. And he's been trying to avoid a scandal."

Benton shrugged, now uncaring. "Whatever. Are you going to get dressed? May I come help?"

"No," she said, and vanished.

He got up, roamed the workroom with his hands deep in his pockets, scuffling woodshavings. He was also whistling, but it was an absent whistle. "Eleanor—"

"Yes?"

"If I tell you something I think is funny, will you laugh?"

"Is this a character test?" Her voice sounded muffled; it came from the depth of a sweater.

"Maybe."

"Try me."

"When I was roaming around in the snow I went by Aunt Julia's. I—found Jill in bed with Mondaine."

"Do I laugh, now?"

"Not yet. They both saw me. Jill screeched. I think she thought I was a ghost. Now, laugh."

Eleanor was pulling on slacks and not really thinking. Obediently she went, "Ha, ha."

Then she looked up because he was standing in the door. His expression was grim. "Is that why you are here?" he asked.

She moved a large paw, and sat on the edge of the cot to don her shoes. "No. But I knew about it."

"You knew—" He stopped. His fists doubled.

Quickly she said, "But I didn't care. That's the important point. Tony was going to buy the shop from Jill. If that's how he was managing it, okay. I couldn't survive with Jill. I would stand a better chance of surviving with Tony."

His face was still set. "I suppose I shouldn't ask how you planned to survive."

"You ass!" she said, and meant it. "Get off my back! I'm talking about the shop. You saw what Jill would do—and I was having no luck whatsoever getting a job anywhere else—besides, I couldn't just abandon Ben, for heaven's sake. His pension is minuscule. If Tony decided to fire him, he'd be—be in a home, or something."

Her angry voice opened Charlie's eyes. Concerned, he laid his large fluffy head on her knee, nuzzling it. She hugged him, and deliberately calmed herself.

"Bent," she said, "you have no idea what it's been like around here. Please—give me a break. Suddenly I've found myself with no sure place to live, an uncertain income and behind on Bobby's medical payments. I've been coping the very best I knew how."

He took a deep breath, swiping a large hand through thick white hair. "Yeah," he said, and she understood the tone of voice. It meant he really didn't grasp the situation yet, but neither did he want to argue any more. Men—damn them all!

She had to make a point.

His going on, saying with a sigh, "I just screwed up. Then this wouldn't have happened. None of it," didn't alter the situation a bit.

She said, "No. You didn't. Not really. It wasn't in your control. I was the one who leaned on everyone else, let them manage my life for me. I was the one who had to learn, hey—it's *my* life. Therefore, it's up to me."

A little coldly he answered, "Marrying Mondaine is some marvelous option!" He was jerking his massive head at the ring sending off rainbows as she petted Charlie's ruff.

"I hadn't said I'd marry him. He handed it to me, he said don't tell Jill, and we'd talk about it later. I'd never worn it until last night when, God damn it if you must know, I was trying to get my mind off you."

Their eyes locked. And despite herself, tears came to hers. She stood up, walked over, and reached to frame his thunderous face with both hands. "Benton," she said to him, "When you died—I died. Wounds heal. I realize that. After a year—two years—I don't know what I would have

490

done. With—with anyone. But they hadn't healed yet, Bent." She stood on tiptoe, lifted her mouth. "Heal me some more—"

Twenty-six

The rasping crunch of the workroom door opening reluctantly against an obstinate riffle of snow was hardly a welcome interruption—particularly as it was overlaid with a shrill, "My God—I told you—it is him—he is alive—oh, damn, Bent, why did you have to come back—you're screwing up everything!"

Behind a distraught Jill Bonford was a tight-faced Tony Mondaine, muffled to reddened ears in his heavy trenchcoat, and not too plainly thrilled at seeing Benton Bonford, himself. As Jill turned back to him, her leather coattails whirling, and buried her face on his shoulder, he put an automatic arm about her but his voice was short. "Jill, shut up. Get hold of yourself."

From the dark eyes in that stony face the

red star glowed—the dangerous look that Eleanor had grown to know rather well. Almost unconsciously as she saw it she moved closer to Benton—a move impossible to misinterpret.

Tony did not misinterpret it. In a voice as thin as wire, he said, "Well, Bonford. I see the 'report of your death has been greatly exaggerated.' "

"Yes."

Benton had stiffened; Eleanor felt it. But he didn't move, and his own voice was devoid of expression.

Tony then murmured, "How—fortuitous."

He glanced down at the feathered silk head pressed against his damp shoulder. "Your wife does not, I note, seem particularly—overjoyed."

"That's because she is no longer my wife."

"Ah." If one word ever spoke volumes, that was it. Now it was Jill's time to stiffen. And the eyes she turned upward to Tony were anxious.

Almost cheerily Benton said into the vacuum, "So—you want her, she's available."

Tony's dark eyes rested lightly—very

lightly—on Eleanor. "I thought I was in the process of acquiring one elsewhere."

Eleanor opened her mouth, but the pressure of Benton's hand on hers forestalled speech. He said, "I think you'll find the process halted."

"Or obfuscated."

"No. Halted."

But Tony looked past Benton Bonford as though he wasn't even there and said directly to Eleanor, "Sotheby's have asked me to affiliate with them. I want you, Eleanor. You know that. I also need you. Use your head, darling. The world you know is my world—not this tractor jockey's."

Jill had suddenly raised her own head; she was looking up at him with wide, startled eyes. She said abruptly, "Thanks a lot."

He answered calmly, never taking his own dark eyes from the woman across the room, "Eleanor understands."

Strangely, Eleanor did. She also believed what he said—he thought he did need her. He also thought he wanted her—probably, she mused, to his surprise. One took Anthony Mondaine for precisely what he was, then went from there. Except that Eleanor Wright, although she understood it, didn't have to do so any more. There was just one thing left.

Quite gently, she said, "Tony—listen."

"My dear, don't I always?"

"No. Especially when you're being an ass. You're being an ass, now. Listen, damn it."

He shrugged.

She said. "Last night—for my birthday—Ben gave me the Picasso."

He didn't answer with any such nonsense as, What Picasso? He only said, "Indeed—Christ!" And his eyes searched the room.

He found the painting. Freeing himself from Jill, he went towards it. Swiftly.

Benton was swifter. Eleanor hadn't known such a large man could move so fast. He was at the desk before Tony, leaning against it very, very casually.

Tony saw the envelope still propped against the painting. Reaching around Benton, he picked it up, read the scrawl. Then he went quite visibly pale, and sighed, a sound almost like a shudder. He said to Benton, "Your trip to Russia."

"Yes."

Their eyes locked.

Tony cursed softly, bitterly, street curses,

shaking his head. "What incredible, unbelievable bad luck. It's almost past reason."

"Not quite."

"It was a mistake. Eleanor, you know it was a mistake. I personally would never have sold such a thing to Julia."

Benton was now shaking his head. He said, "The sale was a mistake. The repro painting was deliberate."

Now Tony's breath came out in a hiss. "Bonford, for God's sake—what do you want? Blood? You've got blood! I've been sweating it for six weeks."

Jill was standing abandoned in the middle of the floor, lost, bewildered, uncomprehending. Suddenly she was at the desk also, thrusting herself between the two men, crying out petulantly, "Who cares? Who cares about a damned stupid painting? What are you going to do about me? Benton, I'm broke. I've spent everything— the first installment on your dumb farm— the stuff in the house—everything. I'll leave. But you can't expect me to go with nothing and you'll be damned sorry if you do."

Quite abruptly, Benton laughed. It was a genuine sound of laughter from deep in his chest. Tony Mondaine looked at him as though he was mad, and Jill looked with startled, panicky uncertainty.

"Of course we can't expect you to go with nothing," Benton said to his ex-wife. "Not with all the promises that certainly have been made in—ah—certain quarters."

He tipped back her silky blond head, kissed her heartily and bundled the Picasso into her unwilling hands. He said,

"There you are, my dear—one masterpiece, worth thousands of dollars. Mondaine himself will pay you thousands of dollars for it. Just ask him."

Anthony Mondaine was standing as rigidly still as though struck by lightning. To Benton he said through clenched teeth, "You unconscionable bastard."

Jill had turned her beautifully fringed eyes on him—eyes suddenly speculative. "Really? Is it worth a lot of money?"

Affably Benton answered her, "It sure is, honey. To him."

"Like—like *The Last Supper*—or the *Mona Lisa*?"

"In effect."

"Could I sell it to a museum?"

"I'd check with Mondaine, first. He'd probably make you a better offer."

"Would you, Tony?"

Tony looked at Benton with an expression of absolute loathing. "Clever," he said between clenched white teeth. "Yes, my dear, I probably would. Shall we go have some breakfast and talk about it? I can see no further advantage in staying here."

"Wait!"

Suddenly Eleanor had come to life, was hurrying across the workroom swiftly, with purpose, skirting the kas and the Chinese garden seat.

"Here," she said, stripping the diamond and sapphire ring from her finger. "Here, Jill. Here's something else. It's very old, and very valuable."

Jill Bonford looked at the bauble in her palm, turned it so the sapphires scattered blue sparks and the diamond shot a tongue of flame. "My God," she said in awe. "It's real."

"Yes, it is," said Eleanor. "Isn't it, Tony?"

Tight-lipped, Tony Mondaine could only nod. He was so angry, so consumed with rage he could not trust himself to speak. Jill turned her eyes steadily on Eleanor.

"You want me to have it. Why? So I'll never come back? Don't worry on that score. This Podunk Center thrills me like a limp noodle. But—I don't understand the ring."

"Call it—" Eleanor hesitated. "Call it insurance. Something to tide you over until you—you get located. I'm sure Tony can be a great deal of help. He has all sorts of connections—in St. Louis, especially. Why don't you try your luck there?"

"All right," said Jill Bonford, and smiled upward at Tony Mondaine. "Perhaps I will."

She put the ring on her own slender finger with its long, red nails, Then shifting the painting to the other arm, she held out her hand to admire the flash. "Well. Since you're both being so generous, to get rid of me—anything else?"

"No," said Eleanor and Benton simultaneously. They looked at each other and laughed, almost like mischievous children.

Tony Mondaine said coldly, "Thank God for small favors. All right. You win. I'll look after this infant—at least for a while. I suppose you think it's what I richly deserve."

"Let's say, rather," said Eleanor gently, "that you deserve each other."

She wasn't touching Benton. But she

could sense him, warm and solid behind her.

Tony turned up his coat collar, wrenched at the almost frozen door.

It had stopped snowing. Pink and pearly streaks of morning light streamed across the glistening drifts of the alleyway. Black starlings lined the eaves, croaking their displeasure. A UPS truck was pulling in behind the hardware store.

Life went on.

Tony shivered, and said to Jill, "Step along, infant."

Jill went out, saying, "Brrr!" Tony started. Stopped.

He looked back at the two by the desk—the enormous, implacable man, the woman with the calm blue eyes beneath the brief, soft swing of ashy hair. His handsome face was now only wry, and he shook his head.

He said, "I don't believe it. This is not happening to me."

Then as though it was wrenched from him, he said only to Eleanor, "I could have loved you."

She half smiled. She answered as quietly, "I could not have loved you."

Their gaze locked. Impulsively she went on, "Good luck with Sotheby's!"

She meant it. He knew she meant it. He gave her a half salute, pulled the rasping door shut, and was gone.

The two that were left looked at each other.

Benton reached over her head, and turned off the lamp on the desk. The bars of morning gray, filtering in through snow-blocked windows, touched the deep honey patina of the Welsh dresser, the green dragons writhing on the porcelain garden seat, and—now that the painting was gone—the unexpected, out-of-context, screaming purple of a ceramic cow was saying her silent moo on the desktop.

But Benton wasn't looking at purple cows. He was looking at Eleanor in her thick, blue pullover, at her sober face from which the peach-bloom youth of the other girl had long fled, leaving the clean, sweet lines of a caring woman.

He said to her quietly, sincerely, "I didn't intend to make an enemy of him. I hope I haven't."

She shook her head.

"You haven't. Tony—Tony admits to setbacks. Never defeats. I just hope he is not into this fakery thing so far he can't pull out. It would ruin him—not only with Sotheby's, but with everyone. He has such enormous stature as an antiquarian it would affect us all."

"Us?"

"Yes. The small shops. Like Bonford Antiques."

"You don't mean he'll ever come back here?"

"Of course he will."

"He sure as hell better not sniff around you again."

His face was thunderous. She sighed.

"Oh boy," she said. "What was that remark about coming into the twentieth century?"

His scowl deepened. "I only come so far."

"Then come one step more."

"I hate his damn guts."

"I'm not thrilled with them, myself. But Bent—this is a business, like any other business. You take what you need from an associate and ignore the rest. That's what Tony does. That's what Julia did. That's what I'm learning to do. I'll buy from Marvin Coles if he has anything I want."

His face did not change noticeably.

And suddenly she laughed. "Oh, Benton, are we going to have an interesting relationship! Look, you idiot. I had every chance in the world with Tony Mondaine, but I just wasn't interested. You come along, and within a week I'm falling like a ripe apple into your hands. Doesn't that tell you something?"

It was his turn to laugh, from the depth of his deep chest. "It tells me that's what I get, being mixed up with a city woman," he said. But he was starting to grin, and she took heart.

"Bent—I have to say something else."

"As long as it's not about Mondaine. I've had about a bellyful of him."

"No. It's about you. And me."

"A good start. I'm for it."

He was reaching out. She eluded his big hand and pushed him down in the captain's chair. It creaked, but held, and his pants wouldn't pick up cat hairs. She sat on the garden seat.

"You said you meant to buy the Crane farm. Let me run the shop."

"Right."

"Jill said she'd spent your farm money."

"Just what she could get. There's more. Besides, my lawyer says I could sue. But I don't think I want a Picasso, and am damn sure I don't want a ring. At least, not that one." He was grinning.

She wasn't. "I told you—I owe a bunch. I got behind on Bobby's medical bills."

"We'll pay the suckers."

"No, no. They're my bills. My responsibility."

"Haven't you ever heard about 'for better or for worse'?"

"Bent, you hardly know me—except in the—the biblical sense." She was blushing now, and he found it charming.

Gently he answered, "So we'll learn. A day at a time. We'll work things out. You've missed the operative word, Eleanor. I said we were *partners.*"

Now he was holding her eyes with his, and the look was as palpable as touching.

"I had time to think about my life," he said, "slogging along in the snow trying to forget my feet were frozen. And I knew that's what was missing. Jill wasn't a partner—she was a toy, and my fault as much as hers. I need someone to share things with. You can learn to love my sweet, velvety Charolai cattle and the sight of a cornfield, breaking ground in green rows beneath a springtime sun—and I can learn to admire the polish on that damn Welsh whatever and a chest of drawers that's lasted two hundred years. And maybe we'll do it, too."

"Last two hundred years? I'm afraid we're a little late."

"Then by damn," he said, reaching for her. "Let's get started."

She eluded him one last time, but her heart was singing, knowing the truth of what he'd said. Partners. Partners! And she wished—dear God, she wished Bobby could be here. To see his mom—and to see Benton Bonford.

Something told him what she was thinking.

"Look," he said gently. "Another thing I thought about, falling on my ass down those mountain slopes—we can't have kids. We're too old. But I'll bet there's a couple of them out there—who need us. If we want to look."

The sudden look of sunshine on her face pleased him beyond measure. "I'll teach 'em about no-till, and you teach 'em about those pink glass things and Ben can be a great-grandfather. Is it a deal?"

The slant of daylight touched the silver in his thick hair, the sandpaper of his jaw, the glint of matted white inside the open front of his heavy shirt.

Knowing there were things yet to be coped with, things they couldn't even envision on this cold winter morning, nevertheless, she nodded her head.

"It's a deal," she said, holding him off with both hands braced against that deep chest. Holding him off just a moment longer. "But hey, mister. I remember some other promises. Where's my proper bed? The clean sheets? The music? And the appropriate time?"

He took both her hands from their bracing, pushed them on around him inside his shirt, against his warm hard back. He said into her hair, "There are beds at Aunt Julia's—if we can find one without Charlie in it on a regular basis. The sheets are fine. If the power's off, I can whistle. And since it seems to be starting to snow again, we can possibly have all day."

"Tillie," said Eleanor to the purple cow. "I believe I am being propositioned."

"Propositioned, or abducted; that's your choice," said Benton cheerfully. "With matrimony an eventual result of same. And if that sentiment is not particularly twentieth-century, I don't give a damn."

She loosed herself, after a long, satisfactory kiss, and picked up the purple cow.

"There are things," she said to its absurdly long-lashed face, "about the nineteenth century I don't find too repulsive—and perhaps among them is the married state. Note, I said *perhaps.*"

A partner. She could handle that.

He was handing her coat, calling to Charlie. She put it on, reached up on the shelf and tickled the ginger ears of a sleepy, totally detached tomcat.

"Mind the store until Ben comes," she said.

Charlie trundled out of the storeroom, looking refreshed. Thomaseen's topaz eyes lost their sleepiness. Cat and dog exchanged a long, thoughtful look.

But that was tomorrow's problem. Not today's.

Benton was scribbling a note, setting it up on Ben's Welsh dresser. It said, "Gone home."

Eleanor thought, What a nice word: home.

Very happily, they went.

WATCH AS THESE WOMEN LEARN
TO LOVE AGAIN

HELLO LOVE   (4094, $4.50/$5.50)
by Joan Shapiro

Family tragedy leaves Barbara Sinclair alone with her success. The fight to gain custody of her young granddaughter brings a confrontation with the determined rancher Sam Douglass. Also widowed, Sam has been caring for Emily alone, guided by his own ideas of childrearing. Barbara challenges his ideas. And that's not all she challenges . . . Long-buried desires surface, then gentle affection. Sam and Barbara cannot ignore the chance to love again.

THE BEST MEDICINE   (4220, $4.50/$5.50)
by Janet Lane Walters

Her late husband's expenses push Maggie Carr back to nursing, the career she left almost thirty years ago. The night shift is difficult, but it's harder still to ignore the way handsome Dr. Jason Knight soothes his patients. When she lends a hand to help his daughter, Jason and Maggie grow closer than simply doctor and nurse. Obstacles to romance seem insurmountable, but Maggie knows that love is always the best medicine.

AND BE MY LOVE   (4291, $4.50/$5.50)
by Joyce C. Ware

Selflessly catering first to husband, then children, grandchildren, and her aging, though imperious mother, leaves Beth Volmar little time for her own adventures or passions. Then, the handsome archaeologist Karim Donovan arrives and campaigns to widen the boundaries of her narrow life. Beth finds new freedom when Karim insists that she accompany him to Turkey on an archaeological dig . . . and a journey towards loving again.

OVER THE RAINBOW   (4032, $4.50/$5.50)
by Marjorie Eatock

Fifty-something, divorced for years, courted by more than one attractive man, and thoroughly enjoying her job with a large insurance company, Marian's sudden restlessness confuses her. She welcomes the chance to travel on business to a small Mississippi town. Full of good humor and words of love, Don Worth makes her feel needed, and not just to assess property damage. Marian takes the risk.

A KISS AT SUNRISE   (4260, $4.50/$5.50)
by Charlotte Sherman

Beginning widowhood and retirement, Ruth Nichols has her first taste of freedom. Against the advice of her mother and daughter, Ruth heads for an adventure in the motor home that has sat unused since her husband's death. Long days and lonely campgrounds start to dampen the excitement of traveling alone. That is, until a dapper widower named Jack parks next door and invites her for dinner. On the road, Ruth and Jack find the chance to love again.

Available wherever paperbacks are sold, or order direct from the Publisher. Send cover price plus 50¢ per copy for mailing and handling to Penguin USA, P.O. Box 999, c/o Dept. 17109, Bergenfield, NJ 07621.Residents of New York and Tennessee must include sales tax. DO NOT SEND CASH.

IT'S NEVER TOO LATE FOR LOVE AND ROMANCE

JUST IN TIME (4188, $4.50/$5.50)
by Peggy Roberts

Constantly taking care of everyone around her has earned Remy Dupre the affectionate nickname "Ma." Then, with Remy's husband gone and oil discovered on her Louisiana farm, her sons and their wives decide it's time to take care of her. But Remy knows how to take care of herself. She starts by checking into a beauty spa, buying some classy new clothes and shoes, discovering an antique vase, and moving on to a fine plantation. Next, not one, but two men attempt to sweep her off her well-shod feet. The right man offers her the opportunity to love again.

LOVE AT LAST (4158, $4.50/$5.50)
by Garda Parker

Fifty, slim, and attractive, Gail Bricker still hadn't found the love of her life. Friends convince her to take an Adventure Tour during the summer vacation she enjoys as an English teacher. At a Cheyenne Indian school in need of teachers, Gail finds her calling. In rancher Slater Kincaid, she finds her match. Gail discovers that it's never too late to fall in love . . . for the very first time.

LOVE LESSONS (3959, $4.50/$5.50)
by Marian Oaks

After almost forty years of marriage, Carolyn Ames certainly hadn't been looking for a divorce. But the ink is barely dry, and here she is already living an exhilarating life as a single woman. First, she lands an exciting and challenging job. Now Jason, the handsome architect, offers her a fairy-tale romance. Carolyn doesn't care that her ultra-conservative neighbors gossip about her and Jason, but she is afraid to give up her independent life-style. She struggles with the balance while she learns to love again.

A KISS TO REMEMBER (4129, $4.50/$5.50)
by Helen Playfair

For the past ten years Lucia Morgan hasn't had time for love or romance. Since her husband's death, she has been raising her two sons, working at a dead-end office job, and designing boutique clothes to make ends meet. Then one night, Mitch Colton comes looking for his daughter, out late with one of her sons. The look in Mitch's eye brings back a host of long-forgotten feelings. When the kids come home and spoil the enchantment, Lucia wonders if she will get the chance to love again.

COME HOME TO LOVE (3930, $4.50/$5.50)
by Jane Bierce

Julia Delaine says good-bye to her skirt-chasing husband Phillip and hello to a whole new life. Julia capably rises to the challenges of her reawakened sexuality, the young man who comes courting, and her new position as the head of her local television station. Her new independence teaches Julia that maybe her time-tested values were right all along and maybe Phillip does belong in her life, with her new terms.

Available wherever paperbacks are sold, or order direct from the Publisher. Send cover price plus 50¢ per copy for mailing and handling to Penguin USA, P.O. Box 999, c/o Dept. 17109, Bergenfield, NJ 07621. Residents of New York and Tennessee must include sales tax. DO NOT SEND CASH.

CATCH A RISING STAR!

ROBIN ST. THOMAS

FORTUNE'S SISTERS (2616, $3.95)

It was Pia's destiny to be a Hollywood star. She had complete self-confidence, breathtaking beauty, and the help of her domineering mother. But her younger sister Jeanne began to steal the spotlight meant for Pia, diverting attention away from the ruthlessly ambitious star. When her mother Mathilde started to return the advances of dashing director Wes Guest, Pia's jealousy surfaced. Her passion for Guest and desire to be the brightest star in Hollywood pitted Pia against her own family—sister against sister, mother against daughter. Pia was determined to be the only survivor in the arenas of love and fame. But neither Mathilde nor Jeanne would surrender without a fight. . . .

LOVER'S MASQUERADE (2886, $4.50)

New Orleans. A city of secrets, shrouded in mystery and magic. A city where dreams become obsessions and memories once again become reality. A city where even one trip, like a stop on Claudia Gage's book promotion tour, can lead to a perilous fall. For New Orleans is also the home of Armand Dantine, who knows the secrets that Claudia would conceal and the past she cannot remember. And he will stop at nothing to make her love him, and will not let her go again . . .

SENSATION (3228, $4.95)

They'd dreamed of stardom, and their dreams came true. Now they had fame and the power that comes with it. In Hollywood, in New York, and around the world, the names of Aurora Styles, Rachel Allenby, and Pia Decameron commanded immediate attention—and lust and envy as well. They were stars, idols on pedestals. And there was always someone waiting in the wings to bring them crashing down . . .

Available wherever paperbacks are sold, or order direct from the Publisher. Send cover price plus 50¢ per copy for mailing and handling to Penguin USA, P.O. Box 999, c/o Dept. 17109, Bergenfield, NJ 07621. Residents of New York and Tennessee must include sales tax. DO NOT SEND CASH.

KATHERINE STONE—
Zebra's Leading Lady for Love

BEL AIR (2979, $4.95)
Bel Air—where even the rich and famous are awed by the
wealth that surrounds them. Allison, Winter, Emily: three
beautiful women who couldn't be more different. Three
women searching for the courage to trust, to love. Three women fighting for their dreams in the glamorous and treach-
erous *Bel Air*.

ROOMMATES (3355, $4.95)
No one could have prepared Carrie for the monumental
changes she would face when she met her new circle of
friends at Stanford University. Once their lives intertwined
and became woven into the tapestry of the times, they
would never be the same.

TWINS (3492, $4.95)
Brook and Melanie Chandler were so different, it was hard
to believe they were sisters. One was a dark, serious, ambitious New York attorney; the other, a golden, glamorous,
sophisticated supermodel. But they were more than sisters—they were twins and more alike than even they
knew . . .

THE CARLTON CLUB (3614, $4.95)
It was the place to see and be seen, the only place to be.
And for those who frequented the playground of the very
rich, it was a way of life. Mark, Kathleen, Leslie and
Janet—they worked together, played together, and loved
together, all behind exclusive gates of the *Carlton Club*.

*Available wherever paperbacks are sold, or order direct from the
Publisher. Send cover price plus 50¢ per copy for mailing and
handling to Penguin USA, P.O. Box 999, c/o Dept. 17109,
Bergenfield, NJ 07621. Residents of New York and Tennessee
must include sales tax. DO NOT SEND CASH.*

MAKE THE CONNECTION

WITH

Z-TALK
Online

Come talk to your favorite authors and get the inside scoop on everything that's going on in the world of publishing, from the only online service that's designed exclusively for the publishing industry.

With Z-Talk Online Information Service, the most innovative and exciting computer bulletin board around, you can:

- ♥ CHAT "LIVE" WITH AUTHORS, FELLOW READERS, AND OTHER MEMBERS OF THE PUBLISHING COMMUNITY.

- ♥ FIND OUT ABOUT UPCOMING TITLES BEFORE THEY'RE RELEASED.

- ♥ DOWNLOAD THOUSANDS OF FILES AND GAMES.

- ♥ READ REVIEWS OF ROMANCE TITLES.

- ♥ HAVE UNLIMITED USE OF E-MAIL.

- ♥ POST MESSAGES ON OUR DOZENS OF TOPIC BOARDS.

All it takes is a computer and a modem to get online with Z-Talk. Set your modem to 8/N/1, and dial 212-545-1120. If you need help, call the System Operator, at 212-889-2299, ext. 260. There's a two week free trial period. After that, annual membership is only $ 60.00.

See you online!

KENSINGTON PUBLISHING CORP.